W9-AFC-830

Portrait of Garrick by Loitard, Paris, 1751
Victoria and Albert Museum, Enthoven Collection, Theatre Museum

THE PLAYS OF DAVID GARRICK

A COMPLETE COLLECTION OF THE SOCIAL SATIRES,
FRENCH ADAPTATIONS, PANTOMIMES,
CHRISTMAS AND MUSICAL PLAYS,
PRELUDES, INTERLUDES, AND BURLESQUES,
to which are added
the Alterations and Adaptations of the Plays of Shakespeare and
Other Dramatists from the Sixteenth to the Eighteenth Centuries

VOLUME 4

Garrick's Adaptations of Shakespeare, 1759-1773

EDITED WITH COMMENTARY AND NOTES BY
HARRY WILLIAM PEDICORD AND
FREDRICK LOUIS BERGMANN

SOUTHERN ILLINOIS UNIVERSITY PRESS
CARBONDALE AND EDWARDSVILLE

PRINTED IN THE UNITED STATES OF AMERICA
EDITED BY TERESA WHITE
DESIGNED BY GEORGE LENOX
PRODUCTION SUPERVISED BY RICHARD NEAL

LIBRARY OF CONGRESS CATALOGING IN PUBLICATION DATA (REVISED)

Garrick, David, 1717–1779.
The plays of David Garrick.

Bibliography: p.
Includes indexes.
CONTENTS: v. 1. Garrick's own plays, 1740–1766.—
v. 2. Garrick's own plays, 1769–1775.—v. 3. Garrick's Adaptations
of Shakespeare, 1744–1756.—v. 4. Garrick's adaptations of
Shakespeare, 1759–1773.
I. Pedicord, Harry William, 1912 II. Bergmann, Fredrick
Louis, 1916– III. Title.
PR3465 1980 822'.6 79–28443
ISBN 0–8093–0969–6 (v. 4)

Contents

Illustrations

Acknowledgments

THE EDITORS and the publisher gratefully acknowledge the permissions granted by the following libraries, museums, and publishers: The Folger Shakespeare Library, Washington, D.C., the Lilly Library, Indiana University, the Indiana University Libraries, the University of Pennsylvania Libraries, the University of Illinois Library at Urbana-Champaign, the Library of Congress, and the British Library, London, for permission to reproduce the title pages of the first edition of Garrick's plays; the Folger and the Harvard Theatre Collection, the Theatre Collection of the Victoria and Albert Museum, London, and the Trustees of the British Museum, London, for permission to reproduce the illustrations in these volumes; the Folger Shakespeare Library for permission to quote from manuscripts relating to *The Clandestine Marriage*, and for permission to edit the text of Garrick's prompt copy of *A Midsummer Night's Dream*; the Garrick Club, London, for permission to quote from the manuscript of "The Sisters"; the Huntington Library, San Marino, California, for permission to edit the Prologue to and the text of *The Jubilee*, the texts of *The Institution of the Garter* and *The Meeting of the Company* (and the introductory letter to the play), for permission to quote from the Huntington's copy of *Lethe*, and for permission to reprint the Huntington's copy of the Prologue to *The Tempst: An Opera*; the Trustees of the Boston Public Library for permission to edit *Harlequin's Invasion*; Doubleday for permission to quote from the Preface to *Maurice Evans' G.I. Production of Hamlet by William Shakespeare*, copyright 1946 by Maurice Evans and reprinted by permission of Doubleday and Company, Inc.; the Modern Language Association of America for permission to quote from "Garrick's Long Lost Alteration of *Hamlet*" by George Winchester Stone, Jr. (*PMLA*, 49 [1934], 890–921), copyright 1934 by the Modern Language Association of America and reprinted by permission of the Association.

The Garrick Canon

Dates indicate the season each play or adaption was first presented.

GARRICK'S OWN PLAYS

1. Lethe; or Esop in the Shades. A Dramatic Satire (1740)
2. The Lying Valet (1741)
3. Miss in Her Teens; or, The Medley of Lovers. A Farce (1747)
4. Lilliput. A Dramatic Entertainment (1756)
5. The Male-Coquette; or, Seventeen Hundred Fifty-Seven (1757)
6. The Guardian. A Comedy (1759)
7. Harlequin's Invasion; or, A Christmas Gambol (1759)
8. The Enchanter; or, Love and Magic. A Musical Drama (1760)
9. The Farmer's Return from London. An Interlude (1762)
10. The Clandestine Marriage. A Comedy (1766)
11. Neck or Nothing. A Farce (1766)
12. Cymon. A Dramatic Romance (1767)
13. Linco's Travels. An Interlude (1767)
14. A Peep Behind the Curtain; or, The New Rehearsal (1767)
15. The Jubilee (1769)
16. The Institution of the Garter; or, Arthur's Roundtable Restored (1771)
17. The Irish Widow (1772)
18. A Christmas Tale. A New Dramatic Entertainment (1773)
19. The Meeting of the Company; or, Bayes's Art of Acting (1774)
20. Bon Ton; or, High Life Above Stairs (1775)
21. May-Day; or, The Little Gipsy. A Musical Farce (1775)
22. The Theatrical Candidates. A Musical Prelude (1775)

GARRICK'S ADAPTATIONS OF SHAKESPEARE

23. Macbeth (1744)
24. Romeo and Juliet (1748)
25. The Fairies. An Opera (1755)

26. Catharine and Petruchio (1756)
27. Florizel and Perdita. A Dramatic Pastoral (1756)
28. The Tempest. An Opera (1756)
29. King Lear (1756)
30. Antony and Cleopatra (1759)
31. Cymbeline (1761)
32. A Midsummer Night's Dream (1763)
33. Hamlet (1772)
34. The Tempest (1773)

GARRICK'S ALTERATIONS OF OTHERS

35. The Rehearsal (1742)
36. The Alchymist (1743)
37. The Provok'd Wife (1744)
38. The Roman Father (1750)
39. Alfred. A Masque (1751)
40. Every Man in His Humour (1751)
41. Zara (1754)
42. The Chances (1754)
43. Rule a Wife and Have a Wife. A Comedy (1756)
44. Isabella; or, The Fatal Marriage (1757)
45. The Gamesters. A Comedy (1757)
46. Mahomet (1765)
47. The Country Girl (1766)
48. King Arthur; or, The British Worthy (1770)
49. Albumazar. A Comedy (1773)

Chronology

Year	Events	Garrick
1685		David Garric arrives in London from Bordeaux.
1687		Peter Garrick, son of David Garric, born in France, arrives in England.
1707		Peter Garrick married to Arabella Clough of Lichfield.
1717		David Garrick born in the Angel Inn, Hereford, 19 February.
1718	France and England declare war against Spain.	
1720	Failure of South Sea Company and Law's Mississippi Company in Paris.	
1722	Jacobite Plot.	
1724	The Drapier's Letters and Wood's Halfpence.	
1725	Treaty of Hanover.	Brother George Garrick born 22 August.

1727	Accession of George II.	David attends Lichfield Grammar School.
1728		David sent to Lisbon, Portugal, to enter Uncle's wine business. After a brief stay returns to England.
1729	Resolutions against the reporting of Parliamentary debates.	David re-enters Lichfield Grammar School.
1730	Walpole and Townshend quarrel, Townshend resigns.	
1731	Full Walpole administration.	
1735	Porteous Riots in Edinburgh.	David enrolled under Samuel Johnson at Edial Hall.
1736		Father returns from Army and David drops out of Edial. Johnson's academy a failure.
1737	Censorship established with the passing of the Theatrical Licensing Act.	Garrick and Samuel Johnson set out for London on 2 March. Garrick enrolled as student at Lincoln's Inn on 9 March.
1738	Jenkins's Ear.	
1739	England declares war against Spain.	
1740		Garrick's first play, *Lethe; or, Esop in the Shades*, produced at Drury Lane, 1 April.
1741		Charles Macklin's revolutionary performance as Shylock, Drury Lane, 14 February. Garrick plays summer engagement at Ipswich under name of Lyddall—Capt. Duretête in

		Farquhar's *The Inconstant*, 21 July. Garrick's debut as Richard III at Goodman's Fields, 19 October. Appears in seven other roles during the season. *The Lying Valet* produced at Goodman's Fields, 30 November. Garrick retires from wine trade in London.
1742	Resignation of Walpole.	Garrick plays three performances at Drury Lane: Bayes, 26 May; Lear, 28 May; Richard III, 31 May. Plays summer season at Smock Alley Theatre, Dublin. Returns to London as a member of the Drury Lane company, opening with Chamont in Otway's *The Orphan* and playing twelve other roles before end of season.
1743	Defeat of French at Dettingen.	Actors' strike against manager Fleetwood at Drury Lane. Garrick plays second season at Smock Alley, Dublin.
1745		Plays Dublin, 9 December to 3 May 1746.
1746		Mlle. Violetti arrives from Continent in February to dance at Haymarket Theatre. Garrick and James Quin compete in performance of Rowe's *The Fair Penitent* at Covent Garden, 14 November.
1747		*Miss in Her Teens* produced at Covent Garden, 17 January.

		James Lacy and David Garrick become joint-patentees of Drury Lane, 9 April. New managers alter and refurbish Drury Lane Theatre.
1748	Peace of Aix-la-Chapelle.	
1749		Garrick and Violetti married, 22 June, and reside at 27 Southampton Street, Covent Garden. The "Battle of the Romeos."
1751	Death of Frederick, Prince of Wales.	Garricks set out for trip to the Continent, 19 May.
1753	Founding of the British Museum.	
1754	Death of Pelham, who is succeeded by Newcastle as Prime Minister.	Garrick leases villa at Hampton.
1755	Publication of Johnson's *Dictionary*.	The Chinese Festival Riots at Drury Lane, 8–18 November. Garrick buys Hampton villa.
1756	Seven Years' War begins.	
1760	Accession of George III.	
1762	War against Spain.	Drury Lane Theatre altered and enlarged. Half-Price Riots at Drury Lane and Covent Garden.
1763	John Wilkes and *The North Briton*.	Garricks tour the Continent 1763–65.
1764		Garrick stricken with typhoid fever in Munich.
1765	The Stamp Act.	Publication of *The Sick Mon-*

		key precedes Garrick's return from abroad. Returns to stage by command as Benedict in *Much Ado About Nothing*, 14 November.
1766	Repeal of the Stamp Act.	
1768		*The Dramatic Works of David Garrick* published in three volumes.
1769	The letters of "Junius."	Garrick becomes Steward of Shakespeare Jubilee at Stratford-upon-Avon, 6–9 September. Stages *The Jubilee* at Drury Lane on 14 October.
1772		Garrick buys house in Adam Brothers' Adelphi Terrace; moves in on 28 February. Isaac Bickerstaff flees to France in disgrace, and Garrick is attacked by William Kenrick's publication of *Love in the Suds*. Garrick goes to court and Kenrick publishes apology on 26 November.
1773	The Boston Tea-Party.	
1774	Death of Oliver Goldsmith.	*The Dramatic Works of David Garrick* published in two volumes by R. Bald, T. Blaw and J. Kurt.
1775	War of American Independence.	Drury Lane altered and decorated by the Adam Brothers.
1776		Garrick's sale of Drury Lane patent announced in the press on 7 March—to Richard Brinsley Sheridan, Thomas Linley

		and Dr. James Ford. Garrick's farewell performances upon retirement, 1 April to 10 June. Final performance as Don Felix in Mrs. Centlivre's *The Wonder*, 10 June.
1777	Burgoyne surrenders at Saratoga.	Garrick reads *Lethe* before the Royal Family at Windsor Castle in February.
1778	Alliance of France and Spain with the United States.	
1779		Garrick dies at Adelphi Terrace home on 20 January. Burial in Poets Corner, Westminster Abbey on 1 February. Roubillac statue of Shakespeare and large collection of old plays willed to the British Museum. George Garrick dies on 3 February.

Antony and Cleopatra

An Historical Play

1759

ANTONY *and* CLEOPATRA;

an historical Play,

written by

WILLIAM SHAKESPEARE:

fitted for the Stage by abridging only;

and now acted, at the

Theatre-Royal in Drury-*Lane,*

by his Majesty's Servants.

No grave upon the earth shall clip in it
A pair so famous. *p.* 99.

LONDON:

Printed for J. *and* R. TONSON *in the Strand.*

MDCCLVIII.

Facsimile title page of the First Edition
Folger Shakespeare Library

[Dedicatory Poem]

To the right honorable, and worthy of
*all Titles, the Countess of * *.*

Why, from the throne where BEAUTY sits SUPREME
and countless emanations deals below,
infused and fixed in Woman's shining frame,
doth so large portion of his wonder flow?
Why, but to rule the tread of human woe
and point our erring feet where joys abide.
But (ah, the pity!) to a traitor flame,
weak, wavering, wild, the heaven-born ray is tied,
and man, confiding man, from bliss estranged wide.

10 Daughters of Britain, scorn the garish fire,
exile the meteor to its Pharian grave;
sincerer flames from Virtue's heights aspire,
that brighten beauty and from sorrow save.
High o'er the rest, see what fair hand doth wave
a deathless torch and calls you to the shrine,
where only beauty only bliss entire!
follow the branch of much-loved * *'s line,
and from those altars mend, with her, the ray divine.

Oct. 3d 1757. IGNOTO.

The dedicatory poem follows the title page in *D*1. It is printed at the end of the play in *D*1a and *D*1b and is omitted entirely in, *D*3.

[Song]

The SONG at p. 39. being thought too short, an addition was made to it while the play was in rehearsal, and it is performed as follows:

1.

Come, thou monarch of the vine,
plumpy Bacchus, *with pink eyne;*
thine it is to cheer the soul,
made, by thy enlarging bowl,
free from wisdom's fond control,
Bur. *free from wisdom's fond control.*

2.

Monarch, come; and with thee bring
10 *tipsy dance, and revelling.*
In thy vats our cares be drowned;
with thy grapes our hairs be crowned;
cup us 'till the world go round.
Bur. *cup us 'till the world go round.*

CORRIGENDA.

p. 26, l. 7, r. *of our* D° l. 10, r. *of your*
p. 30, l. 32, r. *well.* p. 31, l. 32, r. *report:*

0.1. too short] the original song consists of the first two and the last four lines. In *D*1a the revised song is placed at the end of the play. In *D*1b the song and the corrigenda are placed at the end of the play. In *D*2, *D*3 both the song and the corrigenda are omitted.

[Short Title]

Antony *and* Cleopatra,

an historical play.

No short-title page in *D2*, *D3*.

Persons represented

	OCTAVIUS CAESAR,	*Triumvirs.*	Mr. Fleetwood.
	MARCUS ANTONIUS,	*Triumvirs.*	Mr. Garrick.
	M. AEMIL. LEPIDUS;	*Triumvirs.*	Mr. Blakes.
	SEXTUS POMPEIUS:		Mr. Austin.
	MENAS, *his Follower.*		Mr. Burton.
	DOLABELLA,	*Caesarians.*	Mr. Mozeen.
	THYREUS,	*Caesarians.*	Mr. Holland.
	MECAENAS,	*Caesarians.*	Mr. Atkins.
	AGRIPPA,	*Caesarians.*	Mr. Packer.
10	PROCULEIUS;	*Caesarians.*	Mr. Austin.
	ENOBARBUS,	*Antonians.*	Mr. Berry.
	CANIDIUS,	*Antonians.*	Mr. Wilkinson.
	DIOMEDE,	*Antonians.*	Mr. Bransby.
	EROS, *and*	*Antonians.*	Mr. Davies.
	DERCETAS;	*Antonians.*	Mr. Blakes.
	a Soothsayer.		Mr. Burton.
	ALEXAS;	*Officers of* Cleopatra's *Household*	Mr. Ackman.
	MARDIAN, *an Eunuch*;	*Officers of* Cleopatra's *Household*	Mr. Perry.
	SELEUCUS;	*Officers of* Cleopatra's *Household*	Mr. Burton.

0. *Persons represented*] *D*1, *D*2 name cast; *D*3, *D*4 omit cast.

6. Dolabella] he takes the lines of Demetrius.

7. Thyreus] he takes the lines of Philo, and also those of Enobarbus in the description of Cleopatra sailing down the Cydnus. Omitted from the dramatis personae are Taurus, Demetrius, Philo, Ventidius, Silius, Scarus, Euphronius, Varrius, and Menecrates. The Clown is omitted inadvertantly from the list of *Persons represented.*

20 *Attendants, Messengers, Officers, and Soldiers.*

CLEOPATRA, *Queen* of Egypt:	Mrs. Yates.
CHARMIAN, and IRAS, } *her Women.*	Miss Hippisley.
	Miss Mills.
OCTAVIA, Caesar's *Sister.*	Mrs. Glen.

Divers other Attendants, Soldiers, Etc.

Scene, dispersed in several Parts of the Roman *Empire.*

Antony and Cleopatra

ACT I.

SCENE I. Alexandria. *A room in* Cleopatra's *palace.*

Enter Thyreus *and* Dolabella, *sent from* Caesar.

THYREUS. Nay, but this dotage of our general's
O'erflows the measure. Those his goodly eyes,
That o'er the files and musters of the war
Have glowed like plated Mars, now bend, now turn
The office and devotion of their view
Upon a tawny front. His captain's heart,
Which in the scuffles of great fights hath burst
The buckles on his breast, reneges all temper
And is become the bellows and the fan
10 To cool a gipsy's lust. Look where they come.

Flourish. Enter Antony, Cleopatra, *and their trains, eunuchs fanning her.*

Take but good note, and you shall see in him
The triple pillar of the world transformed
Into a strumpet's fool. Behold and see.
CLEOPATRA. If it be love indeed, tell me how much.
ANTONY. There's beggary in the love that can be reckoned.
CLEOPATRA. I'll set a bourn how far to be beloved.
ANTONY. Then must thou needs find out new heaven, new earth.

Enter an Attendant.

1. Thyreus] *D1*, *D2*; Philo *D3*, *D4*, *S.*

ATTENDANT. News, my good lord, from Rome.
ANTONY. 'T grates me. The sum.
20 CLEOPATRA. Nay hear them, Antony.
Fulvia perchance is angry. Or, who knows
If the scarce-bearded Caesar have not sent
His powerful mandate to you. Do this, or this;
Take in that kingdom and enfranchise that;
Perform't, or else we damn thee.
ANTONY. How, my love!
CLEOPATRA. Perchance? nay, and most like.
You must not stay here longer, your dismission
Is come from Caesar; therefore hear it. Antony,
30 Where's Fulvia's process? Caesar's, I would say? Both?
Call in the messengers.—As I am Egypt's Queen,
Thou blushest, Antony; and that blood of thine
Is Caesar's homager. So thy cheek pays shame
When shrill-tongued Fulvia scolds.—The messengers.
ANTONY. Let Rome in Tyber melt, and the wide arch
Of the ranged empire fall! Here is my space;
Kingdoms are clay. Our dungy earth alike
Feeds beast as man. The nobleness of life
Is to do thus [*embracing her*] when such a mutual pair
40 And such a twain can do't, in which I bind,
On pain of punishment, the world to weet
We stand up peerless.
CLEOPATRA. Excellent falshood!
Why did he marry Fulvia and not love her?
I seem the fool I am not. Antony
Will be himself.
ANTONY. But stirred by Cleopatra.
Now, for the love of Love and his soft hours,
Let's not confound the time with conference harsh.
50 There's not a minute of our lives should stretch

19. 'T grates] here in *D1* is the first example of Edward Capell's system of enabling the reader to read the play more dramatically. There is a dash at the top of and just preceding the " 'T," indicating a change of address. In the same line appears the second example of the system, a dash at the bottom of and just preceding "The" in Antony's "The sum," indicating a change of address within a speech. See the commentary to this play for a brief explanation of the system.

20. them] *D1*, *D2*, *D3*, *S*; it *D4*.

36. Here is] here is the first instance of Capell's using the cross to indicate a thing pointed to. It is placed between the two words.

Without some pleasure now. What sport tonight?
CLEOPATRA. Hear the ambassadors.
ANTONY. Fie, wrangling Queen!
Whom every thing becomes, to chide, to laugh,
To weep; whose every passion fully strives
To make itself, in thee, fair and admired!
No messenger but thine; and all alone
Tonight we'll wander through the streets and note
The qualities of people. Come, my Queen;
60 Last night you did desire it. Speak not to us.

Exeunt Antony, Cleopatra, *and trains.*

DOLABELLA. Triumphant lady! Fame, I see, is true.
THYREUS. Too true. Since she first met Mark Antony
Upon the river Cydnus, he has been hers.
DOLABELLA. There she appeared indeed; or my reporter
Devised well for her.
THYREUS. I will tell you, sir.
The barge she sat in, like a burnished throne,
Burnt on the water. The poop was beaten gold,
Purple the sails, and so perfumed that
70 The winds were love-sick with them. The oars were silver,
Which to the tune of flutes kept stroke and made
The water which they beat to follow faster,
As amorous of their strokes. For her own person,
It beggared all description: she did lie
In her pavilion, cloth-of-gold of tissue,
O'er-picturing that Venus where we see
The fancy outwork nature. On each side her
Stood pretty dimpled boys, like smiling Cupids,
With divers-colored fans, whose wind did seem

---

51. What] *D*1, *D*2, *D*3, *S*; Now, what *D*4.

61–63. Triumphant. . . . hers] *D*1, *D*2, revised from *S*: "MAEC. She's a most triumphant lady, if report be square to her. / ENO. When she first met Mark Antony, she purs'd up his heart, upon the river of Cydnus." Thereafter four lines are omitted:

DEM. Is Caesar with Antonius priz'd so slight?
PHI. Sir, sometimes when he is not Antony
He comes too short of that great property
Which still should go with Antony.

Here is introduced Enobarbus's description of Cleopatra meeting Antony on the River Cydnus from *S* II, ii, 188–238, fifty-two lines in eighteenth-century typesetting. Enobarbus's speech is given to Thyreus, and those of Agrippa and Maecenas to Dolabella. *D*3, *D*4 follow *S*.

80 To glow the delicate cheeks which they did cool,
And what they undid did.

DOLABELLA. O rare for Antony!

THYREUS. Her gentlewomen, like the Nereids,
So many mermaids, tended her i'the eyes
And made their bends adornings. At the helm
A seeming mermaid steers; the silken tackle
Swell with the touches of those flower-soft hands
That yarely frame the office. From the barge,
A strange invisible perfume hits the sense
90 Of the adjacent wharfs. The city cast
Her people out upon her; and Antony,
Enthroned i'the market place, did sit alone,
Whistling to the air, which, but for vacancy,
Had gone to gaze on Cleopatra too
And made a gap in nature.

DOLABELLA. Rare Egyptian!

THYREUS. Upon her landing, Antony sent to her,
Invited her to supper. She replied,
It should be better he became her guest,
100 Which she intreated. Our courteous Antony,
Whom never the word *no* woman heard speak,
Being barbered ten times o'er, goes to the feast,
And for his ordinary pays his heart
For what his eyes eat only.

DOLABELLA. Royal wench!
She made great Julius lay his sword to bed;
He ploughed her, and she cropped. Now Antony
Must leave her utterly.

THYREUS. Never; he will not.
110 Age cannot wither her, nor custom stale
Her infinite variety. Other women cloy
The appetites they feed, but she makes hungry
Where most she satisfies.

DOLABELLA. Well, I am sorry,
He too approves the common liar, who
Thus speaks of him at Rome. But I will hope
Of better deeds tomorrow. Rest you happy!

Exeunt severally.

---

114. Well, I am] *D1*, *D2*; I am full *D3*, *D4*, *S* (but in II, ii).
115. He too] *D1*, *D2*; That he *D3*, *D4*, *S* (but in II, ii).

SCENE II. *The same. Another room.*
Enter Alexas, Iras, Charmian,
a Soothsayer, *and others.*

CHARMIAN. Alexas, sweet Alexas, most anything Alexas, almost most absolute Alexas, where's the soothsayer that you praised so to the Queen? Oh that I knew this husband which, you say, must charge his horns with garlands!

ALEXAS. Soothsayer–

SOOTHSAYER. Your will?

CHARMIAN. Is this the man? Is't you, sir, that know things?

SOOTHSAYER. In nature's infinite book of secrecy
A little I can read.

10 ALEXAS. Show him your hand.

Enter Enobarbus.

ENOBARBUS (*to some within*). Bring in the banquet quickly; wine enough
Cleopatra's health to drink.

CHARMIAN. Good sir, give me good fortune.

SOOTHSAYER. I make not, but foresee.

CHARMIAN. Pray then, foresee me one. Let me be married to three kings in a forenoon and widow them all. Let me have a child at fifty, to whom Herod of Jewry may do homage. Find me to marry with Octavius Caesar, and companion me with my mistress.

20 SOOTHSAYER. You shall out-live the lady whom you serve.

CHARMIAN. O excellent! I love long life better than figs.

SOOTHSAYER. You have seen and proved a fairer former fortune
Than that which is to approach.

CHARMIAN. Then, belike, my children shall have no names.–
Nay, come, tell Iras hers.

ALEXAS. We'll know all our fortunes.

ENOBARBUS. Mine, and most of our fortunes, tonight, shall be drunk to bed.

IRAS. There's a palm presages chastity, if nothing else.

30 CHARMIAN. E'en as the o'er-flowing Nilus presageth famine.

IRAS. Go, you wild bed-fellow; you cannot soothsay.

CHARMIAN. Nay, if an oily palm be not a fruitful prognostication, I can-

---

1. CHARMIAN] *D1*, *D2*, *S*; *D3*, *D4* omit first sixty-nine lines of the Garrick version (ninety-five in their typesetting, which contains fewer lines set as prose). Francis Gentleman's note in *D3*, *D4* reads, "The whole of this scene might well be spared in representation; it has a blameable relish of indecency."

not scratch mine ear. Prythee, tell her but a workday fortune.

SOOTHSAYER. Your fortunes are alike.

IRAS. But how, but how? Give me particulars.

SOOTHSAYER. I have said.

IRAS. Am I not an inch of fortune better than she?

CHARMIAN. Well, if you were but an inch of fortune better than I, where would you choose it?

40 IRAS. Not in my husband's nose.

CHARMIAN. Our worser thoughts heavens mend! Alexas, come, his fortune, his fortune. O let him marry a woman that cannot go, sweet Isis, I beseech thee! And let her die too, and give him a worse! And let worse follow worse, 'till the worst of all follow him laughing to his grave, fifty-fold a cuckold! Good Isis, hear me this prayer, though thou deny me a matter of more weight; good Isis, I beseech thee!

IRAS. Amen. Dear goddess, hear that prayer of the people! For, as it is a heart-breaking to see a handsome man loose-wived, so it is a deadly

50 sorrow to behold a foul knave uncuckolded. Therefore, dear Isis, keep decorum, and fortune him accordingly!

CHARMIAN. Amen.

ALEXAS. Lo now, if it lay in their hands to make me a cuckold, they would make themselves whores, but they'd do't.

ENOBARBUS. Hush! here comes Antony.

CHARMIAN. Not he, the Queen.

Enter Cleopatra, *attended.*

CLEOPATRA. Saw you my lord?

ENOBARBUS. No, lady.

CLEOPATRA. Was he not here?

60 CHARMIAN. No, madam.

CLEOPATRA. He was disposed to mirth; but on the sudden
A Roman thought hath strook him. Enobarbus!

ENOBARBUS. Madam.

CLEOPATRA. Seek him, and bring him hither. Where's Alexas?

ALEXAS. Here, lady, at your service. My lord approaches.

Enter Antony, *with a* Messenger, Attendants *following.*

CLEOPATRA. We will not look upon him. Go with us.

---

33. workday] *D1*; worky-day *D2*, *D3*, *D4*, *S*.

57. CLEOPATRA] *D4* begins scene iii here but indicates omission of the next ten lines (twelve in *D4* setting).

Exeunt Cleopatra, Enobarbus, Alexas, Iras,
Charmian, Soothsayer, *and the rest.*

MESSENGER. Fulvia thy wife first came into the field.
ANTONY. Against my brother Lucius?
MESSENGER. Ay. But soon
70 That war had end, and the time's state made friends
Of them, jointing their forces against Caesar,
Whose better issue in the war from Italy
Upon the first encounter drave them.
ANTONY. Well,
What worst?
MESSENGER. The nature of bad news infects the teller.
ANTONY. When it concerns the fool or coward. On!
Things that are past are done, with me. 'Tis thus:
Who tells me true, though in his tale lie death,
80 I hear him as he flattered.
MESSENGER. Labienus
Hath with his Parthian force, through extended Asia,
From Euphrates his conquering banner shook
From Syria to Lydia and Ionia,
Whilst–
ANTONY. Antony, thou would'st say–
MESSENGER. O, my lord–
ANTONY. Speak to me home, mince not the general tongue;
Name Cleopatra as she's called in Rome.
90 Rail thou in Fulvia's phrase, and taunt my faults
With such full licence as both truth and malice
Have power to utter. Oh, then we bring forth weeds
When our quick winds lie still and our ills told us
Is as our earing. Fare thee well a while.
MESSENGER. At your noble pleasure.

Exit.

ANTONY. From Sicyon how the news? Speak there.
1ST. ATTENDANT. The man from Sicyon, is there such a one?
2ND ATTENDANT. He stays upon your will.
ANTONY. Let him appear.
100 These strong Egyptian fetters I must break,

Enter another Messenger.

Or lose myself in dotage. What are you?

81. Labienus] *D1*, *D2*; Labienus (This is stiff news) *D3*, *D4*, *S*.

MESSENGER. Fulvia thy wife is dead.
ANTONY. Where died she?
MESSENGER. In Sicyon.
Her length of sickness, with what else more serious
Importeth thee to know, this bears. [*Gives a letter.*]
ANTONY. Forbear me.

Exit Messenger.

There's a great spirit gone. Thus did I desire it.
What our contempts do often hurl from us,
110 We wish it ours again; the present pleasure,
By revolution lowering, does become
The opposite of itself. She's good, being gone;
The hand could pluck her back that shoved her on.
I must from this enchanting Queen break off;
Ten thousand harms, more than the ills I know,
My idleness doth hatch.—Ho, Enobarbus!

Enter Enobarbus.

ENOBARBUS. What's your pleasure, sir?
ANTONY. I must with haste from hence.
ENOBARBUS. Why, then we kill all our women. We see how mortal an
120 unkindness is to them; if they suffer our departure, death's the word.
ANTONY. I must be gone.
ENOBARBUS. Under a compelling occasion, let women die. It were pity to cast them away for nothing; though, between them and a great cause, they should be esteemed nothing. Cleopatra, catching but the least noise of this, dies instantly. I have seen her die twenty times upon far poorer moment.
ANTONY. She is cunning past man's thought. Fulvia is dead.
ENOBARBUS. Sir?
ANTONY. Fulvia is dead.
130 ENOBARBUS. Fulvia?
ANTONY. Dead.
ENOBARBUS. Why, sir, give the gods a thankful sacrifice. If there were no more women but Fulvia, then had you indeed a cut, and the case were to be lamented. This grief is crowned with consolation; your old smock brings forth a new petticoat, and, indeed, the tears live in

---

126. poorer moment] *D*1, *D*2 omit thirteen lines following, retaining only one (line 126) from this exchange between Antony and Enobarbus.

132. sacrifice] *D*1, *D*2 omit four lines following; *D*3, *D*4 indicate omission of entire ten-line speech of Enobarbus. Francis Gentleman notes, "The would-be wit of Enobarbus in this speech had better be omitted."

an onion that should water this sorrow.

ANTONY. The business she hath broached in the state
Cannot endure my absence.

ENOBARBUS. And the business you have broached here cannot be with-
140 out you; especially that of Cleopatra's, which wholly depends on
your abode.

ANTONY. No more light answers. Let our officers
Have notice what we purpose. I shall break
The cause of our expedience to the Queen
And get her love to part. For not alone
The death of Fulvia, with more urgent touches,
Do strongly speak to us; but the letters too
Of many our contriving friends in Rome
Petition us at home. Sextus Pompeius
150 Hath given the dare to Caesar and commands
The empire of the sea. Our slippery people,
Whose love is never linked to the deserver
'Till his deserts are past, begin to throw
Pompey the Great and all his dignities
Upon his son, who, high in name and power,
Higher than both in blood and life, stands up
For the main soldier, whose quality, going on,
The sides o'the world may danger. Much is breeding,
Which, like the courser's hair, hath yet but life,
160 And not a serpent's poison. Say, our pleasure,
To such whose place is under us, requires
Our quick remove from hence.

ENOBARBUS. I shall do't.

Exeunt.

SCENE III. *The same. Another room.*
Enter Cleopatra, Charmian, Iras, *and* Alexas.

CLEOPATRA. Where is he?

CHARMIAN. I did not see him since.

CLEOPATRA. See where he is, who's with him, what he does—
I did not send you. (*To* Iras.) If you find him sad,

---

139. ENOBARBUS] *D3*, *D4* omit the speech and Antony's first sentence, following, four lines. Gentleman says, "This reply to Antony should be suppressed, as conveying a fulsom, needless idea, impertinent to Antony and totally beneath the subject of conversation."

0. SCENE III] *D1*, *D2*, *D3*, *S*; scene iv *D4*.

4. (*To* Iras) *D1*, *D2*.

Say I am dancing; if in mirth, report
That I am sudden sick. Quick, and return.

Exit Alexas.

CHARMIAN. Madam, methinks if you did love him dearly,
You do not hold the method to enforce
The like from him.

10 CLEOPATRA. What should I do I do not?

CHARMIAN. In each thing give him way; cross him in nothing.

CLEOPATRA. Thou teachest like a fool the way to lose him.

CHARMIAN. Tempt him not so too far; I wish, forbear;
In time we hate that which we often fear.

Enter Antony.

But here comes Antony.

CLEOPATRA. I am sick and sullen.

ANTONY. I am sorry to give breathing to my purpose—

CLEOPATRA. Help me away, dear Charmian, I shall fall;
It cannot be thus long; the sides of nature
20 Will not sustain it.

ANTONY. Now, my dearest Queen—

CLEOPATRA. Pray you, stand farther from me.

ANTONY. What's the matter?

CLEOPATRA. I know by that same eye there's some good news.
What says the married woman? You may go?
Would she had never given you leave to come!
Let her not say 'tis I that keep you here.
I have no power upon you; hers you are.

ANTONY. The gods best know—

30 CLEOPATRA. O never was there queen
So mightily betrayed! Yet, at the first,
I saw the treasons planted.

ANTONY. Cleopatra—

CLEOPATRA. Why should I think you can be mine, and true,
Though you in swearing shake the throned gods,
Who have been false to Fulvia? Riotous madness,
To be entangled with those mouth-made vows
Which break themselves in swearing!

ANTONY. Most sweet Queen—

40 CLEOPATRA. Nay, pray you, seek no color for your going,
But bid farewell, and go. When you sued staying,
Then was the time for words. No going then;

---

20. sustain it] *D1*, *D2*, *D3*, *S*; it (*Seeming to faint*) *D4*.

Eternity was in our lips and eyes,
Bliss in our brows' bent; none our parts so poor
But was a race of heaven. They are so still,
Or thou, the greatest soldier of the world,
Art turned the greatest liar.

ANTONY. How now, lady?

CLEOPATRA. I would I had thy inches; thou should'st know
50 There were a heart in Egypt.

ANTONY. Hear me, Queen.
The strong necessity of time commands
Our services a while; but my full heart
Remains in use with you. Our Italy
Shines o'er with civil swords. Sextus Pompeius
Makes his approaches to the port of Rome.
Equality of two domestic powers
Breeds scrupulous faction. The hated, grown to strength,
Are newly grown to love. The condemned Pompey,
60 Rich in his father's honor, creeps apace
Into the hearts of such as have not thrived
Upon the present state, whose numbers threaten;
And quietness, grown sick of rest, would purge
By any desperate change. My more particular,
And that which most with you should safe my going,
Is Fulvia's death.

CLEOPATRA. Though age from folly could not give me freedom,
It does from childishness. Can Fulvia die?

ANTONY. She's dead, my Queen.
70 Look here, and at thy sovereign leisure read
The garboils she awaked; at the last best,
See when and where she died.

CLEOPATRA. O most false love!
Where be the sacred vials thou should'st fill
With sorrowful water? Now I see, I see,
In Fulvia's death, how mine shall be received.

ANTONY. Quarrel no more, but be prepared to know
The purposes I bear; which are, or cease,
As you shall give the advices. By the fire
80 That quickens Nilus' slime, I go from hence
Thy soldier, servant, making peace or war
As thou affect'st.

---

70. Look here] Capell's first use of the double cross to indicate a thing delivered is between these two words.

CLEOPATRA. Cut my lace, Charmian, come!
But let it be; I am quickly ill and well,
So Antony loves.

ANTONY. My precious Queen, forbear,
And give true evidence to his love, which stands
An honorable trial.

CLEOPATRA. So Fulvia told me.
90 I prythee, turn aside and weep for her;
Then bid adieu to me, and say the tears
Belong to Egypt. Good now, play one scene
Of excellent dissembling and let it look
Like perfect honor.

ANTONY. You'll heat my blood. No more.

CLEOPATRA. You can do better yet; but this is meetly.

ANTONY. Now, by my sword—

CLEOPATRA. —and target. Still he mends;
But this is not the best. Look, prythee, Charmian,
100 How this Herculean Roman does become
The carriage of his chafe.

ANTONY. I'll leave you, lady.

CLEOPATRA. Courteous lord, one word.
Sir, you and I must part—but that's not it.
Sir, you and I have loved—but there's not it;
That you know well. Something it is I would—
O, my oblivion is a very Antony,
And I am all forgotten.

ANTONY. But that your royalty
110 Holds idleness your subject, I should take you
For idleness itself.

CLEOPATRA. 'Tis sweating labor
To bear such idleness so near the heart
As Cleopatra this. But, sir, forgive me,
Since my becomings kill me when they do not
Eye well to you. Your honor calls you hence;
Therefore be deaf to my unpitied folly,
And all the gods go with you. Upon your sword
Sit laureled victory, and smooth success
120 Be strewed before your feet.

ANTONY. Let us go. Come;
Our separation so abides and flies
That thou, residing here, go'st yet with me,

---

83. CLEOPATRA] *D3*, *D4* omit thirty-three and a half following lines.

And I, hence fleeting, here remain with thee.
Away.

Exeunt.

SCENE IV. Rome. *A room in* Caesar's *house.*
Enter Octavius Caesar, Lepidus, *and their trains.*

CAESAR. You may see, Lepidus, and henceforth know,
It is not Caesar's natural vice to hate
One great competitor. From Alexandria
This is the news: He fishes, drinks, and wastes
The lamps of night in revel. Is not more manlike
Than Cleopatra, nor the Queen of Ptolemy
More womanly than he. Hardly gave audience or
Vouchsafed to think he had partners. You shall find there
A man who is the abstract of all faults
10 That all men follow.
LEPIDUS. I must not think there are
Evils enough to darken all his goodness.
His faults in him seem as the spots of heaven,
More fiery by night's blackness; hereditary
Rather than purchased; what he cannot change
Than what he chooses.
CAESAR. You are too indulgent. Let us grant it is not
Amiss to tumble on the bed of Ptolemy,
To give a kingdom for a mirth, to sit
20 And keep the turn of tipling with a slave,
To reel the streets at noon and stand the buffet
With knaves that smell of sweat. Say this becomes him
(As his composure must be rare indeed,
Whom these things cannot blemish), yet must Antony
No way excuse his foils when we do bear
So great weight in his lightness. If he filled
His vacancy with his voluptuousness,
Full surfeits, and the dryness of his bones
Call on him for't. But to confound such time,

---

0. SCENE IV] *D*1, *D*2, *D*3, *S*; scene v *D*4.
1. see, Lepidus] that *D*2 was set from *D*1 with Capell's markings intentionally omitted is evident from this, one of two instances where a Capell prompting mark is inadvertantly set. A cross is set between the two words (in error for a double cross). *D*3, *D*4 add (*Giving him a letter to read*).

30 That drums him from his sport and speaks as loud
As his own state, and ours, 'tis to be chid
As we rate boys, who, being mature in knowledge,
Pawn their experience to their present pleasure
And so rebel to judgment.

Enter a Messenger.

LEPIDUS. Here's more news.
MESSENGER. Thy biddings have been done, and every hour,
Most noble Caesar, shalt thou have report
How 'tis abroad. Pompey is strong at sea;
And it appears he is beloved of those
40 That only have feared Caesar. To the ports
The discontents repair, and men's reports
Give him much wronged.
CAESAR. I should have known no less.
It hath been taught us from the primal state
That he which is was wished until he were;
And the ebbed man, ne'er loved 'till ne'er worth love,
Comes deared by being lacked. This common body,
Like to a vagabond flag upon the stream,
Goes to and back, lacquying the varying tide,
50 To rot itself with motion.

Enter another Messenger.

MESSENGER. Caesar, I bring thee word
Menecrates and Menas, famous pirates,
Make the sea serve them, which they ear and wound
With keels of every kind. Many hot inroads
They make in Italy; the borders maritime
Lack blood to think on't, and flush youth revolt.
No vessel can peep forth but 'tis as soon
Taken as seen; for Pompey's name strikes more
Than could his war resisted.
60 CAESAR. Antony,
Leave thy lascivious wassails. When thou once
Wert beaten from Modena, where thou slew'st
Hirtius and Pansa, consuls, at thy heel
Did famine follow, whom thou fought'st against,
Though daintily brought up, with patience more
Than savages could suffer. Thou did'st drink
The stale of horses and the gilded puddle
Which beasts would cough at. Thy palate then did deign

The roughest berry on the rudest hedge;
70 Yea, like the stag, when snow the pasture sheets,
The barks of trees thou browsed'st. On the Alps,
It is reported, thou did'st eat strange flesh,
Which some did die to look on. And all this
(It wounds thine honor that I speak it now)
Was born so like a soldier that thy cheek
So much as lanked not.

LEPIDUS. 'Tis pity of him.

CAESAR. Let his shames quickly
Drive him to Rome. Time is it that we twain
80 Did show ourselves i'the field; and to that end
Assemble we immediate council. Pompey
Thrives in our idleness.

LEPIDUS. Tomorrow, Caesar,
I shall be furnished to inform you rightly
Both what by sea and land I can be able
To 'front this present time.

CAESAR. 'Till which encounter,
It is my business too. Farewell.

LEPIDUS. Farewell, my lord. What you shall know meantime
90 Of stirs abroad, I shall beseech you, sir,
To let me be partaker.

CAESAR. Doubt not, sir;
I knew it for my bond.

Exeunt.

SCENE V. Alexandria. *A room in the palace.*
Enter Cleopatra *supporting herself on* Iras, Charmian *and* Mardian *following.*

CLEOPATRA. Charmian!

CHARMIAN. Madam.

CLEOPATRA. Ha, ha! Give me to drink mandragora.

CHARMIAN. Why, madam?

CLEOPATRA. That I might sleep out this great gap of time

90. sir] *D1*, *D2*, *D3*, *S*; omitted *D4*.
91. To let] *D1*, *D2*, *D3*, *S*; Let *D4*.
92. Doubt not] *D1*, *D2*, *D3*, *S*; Doubt it not *D4*.
0. SCENE V] *D1*, *D2*, *D3*, *S*; scene vi *D4*.

My Antony is away.
CHARMIAN. You think of him
Too much.
CLEOPATRA. O! Treason!
10 CHARMIAN. Madam, I trust not so.
CLEOPATRA. Thou, eunuch Mardian!
MARDIAN. What's your Highness' pleasure?
CLEOPATRA. Not now to hear you sing; I take no pleasure
In aught an eunuch has. 'Tis well for thee
That, being unseminared, thy freer thoughts
May not fly forth of Egypt. Has thou affections?
MARDIAN. Yes, gracious madam.
CLEOPATRA. Indeed! O Charmian,
Where think'st thou he is now? Stands he, or sits he?
20 Or does he walk? Or is he on his horse?
O happy horse, to bear the weight of Antony!
Do bravely, horse; for wot'st thou whom thou mov'st?
The demy Atlas of this earth, the arm
And burgonet of man. He's speaking now,
Or murmuring, "Where's my serpent of old Nile?"
For so he calls me. Now I feed myself
With most delicious poison. Think on me,
That am with Phoebus' amorous pinches black,
And wrinkled deep in time? Broad-fronted Caesar,
30 When thou wast here above the ground, I was
A morsel for a monarch; and great Pompey
Would stand and make his eyes grow in my brow;
There would he anchor his aspect, and die
With looking on his life.

Enter Alexas.

ALEXAS. Sovereign of Egypt, hail!
CLEOPATRA. How much art thou unlike Mark Antony!
Yet, coming from him, that great medicine hath
With his tinct gilded thee.
How goes it with my brave Mark Antony?
40 ALEXAS. Last thing he did, dear Queen,
He kissed, the last of many doubled kisses,
This orient pearl. His speech sticks in my heart.
CLEOPATRA. Mine ear must pluck it thence.
ALEXAS. "Good friend," quoth he,

---

11. Thou, eunuch] *D*3, *D*4 indicate omission of twenty-four following lines.

"Say, the firm Roman to great Egypt sends
This [*gives pearl*] treasure of an oyster, at whose foot,
To mend the pretty present, I will piece
Her opulent throne with kingdoms; all the East,
Say thou, shall call her mistress." So he nodded,
50 And soberly did mount an arm-gaunt steed,
Who neighed so high that what I would have spoke
Was beastly dumbed by him.

CLEOPATRA. What, was he sad or merry?

ALEXAS. Like to the time o'the year between the extremes
Of hot and cold, he was nor sad nor merry.

CLEOPATRA. O well-divided disposition! Note him,
Note him, good Charmian; 'tis the man, but note him!
He was not sad, for he would shine on those
That make their looks by his. He was not merry,
60 Which seemed to tell them his remembrance lay
In Egypt with his joy, but between both.
O heavenly mingle! Be'st thou sad or merry,
The violence of either thee becomes;
So does it no man else. Met'st thou my posts?

ALEXAS. Ay, madam, twenty several messengers.
Why do you send so thick?

CLEOPATRA. Who's born that day
When I forget to send to Antony
Shall die a beggar.—Ink and paper, Charmian.—
70 Welcome, my good Alexas.—Did I, Charmian,
Ever love Caesar so?

CHARMIAN. O that brave Caesar!

CLEOPATRA. Be choked with such another emphasis!
Say "the brave Antony."

CHARMIAN. The valiant Caesar!

CLEOPATRA. By Isis, I will give thee bloody teeth
If thou with Caesar paragon again
My man of men.

CHARMIAN. By your most gracious pardon.
80 I sing but after you.

CLEOPATRA. My salad days,
When I was green in judgment, cold in blood;
To say as I said then! But come, away;
Get me ink and paper. He shall have every day
A several greeting, or I'll unpeople Egypt.

Exeunt.

ACT II.

SCENE I. *A room in* Lepidus' *house.*

Enter Lepidus *and* Enobarbus.

LEPIDUS. Good Enobarbus, 'tis a worthy deed,
And shall become you well, to entreat your captain
To soft and gentle speech.
ENOBARBUS. I shall entreat him
To answer like himself. If Caesar move him,
Let Antony look over Caesar's head
And speak as loud as Mars. By Jupiter,
Were I the wearer of Antonio's beard,
I would not shave't today.
10 LEPIDUS. 'Tis not a time
For private stomaching.
ENOBARBUS. Every time
Serves for the matter that is then born in't.
LEPIDUS. But small to greater matters must give way.
ENOBARBUS. Not if the small come first.
LEPIDUS. Your speech is passion.
But, pray you, stir no embers up. Here comes
The noble Antony.

Enter Antony *and* Canidius.

ENOBARBUS. And yonder Caesar.

Enter Caesar, Agrippa, *and* Mecaenas.

20 ANTONY. If we compose well here, to Parthia.
Hark you, Canidius–
CAESAR. I do not know,
Mecaenas; ask Agrippa.
LEPIDUS. Noble friends,
That which combined us was most great, and let not
A leaner action rend us. What's amiss,
May it be gently heard. When we debate
Our trivial difference loud, we do commit
Murder in healing wounds. Then, noble partners
30 (The rather for I earnestly beseech),
Touch you the sourest points with sweetest terms,

---

0. SCENE I] *D1*, *D2*; scene II *D3*, *D4*, *S*. The entire first *S* scene, fifty-two lines, is omitted *D1*, *D2*. Garrick's version begins act II with scene ii.

21. Hark you, Canidius] *D1*, *D2*; Hark, Ventitius *D3*, *D4*, *S*.

Nor curstness grow to the matter.

ANTONY. 'Tis spoken well.
Were we before our armies, and to fight,
I should do thus.

CAESAR. Welcome to Rome.

ANTONY. Thank you.

CAESAR. Sit.

ANTONY. Sit, sir.

40 CAESAR. Nay then.

[*They sit.*]

ANTONY. I learn you take things ill which are not so,
Or being, concern you not.

CAESAR. I must be laughed at
If, or for nothing or a little, I
Should say myself offended; and with you
Chiefly i'the world; more laughed at that I should
Once name you derogately, when to sound your name
It not concerned me.

ANTONY. My being in Egypt, Caesar,
50 What was't to you?

CAESAR. No more than my residing here at Rome
Might be to you in Egypt. Yet if you there
Did practise on my state, your being in Egypt
Might be my question.

ANTONY. How intend you, practiced?

CAESAR. You may be pleased to catch at mine intent
By what did here befall me. Your wife and brother
Made wars upon me; and their contestation
Was themed for you, you were the word of war.

60 ANTONY. You do mistake your business; my brother never
Did urge me in his act. I did inquire it
And have my learning from some true reports
That drew their swords with you. Did he not rather
Discredit my authority with yours
And make the wars alike against my stomach,
Having alike your cause? Of this, my letters
Before did satisfy you. If you'll patch a quarrel,
As matter whole you have not to make it with,
It must not be with this.

70 CAESAR. You praise yourself
By laying to me defects of judgment, but
You patched up your excuses.

ANTONY. Not so, not so.

I know you could not lack, I am certain on't,
Very necessity of this thought, that I,
Your partner in the cause 'gainst which he fought,
Could not with grateful eyes attend those wars
Which 'fronted mine own peace. As for my wife,
I would you had her spirit in such another.
80 The third o'the world is yours, which with a snaffle
You may pace easy, but not such a wife.

ENOBARBUS. 'Would we had all such wives, that the men might go to wars with the women.

ANTONY. So much uncurbable, her garboils, Caesar,
Made out of her impatience, which not wanted
Shrewdness of policy too, I grieving grant
Did you too much disquiet, for that you must
But say I could not help it.

CAESAR. I wrote to you
90 When rioting in Alexandria. You
Did pocket up my letters and with taunts
Did gibe my missive out of audience.

ANTONY. Sir,
He fell upon me ere admitted; then
Three Kings I had newly feasted, and did want
Of what I was i'the morning; but next day
I told him of myself, which was as much
As to have asked him pardon. Let this fellow
Be nothing of our strife; if we contend,
100 Out of our question wipe him.

CAESAR. You have broken
The article of your oath, which you shall never
Have tongue to charge me with.

LEPIDUS. Soft, Caesar.

ANTONY. No,
Lepidus, let him speak.
The honor is sacred which he talks on now,
Supposing that I lacked it. But on, Caesar;
The article of my oath—

110 CAESAR. To lend me arms and aid when I required them,
The which you both denied.

ANTONY. Neglected, rather;
And then, when poisoned hours had bound me up
From mine own knowledge. As nearly as I may,

82. ENOBARBUS] *D3*, *D4* omit nineteen following lines.
101. You] *D1*, *D2*, *D3*, *S*; No, you *D4*.

I'll play the penitent to you; but mine honesty
Shall not make poor my greatness, nor my power
Work without it. Truth is, that Fulvia,
To have me out of Egypt, made wars here,
For which myself, the ignorant motive, do
120 So far ask pardon as befits mine honor
To stoop in such a case.

LEPIDUS. 'Tis nobly spoken.

MECAENAS. If it might please you to enforce no farther
The griefs between ye: to forget them quite
Were to remember that the present need
Speaks to atone you.

LEPIDUS. Worthily spoken, Mecaenas.

ENOBARBUS. Or, if you borrow one another's love for the instant, you may, when you hear no more words of Pompey, return it again. You
130 shall have time to wrangle in when you have nothing else to do.

ANTONY. Thou are a soldier only; speak no more.

ENOBARBUS. That truth should be silent I had almost forgot.

ANTONY. You wrong this presence; therefore speak no more.

ENOBARBUS. Go to then; your considerate stone.

CAESAR. I do not much mislike the manner, but
The matter of his speech; for't cannot be
We shall remain in friendship, our conditions
So differing in their acts. Yet if I knew
What hoop should hold us staunch, from edge to edge
140 O'the world I would pursue it.

AGRIPPA, Give me leave, Caesar—

CAESAR. Speak, Agrippa.

AGRIPPA. Thou hast a sister by the mother's side,
Admired Octavia. Great Mark Antony
Is now a widower.

CAESAR. Say not so, Agrippa;
If Cleopatra heard you, your reproof
Were well deserved of rashness.

ANTONY. I am not married, Caesar; let me hear
150 Agrippa further speak.

AGRIPPA. To hold you in perpetual amity,
To make you brothers, and to knit your hearts
With an unslipping knot, take Antony
Octavia to his wife, whose beauty claims

---

122. 'Tis nobly . . .] *D*3, *D*4 omit thirteen lines here (fourteen in their type-setting).

141. Give me . . .] *D*3, *D*4 omit ten lines here.

No worse a husband than the best of men,
Whose virtue and whose general graces speak
That which none else can utter. By this marriage
All little jealousies, which now seem great,
And all great fears, which now import their dangers,
160 Would then be nothing. Truths would then be tales,
Where now half tales be truths; her love to both
Would, each to other, and all loves to both,
Draw after her. Pardon what I have spoke;
For 'tis a studied, not a present thought,
By duty ruminated.

ANTONY. Will Caesar speak?

CAESAR. Not 'till he hears how Antony is touched
With what is spoke already.

ANTONY. What power is in Agrippa,
170 If I would say, "Agrippa, be it so,"
To make this good?

CAESAR. The power of Caesar, and
His power unto Octavia.

ANTONY. May I never
To this good purpose, that so fairly shows,
Dream of impediment! Let me have thy hand.
Further this act of grace; and, from this hour
The heart of brothers govern in our loves
And sway our great designs!

180 CAESAR. There is my hand.
A sister I bequeath you, whom no brother
Did ever love so dearly. Let her live
To join our kingdoms and our hearts, and never
Fly off our loves again!

LEPIDUS. Happily! Amen.

ANTONY. I did not think to draw my sword 'gainst Pompey;
For he hath laid strange courtesies, and great,
Of late upon me. I must thank him only,
Lest my remembrance suffer ill report;
190 At heel of that, defy him.

LEPIDUS. Time calls upon us.
Of us must Pompey presently be fought,
Or else he seeks out us.

ANTONY. Where lies he, Caesar?

---

160. Truths would] *D3*, *D4* omit three lines, through "Draw after her."
169. What power . . .] *D3* omits five lines here.
194. lies he, Caesar?] *D1*, *D2*, *D3*; lies he? *D4*, *S*.

CAESAR. About the Mount Misenum.
ANTONY. What's his strength
By land?
CAESAR. Great, and encreasing. But by sea
He is an absolute master.
200 ANTONY. So is the fame.
'Would we had spoke together! Haste we for it.
Yet, ere we put ourselves in arms, dispatch we
The business we have talked of.
CAESAR. With most gladness;
And do invite you to my sister's view,
Whither straight I'll lead you.
ANTONY. Let us, Lepidus,
Not lack your company.
LEPIDUS. Noble Antony,
210 Not sickness should detain me.

Exeunt.

SCENE II. Alexandria. *A room in the palace.*
Enter Cleopatra, Charmian, Iras, *and* Alexas.

CLEOPATRA. Give me some music—music, moody food
Of us that trade in love.
ATTENDANT. The music, ho!

Enter Mardian.

CLEOPATRA. Let it alone; let us to billiards. Come, Charmian.
CHARMIAN. My arm is sore; best play with Mardian.
CLEOPATRA. As well a woman with an eunuch played
As with a woman. Come, you'll play with me, sir?
MARDIAN. As well as I can, madam.
CLEOPATRA. And when good will is showed, though't come too short,
10 The actor may plead pardon. I'll none now.
Give me mine angle. We'll to the river. There,

210. detain me] *D1*, *D2* have the Enobarbus-Agrippa-Maecenas scene in I, i. Seventeen lines are omitted from the scene, beginning with Agrippa's "Rare Egyptian" and ending with Enobarbus's "And, breathless, power breath forth." Seven and a half lines at the end are also omitted.

0. SCENE II] *D1*, *D2*; scene v *D3*, *D4*, *S*. *D1*, *D2*, omit next *S* scene, iii, entirely, forty-eight lines in contemporary typography. *D3*, *D4* use first nine *S* lines (eleven in their typography) at beginning of scene and last two and a half lines at end, eliminating thirty-four and a half lines. *D1*, *D2* also omit *S* scene iv, totaling fourteen lines.

My music playing far off, I will betray
Tawny-finned fishes; my bended hook shall pierce
Their slimy jaws; and, as I draw them up,
I'll think them every one an Antony
And say, "Ah, ha! you're caught."

CHARMIAN. 'Twas merry when
You wagered on your angling; when your diver
Did hang a salt-fish on his hook, which he
20 With fervency drew up.

CLEOPATRA. That time! O times!
I laughed him out of patience; and that night
I laughed him into patience, and next morn,
Ere the ninth hour, I drunk him to his bed,
Then put my tires and mantles on him, whilst
I wore his sword Philippan.

Enter a Messenger.

Oh, from Italy!
Rain thou thy fruitful tidings in mine ears,
That long time have been barren.

30 MESSENGER. Madam, madam!

CLEOPATRA. Antony's dead! If thou say so,
Villain, thou kill'st thy mistress; but well and free,
If thou so yield him, there is gold [*giving gold*] and here
My bluest veins to kiss, a hand that kings
Have lipped, and trembled kissing.

MESSENGER. First, madam, he is well.

CLEOPATRA. Why, there's more gold. [*Giving gold.*] But, sirrah, mark: we use
To say the dead are well. Bring it to that,
40 The gold I give thee will I melt and pour
Down thy ill-uttering throat.

MESSENGER. Good madam, hear me.

CLEOPATRA. Well, go to; I will.
But there's no goodness in thy face. If Antony
Be free and healthful, why so tart a favor
To trumpet such good tidings? If not well,
Thou should'st come like a fury crowned with snakes,
Not like a formal man.

MESSENGER. Wilt please you hear me?

---

24. drunk] *D1*, *D3 S*; drank *D2*, *D4*.
33. thou so] *D1*, *D2*, *D3*, *S*; so thou *D4*.
49. Wilt please . . .] *D3*, *D4* omit six lines, through Cleopatra's next speech.

50 CLEOPATRA. I have a mind to strike thee ere thou speak'st.
Yet if thou say Antony lives, is well,
Or friends with Caesar, or not captive to him,
I'll set thee in a shower of gold and hail
Rich pearls upon thee.
MESSENGER. Madam, he's well.
CLEOPATRA. Well said.
MESSENGER. And friends with Caesar.
CLEOPATRA. Thou'rt an honest man.
MESSENGER. Caesar and he are greater friends than ever.
60 CLEOPATRA. Mark thee a fortune from me.
MESSENGER. But yet, madam—
CLEOPATRA. I do not like "but yet"; it does allay
The good precedence; fie upon "but yet."
"But yet" is as a jailor to bring forth
Some monstrous malefactor. Prythee, friend,
Pour out thy pack of matter to mine ear,
The good and bad together. He's friends with Caesar;
In state of health, thou say'st; and, thou say'st, free.
MESSENGER. Free, madam? No, I made no such report.
70 He's bound unto Octavia.
CLEOPATRA. I am pale, Charmian.
MESSENGER. Madam, he's married to Octavia.
CLEOPATRA. The most infectious pestilence upon thee! (*Strikes him down.*)
MESSENGER. Good madam, patience.
CLEOPATRA. What say you? (*Striking him again.*) Hence,
Horrible villain! or I'll spurn thine eyes
Like balls before me; I'll unhair thy head. (*Hales him up and down.*)
Thou shalt be whipped with wire, and stewed in brine,
Smarting in ling'ring pickle.
80 MESSENGER. Gracious madam,
I that do bring the news made not the match.
CLEOPATRA. Say 'tis not so, a province I will give thee
And make thy fortunes proud. The blow thou had'st
Shall make thy peace for moving me to rage.
And I will boot thee with what gift beside
Thy modesty can beg.

---

60. Mark] Make *S*.

70. unto Octavia] all Garrick versions omit the two following lines: "CLEO. For what good turn? / MESS. For the best turn i' the bed."

73. The most infectious . . .] *D*3 *D*4 indicate omission of nine lines beginning here.

MESSENGER. He's married, madam.
CLEOPATRA. Rogue, thou hast lived too long. (*Draws a dagger.*)
MESSENGER. Nay, then I'll run.
90 What mean you, madam? I have made no fault.

Exit Messenger.

CHARMIAN. Good madam, keep yourself within yourself;
The man is innocent.
CLEOPATRA. Some innocents 'scape not the thunderbolt.
Melt Egypt into Nile, and kindly creatures
Turn all to serpents!—Call the slave again;
Though I am mad, I will not bite him. Call.
CHARMIAN. He is afeard to come.
CLEOPATRA. I will not hurt him.—
These hands do lack nobility, that they strike
100 A meaner than myself, since I myself
Have given myself the cause.—Come hither, sir.

Re-enter Messenger.

Though it be honest, it is never good
To bring bad news. Give to a gracious message
An host of tongues, but let ill tidings tell
Themselves when they be felt.
MESSENGER. I have but done my duty.
CLEOPATRA. Is he married?
I cannot hate thee worser than I do,
If thou again say yes.
110 MESSENGER. He's married, madam.
CLEOPATRA. The gods confound thee! Dost thou hold there still?
MESSENGER. Should I lie, madam?
CLEOPATRA. O I would thou did'st,
So half my Egypt were submerged and made
A cistern for scaled snakes! Go, get thee hence;
Had'st thou Narcissus in thy face, to me
Thou would'st appear most ugly. He is married?
MESSENGER. I crave your highness' pardon.
CLEOPATRA. He is married?
120 MESSENGER. Take no offence that I would not offend you.
To punish me for what you make me do
Seems much unequal. He's married to Octavia.
CLEOPATRA. O that his fault should make a knave of thee,
That say'st but what thou art sure of! Get thee hence.

---

88. Rogue . . .] *D*3, *D*4 indicate omission of fourteen lines beginning here.

The merchandise which thou hast brought from Rome
Are all too dear for me. Lie they upon thy hand,
And be undone by 'em!

Exit Messenger.

CHARMIAN. Good your Highness, patience.
CLEOPATRA. In praising Antony I have dispraised Caesar.
130 CHARMIAN. Many times, madam.
CLEOPATRA. I am paid for't now.
Lead me hence,
I faint; O Iras, Charmian!—'Tis no matter.
Go to the fellow, good Alexas; bid him
Report the feature of Octavia, her years,
Her inclination; let him not leave out
The color of her hair. Bring me word quickly.

Exit Alexas.

Let him for ever go.—Let him not, Charmian;
Though he be painted one way like a Gorgon,
140 The other way's a Mars. (*To* Mardian.) Bid you Alexas
Bring me word how tall she is. Pity me, Charmian,
But do not speak to me. Lead me to my chamber.

SCENE III. *Aboard* Pompey's *galley off* Misenum.
Under a pavilion upon deck, a banquet set out. Music. Servants attending.
Enter Menas *and* Enobarbus, *meeting.*

MENAS. Thy father, Pompey, would neer have made this treaty.—You and I have known, sir.
ENOBARBUS. Menas, I think.
MENAS. The same, sir.
ENOBARBUS. We came hither to fight with you.
MENAS. For my part, I am sorry it is turned to a drinking. Pompey doth this day laugh away his fortune.
ENOBARBUS. If he do, sure he cannot weep it back again.
MENAS. You have said, sir. We looked not for Mark Antony here. Pray

0. SCENE III] *D1*, *D2*; scenes vi, vii *D3*, *D4*, *S*. *D1*, *D2* omit the first 107 lines, of which *D3*, *D4* omit 28.
1. Thy father] line 82 in *S*. *D3*, *D4* indicate omission of the remainder of the scene, fifty-four lines. *D1*, *D2* use the first two *S* lines, revise the next two, and eliminate the next fourteen (86–99 in *S*.)
3. Menas] *D1*, *D2*; At sea *D3*, *D4*, *S*.
4. The same] *D1*, *D2*; We have *D3*, *D4*, *S*.

10 you, is he married to Cleopatra?

ENOBARBUS. Caesar's sister is called Octavia.

MENAS. True, sir; she was the wife of Caius Marcellus.

ENOBARBUS. But now she is the wife of Marcus Antonius.

MENAS. Pray you, sir.–

ENOBARBUS. 'Tis true.

MENAS. Then is Caesar and he for ever knit together.

ENOBARBUS. If I were bound to divine of this unity, I would not prophesy so.

MENAS. I think the policy of that purpose made more in the marriage
20 than the love of the parties.

ENOBARBUS. I think so too. But you shall find the band that seems to tie their friendship together will be the very strangler of their amity. Octavia is of a holy, cold, and still conversation.

MENAS. Who would not have his wife so?

ENOBARBUS. Not he that himself is not so, which is Mark Antony. He will to his Egyptian dish again; then shall the sighs of Octavia blow the fire up in Caesar, and, as I said before, that which is the strength of their amity shall prove the immediate author of their variance. Antony will use his affection where it is; he married but his oc-
30 casion here.

MENAS. And thus it may be. Come, sir, we have healths for you.

ENOBARBUS. I shall take'em, sir. We have used our throats in Egypt.

Music. Enter Caesar, Antony, Lepidus,
Pompey, *and others.*

Here they come. Some of their plants are ill-rooted already; the least wind i'the world will blow them down.

MENAS. Lepidus is high-colored.

ANTONY (*to* Caesar). Thus do they, sir. They take the flow o'the Nile
By certain scales i'the pyramid; they know
By the height, the lowness, or the mean if dearth
Or foison follow. The higher Nilus swells,
40 The more it promises; as it ebbs, the seedsman
Upon the slime and ooze scatters his grain
And shortly comes to harvest.

LEPIDUS. You've strange serpents there.

ANTONY. Ay, Lepidus.

---

32. in Egypt.] *D1*, *D2*; in Egypt. Come, let's away. *D3*, *D4*, *S*.
33. Here they come] *D1*, *D2*; Here they'll be, man *D3*, *D4*, *S*. *D1*, *D2* telescope *S* vi and vii into one scene. *D3*, *D4* list scene vii but indicate omission of entire scene, 163 lines.
35. high-colored] *D1*, *D2* omit next twelve lines of *S*.

LEPIDUS. Your serpent of Egypt is bred now of your mud by the operation of the sun. So is your crocodile.

ANTONY. They are so.

POMPEY. Sit—and some wine.—A health to Lepidus.

LEPIDUS. I am not so well as I should be; but I'll ne'er out.

50 ENOBARBUS. [*aside*]. Not 'till you have slept. I fear me you'll be in 'till then.

LEPIDUS. Nay, certainly, I have heard the Ptolemies' pyramises are very goodly things; without contradiction I have heard that.

MENAS [*aside*]. Pompey, a word.

POMPEY [*aside*]. Say in mine ear. What is't?

MENAS [*aside*]. Forsake thy seat, I do beseech thee, Captain, and hear me speak a word.

POMPEY [*aside*]. Forbear me 'till anon.—This wine for Lepidus.

LEPIDUS. What manner o'thing is your crocodile?

60 ANTONY. It is shaped, sir, like itself; and it is as broad as it hath breadth. It is just so high as it is, and moves with its own organs. It lives by that which nourisheth it; and, the elements once out of it, it transmigrates.

LEPIDUS. What color is it of?

ANTONY. Of it's own color too.

LEPIDUS. 'Tis a strange serpent.

ANTONY. 'Tis so, and the tears of it are wet.

CAESAR [*aside*]. Will this description satisfy him?

ANTONY [*aside*]. With the health that Pompey gives him, else he is a
70 very epicure.

POMPEY (*to* Menas). Go hang, sir, hang. Tell me of that! Away.
Do as I bid you.—Where's this cup I called for?

MENAS [*aside*]. If for the sake of merit thou wilt hear me,
Rise from thy stool.

POMPEY. I think thou'rt mad. (*Rising and stepping aside.*)
The matter?

MENAS [*aside*]. I have ever held my cap off to thy fortunes.

POMPEY [*aside*]. Thou hast served me with much faith. What's else to say?—
80 Be jolly, lords.

ANTONY. These quicksands, Lepidus,
Keep off them, for you sink.

50–51. Not . . . then] here in *D1* is Capell's first use of inverted commas to indicate an aside. Throughout this text the word "*aside*," in brackets, is substituted for Capell's marks.

MENAS [*aside*]. Wilt thou be lord of all the world?
POMPEY [*aside*]. What say'st thou?
MENAS [*aside*]. Wilt thou be lord of the whole world? That's twice.
POMPEY [*aside*]. How should that be?
MENAS [*aside*]. But entertain it.
And, though thou think me poor, I am the man
Will give thee all the world.
90 POMPEY [*aside*]. Thou hast drunk well.
MENAS [*aside*]. No, Pompey, I have kept me from the cup.
Thou art, if thou dar'st be, the earthly Jove.
Whate'er the ocean pales, or sky inclips,
Is thine, if thou wilt ha't.
POMPEY [*aside*]. Show me which way.
MENAS [*aside*]. These three world-sharers, these competitors,
Are in thy vessel. Let me cut the cable,
And when we are put off, fall to their throats.
All then is thine.
100 POMPEY [*aside*]. Ah, this thou should'st have done,
And not have spoke of it! In me 'tis villainy;
In thee 't had been good service. Thou must know
'Tis not my profit that does lead mine honor;
Mine honor, it. Repent that e'er thy tongue
Hath so betrayed thine act. Being done unknown,
I should have found it afterwards well done,
But must condemn it now. Desist, and drink.
MENAS [*aside*]. For this (*looking contemptibly after him*)
I'll never follow thy palled fortunes more.
110 Who seeks and will not take, when once 'tis offered,
Shall never find it more. (*Joins the company.*)
POMPEY. This health to Lepidus.
ANTONY (*to an* Attendant). Bear him ashore.—I'll pledge it for him,
Pompey.
ENOBARBUS. Here's to thee, Menas.
MENAS. Enobarbus, welcome.
POMPEY. Fill, 'till the cup be hid.

Lepidus *born off*.

ENOBARBUS. There's a strong fellow, Menas.
MENAS. Why?
120 ENOBARBUS. He bears
The third part of the world, man, seest not?
MENAS. The third part then is drunk. Would it were all,
That it might go on wheels.

ENOBARBUS. Drink thou; increase the reels.
MENAS. Come.
POMPEY. This is not yet an Alexandrian feast.
ANTONY. It ripens towards it. Strike the vessels, ho!
Here is to Caesar.
CAESAR. I could well forbear't;
130 It's monstrous labor when I wash my brain
And it grows fouler.
ANTONY. Be a child o'the time.
ENOBARBUS (*to* Antony). Ha, my brave Emperor! Shall we dance now
Th' Egyptian bacchanals and celebrate our drink?
POMPEY. Let's ha't, good soldier. (*They rise.*)
ANTONY. Come, let's all take hands
'Till that the conquering wine hath steeped our sense
In soft and delicate Lethe.
ENOBARBUS. All take hands.
140 Make battery to our ears with the loud music;
The while I'll place you. Then the boy shall sing;
The holding every man shall bear as loud
As his strong sides can volly.

Music plays. Enobarbus *places them hand in hand.*

SONG.

Come, thou monarch of the vine,
Plumpy Bacchus, with pink eyne!
In thy vats our cares be drowned.
With thy grapes our hairs be crowned,
Cup us 'till the world go round,
BUR[DEN]. Cup us 'till the world go round.

150 CAESAR. What would you more? Pompey, good night. Good brother,
Let me request you off; our graver business
Frowns at this levity.—Gentle lords, let's part;
You see we have burnt our cheeks. Strong Enobarbe
Is weaker than the wine, and mine own tongue
Splits what it speaks. The wild disguise hath almost
Anticked us all. What needs more words? Good night.

Exeunt Ceasar *and* train.

143.2. SONG] *D1*, *D3*, *D4*, *S* use the six-line song here; *D1* prints the twelve-line version prefatory to the text; *D2* prints the expanded version here.
156. Good night.] *D1*, *D2*; Good night. Good Antony, your hand. *D3*, *D4*, *S*.

POMPEY. I'll try you on the shore.
ANTONY. And shall, sir. [*Aside.*] I will to Egypt.
For though I have made this marriage for my peace,
160 I'the east my pleasure lies.—Give us your hand.
POMPEY. O Antony, you have my father's house—
But what? We are friends again.

Exeunt Pompey *and* Antony.

ENOBARBUS. Take heed you fall not.—
Menas, I'll not on shore.
MENAS. No, to my cabin.—
These drums, these trumpets, flutes—let Neptune hear
We bid a loud farewell to these great fellows.
Sound and be hanged; sound out.

Flourish of loud music.

ENOBARBUS. Ho, says 'a! There's my cap.
170 MENAS. Ho, noble captain! Come.

Exeunt.

SCENE IV. Alexandria. *A room in the palace.*
Enter Cleopatra, Charmian, Iras, *and* Alexas.

CLEOPATRA. Where is the fellow?
ALEXAS. Half afeard to come.
CLEOPATRA. Go to, go to.—Come hither, sir.

Enter Messenger.

ALEXAS. Good majesty,
Herod of Jewry dare not look upon you
But when you are well pleased.
CLEOPATRA. That Herod's head
I'll have. But how, when Antony is gone,
Through whom I might command it? Come thou near.
10 MESSENGER. Most gracious majesty—

158–160. I will. . . . lies] *D1*, *D2*; not in *D3*, *D4*, *S*.
162. friends again.] *D1*, *D2*; friends. *D3*, *D4*, *S*. The next line, "Come down into the boat," is omitted in *D1*, *D2*.
0. SCENE IV] *D1*, *D2*; III, iii, *D3*, *D4*, *S*. Scene i (forty-one lines in eighteenth-century typesetting) and scene ii (eighty lines) of *S* omitted *D1*, *D2*. First twenty-four lines of scene ii and eleven later lines omitted *D3*, *C4*.

CLEOPATRA. Did'st thou behold
Octavia?
MESSENGER. Ay, dread Queen.
CLEOPATRA. Where?
MESSENGER. Madam, in Rome.
I looked her in the face and saw her led
Between her brother and Mark Antony.
CLEOPATRA. Is she as tall as me?
MESSENGER. She is not, madam.
20 CLEOPATRA. Did'st hear her speak? Is she shrill-tongued, or low?
MESSENGER. Madam, I heard her speak; she is low-voiced.
CLEOPATRA. That's not so good.—He cannot like her long.
CHARMIAN. Like her? O Isis! 'tis impossible.
CLEOPATRA. I think so, Charmian: dull of tongue, and dwarfish!
What majesty is in her gait? Remember,
If e'er thou look'dst on majesty.
MESSENGER. She creeps;
Her motion and her station are as one.
She shows a body rather than a life,
30 A statue than a breather.
CLEOPATRA. Is this certain?
MESSENGER. Or I have no observance.
CHARMIAN. Three in Egypt
Cannot make better note.
CLEOPATRA. He's very knowing;
I do perceive't.—There's nothing in her yet.
The fellow has good judgment.
CHARMIAN. Excellent.
CLEOPATRA. Guess at her years, I prythee.
40 MESSENGER. Her years, madam?
She is a widow.
CLEOPATRA. Widow? Charmian, hark!
MESSENGER. And I do think she's thirty.
CLEOPATRA. Bear'st thou her face
In mind? Is't long or round?
MESSENGER. Round even to faultiness.
CLEOPATRA. For the most part too, they are foolish that are so.
Her hair, what color?
MESSENGER. Brown, madam. And her forehead
50 As low as she would wish it.
CLEOPATRA. There's gold for thee. [*Giving gold.*]
Thou must not take my former sharpness ill.
I will employ thee back again; I find thee

Most fit for business. Go, make thee ready while
Our letters are prepared.

Exit Messenger.

CHARMIAN. A proper man.
CLEOPATRA. Indeed, he is so. I repent me much
That so I harried him. Why, methinks, by him,
This creature's no such thing.
60 CHARMIAN. Oh, nothing, madam.
CLEOPATRA. The man hath seen some majesty, and should know.
CHARMIAN. Hath he seen majesty? Isis else defend—
And serving you so long!
CLEOPATRA. I have one thing more to ask him yet, good Charmian.—
But 'tis no matter; thou shalt bring him to me
Where I will write. All may be well enough.
CHARMIAN. I warrant you, madam.

Exeunt.

SCENE V. Rome. *A room in* Caesar's *house.*
Enter Caesar, Mecaenas, *and* Agrippa.

CAESAR. Condemning Rome, he did all this. And once,
In Alexandria—here's [*giving documents*] the manner of it—
I'the market-place, on a tribunal silvered,
Cleopatra and himself in chairs of gold
Were publicly enthroned; at the feet sat
Caesarion, whom they call my father's son,
And all the unlawful issue that their lust
Since then hath made between them. Unto her
He gave the 'stablishment of Egypt, made her
10 Of lower Syria, Caprus, Lydia
Absolute queen.
MECAENAS. This in the public eye?
CAESAR. I'the common show-place, where they exercise.
His sons he there proclaimed the kings of kings.
Great Media, Parthia, and Armenia

0. SCENE V] *D1*, *D2*; III, vi, *D3*, *D4*, *S*. All of *S* III, iv, is omitted in *D1*, *D2* (forty-six lines), as is all of *S* III, v (twenty-five lines). *D3*, *D4* use scene iv but indicate omission of all of scene v.
1. did] *D1*, *D2*; has done *D3*, *D4*, *S*.
And once] *D1*, *D2*; And more *D3*, *D4*, *S*.

He gave to Alexander; to Ptolemy he assigned
Syria, Cilicia, and Phoenicia. She
In the habiliments of the goddess Isis
That day appeared, and oft before gave audience,
20 As 'tis reported, so.

MECAENAS. Let Rome be thus
Informed.

AGRIPPA. Who, queasy with his insolence
Already, will their good thoughts call from him.

CAESAR. The people know it and have now received
His accusations.

AGRIPPA. Whom does he accuse?

CAESAR. Caesar; and that, having in Sicily
Sextus Pompeius spoiled, we had not rated him
30 His part o'the isle. Then does he say he lent me
Some shipping unrestored. Lastly, he frets
That Lepidus of the triumvirate
Should be deposed and, being, that we detain
All his revenue.

AGRIPPA. Sir, this should be answered.

CAESAR. 'Tis done already, and the messenger gone.
I have told him, Lepidus was grown too cruel;
That he his high authority abused,
And did deserve his change. For what I have conquered
40 I grant him part; but then in his Armenia
And other of his conquered kingdoms I
Demand the like.

MECAENAS. He'll never yield to that.

CAESAR. Nor must not then be yielded to in this.

Enter Octavia, *attended.*

OCTAVIA. Hail, Caesar, and my lord! Hail, most dear Caesar!

CAESAR. That ever I should call thee castaway!

OCTAVIA. You have not called me so, nor have you cause.

CAESAR. Why hast thou stol'n upon us thus? You come not
Like Caesar's sister. The wife of Antony
50 Should have an army for an usher and
The neighs of horse to tell of her approach
Long ere she did appear. The trees by the way
Should have borne men, and expectation fainted,
Longing for what it had not. Nay, the dust
Should have ascended to the roof of heaven,

---

27. Whom] *D1*, *D2*, *D3*, *D4*; Who *S*.

Raised by your populous troops. But you are come
A market-maid to Rome and have prevented
The ostent of our love, which, left unshown,
Is often left unloved. We should have met you
60 By sea and land, supplying every stage
With an augmented greeting.

OCTAVIA. Good my lord,
To come thus was I not constrained, but did it
On my free will. My lord Mark Antony,
Hearing that you prepared for war, acquainted
My grieving ear withal; whereon I begged
His pardon for return.

CAESAR. Which soon he granted,
Being an obstruct 'tween his lust and him.

70 OCTAVIA. Do not say so, my lord.

CAESAR. I have eyes upon him,
And his affairs come to me on the wind.
Where, say you, he is now?

OCTAVIA. My lord, in Athens.

CAESAR. No, my most wronged sister; Cleopatra
Hath nodded him to her. He hath given his empire
Up to a whore, who now are levying
The kings o'the earth for war.

OCTAVIA. Ah me, most wretched,
80 That have my heart parted betwixt two friends
That do afflict each other.

CAESAR. Welcome hither.
Your letters did withold our breaking forth,
'Till we perceived both how you were wronged
And we in negligent danger. Cheer your heart;
Be you not troubled with the time, which drives
O'er your content these strong necessities,
But let determined things to destiny
Hold unbewailed their way. Welcome to Rome;
90 Nothing more dear to me. You are abused
Beyond the mark of thought; and the high gods,
To do you justice, make them ministers
Of us and those that love you. Be of comfort,

---

58. ostent] *D1*, *D2*, *D3*, *D4*; ostentation *S*.
66. grieving] *D1*, *D2*, *D3*, *D4*; grieved *S*.
73. he is] *D1*, *D2*, *D3*; is he *D4*, *S*.
78. for war] *D1*, *D2*; *D3*, *D4* follow *S* with eight and a half additional lines.
81. do] *D1*, *D2*, *D3*, *D4*; does *S*.

And ever welcome to us.
AGRIPPA. Welcome, lady.
MECAENAS. Welcome, dear madam.
Each heart in Rome does love and pity you.
Only the adulterous Antony, most large
In his abominations, turns you off
100 And gives his potent regiment to a trull
That noises it against us.
OCTAVIA. Is it so, sir?
CAESAR. Most certain. Sister, welcome. Pray you now,
Be ever known to patience. My dearest sister!

Exeunt.

ACT III.

SCENE I. *Near* Actium. Antony's *camp.*
Enter Cleopatra *and* Enobarbus.

CLEOPATRA. I will be even with thee, doubt it not.
ENOBARBUS. But why, why, why?
CLEOPATRA. Thou hast forespoke my being in these wars
And say'st it is not fit.
ENORARBUS. Well, is it, is it?
CLEOPATRA. Is't not denounced 'gainst us? Why should not we
Be there in person?
ENOBARBUS. Well, I could reply:
If we should serve with horse and mares together,
10 The horse were merely lost; the mares would bear
A soldier and his horse.
CLEOPATRA. What is't you say?
ENOBARBUS. Your presence needs must puzzle Antony,
Take from his heart, take from his brain, from his time,
What should not then be spared. He is already
Traduced for levity, and 'tis said in Rome
That Photinus, an eunuch, and your maids
Manage this war.
CLEOPATRA. Sink Rome, and their tongues rot
20 That speak against us! A charge we bear i'the war,
And, as the president of my kingdom, will
Appear there for a man. Speak not against it;

0. ACT III. SCENE I] *D*1, *D*2; III, vii, *D*3, *D*4, *S*.
7. in person] next eighteen lines indicated for omission in *D*3.

I will not stay behind.
ENOBARBUS. Nay, I have done.
Here comes the Emperor.

Enter Antony *and* Canidius.

ANTONY. Is't not strange, Canidius,
That from Tarentum and Brundusium
He could so quickly cut the Ionian sea
And take in Toryne?—You have heard on't, sweet?
30 CLEOPATRA. Celerity is never more admired
Than by the negligent.
ANTONY. A good rebuke,
Which might have well becomed the best of men
To taunt a slackness.—My Canidius, we
Will fight with him by sea.
CLEOPATRA. By sea! What else?
CANIDIUS. Why will my lord do so?
ANTONY. For that he dares us to't.
ENOBARBUS. So hath my lord dared him to single fight.
40 CANIDIUS. Ay, and to wage this battle at Pharsalia,
Where Caesar fought with Pompey. But these offers,
Which serve not for his vantage, he shakes off,
And so should you.
ENOBARBUS. Your ships are not well manned;
Your mariners are muleteers, reapers, people
Ingrossed by swift impress. In Caesar's fleet
Are those that often have 'gainst Pompey fought;
Their ships are yare; yours heavy. No disgrace
Can fall you for refusing him at sea,
50 Being prepared for land.
ANTONY. By sea, by sea.
ENOBARBUS. Most worthy sir, you therein throw away
The absolute soldiership you have by land;
Distract your army, which doth most consist
Of war-marked footmen; leave unexecuted
Your own renowned knowledge; quite forego
The way which promises assurance; and
Give up yourself merely to chance and hazard
From firm security.
60 ANTONY. I'll fight at sea.
CLEOPATRA. I have sixty sails, Caesar none better.
ANTONY. Come!

62. Come] *D1*, *D2*, *D3*; not in *D4*, *S*.

Our overplus of shipping will we burn,
And with the rest full-manned, from the head of Actium
Beat the approaching Caesar. But if we fail,

Enter an Attendant.

We then can do't at land.—Thy business?
ATTENDANT. The news is true, my lord; he is descried;
Caesar has taken Toryne.
ANTONY. Can he be there in person? 'Tis impossible;
70 Strange that his power should be.—Canidius,
Our nineteen legions thou shalt hold by land,
And our twelve thousand horse. We'll to our ship.

Enter Diomede.

Away, my Thetis.—How now, worthy soldier?
DIOMEDE. O noble Emperor, do not fight by sea;
Trust not to rotten planks. Do you misdoubt
This sword, and these my wounds? Let the Egyptians
And the Phoenicians go a-ducking; we
Have used to conquer standing on the earth
And fighting foot to foot.
80 ANTONY. Well, well, away.

Exeunt Antony, Cleopatra, Enobarbus, *and* Attendant.

DIOMEDE. By Hercules, I think I am i'the right.
CANIDIUS. Soldier, thou art, but this whole action grows
Not in the power on't; so our leader's led,
And we are women's men.
DIOMEDE. You keep by land
The legions and the horse whole, do you not?
CANIDIUS. Marcus Octavius, Marcus Justeius,
Publicola, and Coelius are for sea;
But we keep whole by land. This speed of Caesar's
90 Carries beyond belief.
DIOMEDE. While he was yet in Rome,
His power went out in such distractions as
Beguiled all spies.
CANIDIUS. Who's his lieutenant, hear you?

65.1. Attendant] *D1*, *D2*; Messenger *D3*, *D4*, *S*.
72.1. *Enter* Diomede] *D1*, *D2*; *Enter a* Soldier *D3*, *D4*, *S*. This difference continues through the scene.
81. By Hercules . . .] *D3*, *D4* indicate omission of remainder of scene, nineteen lines.

DIOMEDE. They say one Taurus.
CANIDIUS. Well I know the man.

Re-enter Attendant.

ATTENDANT. The Emperor calls Canidius.
CANIDIUS. With news the time's in labor and throws forth
Each minute some.

Exeunt.

SCENE II. *The same. Plain between both camps.*
Enter Caesar, Taurus, *Officers, and others.*

CAESAR. Taurus!
TAURUS. My lord?
CAESAR. Strike not by land; keep whole. Provoke not battle
'Till we have done at sea. Do not exceed
The prescript of this scroll. [*Giving scroll.*] Our fortune lies
Upon this jump.

Exeunt.

Enter Antony, Enobarbus, *and* Others.

ANTONY. Set we our squadrons on yon' side o'the hill,
In eye of Caesar's battle, from which place
We may the number of the ships behold
10 And so proceed accordingly.

Exeunt.

Enter Canidius, *marching with his land army, one way, and* Taurus, *the lieutenant of* Caesar, *with his, the other way. After their going in is heard the noise of a sea-fight.*
Alarums. Enter Enobarbus.

ENOBARBUS. Naught, naught, all naught! I can behold no longer.
The Antoniad, the Egyptian admiral,
With all their sixty, fly and turn the rudder.
To see't mine eyes are blasted.

Enter Diomede.

---

0. SCENE II] *D1*, *D2*; scene viii *D3*, *D4*, *S*.
14.1. *Enter* Diomede] *D1*, *D2*; *Enter* Scarus *D3*, *D4*, *S*. But *D3*, *D4* indicate omission, beginning here, of twenty-five lines.

DIOMEDE. Gods and goddesses,
All the whole synod of them!
ENOBARBUS. What's thy passion?
DIOMEDE. The greater cantle of the world is lost
With very ignorance; we have kissed away
20 Kingdoms and provinces.
ENOBARBUS. How appears the fight?
DIOMEDE. On our side like the tokened pestilence,
Where death is sure. Yon' ribald nag of Egypt,
Whom leprosy o'ertake, i'the midst o'the fight,
When vantage like a pair of twins appeared,
Both as the same, or rather ours the elder,
The breeze upon her, like a cow in June
Hoists sails and flies.
ENOBARBUS. That I beheld. Mine eyes
30 Did sicken at the sight of it and could not
Endure a further view.
DIOMEDE. She once being looft,
The noble ruin of her magic, Antony,
Claps on his sea-wing and, like a doting mallard,
Leaving the fight in height, flies after her.
I never saw an action of such shame;
Experience, manhood, honor ne'er before
Did violate so itself.
ENOBARBUS. Alack, alack!

Enter Canidius.

40 CANIDIUS. Our fortune on the sea is out of breath
And sinks most lamentably. Had our general
Been what he knew himself, it had gone well.
O, he has given example for our flight
Most grossly by his own.
ENOBARBUS. [*aside*]. Ay, are you therabouts? Why then, good-night
Indeed.
CANIDIUS. Toward Peloponnesus are they fled.
DIOMEDE. 'Tis easy to't, and there I will attend
What further comes.

Exit.

50 CANIDIUS. To Caesar will I render
My legions and my horse; six kings already
Show me the way of yielding.

Exit.

ENOBARBUS. I'll yet follow
The wounded chance of Antony, though my reason
Sits in the wind against me.

Exit.

SCENE III. Alexandria. *A room in the palace.*

Enter Antony *and* Attendants.

ANTONY. Hark, the land bids me tread no more upon't!
It is ashamed to bear me.—Friends, come hither;
I am so lated in the world that I
Have lost my way for ever. I have a ship
Laden with gold; take that, divide it; fly
And make your peace with Caesar.
ATTENDANT. Fly? Not we!
ANTONY. I have fled myself, and have instructed cowards
To run and show their shoulders. Friends, be gone.
10 I have myself resolved upon a course
Which has no need of you; be gone, be gone.
My treasure's in the harbor. Take it.—Oh,
I followed that I blush to look upon.
My very hairs do mutiny, for the white
Reprove the brown for rashness, and they them
For fear and doting.—Friends, be gone; you shall
Have letters from me to some friends that will
Sweep your way for you. Pray you, look not sad
Nor make replies of lothness; take the hint
20 Which my despair proclaims. Let that be left
Which leaves itself. To the sea-side straight away;
I will possess you of that ship and treasure.
Leave me, I pray, a little. Pray you now—
Nay, do so, for indeed I have lost command,
Therefore I pray you. I'll see you by and by. (*Throws himself on a couch.*)

Exeunt Attendants.

Enter Eros, *with* Cleopatra *led by* Iras *and* Charmian.

EROS. Nay, gentle madam, to him. Comfort him.
IRAS. Do, most dear Queen.
CHARMIAN. Do! Why, what else?

---

0. SCENE III] *D1*, *D2*; scene xi *D3*, *D4*, *S.*

CLEOPATRA. Let me sit down. O Juno!

30 ANTONY. No, no, no, no, no!

EROS. See you here, sir?

ANTONY. Oh, fie, fie, fie!

CHARMIAN. Madam—

IRAS. Madam, good Empress!

EROS. Sir, sir!

ANTONY. Yes, my lord, yes.—He at Philippi kept
His sword even like a dancer, while I struck
The lean and wrinkled Cassius; and 'twas I
That the mad Brutus ended. He alone
40 Dealt on lieutenantry and no practise had
In the brave squares of war. Yet now—no matter.

CLEOPATRA. Ah me! Stand by. (*Rising.*)

EROS. The Queen, my lord, the Queen.

IRAS. Go to him, madam, speak to him; he is unqualitied
With very shame.

CLEOPATRA. Well then, sustain me. O!

EROS. Most noble sir, arise; the Queen approaches;
Her head's declined, and death will seize her; but
Your comfort makes the rescue.

50 ANTONY. I have offended reputation,
A most unnoble swerving.

EROS. Sir, the Queen.

ANTONY. O whither hast thou led me, Egypt? (*Starting up.*) See
How I convey my shame out of thine eyes
By looking back on what I have left behind
'Stroyed in dishonor.

CLEOPATRA. Oh, my lord, my lord!
Forgive my fearful sails; I little thought
You would have followed.

60 ANTONY. Egypt, thou knewest too well
My heart was to thy rudder tied by the strings
And thou should'st tow me after. O'er my spirit
Thy full supremacy thou knew'st, and that
Thy beck might from the bidding of the gods
Command me.

CLEOPATRA. Oh, my pardon.

ANTONY. Now I must
To the young man send humble 'treaties, dodge
And palter in the shifts of lowness, who
70 With half the bulk o'the world played as I pleased,
Making and marring fortunes. You did know
How much you were my conqueror and that

My sword, made weak by my affection, would
Obey it on all causes.

CLEOPATRA. Pardon, pardon!

ANTONY. Fall not a tear, I say; one of them rates
All that is won and lost. Give me a kiss;
Even this [*kissing her*] repays me.—We sent our soothsayer.
Is he come back?—Love, I am full of lead.—
80 Some wine, there, and our viands.—Fortune knows
We scorn her most when most she offers blows.

Exeunt.

SCENE IV. *A camp in* Egypt. Caesar's *tent.*

Enter Caesar, Thyreus, Dolabella, *and others.*

CAESAR. Let him appear that's come from Antony.
Know you him?

DOLABELLA. Caesar, 'tis his soothsayer.
An argument that he is plucked, when hither
He sends so poor a pinion of his wing,
Which had superfluous kings for messengers
Not many moons gone by.

Enter Soothsayer.

CAESAR. Approach and speak.

SOOTHSAYER. Such as I am, I come from Antony.
10 I was of late as petty to his ends
As is the morn dew on the myrtle leaf
To his grand sea.

CAESAR. Be it so. Declare thine office.

SOOTHSAYER. Lord of his fortunes he salutes thee and
Requires to live in Egypt; which not granted,
He lessens his request and of thee sues
To let him breath between the heavens and earth
A private man in Athens. This for him.
Next, Cleopatra does confess thy greatness,

---

74. causes] *D1*, *D2*, *D3*; cause *D4*, *S*.
78. soothsayer] *D1*, *D2*; schoolmaster *D3*, *D4*, *S*.
0. SCENE IV] *D1*, *D2*; scene xii *D3*, *D4*, *S*.
3. soothsayer] *D1*, *D2*; schoolmaster *D3*, *D4*, *S*.
7.1. *Enter* Soothsayer] *D1*, *D2*; *Enter* Euphronius *D3*; *Enter* Ambassador *D4*, *S*. This difference is repeated at line 30.

20 Submits her to thy might, and of thee craves
The circle of the Ptolemies for her heirs,
Now hazarded to thy grace.

CAESAR. For Antony,
I have no ears to his request. The Queen
Of audience nor desire shall fail, so she
From Egypt drive her all-disgraced friend,
Or take his life there. This if she perform,
She shall not sue unheard. So to them both.

SOOTHSAYER. Fortune pursue thee!

30 CAESAR. Bring him through the bands.

Exit Soothsayer, *attended.*

To try thy eloquence now's the time. Dispatch.
From Antony win Cleopatra; promise,
And in our name, what she requires; add more,
From thine invention, offers. Women are not
In their best fortunes strong, but want will perjure
The ne'er-touched vestal. Try thy cunning, Thyreus;
Make thine own edict for thy pains, which we
Will answer as a law.

THYREUS. Caesar, I go.

40 CAESAR. Observe how Antony becomes his flaw
And what thou think'st his very action speaks
In every power that moves.

THYREUS. Caesar, I shall.

Exeunt.

SCENE V. Alexandria. *A room in the palace.*

Enter Cleopatra, Enobarbus, Charmian, *and* Iras.

CLEOPATRA. What shall we do, Enobarbus?

ENOBARBUS. Drink, and die.

CLEOPATRA. Is Antony or we in fault for this?

ENOBARBUS. Antony only, that would make his will
Lord of his reason. What though you fled
From that great face of war, whose several ranges

---

0. SCENE V] *D1*, *D2*; scene xiii *D3*, *D4*, *S*.
2. Drink] *D1*, *D2*, *D3*; Think *D4*, *S*.

Frighted each other? Why should he follow you?
The itch of his affection should not then
Have nicked his captainship at such a point,
10 When half to half the world opposed, he being
The mered question. 'Twas a shame no less
Than was his loss to course your flying flags
And leave his navy gazing.

CLEOPATRA. Prythee, peace.

Enter Antony *and* Soothsayer.

ANTONY. Is that his answer?

SOOTHSAYER. Ay, my lord.

ANTONY. The Queen
Shall then have courtesy, so she will yield
Us up.

20 SOOTHSAYER. My lord, he says so.

ANTONY. Let her know't.
To the boy Caesar send this grizzled head,
And he will fill thy wishes to the brim
With principalities.

CLEOPATRA. That head, my lord?

ANTONY. To him again. Tell him he wears the rose
Of youth upon him, from which the world should note
Something particular: his coin, ships, legions,
May be a coward's whose ministries would prevail
30 Under the service of a child as soon
As i' the command of Caesar. I dare him therefore
To lay his gay comparisons apart
And answer me declined, sword against sword,
Ourselves alone. I'll write it. Follow me.

Exeunt Antony *and* Soothsayer.

ENOBARBUS [*aside*]. Yes, like enough high-battled Caesar will
Unstate his happiness and be staged to the show
Against a sworder. I see men's judgments are
A parcel of their fortunes, and things outward
Do draw the inward quality after them
40 To suffer all alike. That he should dream,
Knowing all measures, the full Caesar will

---

7. follow you?] *D1*, *D2*, *D3*; follow? *D4*, *S*.

37. sworder] *D1* has a raised period following to indicate irony, the only instance of Capell's using this "reader prompt" in the play.

Answer his emptiness! Caesar, thou hast subdued
His judgment too.

Enter an Attendant.

ATTENDANT. A messenger from Caesar.

CLEOPATRA. What, no more ceremony! See, my women,
Against the blown rose may they stop their nose
That kneeled unto the buds.—Admit him, sir.

Exit Attendant.

ENOBARBUS [*aside*]. Mine honesty and I begin to square.
The loyalty, well held to fools, does make
50 Our faith mere folly. Yet he that can endure
To follow with allegiance a fallen lord
Does conquer him that did his master conquer
And earns a place i'the story.

Enter Thyreus.

CLEOPATRA. Caesar's will?

THYREUS. Hear it apart.

CLEOPATRA. None but friends; say on boldly.

THYREUS. So, haply, are they friends to Antony.

ENOBARBUS. He needs as many, sir, as Caesar has,
Or needs not us. If Caesar please, our master
60 Will leap to be his friend. Or, as you know
Whose he is we are, and that is Caesar's.

THYREUS. So.
Thus then, thou most renowned: Caesar entreats
Not to consider in what case thou stand'st
Further than he is Caesar.

CLEOPATRA. Go on. Right royal!

THYREUS. He knows that you embrace not Antony
As you did love, but as you feared him.

CLEOPATRA. Oh!

70 THYREUS. The scars upon your honor therefore he
Does pity as constrained blemishes,
Not as deserved.

CLEOPATRA. He is a god and knows
What is most right. Mine honor was not yielded,
But conquered merely.

ENOBARBUS [*aside*]. To be sure of that,
I will ask Antony. Sir, sir, thou art so leaky

That we must leave thee to thy sinking, for
Thy dearest quit thee.

Exit Enobarbus.

80 THYREUS. Shall I say to Caesar
What you require of him? For he partly begs
To be desired to give. It much would please him
That of his fortunes you should make a staff
To lean upon; but it would warm his spirits
To hear from me you had left Antony
And put yourself under his shroud, the great,
The universal landlord.

CLEOPATRA. What's your name?

THYREUS. My name is Thyreus.

90 CLEOPATRA. Most kind messenger,
Say to great Caesar this: In deputation
I kiss his conquering hands. Tell him, I am prompt
To lay my crown at his feet, and there to kneel.
Tell him, from his all-obeying breath I hear
The doom of Egypt.

THYREUS. 'Tis your noblest course.
Wisdom and fortune combatting together,
If that the former dare but what it can,
No chance may shake it. Give me grace to lay
100 My duty on your hand.

CLEOPATRA (*giving her hand*). Your Caesar's father oft,
When he hath mused of taking kingdoms in,
Bestowed his lips on that unworthy place
As it rained kisses.

Re-enter Enobarbus *with* Antony.

ANTONY. Favors, by Jove that thunders!
What art thou, fellow?

THYREUS. One that but performs
The bidding of the fullest man, and worthiest
To have command obeyed.

110 ENOBARBUS [*aside*]. You will be whipped.

ANTONY. Approach, there!—Ah, you kite! Now, gods and devils!
Authority melts from me of late. When I cried "Ho!"
Like boys unto a muss, kings would start forth
And cry, "Your will?"—Have you no ears? I am

Enter Attendants.

Antony yet. Take hence this Jack and whip him.
ENOBARBUS [*aside*]. Tis better playing with a lion's whelp,
Than with an old one dying.
ANTONY. Moon and stars!
Whip him. Wer't twenty of the greatest tributaries
120 That do acknowledge Caesar, should I find them
So saucy with the hand of she there (What's her name
Since she *was* Cleopatra?). Whip him, fellows,
'Till, like a boy, you see him cringe his face
And whine aloud for mercy. Take him hence.
THYREUS. Mark Antony—
ANTONY. Tug him away. Being whipped,
Bring him again. This Jack of Caesar's shall
Bear us an errand to him.

Exeunt Attendants *with* Thyreus.

You were half blasted ere I knew you. Ha!
130 Have I my pillow left unprest in Rome,
Forborn the getting of a lawful race,
And by a gem of women, to be abused
By one that looks on feeders?
CLEOPATRA. Good my lord—
ANTONY. You have been a boggler ever.
But when we in our viciousness grow hard
(O misery on't!) the wise gods seel our eyes,
In our own filth drop our clear judgments, make us
Adore our errors, laugh at us while we strut
140 To our confusion.
CLEOPATRA. Oh, is't come to this?
ANTONY. I found you as a morsel cold upon
Dead Caesar's trencher. Nay, you were a fragment
Of Cneius Pompey's, besides what hotter hours,
Unregistered in vulgar fame, you have
Luxuriously picked out. For I am sure,
Though you can guess what temperance should be,
You know not what it is.
CLEOPATRA. Wherefore is this?
150 ANTONY. To let a fellow that will take rewards
And say, "God quit you!" be familiar with
My play-fellow, your hand; this kingly seal

Re-enter Attendants *with* Thyreus.

---

142. I found . . .] *D3*, *D4* omit forty lines of the "whipping scene."

And plighter of high hearts!—O, is he whipped?
1ST. ATTENDANT. Soundly, my lord.
ANTONY. Cried he, and begged he pardon?
1ST. ATTENDANT. He did ask favor.
ANTONY. If that thy father live, let him repent
Thou wast not made his daughter; and be thou sorry
To follow Caesar in his triumph, since
160 Thou hast been whipped for following him. Henceforth
The white hand of a lady fever thee!
Shake thou to look on't! Get thee back to Caesar;
Tell him thy entertainment. Look thou say
He makes me angry with him; for he seems
Proud and disdainful, harping on what I am,
Not what he knew I was. He makes me angry,
And at this time most easy 'tis to do't,
When my good stars, that were my former guides,
Have empty left their orbs and shot their fires
170 Into the abysm of hell. If he mislike
My speech and what is done, tell him he has
Hipparchus, my enfranched bondman, whom
He may at pleasure whip, or hang, or torture,
As he shall like to quit me. Urge it thou.
Hence with thy stripes, be gone!

Exit Thyreus.

CLEOPATRA. Have you done yet?
ANTONY. Alack, our terrene moon
Is now eclipsed, and it portends alone
The fall of Antony.
180 CLEOPATRA (*to her women*). I must stay his time.
ANTONY. To flatter Caesar, would you mingle eyes
With one that ties his points?
CLEOPATRA. Not know me yet?
ANTONY. Cold-hearted toward me?
CLEOPATRA. Ah, dear, if I be so,
From my cold heart let heaven engender hail
And poison it in the source; and the first stone

---

153. hearts! O] *D1*, *D2* omit five lines here:

that I were
Upon the hill of Basan, to outroar
The horned herd! For I have savage cause,
And to proclaim it civilly, were like
A halter'd neck, which does the hangman thank
For being yare about him.

Drop in my neck: as it determines, so
Dissolve my life! The next Caesarion smite!
190 'Till, by degrees, the memory of my womb,
Together with my brave Egyptians all,
By the discandying of this pelleted storm,
Lie graveless, 'till the flies and gnats of Nile
Have buried them for prey!

ANTONY. I am satisfied.
Caesar sits down in Alexandria, where
I will oppose his fate. Our force by land
Hath nobly held; our severed navy too
Have knit again, and fleet, threat'ning most sea-like.—
200 Where hast thou been, my heart? Dost thou hear, lady?
If from the field I shall return once more
To kiss these lips, I will appear in blood.
I and my sword will earn our chronicle;
There is hope in it yet.

CLEOPATRA. That's my brave lord!

ANTONY. I will be treble-sinewed, hearted, breathed,
And fight maliciously; for when mine hours
Were nice and lucky, men did ransom lives
Of me for jests. But now I'll set my teeth
210 And send to darkness all that stop me. Come,
Let's have one other gaudy night. Call to me
All my sad captains, fill our bowls; once more
Let's mock the midnight bell.

CLEOPATRA. It is my birthday.
I had thought to have held it poor; but since my lord
Is Antony again I will be Cleopatra.

ANTONY. We'll yet do well.

CLEOPATRA. Call all his noble captains to my lord.

ANTONY. Do so, we'll speak to them; and tonight I'll force
220 The wine peep through their scars. Come on, my Queen;
There's sap in't yet. The next time I do fight
I'll make death love me; for I will contend
Even with his pestilent scythe.

Exeunt Antony, Cleopatra, Charmian, Iras, *and* Attendants.

ENOBARBUS. Now he'll outstare the lightning. To be furious
Is to be frighted out of fear; in that mood
The dove will peck the estridge; and I see still
A diminution in our captain's brain
Restores his heart. When valor preys on reason,

It eats the sword it fights with. I will seek
230 Some way to leave him.

Exit.

ACT IV.

SCENE I. *The same. Another room.*

Enter Antony *and* Cleopatra; Charmian, Iras, *and others attending.*

ANTONY. Eros! Mine armor, Eros!
CLEOPATRA. Sleep a little.
ANTONY. No, my chuck. Eros, come; mine armor, Eros!

Enter Eros *with armor.*

Come, my good fellow, put thine iron on.
If fortune be not ours today, it is
Because we brave her. Come.

Eros *arms him.*

CLEOPATRA. Nay, I'll help too.
ANTONY. What's this for? Ah, let be, let be! Thou art
The armorer of my heart. False, false; this, this.
10 CLEOPATRA. Sooth, la, I'll help. Thus it must be.
ANTONY. Well, well,
We shall thrive now. Seest thou, my good fellow?
Go, put on thy defences.
EROS. Briefly, sir.
CLEOPATRA. Is not this buckled well?
ANTONY. O rarely, rarely!
He that unbuckles this, 'till we do please
To doff't for our repose, shall hear a storm.—
Thou fumbl'st, Eros; and my Queen's a squire
20 More tight at this than thou. Dispatch.—O, love,
That thou could'st see my wars today, and knew'st
The royal occupation, thou should'st see

---

0. SCENE I] all Garrick versions omit scene i (eighteen lines); *D1*, *D2* omit scene ii (fifty-five lines); all versions omit scene iii (thirty-four lines). (All line counts refer to eighteenth-century typesetting style.) Scene i in *D1*, *D2* is scene iv in *S*. The latter is indicated for omission *D3*, *D4* (forty-three lines).

16. O rarely] *D1*, *D2*, *D3*; Rarely *D4*, *S*.

Enter an Officer, *armed.*

A workman in't.—Good morrow to thee; welcome;
Thou look'st like him that knows a warlike charge.
To business that we love we rise betime
And go to't with delight.

1ST OFFICER. A thousand, sir,
Early though't be, have on their rivetted trim
And at the port expect you.

Shout within. Trumpets. Enter other Officers, Soldiers, *&c.*

30 2ND OFFICER. The morn is fair.—Good morrow, General.

ALL. Good morrow, General.

ANTONY. 'Tis well blown, lads.
This morning, like the spirit of a youth
That means to be of note, begins betimes.
So, so; come, give me that. This way; well said.
Fare thee well, dame, whate'er becomes of me.
This [*kisses her*] is a soldier's kiss; rebukable
And worthy shameful check it were to stand
On more mechanic compliment. I'll leave thee
40 Now like a man of steel.—You that will fight,
Follow me close; I'll bring you to't. Adieu.

Exeunt Eros, Antony, Officers, *and* Soldiers.

CHARMIAN. Please you, retire into your chamber.

CLEOPATRA. Lead me.
He goes forth gallantly. That he and Caesar might
Determine this great war in single fight!
Then, Antony—but now—well, on.

Exeunt.

SCENE II. *Under the walls of* Alexandria. Antony's *camp.*

Trumpets. Enter Antony *and* Eros, Diomede *meeting them.*

DIOMEDE. The gods make this a happy day to Antony!

ANTONY. 'Would thou and those thy scars had once prevailed
To make me fight at land!

DIOMEDE. Had'st thou done so,

---

0. SCENE II] *D1*, *D2*; scene v *D3*, *D4*, *S*. Entire scene is indicated for omission in *D3*, *D4* (twenty-five lines).

0.1. Diomede] *D1*, *D2*; *a* Soldier *D3 D4*.

The kings that have revolted and the soldier
That has this morning left thee would have still
Followed thy heels.

ANTONY. Who's gone this morning?

DIOMEDE. Who?

10 One ever near thee. Call for Enobarbus,
He shall not hear thee, or from Caesar's camp
Say, "I am none of thine."

ANTONY. What say'st thou?

DIOMEDE. Sir,
He is with Caesar.

EROS. Sir, his chests and treasure
He has not with him.

ANTONY. Is he gone?

DIOMEDE. Most certain.

20 ANTONY. Go, Eros, send his treasure after; do it.
Detain no jot of it, I charge thee. Write to him
(I will subscribe) gentle adieus and greetings.
Say that I wish he never find more cause
To change a master.—O, my fortunes have
Corrupted honest men.—Dispatch.—O Enobarbus!

[*Exeunt.*]

SCENE III. *Before* Alexandria. Caesar's *camp.*

Flourish. Enter Caesar, *with* Agrippa, Enobarbus, *and others.*

CAESAR. Go forth, Agrippa, and begin the fight.
Our will is Antony be took alive;
Make it so known.

AGRIPPA. Caesar, I shall.

Exit Agrippa.

CAESAR. The time of universal peace is near.
Prove this a prosperous day, the three-nooked world
Shall bear the olive freely.

Enter an Officer.

OFFICER. Antony
Is come into the field.

---

0. SCENE III] *D1*, *D2*; scene vi *D3*, *D4*, *S*.
7.1. *an* Officer] *D1*, *D2*; *a* Messenger *D3*, *D4*, S.

10 CAESAR. Go charge Agrippa
Plant those that have revolted in the van
That Antony may seem to spend his fury
Upon himself.

Exeunt Caesar *and train.*

ENOBARBUS. Alexas did revolt. He went to Jewry on
Affairs of Antony; there did persuade
Great Herod to incline himself to Caesar
And leave his master Antony. For this pains
Caesar hath hanged him. Canidius and the rest
That fell away have entertainment, but
20 No honorable trust. I have done ill,
Of which I do accuse myself so sorely
That I will joy no more.

Enter a Soldier

SOLDIER. Enobarbus, Antony
Hath after thee sent all thy treasure, with
His bounty over-plus. The messenger
Came on my guard and at thy tent is now
Unloading of his mules.
ENOBARBUS. I give it you.
SOLDIER. I mock not, Enobarbus;
30 I tell you true. Best you see safe the bringer
Out of the host; I must attend mine office
Or would have done't myself. Your emperor
Continues still a Jove.

Exit Soldier.

ENOBARBUS. I am alone the villain of the earth,
And feel I am so most. O Antony,
Thou mine of bounty, how would'st thou have paid
My better service, when my turpitude
Thou dost so crown with gold! This bows my heart.
If swift thought break it not, a swifter mean
40 Shall out-strike thought; but thought will do't, I feel.
I fight against thee! No. I will go seek
Some ditch wherein to die; the foul'st best fits
My latter part of life.

Exit.

---

29. I mock not] *D1*, *D2*, *D3*; Mock not *D4*, *S*.
30. see safe] *D1*, *D2*, *D3*; saf'd *D4*, *S*.

SCENE IV. *Between the camps. Field of battle.*

Alarums. Enter Agrippa *and forces.*

AGRIPPA. Retire. We have engaged ourselves too far.
Caesar himself has work, and our oppression
Exceeds what we expected.

Retreat. Exeunt.

Alarums. Enter Antony *and forces, with* Diomede, *wounded.*

DIOMEDE. O my brave Emperor, this is fought indeed!
Had we done so at first, we had driven them home
With clouts about their heads.
ANTONY. Thou bleed'st apace.
DIOMEDE. I had a wound here that was like a T,
But now 'tis made an H.

Retreat afar off.

10 ANTONY. They do retire.
DIOMEDE. We'll beat 'em into bench-holes; I have yet
Room for six scotches more.

Enter Eros.

EROS. They are beaten, sir, and our advantage serves
For a fair victory.
DIOMEDE. Let us score their backs
And snatch 'em up, as we take hares, behind.
'Tis sport to maul a runner.
ANTONY. I will reward thee
Once for thy sprightly comfort and ten-fold
20 For thy good valor. Come thee on.
DIOMEDE. I'll halt after.

Exeunt.

SCENE V. *Gates of* Alexandria.

Enter Antony, *marching*; Diomede, *and forces.*

ANTONY. We have beat him to his camp. Run one before
And let the Queen know of our gests. Tomorrow
Before the sun shall see us we'll spill the blood

---

0. SCENE IV] *D1*, *D2*; scene vii *D3*, *D4*, *S*. The entire scene is marked for omission in *D3*, *D4* (twenty-one lines).
4. Diomede] *D1*, *D2*; Scarus *D3*, *D4*, S.
0. SCENE V] *D1*, *D2*; scene viii *D3*, *D4*, *S*. Diomede is substituted for Scarus throughout in *D1*, *D2*.

That has today escaped. I thank you all,
For doughty-handed are you and have fought
Not as you served the cause, but as't had been
Each man's like mine. You have all shown you Hectors.
Enter the city, clip your wives, your friends,
Tell them your feats, whilst they with joyful tears
10 Wash the congealment from your wounds and kiss
The honored gashes whole. (*To* Diomede.) Give me thy hand.

Enter Cleopatra, *attended.*

To this great fairy I'll commend thy acts,
Make her thanks bless thee. [*To* Cleopatra.] O thou day o'the world,
Chain mine armed neck; leap thou, attire and all,
Through proof of harness to my heart, and there
Ride on the pants triumphing.

CLEOPATRA. Lord of lords,
O infinite virtue, com'st thou smiling from
The world's great snare uncaught?

20 ANTONY. My nightingale,
We have beat them to their beds. What, girl? Though grey
Do something mingle with our brown, yet have we
A brain that nourishes our nerves and can
Get goal for goal of youth. Behold this man.
Commend unto his lips thy favoring hand.
Kiss it, my warrior! He hath fought today
As if a god in hate of mankind had
Destroyed in such a shape.

CLEOPATRA. I'll give thee, friend,
30 An armor all of gold; it was a king's.

ANTONY. He has deserved it, were it carbuncled
Like holy Phoebus' car. Give me thy hand.
Through Alexandria make a jolly march;
Bear our hacked targets like the men that owe them.
Had our great palace the capacity
To camp this host, we all would sup together
And drink carouses to the next day's fate,
Which promises royal peril.—Trumpeters,
With brazen din blast you the city's ear;
40 Make mingle with our rattling tabourines,
That heaven and earth may strike their sounds together,
Applauding our approach.

Flourish. Exeunt.

---

22. our brown] *D1, D2, D3*; our younger brown *D4, S.*

SCENE VI. *Outskirts of* Caesar's *camp.*

Sentinels *upon their posts.*
Enter Enobarbus.

3RD SENTINEL. If we be not relieved within this hour,
We must return to the court of guard. The night
Is shiny, and they say we shall embattle
By the second hour i'the morn.

1ST SENTINEL. This last day was
A shrewd one to us.

ENOBARBUS. Oh, bear me witness, night—

2ND SENTINEL [*aside*]. What man is this?

1ST SENTINEL [*aside*]. Stand close and list him.

10 ENOBARBUS. Be witness to me, O thou blessed moon.
When men revolted shall upon record
Bear hateful memory, poor Enobarbus did
Before thy face repent.

3RD SENTINEL [*aside*]. Enobarbus!

2ND SENTINEL [*aside*]. Peace; hark further.

ENOBARBUS. O sovereign mistress of true melancholy,
The poisonous damp of night dispunge upon me,
That life, a very rebel to my will,
May hang no longer on me. Throw my heart
20 Against the flint and hardness of my fault,
Which, being dried with grief, will break to powder
And finish all foul thoughts. O Antony,
Nobler than my revolt is infamous,
Forgive me in thine own particular;
But let the world rank me in register
A master-leaver and a fugitive.
O Antony! O Antony! (*Dies.*)

1ST SENTINEL [*aside*]. Let's speak to him.

3RD SENTINEL [*aside*]. Let's hear him further, for the things he speaks
30 May concern Caesar.

2ND SENTINEL [*aside*]. Let's do so. But he sleeps.

3RD SENTINEL [*aside*]. Swoons rather, for so bad a prayer as his
Was never yet for sleep.

1ST SENTINEL. Go we to him.

2ND SETINEL (*to* Enobarbus). Awake, sir,
Awake; speak to us.

1ST SENTINEL (*shaking him*). Hear you, sir?

3RD SENTINEL. The hand

---

0. SCENE VI] *D1*, *D2*; scene ix *D3*, *D4*, *S*.

Of death hath raught him.

Drum afar off.

40 Hark how the drums demurely wake the sleepers.
Let's bear him to the court of guard; he is
Of note. Our hour is fully out.

2ND SENTINEL. Come on then;
He may recover yet.

Exeunt with the body.

SCENE VII. *Hills without the city.*

Enter Antony *and* Diomede *with forces, marching.*

ANTONY. Their preparation is today for sea;
We please them not by land.

DIOMEDE. For both, my lord.

ANTONY. I would they'd fight i'the fire or i'the air;
We'd fight there too. But this it is; our foot,
Upon the hills adjoining to the city,
Shall stay with us. Order for sea is given;
They have put forth the haven. Hie we on
Where their appointment we may best discover
10 And look on their endeavor.

Exeunt.

Enter Caesar *and his forces, marching.*

CAESAR. But being charged, we will be still by land,
Which, as I take't, we shall, for his best force
Is forth to man his galleys. To the vales,
And hold our best advantage.

Exeunt.

Re-enter Antony *and* Diomede.

ANTONY. Yet they're not joined. Where yonder pine does stand
I shall discover all. I'll bring thee word
Straight how 'tis like to go.

Exit.

---

0. SCENE VII] *D1*, *D2*; scene x *D3*, *D4*; scenes x, xi, xii, *S*.
8. Hie we on] *D1*, *D2*; not in *D3*, *D4*, *S*.

DIOMEDE. Swallows have built
In Cleopatra's sails their nests. The augurers
20 Say they know not, they cannot tell; look grimly
And dare not speak their knowledge. Antony
Is valiant, and dejected; and, by starts,
His fretted fortunes give him hope and fear
Of what he has and has not.

Shouts afar off.
Re-enter Antony, *hastily.*

ANTONY. All is lost!
This foul Egyptian hath betrayed me!
My fleet hath yielded to the foe, and yonder
They cast their caps up and carouse together
Like friends long lost.—Triple-turned whore! 'tis thou
30 Hast sold me to this novice, and my heart
Makes only wars on thee.—Bid them all fly!
For when I am revenged upon my charm,
I have done all. Bid them all fly; begone!

Exit Diomede.

O sun, thy uprise shall I see no more.
Fortune and Antony part here; even here
Do we shake hands. All come to this? The hearts
That spanieled me at heels, to whom I gave
Their wishes, do discandy, melt their sweets
On blossoming Caesar; and this pine is barked,
40 That overtopped them all. Betrayed I am.
(O this false soil of Egypt!) This grave charm,
Whose eye becked forth my wars and called them home,
Whose bosom was my crownet, my chief end,
Like a true gipsy hath at fast and loose
Beguiled me to the very heart of loss.

Enter Cleopatra.

What, Eros! Eros!—Ah, thou spell! Avaunt.
CLEOPATRA. Why is my lord enraged against his love?
ANTONY. Vanish, or I shall give thee thy deserving
And blemish Caesar's triumph. Let him take thee
50 And hoist thee up to the shouting plebeians.

---

41. soil] *D1*, *D2*, *D3*; soul *D4*, *S*.
44. true] *D1*, *D2*; right *D3*, *D4*, *S*.

Follow his chariot, like the greatest spot
Of all thy sex; most monster-like, be shown
For poorest diminutives, for dolts; and let
Patient Octavia plough thy visage up
With her prepared nails.

Exit Cleopatra.

'Tis well thou'rt gone,
If it be well to live. But better't were,
Thou fell'st into my fury; for one death
Might have prevented many.–Eros, ho!–
60 The shirt of Nessus is upon me. Teach me,
Alcides, thou mine ancestor, thy rage.
Let me lodge Lichas on the horns o'the moon
And with those hands that grasped the heaviest club
Subdue my worthiest self. The witch shall die.
To the Roman boy she hath sold me, and I fall
Under this plot. She dies for't.–Eros, ho!

Exit.

SCENE VIII. Alexandria. *A room in the palace.*

Enter Cleopatra, Charmian, Iras, *and* Mardian.

CLEOPATRA. Help me, my women. Oh, he is more mad
Than Telamon for his shield; the boar of Thessaly
Was never so imbost.
CHARMIAN. To the monument!
There lock yourself and send him word you are dead.
The soul and body rive not more in parting
Than greatness going off.
CLEOPATRA. To the monument!
Mardian, go tell him I have slain myself.
10 Say that the last I spoke was "Antony,"
And word it, prythee, piteously. Hence, Mardian,
And bring me how he takes my death. To the monument!

---

65. Roman] *D1*, *D2*, *D3*; young Roman *D4*, *S*.
0. SCENE VIII] *D1*, *D2*; scene xi *D3*, *D4*; scene xiii *S*. *D3*, *D4* indicate omission of entire scene (twelve lines).

SCENE IX. *The same. Another room.*

Enter Antony *and* Eros.

ANTONY. Eros, thou yet behold'st me?
EROS. Ay, noble lord.
ANTONY. Sometime we see a cloud that's dragonish;
A vapor, sometime, like a bear or lion,
A towered citadel, a pendant rock,
A forked mountain, or blue promontory
With trees upon't that nod unto the wind
And mock our eyes with air. Thou hast seen these signs;
They are black Vesper's pageants.
10 EROS. Ay, my lord.
ANTONY. That which is now a horse, even with a thought
The rack dislimns and makes it indistinct
As water is in water.
EROS. It does, my lord.
ANTONY. My good knave, Eros, now thy captain is
Even such a body. Here I am Antony,
Yet cannot hold this visible shape, my knave.
I made these wars for Egypt, and the Queen—
Whose heart I thought I had, for she had mine;
20 Which, whilst it was mine, had annexed unto't
A million more, now lost—she, Eros, has
Packed cards with Caesar, and false-played my glory
Unto an enemy's triumph.
Nay, weep not, gentle Eros; there is left us
Ourselves, to end ourselves.

Enter Mardian.

Oh, thy vile lady!
She has robbed me of my sword.
MARDIAN. No, Antony;
My mistress loved thee, and her fortunes mingled
30 With thine entirely.
ANTONY. Hence, saucy eunuch! Peace!
She hath betrayed me and shall die the death.
MARDIAN. Death of one person can be paid but once,
And that she hath discharged. What thou would'st do

---

0. SCENE IX] *D1*, *D2*; printed scene xii but marked as continuation of scene x in *D3*, *D4*; scene xiv *S*.
7. wind] *D1*, *D2*, *D3*; world *D4*, *S*.

Is done unto thy hand; the last she spake
Was, "Antony! Most noble Antony!"
Then in the midst a tearing groan did break
The name of Antony; it was divided
Between her heart and lips. She rendered life,
40 Thy name so buried in her.

ANTONY. Dead then?

MARDIAN. Dead.

ANTONY. Unarm me, Eros; the long day's task is done,
And we must sleep.—That thou depart'st hence safe
Does pay thy labor richly. Go.

Exit Mardian.

Pluck off!
The seven-fold shield of Ajax cannot keep
The battery from my heart. Oh, cleave, my sides!
Heart, once be stronger than thy continent,
50 Crack thy frail case!—Apace, Eros, apace.—
No more a soldier. Bruised pieces, go;
You have been nobly born.—From me a while.

Exit Eros.

I will o'ertake thee, Cleopatra, and
Weep for my pardon. So it must be, for now
All length is torture. Since the torch is out,
Lie down and stray no farther. Now all labor
Mars what it does; yea, every force entangles
Itself with strength. Seal then, and all is done.—
Eros!—I come, my Queen.—Eros!—Stay for me.
60 Where souls do couch on flowers we'll hand in hand,
And with our sprightly port make the ghosts gaze.
Dido and her Æneas shall want troups,
And all the haunt be ours.—Come, Eros, Eros!

Re-enter Eros.

EROS. What would my lord?

ANTONY. Since Cleopatra died
I have lived in such dishonor that the gods
Detest my baseness. I, that with my sword
Quartered the world, and o'er green Neptune's back

---

43. Unarm me] *D1*, *D2*, *D3*; Unarm *D4*, *S*.
46. Pluck off] *D1*, *D2*, *D3*; Off, pluck off *D4*, *S*.
67. I, that] *D1*, *D2*, *D3*, *S*; I *D4*.

With ships made cities, condemn myself to lack
70 The courage of a woman; less noble-minded
Than she, which, by her death, our Caesar tells,
"I am conqueror of myself." Thou art sworn, Eros,
That, when the exigent should come (which now
Is come, indeed) when I should see behind me
The inevitable prosecution of
Disgrace and horror, that, on my command,
Thou then would'st kill me. Do't; the time is come.
Thou strik'st not me; 'tis Caesar thou defeatest.
Put color in thy cheek.
80 EROS. The gods withold me!
Shall I do that which all the Parthian darts,
Though enemy, lost aim and could not?
ANTONY. Eros,
Would'st thou be windowed in great Rome and see
Thy master thus with pleached arms, bending down
His corrigible neck, his face subdued
To penetrative shame, whilst the wheeled seat
Of fortunate Caesar, drawn before him, branded
His baseness that ensued?
90 EROS. I would not see't.
ANTONY. Come then, for with a wound I must be cured.
Draw that thy honest sword, which thou hast worn
Most useful for thy country.
EROS. Oh, sir, pardon me.
ANTONY. When I did make thee free, swor'st thou not then
To do this when I bade thee? Do it at once,
Or thy precedent services are all
But accidents unpurposed. Draw and come.
EROS. Turn from me then that noble countenance
100 Wherein the worship of the whole world lies.
ANTONY (*turning away his face*). Lo thee.
EROS. My sword is drawn.
ANTONY. Then let it do at once
The thing why thou hast drawn it.
EROS. My dear master,
My captain, and my emperor, let me say,
Before I strike this bloody stroke, farewell.
ANTONY. 'Tis said, man; and farewell.
EROS. Farewell, great chief.

---

70. minded] *D*1, *D*2, *D*3; mind *D*4, *S*.
91. Come then . . .] *D*3, *D*4 indicate omission of seven and a half lines here.

110 Shall I strike now?

ANTONY. Now, Eros.

EROS. Why, there then. (*Falling on his sword.*) Thus I do escape the sorrow

Of Antony's death. (*Dies.*)

ANTONY. Thrice nobler than myself!

Thou teachest me, O valiant Eros, what

I should, and thou could'st not. My queen and Eros

Have, by their brave instruction, got upon me

A nobleness in record. But I will be

120 A bride-groom in my death, and run into't

As to a lover's bed. Come then (*taking* Eros' *sword*), and, Eros,

Thy master dies thy scholar; to do thus (*Running on it.*)

I learnt of thee. How! not yet dead? Not dead?

Enter Guard *and* Dercetas.

The guard? How! Oh, dispatch me!

1ST GUARD. What's the noise?

ANTONY. I have done my work ill, friends. Oh, make an end

Of what I have begun.

2ND GUARD. The star is fallen.

1ST GUARD. And time is at his period.

130 ALL. Alas, and woe!

ANTONY. Let him that loves me strike me dead.

1ST GUARD. Not I.

2ND GUARD. Nor I.

3RD GUARD. Not any one.

Exeunt Guard.

DERCETAS. Thy death and fortunes bid thy followers fly.

This sword [*showing sword*] but shown to Caesar, with this tidings,

Shall enter me with him.

Enter Diomede.

DIOMEDE. Where's Antony?

DERCETAS. There, Diomede, there.

140 DIOMEDE. Lives he? Wilt thou not answer, man?

Exit Dercetas, *with the sword.*

---

123. not yet dead] *D1*, *D2*, *D3*; not dead *D4*, *S*.
124. How] *D1*, *D2*, *D3*; Ho *D4*, *S*.
137.1. DIOMEDE] *D1*, *D2*, *D3*; Diomedes *D4*, *S*.
138. Diomede] *D1*, *D2*, *D3*; Diomed *D4*, *S*.

ANTONY. Art thou there, Diomede? Draw thy sword and give me
Sufficing strokes for death.
DIOMEDE. Most absolute lord,
The Empress Cleopatra sent me to thee.
ANTONY. When did she send thee?
DIOMEDE. Now, my lord.
ANTONY. Where is she?
DIOMEDE. Locked in her monument. She had a prophesying fear
Of what hath come to pass. For when she saw
150 (Which never shall be found) you did suspect
She had disposed with Caesar, and that your rage
Would not be purged, she sent you word she was dead;
But, fearing since how it might work, hath sent
Me to proclaim the truth; and I am come,
I dread, too late.
ANTONY. Too late, good Diomede. Call my guard, I prythee.
DIOMEDE. What ho, the emperor's guard! The guard, what ho!

Enter some of the Guard.

Come, your lord calls.
ANTONY. Bear me, good friends, where Cleopatra bides;
160 'Tis the last service that I shall command you.
1ST GUARD. Woe are we, sir, you may not live to wear
All your true followers out.
ALL. Most heavy day!
ANTONY. Nay, good my fellows, do not please sharp fate
To grace it with your sorrows. Bid that welcome
Which comes to punish us, and we punish it
Seeming to bear it lightly. Take me up.
I have led you oft; carry me now, good friends,
And have my thanks for all.

Exeunt, bearing Antony.

SCENE X. *The same. A monument.*

Enter, at a window above, Cleopatra, Charmian, *and* Iras.

CLEOPATRA. O Charmian, I will never go from hence.
CHARMIAN. Be comforted, dear madam.

---

161. Woe are] *D1*, *D2*, *D3*; Woe, woe are *D4*, *S*.
0. SCENE X] *D1*, *D2*; scene xiii *D3*, *D4*; scene xv *S*. *D3*, *D4* indicate omission of entire scene (103 lines).

CLEOPATRA. No, I will not.
All strange and terrible events are welcome,
But comforts we despise; our size of sorrow,
Proportioned to our cause, must be as great

Enter Diomede.

As that which makes it.—How now? Is he dead?
DIOMEDE. His death's upon him, but not dead. Look out
O'the other side your monument.—But see,
10 His guard have brought him hither.

Enter Antony, *borne by the* Guard.

CLEOPATRA. O sun, sun,
Burn the great sphere thou mov'st in! Darkling stand
The varying shore o'the world! O Antony,
Antony, Antony! Charmian, help; help, Iras!
Help, friends below! Let's draw him hither.
ANTONY. Peace!
Not Caesar's valor hath o'erthrown Antony,
But Antony's hath triumphed on itself.
CLEOPATRA. So it should be, that none but Antony
20 Should conquer Antony. But woe 'tis so!
ANTONY. I am dying, Egypt, dying; only yet
I here importune death a while, until
Of many thousand kisses the poor last
I lay upon thy lips. Come down.
CLEOPATRA. I dare not—
Dear, dear my lord, your pardon that I dare not—
Lest I be taken. Not the imperious show
Of the full-fortuned Caesar ever shall
Be brooched with me; if knives, drugs, serpents, have
30 Edge, sting, or operation, I am safe.
Your wife Octavia, with her modest eyes
And still conclusion, shall acquire no honor
Demuring upon me. But come, come, Antony!
Help me, my women. We must draw thee up.
Assist, good friends.

---

11. O sun, sun] *D1*, *D2*, *D3*; O sun *D4*, S.
14. Antony, Antony . . .] *D1*, *D2*, *D3*; Antony, Antony! / Help, Charmian, help; Iras, help *D4*; Antony, Antony! Help, Charmian; help, Iras; help! *S*.
21. only yet] *D1*, *D2*, *D3*; only *D4*, *S*.
24. thy lips. Come down.] *D1*, *D2*, *D3*; thy lips. *D4*, *S*.

Garrick and Mrs. Yates in *Antony and Cleopatra*
Folger Shakespeare Library

Cleopatra *and her women throw out certain tackle, into which the people below put* Antony, *and he is drawn up.*

ANTONY. O quick, or I am gone.
CLEOPATRA. Here's sport, indeed! How heavy weighs my lord!
Our strength is all gone into heaviness;
That makes the weight. Had I great Juno's power,
40 The strong-winged Mercury should fetch thee up
And set thee by Jove's side. Yet come a little.
Wishers were ever fools. O come, come, come!
And welcome, welcome! Die where thou hast lived.
Quicken with kissing. [*Kisses him.*] Had my lips that power,
Thus would I wear them out.
ALL. A heavy sight!
ANTONY. I am dying, Egypt, dying.
Give me some wine, and let me speak a little.
CLEOPATRA. No, let me speak, and let me rail so high
50 That the false huswife Fortune break her wheel,
Provoked by my offence.
ANTONY. One word, sweet queen.
Of Caesar seek your honor with your safety. Oh!
CLEOPATRA. They do not go together.
ANTONY. Gentle, hear me!
None about Caesar trust but Proculeius.
CLEOPATRA. My resolution and my hands I'll trust;
None about Caesar.
ANTONY. The miserable change now at my end
60 Lament nor sorrow at; but please your thoughts
In feeding them with those my former fortunes,
Wherein I lived the greatest prince o'the world,
The noblest; and do now not basely die,
Not cowardly put off my helmet to
My countryman, a Roman by a Roman
Valiantly vanquished. Now my spirit is going.
I can no more. (*Sinks.*)
CLEOPATRA. Noblest of men, wou't die?
Hast thou no care of me? Shall I abide
70 In this dull world, which in thy absence is

61. former fortunes] *D1*, *D2*, *D3*, *S*; fortunes *D4*.
67. (*Sinks*)] *D1*, *D2*, *D3*; (*Dies*) *D4*.
68. wou't] *D1*, *D2*, *D3*; woo't *D4*, *S*.

Antony *dies.*

No better than a sty? O see, my women,
The crown o'the earth doth melt. My lord!
O withered is the garland of the war;
The soldier's pole is fall'n! Young boys and girls
Are level now with men. The odds is gone,
And there is nothing left remarkable
Beneath the visiting moon.

CHARMIAN. O quietness, lady!

Cleopatra *swoons.*

IRAS. She is dead too, our sovereign.

80 CHARMIAN. Lady!

IRAS. Madam!

CHARMIAN. O madam, madam, madam!

IRAS. Royal Egypt!
Emperess!

CHARMIAN (*seeing her recover*). Peace, peace, Iras.

CLEOPATRA. No more but e'en a woman, and commanded
By such poor passion as the maid that milks
And does the meanest chares. It were for me
To throw my scepter at the injurious gods,
90 To tell them that this world did equal theirs
'Till they had stol'n our jewel. All's but naught.
Patience is sottish, and impatience does
Become a dog that's mad. Then is it sin
To rush into the secret house of death
Ere death dare come to us?—How do you, women?
What, what? Good cheer! Why, how now, Charmian?
My noble girls! Ah, women, women, look,
Our lamp is spent; it's out.—Good sirs, take heart.—
We'll bury him. And then, what's brave, what's noble,
100 Let's do it after the high Roman fashion
And make death proud to take us. Come, away.
This case of that huge spirit now is cold.
Ah, women, women! Come; we have no friend
But resolution and the briefest end.

Exeunt, those above bearing off the body.

88. chares] *D1*, *D2*, *D3*, *S*; charges *D4*.

ACT V. SCENE I. *Camp before* Alexandria.

Enter Caesar, *with* Dolabella, Agrippa, Mecaenas, Gallus, Proculeius, *and others.*

CAESAR. Go to him, Dolabella, bid him yield;
Being so frustrated, tell him he mocks
The pauses that he makes.
DOLABELLA. Caesar, I shall.

Exit Dolabella.

Enter Dercetas, *with* Antony's *sword.*

CAESAR. Wherefore is that? And what art thou that dar'st
Appear thus to us?
DERCETAS. I'm called Dercetas;
Mark Antony I served, who best was worthy
Best to be served. Whilst he stood up and spoke
10 He was my master, and I wore my life
To spend upon his haters. If thou please
To take me to thee, as I was to him
I'll be to Caesar; if thou pleasest not,
I yield thee up my life.
CAESAR. What is't thou say'st?
DERCETAS. I say, O Caesar, Antony is dead.
CAESAR. The breaking of so great a thing should make
A greater crack in nature. The round world
Should have shook lions into civil streets
20 And citizens to their dens. The death of Antony
Is not a single doom; in that name lay
A moiety of the world.
DERCETAS. He is dead, Caesar;
Not by a public minister of justice,
Nor by a hired knife; but that self-hand
Which writ his honor in the acts it did
Hath, with the courage which the heart did lend it,
Splitted the heart itself. This [*showing sword*] is his sword;
I robbed his wound of it. Behold it stained
30 With his most noble blood.
CAESAR. Look you sad, friends?
The gods rebuke me, but it is a tidings

---

2. frustrated] *D1*, *D2*, *D3*; frustrate *D4*, *S.*
18. crack in nature] *D1*, *D2*, *D3*; crack *D4*, *S.*

To wash the eyes of kings!
AGRIPPA. And strange it is
That nature must compell us to lament
Our most persisted deeds.
MECAENAS. His taints and honors
Weighed equal with him.
AGRIPPA. A rarer spirit never
40 Did steer humanity; but you, gods, will give us
Some faults to mark us men. Caesar is touched.
MECAENAS. When such a spacious mirror's set before him,
He needs must see himself.
CAESAR. O Antony,
I have followed thee to this!—But we do launch
Diseases in our bodies. I must perforce
Have shown to thee such a declining day
Or look on thine: we could not stall together
In the whole world. But yet let me lament,
50 With tears as sovereign as the blood of hearts,
That thou, my brother, my competitor
In top of all design, my mate in empire,
Friend and companion in the front of war,
The arm of mine own body, and the heart
Where mine his thoughts did kindle—that our stars,
Unreconciliable, should divide
Our equalness to this. Hear me, good friends—

Enter Mardian.

But I will tell you at some meeter season;
The business of this man looks out of him.
60 We'll hear him what he says. Whence are you, sir?
MARDIAN. A poor Egyptian. The Queen my mistress,
Confined in all she has, her monument,
Of thy intents desires instruction,
That she preparedly may frame herself
To the way she's forced to.
CAESAR. Bid her have good heart;
She soon shall know of us, by some of ours,
How honorably and how kindly we
Determined have for her; for Caesar cannot

38. Weighed] *D1*, *D2*, *D3*; Waged *D4*, *S*.
45. launch] *D1*, *D2*; lance *D3*, *D4*; lanch S.
57.1. *Enter* Mardian] *D1*, *D2*; . . . *a Messenger* *D3*, *D4*; . . . *an Egyptian S*.

70 Leave to be gentle.

MARDIAN. So the gods preserve thee!

Exit.

CAESAR. Come hither, Proculeius. Go and say
We purpose her no shame. Give her what comforts
The quality of her passion shall require,
Lest, in her greatness, by some mortal stroke
She do defeat us. For her life in Rome
Would be eternaling our triumph. Go,
And with your speediest bring us what she says
And how you find of her.

80 PROCULEIUS. Caesar, I shall.

Exit.

CAESAR. Gallus, go you along.

Exit Gallus.

Where's Dolabella?
To second Proculeius?

ALL. Dolabella!

CAESAR. Let him alone, for I remember now
How he's employed. He shall in time be ready.
Go with me to my tent, where you shall see
How hardly I was drawn into this war,
How calm and gentle I proceeded still
90 In all my writings. Go with me and see
What I can show in this.

Exeunt.

SCENE II. Alexandria. *A room in the monument.*

Enter Cleopatra, Charmian, *and* Iras.

CLEOPATRA. My desolation does begin to make
A better life. 'Tis paltry to be Caesar;
Not being Fortune, he's but Fortune's knave,
A minister of her will. And it is great
To do that thing that ends all other deeds,
Which shackles accidents and bolts up change,

---

70. Leave] *D1*, *D2*, *D3*; live *D4*, *S*. gentle] *D1*, *D2*, *D3*; ungentle *D4*, *S*.
77. eternaling] *D1*, *D2*; eternalizing *D3*; eternal in *D4*, *S*.

Which sleeps, and never palates more the dung,
The beggar's nurse and Caesar's.

Enter Proculeius *and* Gallus, *with soldiers, to the door of the monument, without.*

PROCULEIUS. Caesar sends greeting to the Queen of Egypt
10 And bids thee study on what fair demands
Thou mean'st to have him grant thee.
CLEOPATRA. What's thy name?
PROCULEIUS. My name is Proculeius.
CLEOPATRA. Antony
Did tell me of you, bade me trust you; but
I do not greatly care to be deceived,
That have no use for trusting. If your master
Would have a queen his beggar, you must tell him
That majesty, to keep decorum, must
20 No less beg than a kingdom. If he please
To give me conquered Egypt for my son,
He gives me so much of mine own as I
Will kneel to him with thanks.
PROCULEIUS. Be of good cheer;
You are fall'n into a princely hand. Fear nothing.
Make your full reference freely to my lord,
Who is so full of grace that it flows over
On all that need. Let me report to him
Your sweet dependancy, and you shall find
30 A conqueror that will pray in aid for kindness
Where he for grace is kneeled to.
CLEOPATRA. Pray you, tell him
I am his fortune's vassal, and I send him
The greatness he has got. I hourly learn
A doctrine of obedience, and would gladly
Look him i'the face.
PROCULEIUS. This I'll report, dear lady.
Have comfort, for I know your plight is pitied
Of him that caused it. Fare you well. [*Aside.*] Hark, Gallus!
40 You see how easily she may be surprised;
Guard her 'till Caesar come.

Exit Proculeius.

---

39. Fare you well] *D1*, *D2*, *D3*, *S*; omitted *D4*.
Hark, Gallus] although this corrupt passage has been variously interpreted, sometimes "Gallus" being considered a speaking cue and assigned the next line, in any event the word "Hark" is not in *S*.

Gallus *maintains converse with* Cleopatra.

Re-enter in the monument, from behind,
Proculeius *and soldiers, hastily.*

IRAS. O royal Queen!
CHARMIAN. O Cleopatra! thou art taken, Queen!
CLEOPATRA. Quick, quick, good hands. (*Drawing a dagger.*)
PROCULEIUS. Hold, worthy lady, hold. (*Staying her.*)
Do not yourself such wrong, who are in this
Relieved, but not betrayed.
CLEOPATRA. What, of death too,
That rids our dogs of languish?
50 PROCULEIUS. Cleopatra,
Do not abuse my master's bounty by
The undoing of yourself. Let the world see
His nobleness well acted, which your death
Will never let come forth.
CLEOPATRA. Where art thou, death?
Come hither, come! Come, come, and take a queen
Worth many babes and beggars!
PROCULEIUS. O temperance, lady!
CLEOPATRA. Sir, I will eat no meat; I'll not drink, sir;
60 If idle talk will once be necessary,
I'll not speak neither. This mortal house I'll ruin,
Do Caesar what he can. Know, sir, that I
Will not wait pinioned at your master's court,
Nor once be chastised with the sober eye
Of dull Octavia. Shall they hoist me up
And show me to the shouting varletry
Of censuring Rome? Rather a ditch in Egypt
Be gentle grave unto me; rather on Nilus' mud
Lay me stark naked, and let the water-flies
70 Blow me into abhorring; rather make
My country's high pyramids my gibbet,
And hang me up in chains!
PROCULEIUS. You do extend
These thoughts of horror farther than you shall
Find cause for it in Caesar.

Enter Dolabella.

---

42. O royal Queen] *D1*, *D2*, *D3*; Royal Queen *D4*, *S.*
75. cause for it] *D1*, *D2*, *D3*; cause *D4*, *S.*

DOLABELLA. Proculeius,
What thou hast done thy master Caesar knows,
And he hath sent for thee. As for the Queen,
I'll take her to my guard.

80 PROCULEIUS. So, Dolabella,
It shall content me best. Be gentle to her.
To Caesar I will speak what you shall please,
If you'll employ me to him.

CLEOPATRA. Say, I would die.

Exeunt Proculeius *and Soldiers.*

DOLABELLA. Most noble Empress, you have heard of me?

CLEOPATRA. I cannot tell.

DOLABELLA. Assuredly you have.

CLEOPATRA. No matter, sir, what I have heard or known.
You laugh when boys or women tell their dreams;
90 Is't not your trick?

DOLABELLA. I understand not, madam.

CLEOPATRA. I dreamt there was an Emperor Antony.
O such another sleep, that I might see
But such another man!

DOLABELLA. If it might please you—

CLEOPATRA. His face was as the heavens, and therein stuck
A sun and moon which kept their course and lighted
The little *o* o'the earth.

DOLABELLA. Most sovereign creature—

100 CLEOPATRA. His legs bestrid the ocean; his reared arm
Crested the world. His voice was propertied
As all the tuned spheres, when that to friends;
But when he meant to quail and shake the orb,
He was as rattling thunder. For his bounty,
There was no winter in't; an autumn 'twas,
That grew the more by reaping. His delights
Were dolphin-like; they showed his back above
The element they lived in. In his livery
Walked crowns and crownets; realms and islands
110 As plates dropt from his pocket.

DOLABELLA. Cleopatra!

87. you have] *D1*, *D2*; know me *D3*, *D4*, *S*.
95. you] *D1*, *D2*, *D3*; ye *D4*, *S*.
98. little *o* o'the] *D1*, *D2*, *D3*; little *O*, the *D4*, *S*.

CLEOPATRA. Think you there was, or might be, such a man
As this I dreamt of?
DOLABELLA. Gentle madam, no.
CLEOPATRA. You lie, up to the hearing of the gods!
But if there be, or ever were, one such,
It's past the size of dreaming. Nature wants stuff
To vie strange forms with fancy; yet to imagine
An Antony were nature's piece 'gainst fancy,
120 Condemning shadows quite.
DOLABELLA. Hear me, good madam.
Your loss is as yourself, great; and you bear it
As answering to the weight. 'Would I might never
O'ertake pursued success but I do feel,
By the rebound of yours, a grief that smites
My very heart at root.
CLEOPATRA. I thank you, sir.
Know you what Caesar means to do with me?
DOLABELLA. I am loth to tell you what I would you knew.
130 CLEOPATRA. Nay, pray you, sir.
DOLABELLA. Though he be honorable—
CLEOPATRA. He'll lead me in triumph.
DOLABELLA. Madam, he will; I know it.
(*Within.*) Make way there! Caesar!

Enter Caesar *and train of Romans,*
and Seleucus.

CAESAR. Which is the Queen of Egypt?
DOLABELLA. It is the Emperor, madam.
CAESAR (*to* Cleopatra, *raising her*). Arise, you shall not kneel.
I pray you, rise. Rise, Egypt.
CLEOPATRA. Sir, the gods
140 Will have it thus; my master and my lord
I must obey.
CAESAR. Take to you no hard thoughts.
The record of what injuries you did us,
Though written in our flesh, we shall remember
As things but done by chance.
CLEOPATRA. Sole sir o'the world,
I cannot project mine own cause so well
To make it clear, but do confess I have

125. smites] *D1*, *D2*, *D3*, *S*; shoots *D4*.
132. me in] *D1*, *D2*, *D3*; me then in *D4*, *S*.

Been laden with like frailties which before
150 Have often shamed our sex.

CAESAR. Cleopatra, know
We will extenuate rather than enforce.
If you apply yourself to our intents,
Which towards you are most gentle, you shall find
A benefit in this change. But if you seek
To lay on me a cruelty by taking
Antony's course, you shall bereave yourself
Of my good purposes and put your children
To that destruction which I'll guard them from,
160 If thereon you rely. I'll take my leave.

CLEOPATRA. And may, through all the world. 'Tis yours, and we,
Your 'scutcheons and your signs of conquest, shall
Hang in what place you please. Here, my good lord.

CAESAR. You shall advise me in all for Cleopatra.

CLEOPATRA. This is the brief of money, plate, and jewels
I am possest of. 'Tis exactly valued;
Not petty things omitted.—Where's Seleucus?

SELEUCUS. Here, madam.

CLEOPATRA. This is my treasurer; let him speak, my lord,
170 Upon his peril, that I have reserved
To myself nothing. Speak the truth, Seleucus.

SELEUCUS. Madam,
I had rather seal my lips than to my peril
Speak that which is not.

CLEOPATRA. What have I kept back?

SELEUCUS. Enough to purchase what you have made known.

CAESAR. Nay, blush not, Cleopatra; I approve
Your wisdom in the deed.

CLEOPATRA. See, Caesar! O, behold
180 How pomp is followed! Mine will now be yours;
And should we shift estates, yours would be mine.
The ingratitude of this Seleucus does
E'en make me wild. O slave, of no more trust
Than love that's hired! What, go'st thou back? thou shalt
Go back, I warrant thee; but I'll catch thine eyes,
Though they had wings. Slave! soulless villain! dog!
O rarely base! (*Flying at him.*)

---

163. Here] *D2* again inadvertantly prints a dagger following, the second suggestion that the text was set from *D1*.

182. The ingratitutde . . .] *D3*, *D4* indicate the omission of seven following lines.

CAESAR (*interposing*). Good Queen, let us intreat you.
CLEOPATRA. O Caesar, what a wounding shame is this,
190 That thou vouchsafing here to visit me,
Doing the honor of thy lordliness
To one so mean, that mine own servant should
Parcel the sum of my disgraces by
Addition of his envy! Say, good Caesar,
That I some lady trifles have reserved,
Immoment toys, things of such dignity
As we greet modern friends withal; and say
Some nobler token I have kept apart
For Livia and Octavia to induce
200 Their mediation; must I be unfolded
By one that I have bred? The gods! It smites me
Beneath the fall I have. [*To* Seleucus.] Wert thou a man,
Thou would'st have mercy on me.
CAESAR. Forbear, Seleucus.

Exit Seleucus.

CLEOPATRA. Be it known that we, the greatest, are misthought
For things that others do; and when we fall,
We answer others' merits; in our name
Are therefore to be pitied.
CAESAR. Cleopatra,
210 Not what you have reserved, nor what acknowledged,
Put we i'the roll of conquest. Still be it yours;
Bestow it at your pleasure and believe
Caesar's no merchant, to make prize with you
Of things that merchants sold. Therefore be cheered;
Make not your thoughts your prisons. No, dear Queen,
For we intend so to dispose you as
Yourself shall give us counsel. Feed, and sleep.
Our care and pity is so much upon you
That we remain your friend. And so adieu.
220 CLEOPATRA. My master, and my lord.
CAESAR. Not so. Adieu.

Exeunt Caesar, Dolabella
and train.

---

202. I have] *D1* omits Cleopatra's following aside to Seleucus: "—Prithee go hence! / Or I shall show the cinders of my spirits / Through th'ashes of my chance."

207. others'] *D1*, *D2*, *D3*; others *D4*. name] *D1*, *D3*, *S*; names *D2*, *D4*.

CLEOPATRA. He words me, girls, he words me, that I should not
Be noble to myself. But hark thee, Charmian.
IRAS. Finish, good lady; the bright day is done,
And we are for the dark.
CLEOPATRA. Hie thee again.
I have spoke already, and it is provided.
Go, put it to the haste.
CHARMIAN. Madam, I will. (*Going.*)

Re-enter Dolabella.

230 DOLABELLA. Where is the Queen?
CHARMIAN. Behold, sir.

Exit.

CLEOPATRA. Dolabella?
DOLABELLA. Madam, as thereto sworn by your command,
Which my love makes religion to obey,
I tell you this. Caesar through Syria
Intends his journey; and within three days
You with your children will he send before.
Make your best use of this. I have performed
Your pleasure and my promise.
240 CLEOPATRA. Dolabella,
I shall remain your debtor.
DOLABELLA. I your servant.
Adieu, good Queen; I must attend on Caesar.
CLEOPATRA. Farewell, and thanks.

Exit Dolabella.

Now Iras, what think'st thou?
Thou, an Egyptian puppet, shalt be shown
In Rome, as well as I. Mechanic slaves
With greasy aprons, rules, and hammers shall
Uplift us to the view; in their thick breaths,
250 Rank of gross diet, shall we be enclouded
And forced to drink their vapor.
IRAS. The gods forbid!
CLEOPATRA. Nay, 'tis most certain, Iras. Saucy lictors
Will catch at us, like strumpets, and scald rimers
Ballad us out o'tune. The quick comedians
Extemporally will stage us and present
Our Alexandrian revels. Antony
Shall be brought drunken forth, and I shall see

Some squeaking Cleopatra boy my greatness
260 I'the posture of a whore.

IRAS. O the good gods!

CLEOPATRA. Nay, this is certain.

IRAS. I'll never see't, for I am sure my nails
Are stronger than mine eyes.

CLEOPATRA. Why, that's the way
To fool their preparation and to conquer
Their most assured intents.—Now, Charmian?

Re-enter Charmian.

Show me, my women, like a queen. Go fetch
My best attires. I am again for Cydnus,
270 To meet Mark Antony. Sirrah Iras, go.
Now, noble Charmian, we'll dispatch indeed,
And when thou hast done this chare I'll give thee leave
To play 'till doomsday. Bring our crown and all.

Exit Iras.

Charmian *falls to adjusting* Cleopatra's *dress. Noise within.*

Wherefore's this noise?

Enter some of the Guard.

1ST GUARD. Here is a rural fellow
That will not be denied your highness' presence.
He brings you figs.

CLEOPATRA. Let him come in.

Exeunt Guard.

How poor an instrument
280 May do a noble deed! He brings me liberty.
My resolution's placed, and I have nothing
Of woman in me. Now from head to foot
I am marble-constant; now the fleeting moon
No planet is of mine.

Re-enter Guard, *with the* Clown.

1ST GUARD. This is the man.

CLEOPATRA. Avoid, and leave him.

Exit Guard.

---

267. assured] *D1*, *D2*, *D3*; absurd *D4*, *S.*
274.1. *some of the* Guard] *D1*, *D2*; *one of the Guard D3*, *D4*; *a* Guardsman *S.*
284.1. *with the* Clown] *D1*, *D2*; . . . *a Clown D3*, *D4*; *and* Clown *S.*

Hast thou the pretty worm of Nilus there,
That kills and pains not?

CLOWN. Truly, I have him; but I would not be the party that should
290 desire you to touch him, for his biting is immortal. Those that do die of it do seldom or never recover.

CLEOPATRA. Remember'st thou any that have died on't?

CLOWN. Very many, men and women too. I heard of one of them no longer than yesterday, a very honest woman, but something given to lie, as a woman should not do but in the way of honesty, how she died of the biting of it, what pain she felt. Truly, she makes a very good report o'the worm. But he that will believe all that they say, shall never be saved by half that they do. But this is most fallible; the worm's an odd worm.

300 CLEOPATRA. Get thee hence; farewell.

CLOWN. I wish you all joy of the worm. (*Setting down his basket.*)

CLEOPATRA. Farewell.

CLOWN. You must think this, look you, that the worm will do his kind.

CLEOPATRA. Ay, ay; farewell.

CLOWN. Look you, the worm is not to be trusted but in the keeping of wise people; for indeed there is no goodness in the worm.

CLEOPATRA. Take thou no care; it shall be heeded.

CLOWN. Very good. Give it nothing, I pray you, for it is not worth the feeding.

310 CLEOPATRA. Well, get thee gone; farewell.

CLOWN. Yes, forsooth. I wish you joy of the worm.

Exit.

Re-enter Iras, *with the robe, &c.*

CLEOPATRA. Give me my robe, put on my crown; I have
Immortal longings in me. Now no more
The juice of Egypt's grape shall moist this lip.
Yare, yare, good Iras; quick. Methinks I hear
Antony call; I see him rouse himself
To praise my noble act. I hear him mock
The luck of Caesar, which the gods give men
To excuse their after wrath. Husband, I come.

---

289. that should] *D*1, *D*2, *D*3, S; should *D*4.

303. You must] *D*3, *D*4 mark eighteen lines for omission beginning here.

309. feeding] *D*1, *D*2 omit seven lines here, and *D*4 indicates their omission with inverted commas: "CLEO. Will it eat me? / CLOWN. You must not think I am so simple but I know the devil himself will not eat a woman. I know that a woman is a dish for the gods, if the devil dress her not. But, truly, these same whoreson devils do the gods great harm in their women, for in every ten that they make, the devils mar five."

Goes to a bed, or sofa, which she ascends; her women compose her on it. Iras *sets the basket, which she has been holding upon her own arm, by her.*

320 Now to that name my courage prove my title!
I am fire and air; my other elements
I give to baser life. So, have you done?
Come then, and take the last warmth of my lips.
Farewell, kind Charmian. Iras, long farewell. (*Kissing them.*)

Iras *falls.*

Have I the aspic in my lips? Dost fall?
If thou and nature can so gently part,
The stroke of death is as a lover's pinch,
Which hurts and is desired. Dost thou lie still?
If thus thou vanquishest, thou tell'st the world
330 It is not worth leave-taking.

CHARMIAN. Dissolve, thick cloud, and rain, that I may say
The gods themselves do weep!

CLEOPATRA. This proves me base.
If she first meet the curled Antony,
He'll make demand of her and spend that kiss
Which is my heaven to have. Come, mortal wretch (*To the asp, applying it to her breast.*),
With thy sharp teeth this knot intrinsicate
Of life at once untie. Poor venomous fool (*Stirring it.*)
Be angry and dispatch. O could'st thou speak,
340 That I might hear thee call great Caesar ass
Unpolicied!

CHARMIAN. O Eastern star!

CLEOPATRA. Peace, peace!
Dost thou not see my baby at my breast,
That sucks the nurse asleep?

CHARMIAN. O break! O break!

CLEOPATRA. As sweet as balm, as soft as air, as gentle—
O Antony! Nay, I will take thee too. (*Applying another asp to her arm.*)
What should I stay—(*Dies.*)

350 CHARMIAN. In this vile world?—So fare thee well.—
Now boast thee, death; in thy possession lies
A lass unparalleled.—Downy windows, close;
And golden Phoebus never be beheld

---

350. vile world] *D1*, *D2*, *D3*; wild world *D4*, *S.*

Of eyes again so royal! Your crown's awry;
I'll mend it, and then play.

Enter some of the Guard.

1ST GUARD. Where is the Queen?
CHARMIAN. Speak softly; wake her not.
1ST GUARD. Caesar hath sent—
CHARMIAN. Too slow a messenger. (*Applying the asp.*)
360 O come apace, dispatch. I partly feel thee.
1ST GUARD. Approach, ho! All's not well. Caesar's beguiled.
2ND GUARD. There's Dolabella sent from Caesar. Call him.
1ST GUARD. What work is here! Charmian, is this well done?
CHARMIAN. It is well done, and fitting for a princess
Descended of so many royal kings.
Ah, soldiers! (*Dies.*)

Enter Dolabella.

DOLABELLA. How goes it here?
2ND GUARD. All dead.
DOLABELLA. Caesar, thy thoughts
370 Touch their effects in this. Thyself art coming
To see performed the dreaded act which thou
So sought'st to hinder.

(*Within.*) A way there, way for Caesar!

Enter Caesar *and train.*

DOLABELLA. O, sir, you are too sure an augurer;
That you did fear is done.
CAESAR. Brav'st at the last,
She leveled at our purposes and, being royal,
Took her own way. The manner of their deaths?
I do not see them bleed.
380 DOLABELLA. Who was last with them?
380 1ST GUARD. A simple countryman that brought her figs;
This [*showing basket*] was his basket.
CAESAR. Poisoned then.
1ST GUARD. O Caesar,
This Charmian lived but now; she stood and spake.
I found her trimming up the diadem
On her dead mistress; tremblingly she stood,
And on the sudden dropped.
CAESAR. O noble weakness!
390 If they had swallowed poison, 'twould appear

390 By external swelling; but she looks like sleep,
As she would catch another Antony
In her strong toil of grace.

DOLABELLA. Here, on her breast
There is a vent of blood, and something blown.
The like is on her arm.

1ST GUARD. This is an aspic's trail (*pointing to the floor*)
And these fig leaves have slime upon them, such
As the aspic leaves upon the caves of Nile.

400 CAESAR. Most probable,
That so she died, for her physician tells me
She hath pursued conclusions infinite
Of easy ways to die. Take up her bed,
And bear her women from the monument.
She shall be buried by her Antony.
No grave upon the earth shall clip in it
A pair so famous. High events as these
Strike those that make them; and their story is
No less in pity than his glory, which
410 Brought them to be lamented. Our army shall,
In solemn show, attend this funeral,
And then to Rome. Come, Dolabella, see
High order in this great solemnity.

Exeunt.

From the Press of Dryden Leach,
in Crane Court, Fleet-street. Oct. 23, 1758.

Conjectural Readings

p.	*l.*	
4,	23.	the raised empire
6,	9.	adorings
12,	13.	her leave to
14,	17.	a ray of
15,	5.	should salve my
17,	7.	A great
25,	2.	reporters
45,	23.	noses
49,	28.	*Antonias*,
50,	13.	fail,
52,	22.	the man *Brutus*
53,	7.	Strewed (or, Strowed) in
56,	20.	caparifons
57,	27.	embraced
61,	8.	enfranchised
62,	3.	and float,
64,	18.	cheek
67,	14.	work, our opposition
70,	6.	disperge
D°	29.	drum's din early wakes
75,	26.	her *Sichæus*
78,	5.	these tidings,
D°	19.	*dele*, prophesying
82,	8.	passions,
84,	17.	looked on
86,	24.	thanks for.
89,	29.	was nature's
99,	I.	By some external swelling: but she looks Like sleep, as she *&c.*

Cymbeline

A Tragedy

1762

CYMBELINE.

A

TRAGEDY.

By SHAKESPEAR

With ALTERATIONS.

LONDON:

Printed for J. and R. TONSON in the Strand.

M DCC LXII.

Facsimile title page of the First Edition
Folger Shakespeare Library

Advertisement

The admirers of Shakespear must not take it ill that there are some scenes, and consequently many fine passages, omitted in this edition of *Cymbeline*. It was impossible to retain more of the play and bring it within the compass of a night's entertainment. The chief alterations are in the division of the acts, in the shortening of many parts of the original, and transposing some scenes. As the play has met with so favourable a reception from the public, it is hoped that the alterations have not been made with great impropriety.

10 N.B. The scene printed in *italics* in the fifth act was omitted in the representation after the first night, but it is thought proper to print it.

6. of many parts] *D*1, *D*3, *D*4, *O*1; of omitted *D*2, *W*1, *W*2.

Dramatis Personae

MEN.

	Cymbeline, *King of Britain.*	*Mr.* Davies.
	Cloten, *son to the Queen by a former husband.*	*Mr.* King.
	Leonatus Posthumus, *a gentleman in love with the Princess, and privately married to her.*	*Mr.* Garrick.
	Guiderius } *disguised under the names of* Polidore *and* Cadwal,	*Mr.* O'Brian.
	Arviragus } *supposed sons to* Bellarius.	*Mr.* Palmer.
10	Bellarius, *a banished lord, disguised under the name of* Morgan.	*Mr.* Havard.
	Philario, *an* Italian, *friend to* Posthumus.	*Mr.* Kennedy.
	Iachimo, *friend to* Philario.	*Mr.* Holland.
	Caius Lucius, *ambassador from* Rome.	*Mr.* Bransby.
	Pisanio, *servant to* Posthumus.	*Mr.* Packer.
	A French *Gentleman, friend to* Philario.	*Mr.* Scrase.
	Cornelius, *a Doctor, servant to the Queen.*	*Mr.* Burton.
20	Two Gentlemen.	*Mr.* Ackman, *Mr.* Fox

WOMEN.

Queen, Wife to Cymbeline.	*Mrs.* Bennet.
Imogen, *daughter to* Cymbeline *by a former Queen.*	*Miss* Bride.

Helen, *woman to* Imogen. *Miss* Hippisley.

Lords, ladies, Roman *Senators, Tribunes, Captains,*
soldiers, messengers, and other attendants.

The SCENE, *partly in* Rome; *partly in* Britain.

Cymbeline

ACT I.

SCENE I. *A palace.*

Enter Pisanio *and a Gentleman.*

PISANIO. You do not meet a man but frowns. Our looks
No more obey the hearts than our courtiers,
But seem as does the king's.
GENTLEMAN. But what's the matter?
PISANIO. Are you so fresh a stranger as to ask that?
His daughter, and the heir of's kingdom (whom
He purposed to his wife's sole son, a widow
That late he married) hath referred herself
Unto a poor but worthy gentleman. She's wedded,
10 Her husband banished, she imprisoned. All
Is outward sorrow, though I think the king
Be touched at very heart.
GENTLEMAN. None but the king?
PISANIO. There is not a courtier,
Although they wear their faces to the bent
Of the king's looks, hath a heart that is not
Glad at the thing he scowl[s] at.
GENTLEMAN. And why so?
PISANIO. He that hath missed the princess is a thing
20 Too bad for bad report; and he that hath her
(I mean that married her) is a creature such
As, to seek through the regions of the earth
For one his like, there would be something failing
In him that should compare.

GENTLEMAN. His name and birth?
PISANIO. That I can well inform you, having lived
A faithful servant in the family.
His father was Sicilius, who served
Against the Romans with Cassibelan
30 And gained the sur-addition Leonatus.
He had, besides this gentleman in question,
Two other sons, who in the wars o'th' time
Died with their swords in hand. For which their father,
Then old and fond of issue, took such sorrow
That he quit being, and his gentle lady,
Big of this gentleman our theme, deceased
As he was born. The king he takes the babe
To his protection, calls him Posthumus,
Breeds him and makes him of his bed-chamber,
40 Puts to him all the learnings that his time
Could make him the receiver of; which he took
As we do air, fast as 'twas ministered;
His spring became a harvest. He lived in court,
Which rare it is to do, most praised, much loved,
A sample to the youngest; to th' more mature
A glass that featured them, and to the graver,
A child that guided dotards.
GENTLEMAN. I honor him, even out of your report.
But to my mistress, is she the sole child to the king?
50 PISANIO. His only child.
He had two sons (if this be worth your hearing,
Mark it), the eldest of them at three years old,
I'th' swathing clothes the other, from their nursery
Were stol'n, and to this hour no guess in knowledge
Which way they went.
GENTLEMAN. How long is this ago?
PISANIO. Some twenty years.
GENTLEMAN. That a king's children should be so conveyed!
So slackly guarded, and the search so slow
60 That could not trace them—
PISANIO. Howsoe'er 'tis strange,
Or that the negligence may well be laughed at,
Yet is it true, sir.
GENTLEMAN. I do well believe you.

---

44. most] *D2*, *D3*, *D4*, *D5*, *W1*, *W2*, *O1*; much *D1*.

PISANIO. Here comes my lord,
The queen, and princess; you must forbear.

Enter the Queen, Posthumus, Imogen, *and attendants.*

QUEEN. No, be assured you shall not find my daughter,
After the slander of most stepmothers,
Ill-eyed unto you. You're my prisoner, but
70 Your goaler shall deliver you the keys
That lock up your restraint. For you, good Posthumus,
So soon as I can win th'offended king,
I will be known your advocate. Marry, yet
The fire of rage is in him, and 'twere good
You leaned unto his sentence with what patience
Your wisdom may inform you.
POSTHUMUS. Please your Highness,
I will from hence today.
QUEEN. You know the peril.
80 I'll fetch a turn about the garden, pitying
The pangs of barred affections, though the king
Hath charged you should not speak together.

Exit.

IMOGEN. Dissembling courtesy! How fine this tyrant
Can tickle where she wounds. My dearest husband,
You must be gone;
And I shall here abide the hourly shot
Of angry eyes, not comforted to live,
But that there is this jewel in the world
That I may see again.
90 POSTHUMUS. My queen! My mistress!
Oh, Lady, weep no more, lest I give cause
To be suspected of more tenderness
Than doth become a man. I will remain
The loyal'st husband that did e'er plight troth.
My residence in Rome, at one Philario's,
Who to my father was a friend, to me
Known but by letter, thither write, my love,
And with mine eyes I'll drink the words you send,
Though ink be made of gall.

Enter Queen.

67. my] *D1*, *D2*, *D3*, *D4*; me *W1*, *W2*, *D5*, *O1*.

100 QUEEN. Be brief, I pray you;
If the king come I shall incur I know not
How much of his displeasure. (*Aside.*) Yet I'll move him
To walk this way. I never do him wrong
But he does buy my injuries to be friends,
Pays dear for my offences.

Exit.

POSTHUMUS. Should we be taking leave,
As long a term as yet we have to live,
The loathness to depart would grow. Adieu!
IMOGEN. Nay, stay a little.
110 Were you but riding forth to air yourself
Such parting were too petty. Look here, my love,
This diamond was my mother's. Take it, heart,
But keep it till you woo another wife
When Imogen is dead.
POSTHUMUS. How, how! Another?
You gentle gods, give me but this I have,
And sear up my embracements from a next
With bonds of death. (*Putting on the ring.*) Remain,
remain thou here
120 While sense can keep thee on. And sweetest, fairest,
As I my poor self did exchange for you
To your so infinite loss, so in our trifles
I still win of you. For my sake, wear this,
It is a manacle of love. I'll place it (*Putting a bracelet on her arm.*)
Upon this fairest prisoner.
IMOGEN. Oh, the gods!
When shall we meet again?

Enter Cymbeline *and lords.*

POSTHUMUS. Alack, the king!
CYMBELINE. Thou basest thing! Avoid, hence from my sight!
130 If, after this command, thou fraught the court
With thy unworthiness, thou diest. Away!
Thou'rt poison to my blood!
POSTHUMUS. The gods protect you,
And bless the good remainders of the court.
I am gone.

Exit.

101. come] *D1*, *D2*, *W1*; comes *D3*, *D4*, *D5*, *W2*, *O1*.

IMOGEN. There cannot be a pinch in death
More sharp than this is.
Pisanio, go see your lord on board.

Exit Pisanio.

CYMBELINE. Oh, disloyal thing
140 That should'st repair my youth, thou heap'st
A yar' age on me.
IMOGEN. I beseech you, Sir,
Harm not yourself with your vexation;
I am senseless of your wrath. A touch more rare
Subdues all pangs, all fears.
CYMBELINE. That might'st have had the sole son of my queen.
IMOGEN. Oh, bless'd, that I might not.
CYMBELINE. Thou took'st a beggar, wouldst have made my throne
A seat for baseness.
150 IMOGEN. No, I rather added
A lustre to it.
CYMBELINE. Oh, thou vile one!
IMOGEN. Sir,
It is your fault that I have loved Posthumus.
You bred him as my playfellow, and he is
A man worth any woman, overbuys me
Almost the sum he pays.
CYMBELINE. What, art thou mad?
IMOGEN. Almost, sir, heaven restore me! Would I were
160 A neatherd's daughter and my Posthumus
Our neighbor-shepherd's son.

Enter Queen.

CYMBELINE. Thou foolish thing!
They were again together; you have done
Not after our command. Away with her
And pen her up.
QUEEN. 'Beseech your patience. Peace,
Dear lady daughter, peace. Sweet sovereign,
Make yourself some comfort
Out of your best advice.
170 CYMBELINE. Nay, let her languish
A drop of blood a day, and being aged
Die of this folly.

Exit.

141. yar'] *D1*, *D2*, *D3*, *D4*, *W1*, *W2*; year's *O1*; years *D5*.

QUEEN. Fie, fie, you must give way. Here is Pisanio,

Enter Pisanio.

Your faithful servant, and I dare lay mine honor
He will remain so.
PISANIO. I humbly thank your Highness.

Exit Queen.

IMOGEN. Well, good Pisanio,
Thou saw'st thy lord on board. What was the last
That he spake to thee?
180 PISANIO. 'Twas his lovely princess.
IMOGEN. Then waved his handkerchief?
PISANIO. And kissed it, madam.
IMOGEN. Senseless linen, happier therein than I.
And that was all?
PISANIO. No, madam. For so long
As he could make me with this eye or ear
Distinguish him from others, he did keep
The deck, with glove, or hat, or handkerchief
Still waving, as the fit and stirs of's mind
190 Could best express how slow his soul sailed on,
How swift his ship.
IMOGEN. Thou should'st have made him
As little as a crow, or less, ere left
To after eye him.
PISANIO. Madam, so I did.
IMOGEN. I would have broke mine eye-strings;
Cracked them but to look upon him, till the diminution
Of space had pointed him sharp as my needle;
Nay followed him till he had melted from
200 The smallness of a gnat to air, and then,
Then turned mine eye and wept. But, good Pisanio,
When shall we hear from him?
PISANIO. Be assured, madam,
With his next vantage.
IMOGEN. I did not take any leave of him, but had
Most pretty things to say. Ere I could tell him
How I would think on him at certain hours,
Such thoughts, and such; or I could make him swear
The she's of Italy should not betray
210 Mine interest in his honor; or have charged him
At the sixth hour of morn, at noon, at midnight,

T' encounter me with orisons, (for then
I am in heaven for him); or ere I could
Give him that parting kiss which I had set
Betwixt two charming words, come in my father,
And, like the tyrannous breathing of the north,
Shakes all our buds from growing. See the queen.
Those things I bid you do, get them dispatched.

Exeunt.

Enter Queen *and* Cornelius, *with a phial.*

QUEEN. Now, Master Doctor, have you brought those drugs?
220 CORNELIUS. Pleaseth your highness, aye.
But I beseech your grace, without offence
My conscience bids me ask wherefore you have
Commanded of me these most poisonous compounds?
QUEEN. I wonder, Doctor,
Thou ask'st me such a question. Have I not been
Thy pupil long? I will but try the force
And vigor of thy compounds, and apply
Allayments to their acts, and by them gather
Their virtues and effects.

Enter Pisanio.

230 (*Aside.*) Here comes a flattering rascal. Upon him
Will I first work. He's for his master's sake
An enemy to my son. A sly and constant knave
Not to be shaked, the agent for his master
And the remembrancer of her to hold
The hand fast to her lord.—How now, Pisanio?
Doctor, your service for this time is ended.
CORNELIUS (*aside*). I do suspect you, Madam.
But you shall do no harm.
QUEEN (*to* Pisanio). Hark thee, a word.
240 CORNELIUS [*aside*]. I will not trust one of her malice with
A drug of such damned nature. Those she has
Will stupify and dull the sense a while,
But there is no danger in that show of death
More than the locking up the spirits a time,
'To be more fresh, reviving. She is fooled
With a most false effect; and I the truer
So to be false with her.

Exit.

QUEEN. Weeps she still, say'st thou? Dost thou think in time
She will not quench and let instructions enter
250 Where folly now possesses? Do thou work!
When thou shalt bring me word she loves my son,
I'll tell thee on the instant thou art then
As great as is thy master; greater, for
His fortunes all lie speechless, and his name
Is at last gasp. And what shalt thou expect,
To be depender on a thing that leans?
Who cannot be new-built and has no friends
So much as but to prop him? Thou takest up

Pisanio *looking on the phial.*

Thou know'st not what; but take it for thy labor.
260 It is a thing I make which hath the king
Five times redeemed from death. I do not know
What is more cordial. Nay, prithee, take it.
It is an earnest of a farther good
That I mean to thee. Tell thy mistress how
The case stands with her. Do't as from thyself.
I'll move the king
To any shape of thy preferment, such
As thou'lt desire. Think on my words.
(*Aside.*) I have given him that
270 Which, if he take, shall quite unpeople her
Of liegers for her sweet, and which she after,
Except she bend her humor, shall be assured
To taste of, too. Fare thee well, Pisanio.
Think on my words.

Exit Queen.

PISANIO. And shall do;
But when to my good lord I prove untrue,
I'll choke myself; there's all I'll do for you.
By this he is at Rome, and good Philario,
With open arms and grateful heart, receives
280 His friend's reflected image in his son,
Old Leonatus in young Posthumus.
Sweet Imogen, what thou endur'st the while
Betwixt a father by thy stepdame governed,
A mother hourly coining plots, a wooer

---

258. prop] *D1*, *D2*, *D3*, *D4*, *D5*, *O1*; prompt *W1*, *W2*.

More hateful than the foul expulsion is
Of thy dear husband—Heaven keep unshaken
That temple, thy fair mind, that thou may'st stand
T'enjoy thy banished lord and this great land.

Exit.

SCENE II. Philario's *house in* Rome.

Philario, Iachimo, *and a* Frenchman, *at a banquet.*

IACHIMO. Believe it, sir, I have seen him in Britain, and he was then but crescent, not expected to prove so worthy as since he has been allowed the name of. But I could then have looked on him without the help of admiration, though the catalogue of his endowments had been tabled by his side, and I to peruse him by items.

PHILARIO. You speak of him when he was less furnished than now he is.

FRENCHMAN. I have seen him in France; we had very many there could behold the sun with as firm eyes as he.

IACHIMO. This matter of marrying his king's daughter, wherein he must
10 be weighed rather by her value than his own, words him, I doubt not, a great deal from the matter.

FRENCHMAN. And then, his banishment.

IACHIMO. Aye, and the approbation of those that weep this lamentable divorce under her colors are wonderfully to extend him; be it but to fortify her judgment, which else an easy battery might lay flat, for taking a beggar without more quality. But how comes it, he is to sojourn with you? How creeps acquaintance?

PHILARIO. His father and I were soldiers together, to whom I have been often bound for no less than my life.

Enter Posthumus.

20 Here comes the Briton. Let him be so entertained amongst you as suits with gentlemen of your knowing to a stranger of his quality. I beseech you all, be better known to this gentleman whom I commend to you as a noble friend of mine. How worthy he is, I will leave to appear hereafter, rather than story him in his own hearing.

FRENCHMAN. Sir, we have been known together in Orleans.

POSTHUMUS. Since when I have been debtor to you for courtesies, which I will be ever to pay and yet pay still.

FRENCHMAN. Sir, you o'errate my poor kindness. I was glad I did atone

my countryman and you; it had been pity you should have been put
30 together with so mortal a purpose as then each bore, upon importance of so slight and trivial a nature.

POSTHUMUS. By your pardon, sir, I was then a young traveler; but upon my mended judgment, (if I offend not to say it is mended) my quarrel was not altogether slight.

FRENCHMAN. Faith, yes, to be put to the arbitrement of swords.

IACHIMO. Can we with manners ask what was the difference?

FRENCHMAN. Safely, I think. 'Twas a contention in public which may without contradiction suffer the report. It was much like an argument that fell out last night, where each of us fell in praise of our
40 country mistresses, this gentleman at that time vouching (and upon warrant of bloody affirmation) his to be more fair, virtuous, wise, chaste, constant, qualified, and less attemptable than any, the rarest of our ladies in France.

IACHIMO. That lady is not now living, or this gentleman's opinion by this worn out.

POSTHUMUS. She holds her virtue still, and I my mind.

IACHIMO. You must not so far prefer her 'fore ours of Italy.

POSTHUMUS. Being so far provoked as I was in France, I would abate her nothing, though I profess myself her adorer not her friend.

50 IACHIMO. As fair and as good, a kind of hand-in-hand comparison, had been something too fair and too good for any lady in Britain. If she went before others I have seen, as that diamond of yours outlustres many I have beheld, I could believe she excelled many. But I have not seen the most precious diamond that is, nor you the lady.

POSTHUMUS. I praised her as I rated her; so do I my stone.

IACHIMO. What do you esteem it at?

POSTHUMUS. More than the world enjoys.

IACHIMO. Either your paragoned mistress is dead or she's outprized by a trifle.

60 POSTHUMUS. You are mistaken. The one may be sold or given, if there were wealth enough for the purchase or merit for the gift; the other is not a thing for sale, and only the gift of the gods.

IACHIMO. Which the gods have given you?

POSTHUMUS. Which by their graces I will keep.

IACHIMO. You may wear her in title yours; but, you know, strange fowl light upon neighboring ponds. Your ring may be stolen, too; so, of your brace of unprizeable estimations, the one is but frail and the other casual. A cunning thief, or a that-way-accomplished courtier, would hazard the winning both of first and last.

70 POSTHUMUS. Your Italy contains none so accomplished a courtier to

convince the honor of my mistress; if in the holding or loss of that you term her frail, I do nothing doubt you have store of thieves, notwithstanding I fear not my ring.

PHILARIO. Let us leave here, gentlemen.

POSTHUMUS. Sir, with all my heart. This worthy signior, I thank him, makes no stranger of me; we are familiar at first.

IACHIMO. With five times so much conversation, I should get ground of your fair mistress, make her go back even to the yielding, had I admittance and opportunity to friend.

80 POSTHUMUS. No, no.

IACHIMO. I dare thereupon pawn the moiety of my estate to your ring, which in my opinion o'ervalues it something; but I make my wager rather against your confidence than her reputation. And to bar your offence herein too, I durst attempt it against any lady in the world.

POSTHUMUS. You are a great deal abused in too bold a persuasion; and I doubt not you'd sustain what you're worthy of by your attempt.

IACHIMO. What's that?

POSTHUMUS (*angrily*). A repulse; though your attempt, as you call it, deserves more—a punishment too.

90 PHILARIO. Gentlemen, enough of this. It came in too suddenly; let it die as it was born, and I pray you be better acquainted.

IACHIMO. Would I had put my estate and my neighbor's on th' approbation of what I have spoke.

POSTHUMUS. What lady would you choose to assail?

IACHIMO. Yours; whom in constancy you think stands so safe. I will lay you ten thousand ducats to your ring, that, commend me to the court where your lady is, with no more advantage than the opportunity of a second conference, and I will bring from thence that honor of hers which you imagine so reserved.

100 POSTHUMUS. I will wager against your gold, gold to it. My ring I hold as dear as my finger, 'tis part of it.

IACHIMO. You are afraid, and therein the wiser. If you buy ladies' flesh at a million a dram, you cannot preserve it from tainting; but I see you have some religion in you, that you fear.

POSTHUMUS. This is but a custom in your tongue; you bear a graver purpose, I hope.

IACHIMO. I am the master of my speeches and would undergo what's spoken, I swear.

POSTHUMUS. Will you? Let there be covenants drawn between us. My
110 mistress exceeds in goodness the hugeness of your unworthy thinkings. I dare you to this match! Here's my ring.

---

81. pawn] *D1*, *D2*, *D3*, *D4*, *D5*, *O1*; pardon *W1*, *W2*.

PHILARIO. I will have it no lay.

IACHIMO. By the gods, it is one. If I bring you not sufficient testimony that I have enjoyed the dearest bodily part of your mistress, my ten thousand ducats are yours; so is your diamond, too. If I come off and leave her in such honor as you have trust in, she your jewel, this your jewel, and my gold are yours, provided I have your commendation for my more free entertainment.

POSTHUMUS. I embrace these conditions; let us have articles betwixt us.
120 Only, thus far you shall answer. If you make your voyage upon her and give me directly to understand you have prevailed, I am no further your enemy; she is not worth our debate. If she remain unseduced, you not making it appear otherwise, for your ill opinion and the assault you have made to her chastity, you shall answer me with your sword.

IACHIMO. Your hand; a covenant. We will have these things set down by lawful counsel, and I'll straight away for Britain lest the bargain should catch cold and starve. I will fetch my gold and have our two wagers recorded.

130 POSTHUMUS. Agreed.

Exit Posthumus *and* Iachimo.

FRENCHMAN. Will this hold, think you?

PHILARIO. Signior Iachimo will not from it. Pray let us follow 'em.

Exeunt.

ACT II.

SCENE I. Britain. *A Chamber in the palace.*

Enter Imogen *alone.*

IMOGEN. A father cruel, and a stepdame false,
A foolish suitor to a wedded lady,
That hath her husband banished. Oh, that husband!
My supreme crown of grief, and those repeated
Vexations of it! Had I been thief-stol'n,
As my two brothers, happy! but most miserable
Is the desire that's glorious. Blessed be those,
How mean soe'er, that have their honest wills,
Which seasons comfort. Who may this be?

Enter Pisanio *and* Iachimo.

0.1. ACT II. SCENE I] *D*1, *D*2, *D*3, *D*4, *D*5, *O*1, *W*1; V, i, *W*2.

10 PISANIO. Madam, a noble gentleman of Rome
Comes from my lord with letters.
IACHIMO. Change you, madam?
The worthy Leonatus is in safety
And greets your highness dearly.
IMOGEN. Thanks, good sir.
You're kindly welcome. (*Reads aside.*)
IACHIMO (*aside*). All of her that is out of door, most rich!
If she be furnished with a mind so rare,
She is alone the Arabian bird, and I
20 Have lost the wager. Boldness be my friend!
Arm me, audacity, from head to foot.
IMOGEN (*reads*). "He is one of the noblest note, to whose kindnesses I am most infinitely tied. Reflect upon him accordingly, as you value your trust. Leonatus."
So far I read aloud.
But even the very middle of my heart
Is warmed by the rest, and takes it thankfully.
You are as welcome, worthy sir, as I
Have words to bid you, and shall find it so
30 In all that I can do.
IACHIMO. Thanks, fairest lady.
What, are men mad? Hath nature given them eyes
To see this vaulted arch, and the rich crop
Of sea and land, which can distinguish 'twixt
The fiery orbs above and the twinn'd stones
Upon the humble beach? And can we not
Partition make 'twixt fair and foul?
IMOGEN. What makes your admiration?
IACHIMO. It cannot be i'th' eye; for apes and monkeys,
40 'Twixt two such she's, would chatter this way and
Contemn with mows the other. Nor i'th' judgment,
For idiots in this case of favor would
Be wisely definite. Nor in the appetite—
IMOGEN. What is the matter, trow?
IACHIMO. The cloyed will,
That satiate yet unsatisfied desire,
Ravening first the lamb,
Longs after for the garbage.
IMOGEN. What, dear sir,
50 Thus raps you? Are you well?
IACHIMO. Thanks, madam; well. [*To* Pisanio.] Beseech you, sir,
Desire my man's abode, where I did leave him.

He's strange and sheepish.
PISANIO. I was going, sir,
To give him welcome.

Exit Pisanio.

IMOGEN. Continues well my lord his health, beseech you?
IACHIMO. Well, madam.
IMOGEN. Is he disposed to mirth? I hope he is.
IACHIMO. Exceeding pleasant; none a stranger there,
60 So merry and so gamesome; he is called
The Britain reveler.
IMOGEN. When he was here
He did incline to sadness, and oft times
Not knowing why.
IACHIMO. I never saw him sad.
There is a Frenchman, his companion, one
An eminent monsieur, that it seems much loves
A Gallian girl at home. He furnaces
The thick sighs from him, while the jolly Briton
70 (Your lord, I mean) laughs from's free lungs, cries "Oh!
Can my sides hold, to think that man who knows
By history, report, or his own proof
What woman is, yea, what she cannot choose
But must be, will his free hours languish out
For assured bondage?"
IMOGEN. Will my lord say so?
IACHIMO. Aye, madam, with his eyes in flood with laughter.
It is a recreation to be by
And hear him mock the Frenchman. But, heaven knows,
80 Some men are much to blame.
IMOGEN. Not he, I hope.
IACHIMO. Not he. But yet heaven's bounty towards him might
Be used more thankfully. In himself 'tis much;
In you, whom I account his beyond all talents,
Whilst I am bound to wonder, I am bound
To pity, too.
IMOGEN. What do you pity, sir?
IACHIMO. Two creatures heartily.
IMOGEN. Am I one, sir?
90 You look on me: what wrack discern you in me
Deserves your pity?
IACHIMO. Lamentable! What,
To hide me from the radiant sun, and solace

I'th' dungeon by a snuff?

IMOGEN. 'Pray you, sir,
Deliver with more openness your answers
To my demands. Why do you pity me?

IACHIMO. That others do,
I was about to say, enjoy your—but
100 It is an office of the gods to venge it,
Not mine to speak on't.

IMOGEN. You do seem to know
Something of me or what concerns me; pray you
(Since doubting things go ill often hurts more,
Than to be sure they do) discover to me
What doth you spur and stop.

IACHIMO. Had I this cheek
To bathe my lips upon; this hand, whose touch,
Whose very touch would force the feeler's soul
110 To th' Oath of Loyalty; this object which
Takes prisoner the wild motion of mine eye,
Fixing it only here; should I, (damn'd, then)
Slaver with lips as common as the stairs
That mount the capitol? join grips with hands
Made hard with hourly falsehood as with labor?
Then glad myself by peeping in an eye
Base and unlust'rous as the smokey light
That's fed with stinking tallow? It were fit
That all the plagues of hell should at one time
120 Encounter such revolt.

IMOGEN. My lord, I fear,
Has forgot Britain.

IACHIMO. And himself. Not I,
Inclined to this intelligence, pronounce
The beggary of his change; but 'tis your graces
That from my mutest conscience to my tongue
Charm this report out.

IMOGEN. Let me hear no more.

IACHIMO. Oh, dearest soul! your cause doth strike my heart
130 With pity that doth make me sick. A lady
So fair, and fastened to an empery,
Would make the greatest king double,—to be partnered
With tomboys hired with that self exhibition

---

114. grips] *D3*, *D4*, *D5*, *W1*, *O1*; gripes *D1*, *D2*, *W2*.
117. smokey] *D1*, *D2*, *D3*, *D4*, *D5*, *W1*, *O1*; moakey *W2*.

Which your own coffers yield! with diseased venturers
To play with all infirmities for gold,
Which rottenness lends nature! Be revenged,
Or she that bore you was no queen, and you
Recoil from your great stock.

IMOGEN. Revenged?

140 How should I be revenged if this be true?
As I have such a heart that both mine ears
Must not in haste abuse; if it be true,
How shall I be revenged?

IACHIMO. Should he make me
Live like Diana's priestess 'twixt cold sheets,
Whiles he is vaulting variable ramps
In your despite, upon your purse! Revenge it.
I dedicate myself to your sweet pleasure,
More noble than that runagate to your bed,
150 And will continue fast to your affection,
Still close as sure.

IMOGEN. What ho, Pisanio!—

IACHIMO. Let me my service tender on your lips.

IMOGEN. Away, I do condemn mine ears that have
So long attended thee. If thou wert honorable,
Thou would'st have told this tale for virtue, not
For such an end thou seek'st, as base as strange.
Thou wrong'st a gentleman who is as far
From thy report as thou from honor, and
160 Solicit'st here a lady that disdains
Thee and the devil alike. What ho, Pisanio!—
The king, my father, shall be made acquainted
Of thy assault. If he shall think it fit
A saucy stranger in his court to mart
As in a Romish stew, and to expound
His beastly mind to us, he hath a court
He little cares for, and a daughter whom
He not respects at all. What ho, Pisanio!—

IACHIMO. Oh happy Leonatus, I may say!
170 The credit that thy lady hath of thee
Deserves thy trust, and thy most perfect goodness
Her assured credit. Blessed live you long!
A lady to the worthiest sir that ever
Country called his, and you his mistress, only
For the most worthiest fit. Give me your pardon.
I have spoke this to know if your affiance

Were deeply rooted and shall make your lord,
That which he is, new o'er. And he is one
The truest mannered, such a holy witch
180 That he enchants societies into him.
Half all men's hearts are his.

IMOGEN. You make amends.

IACHIMO. He sits amongst men like a descended god.
He hath a kind of honor sets him off,
More than a mortal seeming. Be not angry,
Most mighty princess, that I have adventured
To try your taking of a false report.
The love I bear him
Made me to fan you thus; but the gods made you,
190 Unlike all others, chaffless. Pray, your pardon.

IMOGEN. All's well, sir; take my power i'th' court for yours.

IACHIMO. My humble thanks. I had almost forgot
T'intreat your grace, but in a small request,
And yet of moment too, for it concerns
Your lord; myself and other noble friends
Are partners in the business.

IMOGEN. Pray, what is it?

IACHIMO. Some dozen Romans of us, and your lord,
(The best feather of our wing) have mingled sums
200 To buy a present for the emperor;
Which I, the factor for the rest, have done
In France. 'Tis plate of rare device and jewels
Of rich and exquisite form, the values great.
And I am something curious, being strange,
To have them in safe stowage. May it please you
To take them in protection.

IMOGEN. Willingly;
And pawn mine honor for their safety, since
My lord hath interest in them. I will keep them
210 In my chamber.

IACHIMO. They are in a coffer
Attended by my men. I will make bold
To send them to you only for this night.
I must abroad tomorrow.

IMOGEN. Oh no, no.

IACHIMO. Yes, I beseech you, or I shall short my word
By lengthening my return. From Gallia
I crossed the seas on purpose, and on promise
To see your Grace.

220 IMOGEN. I thank you for your pains;
But not away tomorrow.
IACHIMO. Oh, I must, madam.
Therefore I shall beseech you, if you please
To greet your lord with writing, do't tonight.
I have outstayed my time, which is material
To th' tender of our present.
IMOGEN. I will write.
Send your coffer to me; it shall be kept,
And truly yielded you. You're very welcome.

Exeunt.

SCENE II. *A palace.*

Enter Cloten *and two lords.*

CLOTEN. Was there ever man had such luck! When I kissed the Jack upon an Up-cast, to be hit away! I had an hundred pound on't; and then a whoreson jackanapes must take me up for swearing, as if I had borrowed mine oaths of him and might not spend them at my pleasure.

FIRST LORD. What got he by that? You have broke his pate with your bowl.

SECOND LORD (*aside*). If his wit had been like him that broke it, it would have run all out.

10 CLOTEN. When a gentleman is disposed to swear, it is not for any standers-by to curtail his oaths. Ha?

SECOND LORD. No, my lord. [*Aside.*] Nor crop the ears of them.

CLOTEN. Whoreson dog! I give him satisfaction? Would he had been one of my rank. Pox on't! I had rather not be so noble as I am; they dare not fight with me because of the queen, my mother. Every jack-slave hath his belly full of fighting, and I must go up and down like a cock that nobody can match.

SECOND LORD. It is not fit your lordship should undertake every companion that you give offence to.

20 CLOTEN. No, I know that. But it is fit I should commit offence to my inferiors.

FIRST LORD. Aye, it is fit for your lordship only.

CLOTEN. Why, so I say.

SECOND LORD. Here comes the king.

Enter Cymbeline *and* Queen.

CLOTEN. Goodnight to your Majesty and gracious mother.

CYMBELINE. Attend you here the door of our stern daughter?
Will she not forth?

CLOTEN. She vouchsafes no notice; but I will assail her before morning with mask and music.

30 CYMBELINE. The exile of her minion is too new,
She hath not yet forgot him; some more time
Must wear the print of his remembrance out,
And then she's yours.

Enter Messenger, *and whispers the First Lord.*

QUEEN. You are most bound to the king,
Who lets go by no vantages that may
Prefer you to his daughter.

FIRST LORD. So like you, sir, ambassadors from Rome,
The one is Caius Lucius.

CYMBELINE. A worthy fellow,
40 Albeit he comes on angry purpose now;
But that's no fault of his. Our dear son,
When you have given good morning to your mistress,
Attend the Queen and us; we shall have need
T'employ you towards this Roman.
Betimes tomorrow we'll hear th' Embassy.
Come, our Queen.

Exeunt King *and* Queen.

FIRST LORD. Did you hear of another stranger that's come to court tonight?

CLOTEN. Another stranger, and I not know on't?

50 SECOND LORD (*aside*). He's a strange fellow himself and knows it not.

FIRST LORD. There's an Italian come, and 'tis thought one of Leonatus' friends.

CLOTEN. Leonatus! A banished rascal; and he's another, wheresoever he be. Who told you of this stranger?

FIRST LORD. One of your lordship's pages.

CLOTEN. Is it fit I went to look upon him? Is there no derogation in't?

SECOND LORD. You cannot derogate, my lord.

CLOTEN. Not easily, I think.

SECOND LORD (*aside*). You are a fool, granted, therefore cannot dero-
60 gate.

CLOTEN. Come, I'll go see this Italian, and if he'll play, I'll game with

49. on't] *D1*, *D2*, *D3*, *D4*, *D5*, *O1*, *W1*; an't *W2*.

him, and tomorrow with our father we'll hear th' Ambassador.
Come, let's go.

FIRST LORD. I'll attend your lordship.

Exit Cloten *and* First Lord.

SECOND LORD. That such a crafty devil as is his mother,
Should yield the world this ass; a woman that
Bears all down with her brain, and this her son
Cannot take two from twenty for his heart
And leave eighteen! Alas, poor Princess,
70 Thou divine Imogen, what thou endur'st.

Exit.

SCENE III. *A magnificent bedchamber, in one part of it a large trunk.*

Imogen *is discovered reading in her bed, a lady attending.*

IMOGEN. Who's there? My woman, Helen?
LADY. Please you, madam—
IMOGEN. What hour is it?
LADY. Almost midnight, madam.
IMOGEN. I have read three hours, then. Mine eyes are weak,
Fold down the leaf where I have left; to bed.
Take not away the taper, leave it burning.
And if thou canst awake by four o'th' clock,
I prithee call me. Sleep hath seized me wholly.

Exit Lady.

10 From fairies and the tempters of the night,
Guard me, beseech ye.
To your protection I commend me, gods. (*Sleeps.*)

Iachimo *rises from the coffer.*

IACHIMO. The crickets sing, and man's o'er-labored sense
Repairs itself by rest. Our Tarquin thus
Did softly press the rushes, ere he waken'd
The chastity he wounded. Cytherea,
How bravely thou becom'st thy bed! Fresh lily!
And whiter than the sheets! That I might touch,
But kiss, one kiss! Rubies unparagoned
20 How dearly they do't. 'Tis her breathing
Perfumes the chamber thus. The flame o'th' taper
Bows toward her and would under-peep her lids,

To see th' inclosed lights now canopied
Under the windows, white and azure laced
With blue of heav'ns own tinct. But my design's
To note the chamber. I will write all down.
Such and such pictures—there the window,—such
Th' adornment of her bed—the arras, figures—
Why such and such—and the contents o'th' story—
30 Ah, but some natural notes about her body,
Above ten thousand meaner moveables
Would testify t' enrich my inventory.
Oh sleep, thou ape of death, lie dull upon her,
And be her sense but as a monument,
Thus in the chapel lying. Come off, come off,—
(*Taking off her bracelet.*) As slippery as the Gordian knot was hard.
'Tis mine, and this will witness outwardly,
As strongly as the conscience does within,
To th' madding of her lord. On her left breast
40 A mole cinque-spotted, like the crimson drops
I'th' bottom of a cowslip. Here's a voucher,
Stronger than ever law could make. This secret
Will force him think I've picked the lock and ta'en
The treasure of her honor. More—to what end?
Why should I write this down, that's riveted,
Screwed to my memory? She hath been reading late,
The Tale of Tereus; here the leaf's turned down
Where Philomel gave up. I have enough.
To th' trunk again, and shut the spring of it.
50 Swift, swift, you dragons of the night, that dawning
May bear its raven's eye. I lodge in fear,
Though this a heav'nly angel, hell is here.

Clock strikes.

One, two, three. Time, time.

He goes into the trunk; the scene closes.

SCENE IV. *The palace.*

Enter Cloten *and* Lords.

FIRST LORD. Your lordship is the most patient man in loss, the coldest that ever turned up ace.

CLOTEN. It would make any man cold so to lose.

FIRST LORD. But not every man patient after the noble temper of your lordship. You are most hot and furious when you win.

CLOTEN. Winning will put any man into courage. If I could get this foolish Imogen, I shall have gold enough. It's almost morning, is't not?

FIRST LORD. It is, my lord.

10 CLOTEN. I would the masquers and musicians were come. I am advised to give her music a' mornings; they say it will penetrate. (*A flourish.*)

FIRST LORD. Here they are, my lord.

CLOTEN. Come, let's join them.

Exeunt.

SCENE V. *An open place in the palace.*

Cloten, *Lords, Singers and Masquers discovered.*

CLOTEN. Come on, tune, first a very excellent good conceited thing, after a wonderful sweet air, with admirable rich words to it, and then let her consider.

Song.

Hark, hark, the Lark, at heav'ns gate sings,
　　And Phoebus 'gins arise,
His steeds to water at those springs,
　　On chaliced flowers that lies;
And winking Marybuds begin to ope their golden eyes,
With everything that pretty is, my Lady sweet arise,
10　　Arise, arise!

So, get you gone. If this penetrate, I will consider your music the better; if it do not, it is a vice in her ears, which horse-hairs and cat-guts, nor the voice of unpaved eunuch to boot, can never amend. Come, now to our dancing, and if she is unmoveable with this, she is an immoveable princess and not worth my notice.

A dance.

(*Knocks at her door.*) Leave us to ourselves.

Exeunt Lords, etc.

If she be up, I'll speak with her; if not,
Let her lie still and dream. By your leave, ho!

I know her women are about her. What
20 If I do line one of their hands? 'Tis gold
Which buys admittance, oft it doth, yea, and makes
Diana's rangers false themselves, and yield up
Their deer to th' stand o'th' stealer. And 'tis gold
Which makes the true man killed and saves the thief,
Nay, sometimes hangs both thief and true man. What
Can it not do and undo? I will make
One of her women lawyer to me, for
I yet not understand the case myself.
By your leave. (*Knocks.*)

Enter a Lady.

30 LADY. Who's there that knocks?
CLOTEN. A gentleman.
LADY. No more?
CLOTEN. Yes, and a gentlewoman's son.
LADY. That's more
Than some, whose tailors are as dear as yours,
Can justly boast of. What's your Lordship's pleasure?
CLOTEN. Your lady's person. Is she ready?
LADY. Aye,
To keep her chamber.
40 CLOTEN. There is gold for you;
Sell me your good report.
LADY. How! My good name? or to report of you
What I shall think is good? The princess!

Enter Imogen.

CLOTEN. Goodmorrow fairest; sister, your sweet hand.
IMOGEN. Goodmorrow, sir; you lay out too much pains
For purchasing but trouble.
CLOTEN. Still, I swear I love you.
IMOGEN. If you'd but said so, 'twere as deep with me.
If you swear still, your recompence is still
50 That I regard it not.
CLOTEN. This is no answer.
IMOGEN. But that you shall not say I yield being silent,
I would not speak. I pray you, spare me; faith,

---

28. yet not] *D1*, *D2*, *D3*, *D4*, *D5*, *O1*, *W1*; "not" omitted *W2*.
35. some] *D1*, *D2*, *D3*, *D4*, *D5*, *O1*, *W1*; those *W2*.
51. This line omitted *W1*, *W2*.

I shall unfold equal discourtesy
To your best kindness. One of your great knowing
Should learn, being taught, forbearance.

CLOTEN. To leave you in you[r] madness, 'twere my sin.
I will not.

IMOGEN. Fools cure not mad folks.

60 CLOTEN. Do you call me fool?

IMOGEN. As I am mad, I do.
If you'll be patient, I'll no more be mad.
That cures us both. I am much sorry, sir,
You put me to forget a lady's manners,
But I who know my heart do here pronounce
By th' very truth of it, I care not for you.

CLOTEN. The contract you pretend with that base wretch,
(One bred of alms and fostered with cold dishes,
With scraps o'th' court) it is no contract, none.

70 IMOGEN. Profane fellow!
Wert thou the son of Jupiter, and no more
But what thou art besides, thou wert too base
To be his groom.

CLOTEN. The south-fog rot him.

IMOGEN. He never can meet more mischance than come
To be but named of thee. His meanest garment
That ever hath but clipped his body, is dearer
In my respect than all thou hast to boast of.
(*Missing her bracelet.*) How now, Pisanio!

Enter Pisanio.

80 CLOTEN. His garment? Now, the devil.

IMOGEN [*to* Pisanio]. To Dorothy, my woman, hie thee presently.

CLOTEN. His garment?

IMOGEN [*to* Pisanio]. I am sprighted with a fool.
Fretted and angered worse. Go bid my woman
Search for a jewel that too casually
Hath left my arm. It was thy master's. Shrew me,
If I would lose it for a revenue
Of any king's in Europe. I do think
I saw't this morning; confident I am
90 Last night 'twas on my arm; I kissed it then.

PISANIO. 'Twill not be lost.

IMOGEN. I hope so; go and search.

Exit Pisanio.

CLOTEN. You have abused me. His meanest garment!
I will inform your father.

IMOGEN. Your mother, too;
She's my good lady and will conceive, I hope,
But the worst of me. So I leave you, sir,
To th' worst of discontent.

Exit.

CLOTEN. I'll be revenged.
100 His meanest garment? Well.

Exit.

ACT III.

SCENE I. *A chamber in* Rome.

Enter Posthumus *and* Philario.

POSTHUMUS. Fear it not, sir; I would I were so sure
To win the king as I am bold her honor
Will remain hers.

PHILARIO. What means do you make to him?

POSTHUMUS. Not any, but abide the change of time,
Quake in the present winter's state and wish
That warmer days would come. In these feared hopes,
I barely gratify your love; they failing,
I must die much your debtor.

10 PHILARIO. Your very goodness and your company
O'erpays all I can do. By this your king
Hath heard of great Augustus. Caius Lucius
Will do's commission throughly. And I think
He'll grant the tribute; or your countrymen
Will look upon our Romans, whose remembrance
Is yet fresh in their grief.

POSTHUMUS. I do believe,
Statist though I am none, nor like to be,
That this will prove a war; they'll send no tribute.
20 Our countrymen the Britons
Are men more ordered than when Julius Caesar
Smiled at their lack of skill, but found their courage
Worthy his frowning at. Their discipline,

---

14. or] *D1*, *D2*, *D3*, *D4*, *D5*, *O1*, *W1*; ere *W2*.

Now mingled with their courage, will make known
To their approvers they are people such
As mend upon the world; and more than that,
They have a king whose love and justice to them
May ask and have their treasures and their blood.

Enter Iachimo.

PHILARIO. See Iachimo.
30 POSTHUMUS. The swiftest harts have posted you by land;
And winds of all the corners kissed your sails,
To make your vessel nimble.
PHILARIO. Welcome, sir.
POSTHUMUS. I hope the briefness of your answer made
The speediness of your return.
IACHIMO. Your lady
Is one of the fairest that ever I looked upon.
POSTHUMUS. And therewithal the best, or let her beauty
Look through a casement to allure false hearts,
40 And be false with them.
IACHIMO. Here are letters for you.
POSTHUMUS. Their tenor good, I trust.
IACHIMO. 'Tis very like.

Posthumus *reads the letters.*

PHILARIO. Was Caius Lucius in the British court
When you were there?
IACHIMO. He was expected then,
But not approached.
POSTHUMUS. All is well yet.
Sparkles this stone as it was wont, or is't not
50 Too dull for your good wearing?
IACHIMO. If I had lost it,
I should have lost the worth of it in gold;
I'll make a journey twice as far, t'enjoy
A second night of such sweet shortness as
Was mine in Britain, for the ring is won.
POSTHUMUS. The stone's too hard to come by.
IACHIMO. Not a whit,
Your lady being so easy.
POSTHUMUS. Make not, sir,
60 Your loss your sport. I hope you know that we
Must not continue friends.
IACHIMO. Good sir, we must,

If you keep covenant. Had I not brought
The knowledge of your mistress home, I grant
We were to question farther; but I now
Profess myself the winner of her honor,
Together with your ring; and not the wronger
Of her or you, having proceeded but
By both your wills.

70 POSTHUMUS. If you can make't apparent
That you have tasted her in bed, my hand
And ring is yours. If not, the foul opinion
You had of her pure honor gains or loses
Your sword or mine, or masterless leaves both
To who shall find them.

IACHIMO. Sir, my circumstances
Being so near the truth as I will make them,
Must first induce you to believe; whose strength
I will confirm with oath, which I doubt not
80 You'll give me leave to spare, when you shall find
They need it not.

POSTHUMUS. Proceed.

IACHIMO. First, her bed-chamber,
Where I confess I slept not, but profess
Had that was well worth watching. It was hanged
With richest stuff, the colors blue and silver:
A piece of work
So bravely done, so rich, that it did strive
In workmanship and value.

90 POSTHUMUS. This is true;
And this you might have heard of here, by me,
Or by some other.

IACHIMO. More particulars
Must justify my knowledge.

POSTHUMUS. So they must,
Or do your honor injury.

IACHIMO. The chimney
Is South the chamber, and the chimney-piece
Chaste Diana bathing; never saw I figures
100 So likely to report themselves. The painter
Was as another nature dumb; outwent her,
Motion and breath left out.

POSTHUMUS. This is a thing
Which you might from relation likewise reap,

Being, as it is, much spoke of.
IACHIMO. The roof o'th' chamber
With golden cherubims is fretted.
POSTHUMUS. What's this t'her honor?
Let it be granted you have seen all this,
110 (Praise be to your remembrance) the description
Of what is in her chamber nothing saves
The wager you have laid.
IACHIMO. Then, if you can, (*Pulling out the bracelet.*)
Be pale. I beg but leave to air this jewel. See!
And now 'tis up again; it must be married
To that your diamond.
POSTHUMUS. Jove!—
Once more let me behold it. Is it that
Which I left with her?
120 IACHIMO. Sir, I thank her, that.
She stripped it from her arm; I see her yet.
Her pretty action did out-self her gift,
And yet enriched it too. She gave it me,
And said she prized it once.
POSTHUMUS. Maybe she plucked it off
To send it me.
IACHIMO. She writes so to you, doth she?
POSTHUMUS. Oh, no, no, no, 'tis true. Here take this too
(*Gives the ring.*) It is a basilisk unto mine eye,
130 Kills me to look on't. Let there be no honor
Where there is beauty; truth where semblance; love
Where there's another man. The vows of women
Of no more bondage be, to where they are made,
Than they are to their virtues, which is nothing.
Oh, above measure false!
PHILARIO. Have patience, sir,
And take your ring again. 'Tis not yet won.
It may be probable she lost it; or
Who knows, one of her women, being corrupted,
140 Hath stol'n it from her.
POSTHUMUS. Very true;
And so, I hope, he came by't. Back my ring:
Render to me some corporal sign about her
More evident than this; for this was stole.
IACHIMO. By Jupiter, I had it from her arm.
POSTHUMUS. Hark you, he swears; by Jupiter he swears.

'Tis true—nay, keep the ring—'tis true; I am sure
She could not lose it; her attendants are
All honorable. They induced to steal it!
150 And by a stranger!—No, he hath enjoyed her,
The cognizance of her incontinency
Is this: she hath bought the name of whore thus dearly.
There, take thy hire; and all the fiends of hell
Divide themselves between you!

PHILARIO. Sir, be patient.
This is not strong enough to be believed
Of one persuaded well of—

POSTHUMUS. Never talk on't;
She hath been colted by him.

160 IACHIMO. If you seek
For further satisfying, under her breast—
Worthy the pressing—lies a mole, right proud
Of that most delicate lodging. By my life,
I kissed it; and it gave me present hunger
To feed again, though full. You do remember
This stain upon her?

POSTHUMUS. Aye, and it doth confirm
Another stain, as big as hell can hold,
Were there no more but it.

170 IACHIMO. Will you hear more?

POSTHUMUS. Spare your arithmetic. Never count the turns:
Once, and a million!

IACHIMO. I'll be sworn—

POSTHUMUS. No swearing.
If you will swear you have not done't, you lie;
And I will kill thee if thou dost deny
Thou'st made her strumpet.

IACHIMO. I'll deny nothing.

POSTHUMUS. Oh that I had her here, to tear her limb-meal!
180 I will go there and do't i'th' court before
Her father—I'll do something—

Exit.

PHILARIO. Quite besides
The government of patience. You have won.
Let's follow him and pervert the present wrath

---

176. kill] *D1*, *D2*, *D3*, *D4*, *D5*, *O1*; quit *W1*, *W2*.

Samuel Reddish as Posthumous in *Cymbeline*
Folger Shakespeare Library

He hath against himself.
IACHIMO. With all my heart.

Exeunt.

SCENE II. *A chamber* [*in* Philario's *house*].

Enter Posthumus.

POSTHUMUS. Is there no way for men to be but women
Must be half-workers? We are bastards all:
And that most venerable man which I
Did call my father, was I know not where
When I was stamped. Some coiner with his tools
Made me a counterfeit; yet my mother seemed
The Dian of that time. So doth my wife
The nonpareil of this. Oh, vengeance, vengeance!
Me of lawful pleasure she restrained
10 And prayed me oft forbearance; did it with
A pudency so rosy the sweet view on't
Might well have warmed old Saturn, that I thought her
As chaste as unsunned snow. Oh, all the devils!
This yellow Iachimo in an hour—was't not—
Or less,—at first? Perchance he spoke not, but
Like a full-acorned boar, a German one,—
Oh, torture to my mind! Could I find out
The woman's part in me! For there's no motion
That tends to vice in man, but I affirm
20 It is the woman's part; be it lying, note it,
The woman's; flattering, hers; deceiving, hers;
Lust and rank thoughts, hers, hers; revenges hers;
Ambitions, covetings, change of prides, disdain,
Nice longing, slanders, mutability,
All faults that may be named, nay that hell knows
Why, hers, in part or all; or rather all.
For even to vice
They are not constant, but are changing still
One vice, but of a minute old, for one
30 Not half so old as that. I'll write against them,
Detest them, curse them. Yet 'tis greater skill
In a true hate, to pray they have their will.
The very devils cannot plague them better.

Exit.

SCENE III. Britain. *A palace.*

Enter in state, Cymbeline, Queen, Cloten, *and* Lords *at one door*, *and at another*, Caius Lucius *and* Attendants.

CYMBELINE. Now say, what would Augustus Caesar with us?
LUCIUS. When Julius Caesar was in Britain,
Cassibelan, thine uncle, did for him
And his succession grant to Rome a tribute,
Yearly three thousand pounds, which by these lately
Is left untendered.
QUEEN. And to kill the marvel,
Shall be so ever.
CLOTEN. There be many Caesars,
10 Ere such another Julius. Britain's a world
By itself, and we will nothing pay
For wearing our own noses.
Tribute? Why should we pay tribute? If Caesar can hide the sun from us with a blanket, or put the moon in his pocket, we will pay him tribute for light; else, sir, no more tribute.
CYMBELINE. You must know,
'Till the injurious Romans did extort
This tribute, we were free. Say then to Caesar,
Our ancestor was that Mulmutius which
20 Ordained our laws, whose use the sword of Caesar
Hath too much mangled; whose repair and franchise
Shall by the power we hold be our good deed,
Though Rome be therefore angry.
LUCIUS. I am sorry
That I am to pronounce August Caesar
Cymbeline's enemy. War and confusion
In Caesar's name pronounce I 'gainst thee. Look
For fury not to be resisted. Thus defied,
I thank thee for myself.
30 CYMBELINE. Thou art welcome, Caius.
CLOTEN. His Majesty bids you welcome. Make pastime with us a day or two, or longer. If you seek us afterwards in other terms, you shall find us in our salt-water girdle. If you beat us out of it, it is yours; if you fall in the adventure, our crows shall fare the better for you; and there's an end.
LUCIUS. So, sir.

---

34. fare] *D1*, *D2*, *D3*, *D4*, *D5*, *O1*, *W1*; fair *W2*.

CYMBELINE. I know your master's pleasure, and he mine,
All the remain is "Welcome."

Exeunt.

SCENE IV. [Britain.] *A chamber.*

Enter Pisanio *reading a letter.*

PISANIO. How! of adultery? Wherefore write you not
What monsters have accused her? Leonatus!
Oh, master, what a strange infection
Is fall'n into thy ear! What false Italian,
As poisonous tongued as handed, hath prevailed
On thy too ready hearing? Disloyal? No,
She's punished for her truth, and undergoes,
More goddess-like than wife-like, such assaults
As would take in some virtue. Oh, my master,
10 Thy mind to her is now as low as were
Thy fortunes. How? That I should murder her,
Upon the love and truth and vows which I
Have made to thy command? I, her? Her blood?
If it be so to do good service, never
Let me be counted serviceable. How look I,
That I should seem to lack humanity
So much as this fact comes to? (*Reading.*) "Do't: the letter
That I have sent her, by her own command
Shall give the opportunity." Damned paper!
20 Black as the ink that's on thee.
Lo, here she comes!

Enter Imogen.

I am ignorant in what I am commanded.
IMOGEN. How now, Pisanio?
PISANIO. Madam, here is a letter from my lord.
IMOGEN. Who? Thy lord? that is my lord Leonatus?
Oh, learn'd indeed were that astronomer
That knew the stars as I his characters;
He'd lay the future open. You good gods,
Let what is here contained relish of love,
30 Of my lord's health, of his content.
Good wax, thy leave. Blessed be
You bees that make these locks of counsel!

Good news, gods!
(*Reading.*) "Justice, and your father's wrath, should he take me in his dominion, could not be so cruel to me, as you, oh, the dearest of creatures, would even renew me with your eyes. Take notice that I am in Cambria at Milford Haven: what your own love will out of this advise you, follow. So he wishes you all happiness, that remains loyal to his vow, and your increasing in love. Leonatus Posthumus."
40 Oh, for a horse with wings! Hear'st thou, Pisanio?
He is at Milford Haven. Read, and tell me
How far 'tis thither. If one of mean affairs
May plod it in a week, why may not I
Glide thither in a day? Then say, Pisanio,
How far it is to this same blessed Milford?
How may we steal from hence? Prithee, speak.
How many score of miles may we well ride
'Twixt hour and hour?

PISANIO. One score 'twixt sun and sun,
50 Madam's enough for you. (*Aside.*) And too much too.

IMOGEN. Why, one that rode to's execution, man,
Could never go so slow. But this is foolery.
Go, bid my woman feign a sickness, say
She'll home to her father. And provide me present
A riding suit, no costlier than would fit
A franklin's housewife.

PISANIO. Madam, you'd best consider.

IMOGEN. I see before me, man, nor here, nor here,
Nor what ensues, but have a fog in them,
60 That I cannot look through. Away, I prithee;
Do as I bid thee. There's no more to say;
Accessible is none but Milford way.

Exeunt.

SCENE V. [Wales.] *A forest with a cave.*

Enter Bellarius, Guiderius, and Arviragus.

BELLARIUS. A goodly day not to keep house with such
Whose roof's as low as ours. See, boys; this gate
Instructs you how t'adore the heav'ns and bows you
To morning's holy office. Gates of monarchs
Are arched so high that giants may get through

53. woman] *W1*, *W2*; women *D1*, *D2*, *D3*, *D4*, *D5*, *O1*.

And keep their impious turbans on, without
Goodmorrow to the sun. Hail, thou fair heav'n,
We house i'th' rock, yet use thee not so hardly
As prouder livers do.

10 GUIDERIUS. Hail, heav'n!

ARVIRAGUS. Hail, heav'n!

BELLARIUS. Now for our mountain sport. Up to yond hill;
Your legs are young. I'll tread these flats. Consider,
When you above perceive me like a crow,
That it is place which lessens and sets off.
And you may then revolve what tales I told you
Of courts of princes, of the tricks in war,
That service is not service, so being done,
But being so allowed. To apprehend thus,
20 Draws us a profit from all things we see.
And often to our comfort shall we find
The sharded beetle in a safer hold
Than is the full-winged eagle. Oh, this life
Is nobler than attending for a check,
Richer than doing nothing for a bauble,
Prouder than rustling in unpaid-for silk.
Such gain the cap of him that makes them fine,
Yet keeps his book uncrossed; no life to ours.

GUIDERIUS. Out of your proof you speak. We poor unfledged
30 Have never winged from view o' th' nest; nor know not
What air's from home. Haply this life is best,
If quiet life is best; sweeter to you
That have a sharper known; well corresponding
With your stiff age. But unto us it is
A cell of ignorance; traveling a-bed,
A prison for a debtor, that not dares
To stride a limit.

ARVIRAGUS. What should we speak of
When we are old as you? when we shall hear
40 The rain and wind beat dark December? How,
In this our pinching cave, shall we discourse
The freezing hours away? We have seen nothing.

BELLARIUS. How you speak!
Did you but know the city's usuries
And felt them knowingly; the art o' th' court,

32. quiet] omitted *W1*, *W2*.

As hard to leave as keep; whose top to climb
Is certain falling, or so slipp'ry that
The fear's as bad as falling. The toil o' th' war,
A pain that only seems to seek out danger
50 I' th' name of fame and honor; which dies i' th' search,
And hath as oft a sland'rous epitaph
As record of fair act; nay, many time
Doth ill deserve by doing well; what's worse,
Must curtsy at the censure. Oh, boys, this story
The world may read in me. My body's marked
With Roman swords; and my report was once
First with the best of note. Cymbeline loved me,
And when a soldier was the theme, my name
Was not far off. Then was I as a tree
60 Whose boughs did bend with fruit. But in one night,
A storm or robbery, call it what you will,
Shook down my mellow hangings, nay, my leaves,
And left me bare to weather.

GUIDERIUS. Uncertain favor!

BELLARIUS. My fault being nothing, as I have told you oft,
But that two villains, whose false oaths prevailed
Before my perfect honor, swore to Cymbeline
I was confederate with the Romans. So
Followed my banishment, and this twenty years,
70 This rock and these demesnes have been my world,
Where I haved lived at honest freedom, paid
More pious debts to heav'n than in all
The fore-end of my time. But, up to th' mountains,
This is not hunters' language. He that strikes
The venison first shall be the lord o'th' feast,
To him the other two shall minister,
And we will fear no poison which attends
In place of greater state. I'll meet you in the valleys.

Exeunt Guiderius *and* Arviragus.

How hard it is to hide the sparks of nature!
80 These boys know little they are sons to th' king;
And Cymbeline dreams not they are alive.
They think they are mine, and tho' trained up thus meanly
I' th' cave there on the brow, their thoughts do hit

46. top] *D1, D2, D3, D4, D5, O1*; tomb *W1, W2*.

The roofs of palaces, and nature prompts them
In simple and low things, to prince it much
Beyond the trick of others. This Polidore,
(The heir of Cymbeline and Britain, whom
The king his father called Guiderius) Jove!
When on my three-foot stool I sit, and tell
90 The warlike feats I've done, his spirits fly out
Into my story. Say "Thus mine enemy fell,
And thus I set my foot on's neck," even then
The princely blood flows in his cheek, he sweats,
Strains his young nerves, and puts himself in posture
That acts my words. The younger brother, Cadwal,
(Once, Arviragus) in as like a figure
Strikes life into my speech and shows much more
His own conceiving. Hark, the game is roused—
Oh, Cymbeline! Heav'n and my conscience know
100 Thou didst unjustly banish me, whereon
At three and two years old I stole these babes,
Thinking to bar thee of succession, as
Thou reft'st me of my lands. Euriphile,
Thou wast their nurse; they take thee for their mother,
And every day do honor to her grave;
Myself, Belarius, that am Morgan called,
They take for natural father. The game is up.

Exit.

SCENE VI. [Britain.] *The palace.*

Enter Cymbeline, Queen, Cloten, Lucius, *and* Lords.

CYMBELINE. Thus far; and so farewell.
LUCIUS. Thanks, royal sir.
I am right sorry that I must report you
My master's enemy. I desire of you
A conduct over land to Milford Haven.
CYMBELINE. My lords, you are appointed for that office;
The due of honor in no point omit.
So farewell, noble Lucius.

86. Polidore] *D1*, *D2*, *D3*, *D4*, *W1*, *W2*; Cadwall *D5*, *O1*.
88. Guiderius] *D1*, *D2*, *D3*, *D4*, *W1*, *W2*; Arviragus *D5*, *O1*.
95. Cadwal] *D1*, *D2*, *D3*, *D4*, *W1*, *W2*; Paladour *D5*, *O1*.
96. Arviragus] *D1*, *D2*, *D3*, *D4*, *W1*, *W2*; Guiderius *D5*, *O1*.

LUCIUS. Your hand, my lord.
10 CLOTEN. Receive it friendly; but from this time forth
I wear it as your enemy.
LUCIUS. Sir, the event
Is yet to name the winner. Fare you well.

Exit Lucius, *etc.*

QUEEN. He goes hence frowning. But it honors us
That we have given him cause.
CLOTEN. 'Tis all the better,
Your valiant Britons have their wishes in it.
QUEEN. 'Tis not sleepy business,
But must be looked to speedily and strongly.
20 CYMBELINE. Our expectation that it should be thus
Hath made us forward. But, my gentle queen,
Where is our daughter? She has not appeared
Before the Roman, nor to us hath tendered
The duty of the day. She looks as like
A thing more made of malice than of duty,
We've noted it. Call her before us, for
We've been too light in sufferance.

Exit First Lord.

QUEEN. Royal sir,
Since the exile of Posthumus, most retired
30 Hath her life been; the cure whereof, my lord,
'Tis time must do. Beseech your Majesty,
Forbear sharp speeches to her. She's a lady
So tender of rebukes that words are strokes
And strokes death to her.

Re-enter First Lord.

CYMBELINE. Where is she, sir? How
Can her contempt be answered?
FIRST LORD. Please you, sir,
Her chambers are all locked, and there's no answer
That will be given to th' loudest noise we make.
40 QUEEN. My lord, when last I went to visit her,
She prayed me to excuse her keeping close,
Whereto constrained by her infirmity,
She should that duty leave unpaid to you,
Which daily she was bound to proffer. This
She wished me to make known; but our great court

Made me to blame in memory.

CYMBELINE. Her doors locked?

Not seen of late? Grant, heavens, that which I fear

Prove false.

Exit.

50 QUEEN. Son, I say; follow the king.

CLOTEN. That man of hers, Pisanio, her old servant

I have not seen these two days.

QUEEN. Go, look after.

Exit Cloten.

Pisanio, he that stand'st so for Posthumus!
He has a drug of mine; I pray his absence
Proceed by swallowing that; for he believes
It is a thing most precious. But for her,
Where is she gone? Haply, despair hath seized her,
Or winged with fervor of her love, she's flown
60 To her desired Posthumus. Gone she is
To death or to dishonor, and my end
Can make good use of either. She being down,
I have the placing of the British crown.

Exeunt.

SCENE VII. *A wood* [*near Milford Haven*].

Enter Pisanio *and* Imogen.

IMOGEN. Thou told'st me when we came from horse the place

Was near at hand. Oh, where is Posthumus?
Say, good Pisanio, what is in thy mind
That makes thee stare thus? One but painted thus
Would be interpreted a thing perplexed
Beyond self-explication. What's the matter?
Why tender'st thou that paper to me?
If't be summer news,
Smile to't before; if winterly thou need'st
10 But keep that countenance still. My husband's hand!
That drug-damned Italy hath out-crafted him,
And he's at some hard point. Speak, man! Thy tongue
May take off some extremity, which to read
Would be even mortal to me.

PISANIO. Please you, read;
And you shall find me, wretched man, a thing
The most disdained of fortune.

IMOGEN (*reads*). "Thy mistress, Pisanio, hath played the strumpet in my bed; the testimonies whereof lie bleeding in me. I speak not out
20 of weak surmises, but from proof as strong as my grief and as certain as I expect my revenge. That part thou, Pisanio, must act for me, if thy faith be not tainted with the breach of hers. Let thine own hands take away her life: I shall give thee opportunity at Milford Haven. She hath my letter for the purpose; where, if thou fear to strike and to make me certain it is done, thou art the pander to her dishonor, and equally to me disloyal."

PISANIO [*aside*]. What shall I need to draw my sword? The paper
Hath cut her throat already. No, 'tis slander,
Whose edge is sharper than the sword, whose tongue
30 Out-venoms all the worms of Nile, whose breath
Rides on the posting winds and doth belie
All corners of the world. Kings, queens, and states,
Maids, matrons, nay the secrets of the grave
This viperous slander enters.—What cheer, madam?

IMOGEN. False to his bed? What is it to be false?
To lie in watch there and to think on him?
To weep 'twixt clock and clock? If sleep charge nature,
To break it with a fearful dream of him
And cry myself awake? That's false to's bed?

40 PISANIO. Alas, good lady!

IMOGEN. I false? Thy conscience witness, Iachimo,
That didst accuse him of incontinency,
Thou then look'st like a villain. Now, methinks,
Thy favor's good enough. Some jay of Italy,
Whose feathers were her painting, hath betrayed him.
Poor I am stale, a garment out of fashion,
I must be ripped; to pieces with me! Oh,
Men's vows are women's traitors. All good seeming,
By thy revolt, oh, husband, shall be thought
50 Put on for villainy.

PISANIO. Good madam, hear me—

IMOGEN. Come, fellow, be thou honest,
Do thy master's bidding. When thou seest him,
A little witness my obedience. Look!
I draw the sword myself. Take it, and hit

22. breach] *D*1, *D*2, *D*3, *W*1, *W*2; breath *D*4, *D*5, *O*1.

The innocent mansion of my love, my heart,
Fear not; 'tis empty of all things but grief.
Thy master is not there, who was indeed
The riches of it. Do his bidding; strike.
60 Thy may'st be valiant in a better cause;
But now thou seem'st a coward.

PISANIO. Hence, vile instrument!
Thou shalt not damn my hand.

IMOGEN. Why must I die?
And if I do not by thy hand, thou art
No servant of thy master's. Against self-slaughter
There is a prohibition so divine
That cravens my weak hand. Come, here's my heart.
Something's afore't. Soft, soft! we'll no defence.
70 (*Opening her breast.*) What is here?
The scriptures of the loyal Leonatus,
All turned to heresy? Away, away, (*Pulling his letter out of her bosom.*)
Corrupters of my faith; you shall no more
Be stomachers to my heart. Prithee, dispatch.
The lamb entreats the butcher. Where's the knife?
Thou art too slow to do thy master's bidding,
When I desire it too.

PISANIO. Oh gracious lady!
Since I received command to do this business
80 I have not slept one wink.

IMOGEN. Do't, and to bed then.

PISANIO. I'll break mine eye-balls first.

IMOGEN. Wherefore then did'st undertake it?
Why hast thou gone so far
To be unbent when thou hast ta'en thy stand,
Th' elected deer before thee?

PISANIO. But to win time
To lose so bad employment, in the which
I have considered of a course; good lady,
90 Hear me with patience.

IMOGEN. Talk thy tongue weary; speak.
I have heard I am a strumpet, and mine ear,
Therein false struck, can take no greater wound,
Nor tent to bottom that. But speak!

PISANIO. It cannot be,
But that my master is abused. Some villain,
Aye, and singular in his art, hath done you both

This cursed injury.

IMOGEN. Some Roman courtezan.

100 PISANIO. No, on my life.

I'll give him notice you are dead and send him
Some bloody sign of it. For 'tis commanded
I should do so; you shall be missed at court,
And that will well confirm it.

IMOGEN. Why, good fellow,
What shall I do the while? Where bide? How live?
Or in my life what comfort, when I am
Dead to my husband?

PISANIO. If you'll back to the court—

110 IMOGEN. No court, no father.

PISANIO. If not at court,
What shall I do the while? Where bide? How live?

IMOGEN. Hath Britain all the sun that shines?
There's living out of Britain.

PISANIO. I am most glad
You think of other place. Th' ambassador,
Lucius the Roman, comes to Milford Haven
Tomorrow. Now, if you could wear a mien
Dark as your fortune is, you should tread a course
120 Pretty and full of view; yea, happily, near
The residence of Posthumus; so nigh, at least,
That though his action were not visible, yet
Report should render him hourly to your ear
As truly as he moves.

IMOGEN. Oh, for such means!
Though peril to my modesty, not death on't,
I would adventure.

PISANIO. Well, then, there's the point.
You must forget to be a woman, change
130 Command in obedience, fear and niceness,
The handmaids of all women, or more truly
Woman its pretty self, into a waggish courage,
Ready in gibes, quick-answered, saucy and
As quarrelous as the weasel. Nay, you must
Forget that rarest treasure of your cheek,
Exposing it (but oh, the harder heart,
Alack, no remedy!) to the greedy touch
Of common-kissing Titan, and forget

---

133. in] *D1*, *D2*, *D3*, *D4*, *D5*, *O1*; into *W1*, *W2*.

Your laborsome and dainty trims, wherein
140 You made great Juno angry.
IMOGEN. Nay, be brief.
I see into thy end, and am almost
A man already.
PISANIO. First, make yourself but like one.
Fore-thinking this, I have already fit,
('Tis in your cloak-bag) doublet, hat, hose, all
That answer to them. Would you in their serving,
And with what imitation you can borrow
From youth of such a season, 'fore noble Lucius
150 Present yourself, desire his service, tell him
Wherein you're happy, which will make him so,
(If that his head have ear in music) doubtless
With joy he will embrace you, for he's honorable
And doubling that, most holy. For means abroad
You have me, rich; and I will never fail
Beginning nor supply.
IMOGEN. Thou art all the comfort
The gods diet me with. This attempt
I am soldier to, and will abide it with
160 A prince's courage. Away, I prithee.
PISANIO. Well, madam, we must take a short farewell,
Lest, being missed, I be suspected of
Your carriage from the court. My noble mistress,
Here is a phial glass.
What's in't is precious. If you are sick at sea,
Or stomach-qualmed at land, a taste of this
Will drive away distemper. To some shade,
And fit you to your manhood. May the gods
Direct you to the best.
170 IMOGEN. Amen. I thank thee.

Exeunt.

ACT IV.

SCENE I. [Britain.] *A palace.*

Enter Cloten.

CLOTEN. I love and hate her; for she's fair and royal,
I love her; but

166. taste] *D1*, *D2*, *W2*; dram *D3*, *D4*, *D5*, *O1*, *W1*.

Disdaining me and throwing favors on
The low Posthumus, slanders so her judgment,
I will conclude to hate her.

Enter Pisanio.

Who is here? Ah, you precious pander, villain,
Where is thy lady? In a word, or else
Thou art straightway with the fiends.

PISANIO. Oh, my good lord.

10 CLOTEN. Where is thy lady? Or, by Jupiter,
I will not ask again. Close villian,
I'll have this secret from thy heart, or rip
Thy heart to find it. Is she with Posthumus?

PISANIO. Alas, my lord,
How can she be with him? When was she missed?

CLOTEN. Where is she, sir? Satisfy me home,
What is become of her?

PISANIO. Oh, my all worthy lord!

CLOTEN. All worthy villain!
20 Speak, or thy silence on the instant is
Thy condemnation and thy death.

PISANIO. Then, sir,
This paper is the history of my knowledge
Touching her flight.

CLOTEN. Let's see it. I will pursue her
Even to Augustus' throne.

PISANIO (*aside*). Or this, or perish.
She's far enough, and what he learns by this,
May prove his travel, not her danger.

30 CLOTEN. Humh.

PISANIO (*aside*). I'll write to my lord she is dead. Oh, Imogen,
Safe may'st thou wander, safe return again!

CLOTEN. Sirrah, is this letter true?

PISANIO. Sir, as I think.

CLOTEN. It is Posthumus' hand; I know it. Sirrah, if thou would'st not be a villain, but to do me true service, that is, what villainy so'er I bid thee do to perform it, directly and truly, I would think thee an honest man; thou shouldst neither want my means for thy relief nor my voice for thy preferment.

40 PISANIO. Well, my good lord.

CLOTEN. Give me thy hand; here's my purse. Hast any of thy late

39. thy] *D1*, *D2*, *D3*, *D4*, *D5*, *O1*, *W1*; the *W2*.

master's garments in thy possession?

PISANIO. I have, my lord, one at my lodging which he forgot to take with him; it was a favorite of my lady and mistress.

CLOTEN. The first service thou dost me, fetch that suit hither.

PISANIO. I shall, my lord.

Exit.

CLOTEN. Meet thee at Milford Haven? Even there, thou villain, Posthumus, will I kill thee. She said upon a time, that she held the very garment of Posthumus in more respect than my noble and natural
50 person. With that suit upon my back will I ravish her; and when my lust hath dined, to the court I'll foot her home again. My revenge is now at Milford, would I had wings to follow it.

Exit.

SCENE II. *The forest and cave.*

Enter Imogen *in boy's clothes.*

IMOGEN. I see a man's life is a tedious one;
I have tired myself, and for two nights together
Have made the ground my bed. I should be sick,
But that my resolution helps me. Milford,
When from the mountain top Pisanio showed thee,
Thou wast within a ken. Oh, Jove! I think
Foundations fly the wretched, such I mean,
Where they should be relieved. Two beggars told me
I could not miss my way. Will poor folks lie
10 That have afflictions on them? Yet, no wonder,
When rich ones scarce tell true. To lapse in fulness
Is sorer than to lie for need; and falsehood
Is worse in kings than beggars. My dear lord,
Thou art one o'th' false ones; now I think on thee,
My hunger's gone; but even before, I was
At point to sink for food. (*Seeing the cave.*) But what is this?
Here is a path to't—'tis some savage hold;
I were best not call; I dare not call; yet famine
Ere it clean o'erthrow nature makes it valiant.
20 Plenty and peace breed cowards, hardness ever

---

51. lust] *D1*, *D2*, *D3*, *D4*, *W1*, *W2*; appetite *D5*, *O1*.
52. Milford] *D1*, *D2*, *D3*, *D4*, *D5*, *O1*; Milford-Haven *W1*, *W2*.

Of hardiness is mother. Ho! Who's here?
If anything that's civil, speak;
No answer! Then I'll enter.
Best draw my sword; and if mine enemy
But fear my sword like me, he'll scarcely look on't.
Such a foe, good heav'ns! (*She goes into the cave.*)

Enter Bellarius, Guiderius, *and* Arviragus.

BELLARIUS. You, Polidore, have proved best woodsman and
Are master of the feast. Cadwall and I
Will play the cook and servant. Come, our stomachs
30 Will make what's homely savorly; weariness
Can snore upon the flint, when resty sloth
Finds the dawn pillow hard. Now peace be here,
Poor house, that keeps thyself.
GUIDERIUS. There's cold meat in the cave. We'll browse on that
Whilst what we have killed be cooked.
BELLARIUS (*looking in*). Stay; come not in.
But that it eats our victuals, I should think
He were a fairy.
GUIDERIUS. What's the matter, sir?
40 BELLARIUS. By Jupiter, an angel! or, if not,
An earthly paragon. Behold divineness
No elder than a boy.

Enter Imogen *from the cave.*

IMOGEN. Good master, harm me not;
Before I entered here, I called, and thought
To have begged or bought what I have took. Good troth,
I have stol'n nought, nor would not, though I had found
Gold strewed i'th' floor. Here's money for my meat;
I would have left it on the board so soon
As I had made my meal, and parted thence
50 With prayers for the provider.
GUIDERIUS. Money, youth?
ARVIRAGUS. All gold and silver rather turn to dirt,
As 'tis no better reckoned, but of those
Who worship dirty gods.
IMOGEN. I see you're angry:
Know, if you kill me for my fault, I should

---

27. Polidore] *D1*, *D2*, *D3*, *D4*, *W1*, *W2*; Polydour *D5*, *O1*.
34. meat] *D1*, *D2*, *D3*, *D4*, *D5*, *O1*, *W1*; meet *W2*.

have died had I not made it.
BELLARIUS. Whither bound?
IMOGEN. To Milford Haven.
60 BELLARIUS. What's your name?
IMOGEN. Fidele, sir. I have a kinsman who
Is bound for Italy. He embarked at Milford;
To whom being going, almost spent with hunger,
I am fall'n in this offence.
BELLARIUS. Prithee, fair youth,
Think us no churls, nor measure our good minds
By this rude place we live in. Well encountered!
'Tis almost night; you shall have better cheer
Ere you depart; and thanks to stay and eat it.
70 Boys, bid him welcome.
ARVIRAGUS. I'll love him as my brother.
And such welcome as I'd give to him
After long absence, such is yours.
GUIDERIUS. Most welcome.
Be sprightly, for you fall among friends.
IMOGEN. 'Mongst friends,
If brothers. (*Aside.*) Would it had been so, that they
Had been my father's sons, then had my prize
Been less, and so more equal to thee, my Posthumus.
80 BELLARIUS. He wrings at some distress.
GUIDERIUS. Would I could free it.
ARVIRAGUS. Or I, whate'er it be,
What pain it cost, what danger.
BELLARIUS. Hark, boys. (*Whispering.*)
IMOGEN. Great men,
That had a court no bigger than this cave,
That did attend themselves and had the virtue
Which their own conscience sealed them—laying by
That nothing-gift of differing multitudes—
90 Could not out-piece these twain. Pardon me, gods,
I'd change my sex to be companion with them,
Since Posthumus is false.
BELLARIUS. It shall be so.
Boys, we'll go dress our hunt. Fair youth, come in;
Discourse is heavy, fasting; when we have supped,
We'll mannerly demand of thee thy story,
So far as thou wilt speak it.

75. fall] *D1*, *D2*, *D3*, *D4*, *D5*, *O1*, *W1*; all *W2*.

GUIDERIUS. Pray, draw near.
ARVIRAGUS. The night to th' owl and morn to th' lark less welcome.
100 IMOGEN. Thanks, sir.
ARVIRAGUS. I pray, draw near.

Exeunt.

SCENE III. *The forest.*

Enter Cloten *alone.*

CLOTEN. I am near to the place where they should meet, if Pisanio have mapped it truly. How fit his garments serve me! Posthumus, thy head, which is now growing upon thy shoulders, shall within this hour be off, thy mistress enforced, thy garments cut to pieces before her face, and all this done, spurn her home to her father, who may happily be a little angry for my so rough usage; but my mother, having power of his testiness, shall turn all into my commendations. My horse is tied up safe. Out, sword, and to a sore purpose! Fortune put them into my hand. This is the very description of their meeting
10 place, and the fellow dares not deceive me.

Exit.

SCENE IV. *The cave.*

Enter Bellarius, Guiderius, Arviragus, *and* Imogen.

BELLARIUS [*to* Imogen]. You are not well. Remain here in the cave;
We'll come to you after hunting.
ARVIRAGUS [*to* Imogen]. Brother, stay here.
Are we not brothers?
IMOGEN. So man and man should be,
But clay and clay differs in dignity,
Whose dust is both alike. I am very sick.
GUIDERIUS. Go you to hunting. I'll abide with him.
IMOGEN. So sick I am not, yet I am not well.
10 So please you, leave me;
Stick to your journal course. The breach of custom
Is breach of all. I am ill, but your being by me
Cannot amend me. Society is no comfort
To one not sociable. I am not very sick,
Since I can reason of it. Pray you, trust me here.

ARVIRAGUS. Brother, farewell.
IMOGEN. I wish you sport.
ARVIRAGUS. Your health. So, please you, sir.
IMOGEN [*aside*]. These are kind creatures. Gods, what lies have I heard!
20 Our courtiers say all's savage but at court.
I am sick still, heart-sick. Pisanio,
I'll now taste of thy drug. (*Drinks out of the phial.*)
GUIDERIUS. I could not stir him.
He said he was gentle, but unfortunate;
Dishonestly afflicted, but yet honest.
ARVIRAGUS. Thus did he answer me; yet said, hereafter
I might know more.
BELLARIUS. To the field! To the field!
We'll leave you for this time. Go in and rest.
30 ARVIRAGUS. We'll not be long away.
BELLARIUS. Pray, be not sick,
For you must be our housewife.
IMOGEN. Well or ill,
I am bound to you.

Exit.

BELLARIUS. This youth, howe'er distressed, appears t'have had
Good ancestors.
ARVIRAGUS. How angel-like he sings.
Nobly he yokes a smiling with a sigh.
GUIDERIUS. Yet I do note
40 That grief and patience, rooted in him both,
Mingle their spurs together.
ARVIRAGUS. Grow, patience!
And let the stinking elder, grief, untwine
His perishing root from the increasing vine.
BELLARIUS. It is great morning. Come away!—Who's there?

Enter Cloten.

CLOTEN. I cannot find those runagates; that villain
Hath mocked me.

Exit.

BELLARIUS. "Those runagates!"
Means he not us? I partly know him; 'tis
50 Cloten, the son o' th' queen. I fear some ambush.

---

31. sick] *D1*, *D2*, *D3*, *D4*, *D5*, *O1*, *W1*; seek *W2*.

GUIDERIUS. He is but one. You and my brother search
What companies are near. Pray you, away;
Let me alone with him.

Exeunt Bellarius *and* Arviragus.

Re-enter Cloten.

CLOTEN. Soft! What are you
That fly me thus? Some villain mountaineers?
I've heard of such. Thou art a robber,
A law-breaker, a villain: yield thee, thief.
GUIDERIUS. To whom? to thee? What art thou? Have not I
An arm as big as thine? a heart as big?
60 Thy words, I grant, are bigger, for I wear not
My dagger in my mouth. Say what thou art,
Why I should yield to thee.
CLOTEN. Thou villain base,
Know'st me not by my clothes?
GUIDERIUS. No, nor thy tailor, who made those clothes,
Which, as it seems, make thee.
CLOTEN. Thou injurious thief,
Hear but my name, and tremble.
GUIDERIUS. What's thy name?
70 CLOTEN. Cloten, thou villain.
GUIDERIUS. Cloten, then double villain be thy name,
I cannot tremble at it. Were it toad, adder, spider,
'Twould move me sooner.
CLOTEN. To thy further fear,
Nay, to thy mere confusion, thou shalt know
I am son to th' queen.
GUIDERIUS. I am sorry for't; not seeming
So worthy as thy birth.
CLOTEN. Art not afraid?
80 GUIDERIUS. Those that I reverence, those I fear, the wise;
At fools I laugh, not fear them.
CLOTEN. Die the death!
When I have slain thee with my proper hand,
I'll follow those that even now fled hence,
And on the gates of Lud's-town set your heads.
Yield, rustic mountaineer.

Fight and exeunt.

Enter Bellarius *and* Arviragus.

BELLARIUS. No company's abroad.
ARVIRAGUS. None in the world. You did mistake him, sure.
BELLARIUS. No, time hath nothing blurred those lines of favor
90 Which then he wore; the snatches in his voice,
And burst of speaking, were as his. I am absolute
'Twas very Cloten.
ARVIRAGUS. In this place we left them.
[BELLARIUS.] But, see thy brother.

Enter Guiderius.

GUIDERIUS. This Cloten was a fool. Not Hercules
Could have knocked out his brains, for he had none.
BELLARIUS. What hast thou done?
GUIDERIUS. Cut off one Cloten's head,
Son to the queen, after his own report.
100 BELLARIUS. We are all undone.
GUIDERIUS. Why, worthy father, what have we to lose,
But that he swore to take, our lives? The law
Protects not us; then why should we be tender
To let an arrogant piece of flesh threat us,
Play judge and executioner all himself?
For we do fear no law. What company
Discover you abroad?
BELLARIUS. No single soul
Can we set eye on; but in all safe reason
110 He must have some attendants.
It is not probable he'd come alone.
ARVIRAGUS. Let ordinance
Come as the gods foresay it; howsoe'er,
My brother hath done well.
BELLARIUS. I had no mind
To hunt this day: the boy Fidele's sickness
Did make my way long forth.
GUIDERIUS. With his own sword,
Which he did wave against my throat, I have ta'en
120 His head from him. I'll throw't into the creek
Behind our rock, and let it to the sea,
And tell the fishes he's the queen's son, Cloten.
That's all I care.

Exit.

92.1. BELLARIUS] omitted *D1*, *D2*, *D3*, *D4*, *W1*, *W2*; corrected *D5*, *O1*.

BELLARIUS. I fear it will be revenged.
Would, Polidore, thou hadst not done't, though valor
Becomes thee well enough.

ARVIRAGUS. Would I had done't.

BELLARIUS. Well, 'tis done.
We'll hunt no more today, nor seek for danger
130 Where there's no profit. I prithee, to our rock;
You and Fidele play the cooks. I'll stay
Till hasty Polidore return, and bring him
To dinner presently.

ARVIRAGUS. Poor sick Fidele!
I'll willingly to him. To gain his color
I'd let a river of such Cloten's blood,
And praise myself for charity.

Exit.

BELLARIUS. Oh, thou goddess,
Thou divine nature! how thyself thou blazon'st
140 In these two princely boys! They are as gentle
As zephyrs blowing below the violet,
Not wagging his sweet head; and yet as rough
(Their royal blood enchafed), as the rudest wind,
That by the top doth take the mountain pine,
And make him stoop to th' vale. 'Tis wonderful
That an invisible instinct should frame them
To royalty unlearned, honor untaught,
Civility not seen from other, valor
That wildly grows in them, but yields a crop
150 As if it had been sowed. Yet still it's strange
What Cloten's being here to us portends,
Or what his death will bring us.

Enter Guiderius.

GUIDERIUS. Where's my brother?
I have sent Cloten's clotpoll down the stream,
In embassy to his mother; his body's hostage
For his return.

Solemn music.

BELLARIUS. My ingenious instrument!
Hark, Polidore, it sounds! But what occasion
Hath Cadwal now to give it motion? Hark!

160 GUIDERIUS. Is he at home?

BELLARIUS. He went from hence even now.
GUIDERIUS. What does he mean? Since death of my dear'st mother
It did not speak before. All solemn things
Should answer solemn accidents.

Enter Arviragus.

BELLARIUS. Look, here he comes,
And brings the dire occasion in his looks
Of what we blame him for.
ARVIRAGUS. The bird is dead
That we have made so much on. I had rather
170 Have skipped from sixteen years of age to sixty,
Than have seen this.
GUIDERIUS. Oh, sweetest, fairest lily!
And art thou gone, my poor Fidele?
BELLARIUS. What, is he dead? how found you him?
ARVIRAGUS. Stark–smiling as some fly had tickled slumber,
Not as death's dart being laughed at; his right cheek
Reposing on a cushion.
GUIDERIUS. Where?
ARVIRAGUS. O'th' floor;
180 His arms thus leagued, I thought he slept, and put
My clouted brogues from off my feet, whose rudeness
Answered my steps too loud.
GUIDERIUS. If he be gone, he'll make his grave a bed;
With female fairies will his tomb be haunted,
And worms will not come near him.
ARVIRAGUS. With fairest flowers
Whilst summer lasts and I live here, Fidele,
I'll sweeten thy sad grave.
BELLARIUS. Great griefs, I see, medicine the less; for Cloten
190 Is quite forgot. He was a queen's son, boys;
And though he came our enemy, remember
He paid for that. Our foe was princely;
And though you took his life, as being our foe,
Yet bury him as a prince. Go, bring your lily.

Exeunt Guiderius *and* Arviragus.

Oh, melancholy!
Who ever yet could sound thy bottom, find
The ooze to show what coast thy sluggish Carrack
Might easiliest harbor in? Thou blessed thing!

Jove knows what man thou might'st have made. But, oh!
200 Thou died'st, a most rare boy of melancholy.

Enter Guiderius *and* Arviragus *with the body.*

Come, let us lay the bodies each by each.
And strew 'em o'er with flow'rs; and on the morrow
Shall the earth receive 'em.
ARVIRAGUS. Sweet Fidele!
Fear no more th' heat o'th' sun,
Nor the furious winter's blast;
Thou thy worldly task hast done,
And the dream of life is past.
GUIDERIUS. Monarchs, sages, peasants must
210 Follow thee and come to dust.

Exeunt with the body.

SCENE V. *The palace.*

Enter Cymbeline, Lords, *and* Pisanio.

CYMBELINE. Again; and bring me word how 'tis with her.
A fever with the absence of her son;
Madness, of which her life's in danger. Heav'ns!
How deeply you at once do touch me. Imogen,
The great part of my comfort, gone. My queen
Upon a desperate bed, and in a time
When woeful wars point at me. Her son gone,
So needful for this present. It strikes me, past
The hope of comfort. But for thee, fellow,
10 Who needs must know of her departure and
Dost seem so ignorant, we'll enforce it from thee
By a sharp torture.
PISANIO. Sir, my life is yours; set it at your will.
FIRST LORD. Good, my liege,
The day that she was missing he was here.
I dare be bound he's true and shall perform
All parts of his subjection loyally. For Lord Cloten,
There wants no diligence in seeking him;
He will no doubt be found.
20 CYMBELINE. The time is troublesome;
We'll slip you for a season; but our jealousy

Does yet depend.

SECOND LORD. So please your Majesty,
The Roman legions all from Gallia drawn,
Are landed on your coast.

CYMBELINE. Now for the counsel of my son and queen.
I am amazed with matter; let's withdraw
And meet the time as it seeks us. We fear not
What can from Italy annoy us; but
30 We grieve at chances here. Away!

Exeunt.

PISANIO. I've had no letter from my master since
I wrote him Imogen was slain: 'tis strange.
Nor hear I from my mistress, who did promise
To yield me often tidings. Neither know I
What is betide to Cloten, but remain
Perplexed in all. The heavens still must work.
Wherein I'm false I'm honest; not true, to be true.
These present wars shall find I love my country,
Ev'n to the note of th' king, or I'll fall in them.
40 All other doubts by time let them be cleared;
Fortune brings in some boats that are not steered.

Exit.

SCENE VI. *A forest.*

Imogen *and* Cloten *on a bank strewn with flowers.*
Imogen *awakes.*

IMOGEN. Yes, sir, to Milford Haven; which is the way?—
I thank you.—By yond bush?—Pray, how far thither?
'Ods pitikins, can it be six miles yet?—
I have gone all night. 'Faith, I'll lie down and sleep.
But soft! no bedfellow!—Oh gods and goddesses! (*Seeing the body of Cloten.*)
The flowers are like the pleasures of the world;
This bloody man, the care on't. I hope I dream;
For so I thought I was a cave-keeper,
And cook to honest creatures.

5.1. (*Seeing the body*)] *D1, D2, D3, D4, D5, O1*; (*Seeing the boy*) *W1, W2*.

10 I tremble still with fear; but if there be
Yet left in heav'n as small a drop of pity
As a wren's eye—oh, gods! a part of it!—
The dream's here still; even when I wake, it is
Without me, as within me; not imagined, felt.
A headless man!—The garments of my Posthumus?
I know them well; this is his hand—
Murdered—Pisanio!—
'Twas thou conspiring with that devil Cloten
Hast here cut off my lord. Pisanio!—
20 How should this be, Pisanio?—'Tis he!
The drug he gave me, which he said was precious
And cordial to me, have I not found it
Murd'rous to the senses? That confirms it home.
This is Pisanio's deed, and Cloten's deed.
Oh, my lord, my lord! (*Lies down upon the body.*)

Enter Lucius *and captains.*

LUCIUS. But what from Rome?
CAPTAIN. The senate hath stirred up the confiners
And gentlemen of Italy, most willing spirits,
That promise noble service: and they come
30 Under the conduct of bold Iachimo,
Syenna's brother.
LUCIUS. When expect you them?
CAPTAIN. With the next benefit o'th' wind.
LUCIUS. This forwardness
Makes our hopes fair. Soft, ho! what trunk is here
Without his top? The ruin speaks that sometime
It was a worthy building. How! a page!—
Or dead, or sleeping on him? But dead rather:
For nature doth abhor to make his bed
40 With the defunct, or sleep upon the dead.
Let's see the boy's face.
CAPTAIN. He's alive, my lord.
LUCIUS. He'll then instruct us of his body. Young one,
Inform us of thy fortunes, for it seems
They crave to be demanded. Who is this
Thou mak'st thy bloody pillow? What art thou?
IMOGEN. I am nothing; or if not,
Nothing to be were better. This was my master,
A very valiant Briton and a good,

50 That here by mountaineers lies slain. Alas!
There are no more such masters.

LUCIUS. 'Lack, good youth!
Thou movest no less with thy complaining than
Thy master in bleeding. Say thy name, good friend.

IMOGEN. Fidele, sir.

LUCIUS. Thy name well fits thy faith.
Will't take thy chance with me? I will not say
Thou shalt be so well mastered, but be sure
No less beloved. Go with me.

60 IMOGEN. I'll follow, sir. But first, an't please the gods,
I'll hide my master from the fowls as deep
As these poor pickaxes can dig; and when
With wild wood-leaves and weeds I ha' strew'd his grave,
And on it said a century of prayers,
(Such as I can) twice o'er, I'll weep and sigh,
And leaving so his service, follow you,
So please you entertain me.

LUCIUS. Aye, good youth;
And rather father thee than master thee. My friends,
70 The boy hath taught us manly duties; let us
Find out the prettiest daisied plot we can,
And make him with our pikes and partizans
A grave. Come, take him up. Boy, he is preferred
By thee to us, and he shall be interred
As soldiers can. Be cheerful; wipe thine eyes;
Some falls are means the happier to arise.
Bring him along.

Exeunt.

ACT V.
SCENE I. *A forest.*

A march at a distance.

Enter Bellarius, Guiderius *and* Arviragus.

ARVIRAGUS. The noise is round about us.

BELLARIUS. Let us from it.

---

64. and on it . . . prayers] omitted *W*1, *W*2.

We'll higher to the mountains; there secure us.
To the king's party there's no going; newness
Of Cloten's death, we being not known, nor mustered
Among the bands, may drive us to a render
Where we have lived, and so extort from's that
Which we have done, whose answer would be death
Drawn on with torture.

10 GUIDERIUS. This is, sir, a doubt
(In such a time) nothing becoming you,
Nor satisfying us.

ARVIRAGUS. It is not likely
That when they hear the Roman horses neigh,
Behold their quartered fires, have both their eyes
And ears so cloyed importantly as now,
That they will waste their time upon our note,
To know from whence we are.

BELLARIUS. Oh, I am known
20 Of many in the army; and besides the king
Hath not deserved my service nor your loves.

GUIDERIUS. Pray, sir, to the army.
I and my brother are not known; yourself
So out of thought, and thereto so o'ergrown,
Cannot be questioned.

ARVIRAGUS. By this sun that shines,
I'll thither. What thing is it that I never
Did see man die, scarce ever looked on blood
But that of coward hares, hot goats, and venison?
30 I am ashamed to look upon the holy sun, to have
The benefit of his blest beams, remaining
So long a poor unknown.

GUIDERIUS. By heav'ns, I'll go.
If you will bless me, sir, and give me leave,
I'll take the better care; but if you will not,
The hazard therefore due fall on me by
The hands of Romans!

ARVIRAGUS. So say I.

BELLARIUS. No reason I, since of your lives you set
40 So slight a valuation, should reserve
My cracked one to more care. Have with you, boys.
If in your country wars you chance to die,
That is my bed too, lads, and there I'll lie.

Exeunt.

SCENE II. *A field between the British and Roman camps.*

Enter Posthumus *with a bloody handkerchief.*

POSTHUMUS. Yea, bloody cloth, I'll keep thee; for I wished
Thou should'st be colored thus. You married ones,
If each of you would take this course, how many
Must murder wives much better than yourselves
For wrying but a little! Oh, Pisanio!
Every good servant does not all commands—
No bond but to do just ones. Gods! if you
Should have ta'en vengeance on my faults, I never
Had lived to put on this: so had you saved
10 The noble Imogen to repent and struck
Me, wretch more worth your vengeance. But, alack,
You snatch from hence for little faults; that's love
To have them fall no more. You some permit
To second ills with ills, each worse than other,
And make them dreaded to the doers' thrift.
But Imogen is your own. Do your best wills,
And make me blest to obey. I am brought hither
Amongst the Italian gentry, and to fight
Against my lady's kingdom; 'tis enough
20 That, Britain, I have killed thy mistress. Peace!
I'll give no wound to thee. Therefore, good heav'ns,
Hear patiently my purpose: I'll disrobe me
Of these Italian weeds and suit myself
As does a Britain peasant: so I'll fight
Against the part I come with; so I'll die
For thee, O Imogen, for whom my life
Is every breath a death; and thus unknown,
Pitied nor hated, to the face of peril
Myself I'll dedicate. Let me make men know
30 More valor in me than my habits show.
Gods, put the strength o'th' Leonati in me!
To shame the guise o'th' world, I will begin
The fashion, less without and more within.

Exit.

11–15. Lines omitted *D5*, *O1*.

22. I'll disrobe me] *D1*, *D2*, *D3*, *D4*, *W1*, *W2*; I have concealed *D5*, *O1*.

23–24. Of these . . . peasant] *D1*, *D2*, *D3*, *D4*, *W1*, *W2*; "My Italian weeds, under this semblance / of a British peasant" *D5*, *O1*.

29–30. Let me . . . show] *D1*, *D2*, *D3*, *D4*, *W1*, *W2*. Stage direction after "dedicate": (*Trumpet sounds a call*), then "Hark, hark! I'm called" *D5*, *O1*.

SCENE III. *A field of battle.*

A grand fight between the Romans *and* Britons; *the* Romans *are driven off.*

Enter Posthumus *and* Iachimo *fighting.* Iachimo *drops his sword.*

POSTHUMUS. Or yield thee, Roman, or thou die'st.
IACHIMO. Peasant, behold my breast.
POSTHUMUS. No, take thy life and mend it.

Exit Posthumus.

IACHIMO. The heaviness and sin within my bosom
Takes off my manhood. I have belied a lady,
The princess of this country, and the air on't
Revengingly enfeebles me; or could this carl,
A very drudge of nature, have subdued me
In my profession. Knighthoods and honors borne
10 As I wear mine, are titles but of scorn.
With heav'n against me, what is sword or shield;
My guilt, my guilt, o'erpowers me and I yield.

Exit.

SCENE IV. *A wood.*

Enter Pisanio *and* First Lord.

FIRST LORD. This is a day turned strangely.
Came'st thou from where they made the stand?
PISANIO. I did,
Though you, it seems, came from the fliers.
FIRST LORD. I did.
PISANIO. No blame to you, sir, for all was lost,
But that the heav'ns sought. The king himself
Of his wings destitute, the army broken,
And but the backs of Britons seen, all flying
10 Through a straight lane; the enemy full-hearted,
Lolling the tongue with slaughtering, struck down
Some mortally, some slightly touched, some falling
Merely through fear, that the straight pass was damn'd

2. behold] *D*1, *D*2, *D*3, *D*4, *D*5, *O*1, *W*1, *W*2; hold *D*4.
10. straight] *D*1, *D*2, *D*3, *D*4, *D*5, *O*1; strait *W*1, *W*2.

With dead men hurt behind, and cowards living
To die with lengthened shame.

FIRST LORD. Where was this lane?

PISANIO. Close by the battle, ditched and walled with turf,
Which gave advantage to an ancient soldier,
An honest one I warrant. Athwart the lane,
20 He, with two stripling lads more like to run
The country base than to commit such slaughter,
Make good the passage, cried to the fliers, "Stand!
Or we are Romans and will give you that
Like beasts which you shun beastly, and may save
But to look back in frown. Stand, stand!"

FIRST LORD. Were there but three?

PISANIO. There was a fourth man, in a poor rustic habit,
That stood the front with them. These matchless four,
Accommodated by the place, gilded pale looks,
30 Part shame, part spirit renewed, that some turned cowards,
But by example 'gan to look
The way that they did, and to grin like lions
Upon the pikes o'th' hunter. Then began
A stop i'th' chaser, a retire; anon
A rout, confusion thick, and the event
A victory for us.

FIRST LORD. This was strange chance,
An old man, two boys, and a poor rustic.

PISANIO. Nay, do not wonder—but go with me and
40 See these wonders and join the general joy.

Exeunt.

SCENE V. *A Wood.*

Enter Posthumus.

POSTHUMUS. Today how many would have given their honors
To've saved their carcasses! took heel to do't,
And yet died too! I, in mine own woe charmed,
Could not find death where I did hear him groan,
Nor feel him where he struck. This ugly monster,
'Tis strange he hides him in fresh cups, soft beds,
Sweet words; or hath more ministers than we
That drew his knives i'th' war. Well, I will find him;
No more a Briton, I have resumed again,

9. resumed] *D*1, *D*2, *W*1, *W*2; reformed *D*3, *D*4, *D*5, *O*1.

10 The part I came in. Fight I will no more,
But yield me to the veriest hind that shall
Once touch my shoulder. Great the slaughter is
On either side. For me, my ransom's death,
I come to spend my breath;
Which neither here I'll keep, nor bear again,
But end it by some means for Imogen.

Exit.

SCENE VI. Cymbeline's *tent.*

Enter Cymbeline, Bellarius, Guiderius, Arviragus, Pisanio, *and Lords.*

CYMBELINE. Stand by my side, you whom the gods have made
Preservers of my throne. Woe is my heart
That the poor soldier that so richly fought,
Whose rags shamed gilded arms, whose naked breast
Stepped before shields of proof, cannot be found,
He shall be happy that can find him, if
Our grace can make him so.

BELLARIUS. I never saw
Such noble fury in so poor a thing.

10 CYMBELINE. No tidings of him?

PISANIO. He hath been searched among the dead and living,
But no trace of him.

CYMBELINE. To my grief, I am
The heir of his reward, (*to* Bellarius, Guiderius and
Arviragus) which I will add
To you, the liver, heart and brain of Britain,
By whom I grant she lives. 'Tis now the time
To ask of whence you are. Report it.

BELLARIUS. Sir,

20 In Cambria are we born, and gentlemen.
Further to boast were neither true nor modest,
Unless I add, we are honest.

CYMBELINE. Bow your knees.
Arise my knights o'th' battle; I create you
Companions to our person and will fit you
With dignities becoming your estates.

Enter Cornelius *and ladies.*

There's business in these faces. Why so sadly
Greet you our victory? You look like Romans,
And not o'th' court of Britain.

30 CORNELIUS. *Hail, great king!*
To sour your happiness, I must report
The queen is dead.

CYMBELINE. *Dead, say'st thou! How ended she?*

CORNELIUS. *With horror, madly dying, like herself,*
Who, being cruel to the world, concluded
Most cruel to herself. What she confessed
I will report, so please you. These her women
Can trip me, if I err; who with wet cheeks
Were present when she finished.

40 CYMBELINE. *Prithee, say.*

CORNELIUS. *First, she confessed she never loved you, only*
Affected greatness got by you.
Married your royalty, was wife to your place,
Abhorred your person.

CYMBELINE. *She alone knew this:*
And, but she spoke it dying, I would not
Believe her lips in opening it. Proceed.

CORNELIUS. *Your daughter, whom she bore in hand to love*
With such integrity, she did confess
50 *Was as a scorpion to her sight; whose life,*
But that her flight prevented it, she had
Ta'en off by poison.

CYMBELINE. *Oh, most delicate fiend!*
Who is't can read a woman? Is there more?

CORNELIUS. *More, sir, and worse. She did confess she had*
For you a mortal mineral, which being took,
Should by the minute feed on life and lingering
By inches waste you. In which time she purposed,
By watching, weeping, tendance, to o'ercome
60 *You with her show. Yes, and in time to work*
Her son into th' adoption of the crown:
But failing of her end by his strange absence,
Grew shameless, desperate, opened, in despite
Of heav'n and men, her purposes, repented
The ills she hatched, were not effected; so
Despairing died.

CYMBELINE. *Heard you all this, her women?*

LADY. *We did, so please your highness.*

CYMBELINE. *Mine eyes*

70 *Were not in fault, for she was beautiful;*
Mine ears, that heard her flattery; nor my heart,
That thought her like her seeming. It had been vicious
To have mistrusted her: yet, oh my daughter!
That it was folly in me, thou may'st say,
And prove it in thy feeling. Heav'n mend all.

Enter Lucius, Iachimo, *and other* Roman *prisoners,*
Leonatus *behind, and* Imogen.

Thou com'st not, Caius, now for tribute; that
The Britains have razed out, though with the loss
Of many a bold one; whose kinsmen have made suit
That their good souls may be appeased with slaughter
80 Of you their captives, which ourselves have granted.
So think of your estate.

LUCIUS. Consider, sir, the chance of war. The day
Was yours by accident; had it gone with us,
We should not, when the blood was cool, have threatened
Our prisoners with the sword. But since the gods
Will have it thus, that nothing but our lives
May be called ransom, let it come. Sufficeth
A Roman with a Roman's heart can suffer.
Augustus lives to think on't; and so much
90 For my peculiar care. This one thing only
I will entreat: my boy, a Briton born,
Let him be ransomed. Never master had
A page so kind, so duteous, diligent,
So tender over his occasion,
He hath done no Briton harm
Though he hath served a Roman. Save him, sir,
And spare no blood beside.

CYMBELINE. I've surely seen him;
His favor is familiar to me. Boy,
100 Thou hast looked thyself into my grace,
I know not why, nor wherefore,
To say, "Live, boy." Ne'er thank thy master, live;
And ask of Cymbeline what boon thou wilt,
Fitting my bounty and thy state, I'll give it.
Know'st him thou look'st on? Speak,
Wilt have him live? Is he thy kin? thy friend?

IMOGEN. He is a Roman, no more kin to me
Than I to your highness; who being born your vassal,
Am something nearer.

110 CYMBELINE. Wherefore eye'st him so?
IMOGEN. I tell you, sir, in private, if you please
To give me hearing.
CYMBELINE. Aye, with all my heart.
And lend my best attention. What's thy name?
IMOGEN. Fidele, sir.
CYMBELINE. Thou'rt my good youth, my page,
I'll be thy master. Walk with me; speak freely. (*Go aside.*)
BELLARIUS. Is not this boy revived from death?
ARVIRAGUS. One sand another
120 Not more resembles than he th' sweet rosy lad
Who died, and was Fidele. What think you?
GUIDERIUS. The same dead thing alive.
BELLARIUS. Peace, peace; see further.
PISANIO (*aside*). It is my mistress.
Since she is living, let the time run on
To good or bad.
CYMBELINE. Come, stand thou by our side.
Make thy demand aloud. (*To* Iachimo.) Sir, step you forth,
Give answer to this boy, and do it freely,
130 Or, by our greatness and the grace of it,
Which is our honor, bitter torture shall
Winnow the truth from falsehood. On, speak to him.
IMOGEN. My boon is, that this gentleman may render
Of whom he had this ring.
POSTHUMUS (*aside, wondering*). What's that to him?
CYMBELINE. That diamond upon your finger, say,
How came it yours?
IACHIMO. Thou'lt torture me to leave unspoken that
Which to be spoke would torture thee.
140 CYMBELINE. How! me?
IACHIMO. I am glad to be constrained to utter what
Torments me to conceal. By villainy
I got this ring. 'Twas Leonatus' jewel,
Whom thou didst banish; and—which more may grieve thee,
As it doth me—a nobler sir ne'er lived
'Twixt sky and ground. Wilt thou hear more, my lord?
CYMBELINE. All that belongs to this.
IACHIMO. That paragon, thy daughter,
For whom my heart drops blood, and my false spirits
150 Quail to remember. Give me leave; I faint. (*Swoons.*)
CYMBELINE. My daughter! what of her? Renew thy strength.
I had rather thou should'st live, while nature will,

Than die ere I hear more. Strive, man, and speak!
IACHIMO. Upon a time,—unhappy was the clock
That struck the hour!—it was in Rome—accursed
The mansion where!—'twas at a feast,—Oh, would
Our viands had been poisoned, or at least
Those which I heaved to head!—the worthy Posthumus—
CYMBELINE. I stand on fire. Come to the matter.
160 IACHIMO. Your daughter's chastity—there it begins.
He spoke of her, as Dian had hot dreams,
And she alone were cold; whereat I, wretch,
Made scruple of his praise, and waged with him
Pieces of gold 'gainst this which he then wore
Upon his honored finger, to attain
In suit the place of's bed and win this ring
By hers and mine adultery. Away to Britain
Post I in this design. Well may you, sir,
Remember me at court, where I was taught
170 By your chaste daughter the wide difference
'Twixt amorous and villainous.
Yet, to be brief, my practice so prevailed,
That I returned with similar proof, enough
To make the noble Leonatus mad,
By wounding his belief in her renown
With tokens thus, and thus; that he could not
But think her bond of chastity quite cracked,
I having ta'en the forfeit. Whereupon,—
Me thinks I see him now—
180 POSTHUMUS (*coming forward*). Aye, so thou dost,
Italian fiend! Aye me, most credulous fool,
Egregious murderer, thief, any thing
That's due to all the villains past, in being,
To come! Oh, give me cord, knife, or poison,
Some upright justicer! Thou, king, send out
For torturers ingenious; it is I
That all th' abhorred things o'th' earth amend,
By being worse than they. I am Posthumus,
That killed thy daughter. Villain-like, I lie,
190 That caused a lesser villain than myself,
A sacrilegious thief, to do't. The temple
Of virtue was she; yes, and she herself
Spit, and throw stones, cast mire upon me, set
The dogs o'th' street to bait me: every villain
Be called Posthumus Leonatus, and

Be villainy less than 'twas. Oh, Imogen!
My queen, my life, my wife! Oh, Imogen,
Imogen, Imogen!

IMOGEN. Peace, my lord; hear, hear—

200 POSTHUMUS. Away, thou scornful page; there is no peace for me. (*Striking her; she falls.*)

PISANIO. Oh, gentlemen, help!
Mine and your mistress! Oh, my lord Posthumus!
You ne'er killed Imogen 'till now. Help, help!
Mine honored lady!

CYMBELINE. Does the world go round?

POSTHUMUS. How come these staggers on me?

PISANIO. Wake, my mistress.

CYMBELINE. If this be so, the gods do mean to strike me
To death with mortal joy.

210 IMOGEN. Why did you throw your wedded lady from you?
Think that you are upon a rock, and now
Throw me again.

POSTHUMUS. Hang there like fruit, my soul,
'Till the tree die.

CYMBELINE. My child! my child!
My dearest Imogen.

IMOGEN (*kneeling*). Your blessing, sir.

BELLARIUS. Though you did love this youth, I blame you not,
You had a motive for't.

220 CYMBELINE. My tears that fall
Prove holy water on thee! Imogen,
Thy mother's dead.

IMOGEN. I'm sorry for't, my lord.

CYMBELINE. Oh, she was naught; and long of her it was
That we meet here so strangely. But her son
Is gone, we know not how nor where.

GUIDERIUS. Let me end the story; 'twas I that slew him.

CYMBELINE. The gods forefend.
I would not thy good deeds should from my lips
230 Pluck a hard sentence. Prithee, valiant youth,
Deny't again.

GUIDERIUS. I have spoke it, and I did it.

CYMBELINE. He was a prince.

GUIDERIUS. A most uncivil one. The wrongs he did me
Were nothing prince-like; for he did provoke me
With language that would make me spurn the sea,
If it could so roar to me. I cut off's head,

And am right glad he is not standing here
To tell this tale of mine.

240 CYMBELINE. Bind the offender,
And take him from our presence.

BELLARIUS. Stay, sir king,
This man is better than the man he slew,
As well descended as thyself, and hath
More of thee merited than a band of Clotens
Had ever scar for. Let his arms alone,
They were not born for bondage.

CYMBELINE. Why, old soldier,
Wilt thou undo the worth thou art unpaid for,
250 By tasting of our wrath? how of descent
As good as we?

BELLARIUS. I am too blunt and saucy; here's my knee.
Mighty sir,
These two gentlemen that call me father,
And think they are my sons, are none of mine,
They are the issue of your loins, my liege,
And blood of your begetting.

CYMBELINE. How! my issue?

BELLARIUS. So sure as you, your father's. I, old Morgan,
260 Am that Bellarius whom you sometime banished;
Your pleasure was at once my offence, my punishment
Itself, and all my treason. These gentle princes,
For such and so they are, these twenty years
Have I trained up; those arts they have that I
Could put into them. But, gracious sir,
Here are your sons again; and I must lose
Two of the sweet'st companions in the world.
The benediction of these covering heav'ns
Fall on their heads like dew! for they are worthy
270 To inlay heav'ns with stars.

CYMBELINE. Thou weep'st and speak'st.
The service that you three have done is more
Unlike than this thou tell'st. I lost my children:
If these be they, I know not how to wish
A pair of worthier sons. Guiderius had
Upon his neck a mole, a sanguine star.
It was a mark of wonder.

BELLARIUS. This is he!
Who hath upon him still that natural stamp;
280 It was wise nature's end, in the donation,

To be his evidence now.
CYMBELINE. Oh, what am I
A mother to the birth of three? Ne'er mother
Rejoiced deliverance more. Blest may you be,
That, after this strange starting from your orbs,
You may reign in them now. Oh, Imogen,
Thou hast lost by this a kingdom.
IMOGEN. No, my lord;
I have got two worlds by't. Oh, my gentle brothers,
290 Have we thus met? Oh, never say hereafter
But I am truest speaker. You called me brother,
When I was but your sister; I you brothers,
When ye were so indeed.
CYMBELINE. Did you e'er meet?
ARVIRAGUS. Aye, my good lord.
GUIDERIUS. And at first meeting loved.
CYMBELINE. All o'erjoyed
Save these in bonds. Let them be joyful too,
For they shall taste our comfort.
300 IMOGEN. My good master, I will yet do you service.
LUCIUS. Happy be you.
CYMBELINE. The forlorn soldier that so nobly fought,
He would have well becomed this place, and graced
The thankings of a king.
POSTHUMUS. I am, sir,
The soldier that did company these three
In poor beseeming; 'twas a fitment for
The purpose I then followed. That I was he,
Speak, Iachimo, I had you down, and might
310 Have made your finish.
IACHIMO (*kneels*). I am down again:
But now my heavy conscience sinks my knee,
As then your force did. But your ring first,
And here the bracelet of the truest princess
That ever swore her faith. Now take that life,
Beseech you, which I so often owe.
POSTHUMUS. Kneel not to me.
The power that I have on you is to spare you;
The malice towards you to forgive you. Live,
320 And deal with others better.
CYMBELINE. Nobly doomed!
We'll learn our freeness of a son-in-law;
Pardon's the word to all. Laud we the gods;

And let our crooked smokes climb to their nostrils
From our blest altars. Publish we this peace
To all our subjects. Set we forward: let
A Roman and a British ensign wave
Friendly together: so through Lud's town march,
And in the temple of great Jupiter
330 Our peace we'll ratify. Seal it with feasts.
Set on there. Never was a war did cease,
Ere bloody hands were washed, with such a peace.

Exeunt omnes.

Finis

A Midsummer Night's Dream 1763

A

MIDSUMMER-NIGHT'S

DREAM.

By Mr. *WILLIAM SHAKESPEAR.*

LONDON:

Printed for J. TONSON, and the rest of the PROPRIETORS; and sold by the Booksellers of *London* and *Westminster.*

MDCCXXXIV.

Facsimile title page of Garrick's promptbook
Folger Shakespeare Library

Dramatis Personae

THESEUS, *Duke of* Athens
EGEUS, *an* Athenian *Lord*
LYSANDER, *in love with* Hermia
DEMETRIUS, *in love with* Hermia
QUINCE, *the Carpenter*
SNUG, *the Joiner*
BOTTOM, *the Weaver*
FLUTE, *the Bellows-mender*

---

0. DRAMATIS PERSONAE] in his manuscript notes to his alteration of the play, preserved in the Folger Shakespeare Library, Garrick made a tentative, and revised, cast list for the play. It is given here as he made it, with the actual performers in the 1763 production, when different, indicated in brackets:
Lysander, ~~Obrien~~ Vernon; Egeus, ~~Bransby~~ Burton; Theseus, ~~Harvard~~ Bransby; Bottom & Pyramus, Yates; Quince & Progne, Blakes [Love]; Demetrius, Holland > Love [W. Palmer]; Flute & Thisby, ~~To~~[mlinson?] Phillips [Baddeley]; Snout & Wall, ~~Perry~~ ~~Philips~~ Ackman; Philostrate, Packer; Starveling & Moonshine, ~~Perry~~ Parsons; Snug & Lyon, Clough; Philomel; ~~Moonshine~~ Prologue, Vaughan; ~~Wall~~; K. of Fairies, ~~Miss Mathews~~ ~~M. Cautherly~~ ~~M. Burton~~ [Miss Rogers]; Puck, ~~Cautherly~~ ~~Atkins~~ [Master Cape]; 1st Fairy, ~~Hart~~ ~~Miss Matthews~~ [Miss Wright]; Cobweb, ~~Atkins~~ Castle; Hermia, ~~Pritchard~~ ~~Pope~~ ~~Vincent~~ [Miss Young]; Helena, ~~Macklin~~ ~~Miss Vincent~~ Pope [Miss Vincent]; Hippolita, ~~Glen~~ Hopkins; Queen, ~~Miss Lemson~~ Rogers [Miss Ford]; Moth, ~~Pope~~; Peasblossom, ~~Blagdon~~. The 1973 edition (Colman's version) lists the cast as follows: Theseus—Bransby; Egeus—Burton; Lysander—Vernon; Demetrius—W. Palmer; Quince—Love; Bottom—Yates; Flute—Baddeley; Starveling—Parsons; Hippolita—Mrs. Hopkins; Hermia—Miss Young; Helena—Mrs. Vincent; Snout—Ackman; Snug—Clough; Oberon—Miss Rogers; Titania—Miss Ford; Puck—Master Cape; Fairies—Miss Wright, Master Raworth, &c.

SNOUT, *the Tinker*

10 STARVELING, *the Taylor*

HIPPOLITA, *Princess of the* Amazons, *betrothed to* Theseus

HERMIA, *daughter to* Egeus, *in love with* Lysander

HELENA, *in love with* Demetrius.

Attendants.

OBERON, *King of the Fairies*

TITANIA, *Queen of the Fairies*

PUCK, *or* Robin-goodfellow, *a Fairy*

PEASEBLOSSOM
COWWEB
MOTH
20 MUSTARDSEED } Fairies

Other Fairies attending on the King and Queen.

SCENE Athens, *and a wood not far from it.*

A Midsummer Night's Dream

ACT I.

SCENE [I]. Athens.

[CHORUS.]

Enter Theseus *and* Hippolita, *with attendants.*

THESEUS. Now, fair Hippolita, our nuptial hour
Draws on apace; four happy days bring in
Another moon. But oh, methinks how slow
This old moon wanes! She lingers my desires
Like to a step-dame or a dowager,
Long withering out a young man's revenue.
HIPPOLITA. Four days will quickly steep themselves in nights,
And then the moon, like to a silver bow
New bent in heaven, shall behold the night
10 Of our solemnities.
THESEUS. Go, Philostrate,
Stir up th' Athenian youth to merriments,
Awake the pert and nimble spirit of mirth,
Turn melancholy forth to funerals.
The pale companion is not for our pomp.

Exit Philostrate.

---

0. CHORUS] *G* indicates an opening chorus on his alteration, but the text is not given.
7. in nights] the following *S* line is omitted: "Four nights will quickly dream away the time." (Unless otherwise noted, the *S* lines are from the Tonson edition of 1734 as edited by Theobald.)

Hippolita, I wooed thee with my sword
And won thy love doing thee injuries.
But I will wed thee in another key,
With pomp, with triumph, and with revelling.

Enter Egeus, Hermia, Lysander, *and* Demetrius.

20 EGEUS. Happy be Theseus, our renowned Duke!
THESEUS. Thanks, good Egeus. What's the news with thee?
EGEUS. Full of vexation come I with complaint
Against my child, my daughter Hermia.
Stand forth, Demetrius. My noble lord,
This man hath my consent to marry her.
Stand forth, Lysander. And my gracious Duke
This hath bewitched the bosom of my child.
Thou, thou, Lysander, thou hast given her rhymes
And interchanged love-tokens with my child.
30 With cunning hast thou filched my daughter's heart,
Turned her obedience, which is due to me,
To stubborn harshness. And, my gracious Duke,
Be't so she will not here before your Grace
Consent to marry with Demetrius,
I beg the ancient privilege of Athens;
As she is mine, I may dispose of her,
Which shall be either to this gentleman
Or to her death, according to our law
Immediately provided in that case.
40 THESEUS. What say you, Hermia? Be advised, fair maid.
Demetrius is a worthy gentleman.
HERMIA. So is Lysander.
THESEUS. In himself he is;

29. my child] next six *S* lines are omitted:

Thou hast by moonlight at her window sung,
With feigning voice, verses of feigning love,
And stol'n the impression of her fantasie
With bracelets of thy hair, rings, gawds, conceits,
Knacks, trifles, nosegays, sweetmeats (messengers
Of strong prevailment in unhardened youth).

40. fair maid] next five *S* lines are omitted:

To you your father should be as a god,
One that compos'd your beauties; yea, and one
To whom you are but as a form in wax
By him imprinted, and within his power
To leave the figure, or disfigure it.

But in this kind, wanting your father's voice
The other must be held the worthier.

HERMIA. I would my father looked but with my eyes.

THESEUS. Rather your eyes must with his judgment look.

HERMIA. I do intreat your Grace to pardon me.
I know not by what power I am made bold,
50 Nor how it may concern my modesty
In such a presence here to plead my thought.
But I beseech your Grace that I may know
The worst that may befall me in this case
If I refuse to wed Demetrius.

THESEUS. Either to die the death, or to abjure
For ever the society of men.
Therefore, fair Hermia, question your desires,
Know of your youth, examine well your blood,
Whether, not yielding to your father's choice
60 You can endure the livery of a nun
Thrice blessed they that master so their blood,
But earthlier happy is the rose distilled
Than that which, withering on the virgin thorn,
Grows, lives, and dies in single blessedness.

HERMIA. So will I grow, so live, so die, my lord,
Ere I will yield my virgin patent up
Unto his lordship, to whose unwished yoke
My soul consents not to give sovereignty.

[SONG.]

[With mean disguise let others nature hide,
70 And mimic virtue with the paint of art;

---

50. concern] *G* underlined this word, wrote "affect" in the margin, cancelled the word, wrote "impeach" in its place, and probably, judging by the nature of the markings, cancelled that emendation.

60. a nun] *G* cancelled the next three *S* lines: "For aye to be in shady cloister mew'd / To live a barren sister all your life, / Chanting faint hymns to the cold fruitless moon?"

61. blood] the following *S* line is cancelled: "To undergo such maiden pilgrimage."

62. earthlier] *G* corrects Tonson's text, which reads "earlier."

68.1. SONG] *G* merely indicated in the margin of the Tonson text where songs were to be introduced, usually numbering them consecutively. In his manuscript notes, preserved in the Folger Shakespeare Library, he listed the songs to be used. This first one, taken from *G*'s *The Fairies*, has its source in two stanzas of James Hammond's "Elegy IX."

I scorn the cheat of reason's foolish-pride,
And boast the graceful weakness of my heart.
The more I think, the more I feel my pain,
And learn the more each heavenly charm to prize,
While fools, too light for passion, safe remain,
And dull sensation keep the stupid wise.]

THESEUS. Take time to pause, and by the next new moon
(The sealing day betwixt my love and me,
For everlasting bond of fellowship)
80 Upon that day either prepare to die
For disobedience to your father's will,
Or else to wed Demetrius, as he would,
Or on Diana's altar to protest
For aye austerity and single life.
DEMETRIUS. Relent, sweet Hermia; and Lysander, yield
Thy crazed title to my certain right.
LYSANDER. You have her father's love, Demetrius;
Let me have Hermia's. Do you marry him.
EGEUS. Scornful Lysander! True, he hath my love;
90 And what is mine my love shall render him.
And she is mine and all my right of her
I do estate unto Demetrius.
LYSANDER. I am, my lord, as well derived as he,
As well possessed. My love is more than his,
My fortune's every way as fairly ranked
(If not with vantage) as Demetrius'.
And (which is more than all these boasts can be)
I am beloved of beauteous Hermia.
Why should not I then prosecute my right?
100 Demetrius (I'll avouch it to his head)
Made love to Nedar's daughter, Helena,
And won her soul; and she, sweet lady, dotes,
Devoutly dotes, dotes in idolatry,
Upon this spotted and inconstant man.
THESEUS. I must confess that I have heard so much,
And with Demetrius thought t'have spoke thereof;
But being over-full of self-affairs,
My mind did lose it. But, Demetrius, come.
And come, Egeus. You shall go with me;
110 I have some private schooling for you both.
For you, fair Hermia, look you arm yourself
To fit your fancies to your father's will;

Or else the law of Athens yields you up
To death or to a vow of single life.
Come, my Hippolita; what cheer, my love?
Demetrius and Egeus, go along;
I must employ you in some business
Against our nuptials and confer with you
Of something nearly that concerns yourselves.

120 EGEUS. With duty and desire we follow you.

Exeunt

Manent Lysander *and* Hermia.

LYSANDER. Hermia, for ought that ever I could read,
Could ever hear by tale or history,
The course of true love never did run smooth,
But either it was different in blood—
Or else it stood upon the choice of friends—
Or if there were a sympathy in choice,
War, death, or sickness did lay siege to it,
Making it momentary as a sound,
Swift as a shadow, short as a dream,

130 Brief as the lightning in the collied night
That in a spleen unfolds both heaven and earth;
And ere a man hath power to say, Behold!
The jaws of darkness do devour it up,
So quick bright things come to confusion.

HERMIA. If then true lovers have been ever crossed,
Oh, let us teach our trial patience!
Because it is a customary cross
As due to love as thoughts and dreams and sighs,

---

113. you up] the following *S* line, "(Which by no means we may extenuate)," is cancelled.

121. Hermia, for . . .] four preceding lines of interchange between Lysander and Hermia are omitted:

LYS. How now, my love? Why is your cheek so pale?
How chance the roses there do fade so fast?
HER. Belike for want of rain, which I could well
Beteem them from the tempest of my eyes.

124. in blood] three following *S* lines are omitted: "HER. O cross! too high to be enthrall'd to love. / LYS. Or else misgraffed, in respect of years— / HER. O spite! too old to be engag'd too young."

125. of friends] the following *S* line, "O hell! to choose love by another's eye," is omitted.

135. crossed] the next *S* line, "It stands as an edict in destiny," is cancelled.

136. Oh] Then *S*.

Wishes and tears, poor fancy's followers!

140 LYSANDER. A good persuasion; therefore hear me, Hermia.
I have a widow aunt, a dowager.
From Athens is her house removed seven leagues,
And she respects me as her only son.
There, gentle Hermia, may I marry thee,
And to that place the sharp Athenian law
Cannot pursue us. If thou lov'st me, then
Steal forth thy father's house tomorrow night;
And in the wood, a league without the town,
Where I did meet thee once with Helena
150 To do observance to the morn of May,
There will I stay for thee.

[SONG.]

[When that gay season did us lead
To the tanned hay-cock in the mead,
When the merry bells rung round,
And the rebecks brisk did sound,
When young and old came forth to play
On a sunshine holiday.

Let us wander far away
Where the nibbling flocks do stray
160 O'er the mountain's barren breast,
Where laboring clouds do often rest
O'er the meads with daisies pied,
Shallow brooks and rivers wide.]

HERMIA. My good Lysander,
I swear to thee by Cupid's strongest bow,
By his best arrow with the golden head,
By the simplicity of Venus' doves,
By all the vows that ever men have broke,

---

141. a dowager] the next *S* line, "Of great revenue, and she hath no child," is cancelled.

151.1. SONG] this second song, also in *The Fairies*, is taken from Milton's "L'Allegro."

167. Venus' doves] three following lines of *S*,
"By that which knitteth souls and prospers loves / And by that fire which burn'd the Carthage queen / When the false Trojan under sail was seen," are cancelled, possibly by Colman, whose excisions are lighter, more tentative than *G*'s.

168. broke] *G* has cancelled the next line, "In number more than ever women spoke."

In that same place thou hast appointed me,
170 Tomorrow truly will I meet Lysander.

LYSANDER. Keep promise, love. Look, here comes Helena.

Enter Helena.

HERMIA. Good speed, fair Helena, whither away?

HELENA. Call you me fair? That fair again unsay,
Demetrius loves you fair.

[SONG.]

[O Hermia fair, O happy, happy fair,
Your eyes are loadstars, and your tongue's sweet air
More tuneable than lark to shepherd's ear,
When wheat is green, when hawthorn buds appear;
O teach me how you look, and with what art
180 You sway the motions of your lover's heart.]

Sickness is catching: oh, were favor so,
Yours would I catch, fair Hermia.
My ear should catch your voice, my eye your eye,
My tongue should catch your tongue's sweet melody.
O teach me how you look, and with what art
You sway the motion of Demetrius' heart.

---

170. Lysander] with thee *S*. The handwriting suggests that the change is by Colman.

172. Good] God *S*.

174.1. SONG] this third song, again from *The Fairies*, is taken from *S*, I, i, 182–85, 192–93, with "O Hermia fair" added at the beginning and "Demetrius" in the last *S* line changed to "your lover's." The last two lines are inadvertently repeated by *G* as 185–86.

182. Yours would I] *G* here restores Shakespeare's words for Tonson's "Your words I'd" but omits the *S* line ending, "ere I go."

184. sweet melody] two following lines are cancelled, possibly by Colman: "Were the world mine, Demetrius being bated, / The rest I'll give to be to you translated."

186. Demetrius' heart] eight following lines are cancelled:

HER. I frown upon him; yet he loves me still.
HEL. O that your frowns would teach my smiles such skill!
HER. I give him curses; yet he gives me love.
HEL. O that my prayers could such affection move!
HER. The more I hate, the more he follows me.
HEL. The more I love, the more he hateth me.
HER. His folly, Helena, is no fault of mine.
HEL. None but your beauty. Would that fault were mine!

In the seventh line *G* had again restored Shakespeare's reading, "no fault," for "none" in Tonson.

HERMIA. Take comfort. He no more shall see Hermia.
Lysander and myself will fly this place.

[SONG.]

Before the time I did Lysander see,
190 Seemed Athens like a paradise to me;
O then, what graces in my love do dwell,
That he hath turned a heaven into a hell!

LYSANDER. Helen, to you we will unfold our minds;
Tomorrow night, when Phoebe doth behold
Her silver visage in the wat'ry glass,
Decking with liquid pearl the bladed grass
(A time to lovers flights is still propitious),
Through Athens' gate have we devised to steal.
HERMIA. Farewell, sweet play-fellow; pray thou for us.
200 Keep word, Lysander; we must starve our sight
From lover's food 'till morrow deep midnight.

Exit Hermia.

---

187. Hermia] my face *S*. From the autograph the change seems to be Colman's and is in accordance with his opposition to rhyme in the play.

188.1. SONG] the fourth song is directly from *S*, with "unto a hell" changed to "into a hell" (Tonson's "into hell").

193. Helen, to you . . .] Shakespeare's line is, "Helen, to you our minds we will unfold." Again, *G* had corrected the Tonson "to your minds" before the revision, probably in Colman's hand, was made. The change avoids a rhyme.

196–97. Decking with . . .] Colman enclosed these lines in brackets to suggest excision. The changes in the second line, from "A time that lovers' flights doth still conceal" in *S* to "to lovers' flights is still propitious," are probably in Colman's hand.

198. to steal] the first six lines of Hermia's following speech are omitted:

> And in the wood, where often you and I
> Upon faint primrose beds were wont to lie,
> Emptying our bosoms of their counsel sweet,
> There my Lysander and myself shall meet,
> And thence from Athens turn away our eyes
> To seek new friends and strange companions.

Before the excision *G* had changed "swell'd" in line 3 to "sweet."

199. for us] the next line of *S*, "And good luck grant thee thy Demetrius," is cancelled.

201. From lover's . . .] this line, originally marked for omission, is restored by *G*. The last part, " 'till . . . midnight," is marked out and an unreadable change is made, "for many a ——." Whether *G*'s stet was meant to restore the line as Shakespeare had it is not clear.

LYSANDER. I will, my Hermia. Helena, adieu.
As you on him, Demetrius dote on you.

Exit Lysander.

HELENA. How happy some o'er other some can be!
Through Athens I am thought as fair as Hermia.
But what of that; Demetrius thinks not so.
Yet ere he looked on Hermia's eyes, he swore,
He hailed down oaths that he was only mine.
I will go tell him of fair Hermia's flight.
210 Then to the wood will he tomorrow night
Pursue her; and for this intelligence
If I have thanks, it is a dear reward.

[SONG.]

[Against myself why all this art?
To glad my eyes I grieve my heart;
To give him joy I court my bane!
And with his sight enrich my pain.]

Exit Helena.

---

205. as Hermia] as she *S.*

206. not so] thirteen lines are marked for omission:

> He will not know what all but he do know.
> And as he errs, doting on Hermia's eyes,
> So I, admiring of his qualities,
> Things base and vile, holding no quantity,
> Love can transpose to form and dignity.
> Love looks not with the eyes, but with the mind;
> And therefore is wing'd Cupid painted blind.
> Nor hath Love's mind of any judgment taste;
> Wings, and no eyes, figure unheedy haste.
> And therefore is Love said to be a child,
> Because in choice he is so oft beguil'd.
> As waggish boys themselves in game forswear,
> So the boy Love is perjur'd everywhere.

Lines 7–12 make up the seventh song in *The Fairies.*

207. Yet ere . . .] for ere Demetrius look'd on Hermia's eyne *S.*

208. only mine] two following lines are omitted: "And when this hail some heat from Hermia felt, / So he dissolv'd, and shw'rs of oaths did melt." From the markings we judge that Colman first indicated the desirability of excising the lines, probably in deference to contemporary taste, by lightly bracketing them, and then Garrick marked them out with heavy lines.

212. reward] expense *S.* The change seems to be Colman's. The following two lines are omitted: "But herein mean I to enrich my pain, / To have his sight thither and back again."

212.1. SONG] in the prompt *G* marks this fifth song as "New."

[SCENE II.] Quince's *house.*

Enter Quince, Snug, Bottom, Flute, Snout, *and* Starveling.

QUINCE. Is all our company here?

BOTTOM. You were best to call them generally, man by man, according to the scrip.

QUINCE. Here is the scroll of every man's name which is thought fit through all Athens to play in our interlude before the Duke and Duchess on his wedding day at night.

BOTTOM. First, good Peter Quince, say what the play treats on; then read the names of the actors; and so grow on to a point.

QUINCE. Marry, our play is the most lamentable comedy and most cruel
10 death of Pyramus and Thisby.

BOTTOM. A very good piece of work, I assure, and a merry. Now, good Peter Quince, call forth your actors by the scroll. Masters, spread yourselves.

QUINCE. Answer as I call you. Nick Bottom the weaver.

BOTTOM. Ready. Name what part I am for, and proceed.

QUINCE. You, Nick Bottom, are set down for Pyramus.

BOTTOM. What is Pyramus, a lover or a tyrant?

QUINCE. A lover that kills himself most gallantly for love.

BOTTOM. That will ask some tears in the true performing of it. If I do
20 it, let the audience look to their eyes; I will move storms; I will condole in some measure. To the rest—yet my chief humour is for a tyrant. I could play Ercles rarely, or a part to tear a cat in. "To make all split the raging rocks, and shivering shocks shall break the locks of prison gates—and Phibbus' car shall shine from far, and make and mar the foolish Fates"—This was lofty! Now name the rest of the players. This is Ercles' vein, a tyrant's vein. A lover is more condoling.

QUINCE. Francis Flute the bellows-mender.

FLUTE. Here, Peter Quince.

30 QUINCE. Flute, you must take Thisby on you.

FLUTE. What is Thisby, a wand'ring knight?

QUINCE. It is the lady that Pyramus must love.

FLUTE. Nay, faith, let not me play a woman. I have a beard coming.

QUINCE. That's all one. You shall play it in a mask, and you may speak as small as you will.

BOTTOM. An I may hide my face, let me play Thisby too. I'll speak in

---

30. Flute] *G* restore's Shakespeare's reading. The Tonson text omits Flute's name.

a monstrous little voice, "Thisne, Thisne." "Ah, Pyramus my lover dear, thy Thisby dear, and lady dear."

QUINCE. No, no, you must play Pyramus; and Flute, you Thisby.

40 BOTTOM. Well, proceed.

QUINCE. Robin Starveling the tailor.

STARVELING. Here, Peter Quince.

QUINCE. Robin Starveling, you must play Thisby's mother. Tom Snout the tinker.

SNOUT. Here, Peter Quince.

QUINCE. You, Pyramus's father; myself, Thisby's father; Snug the joiner, you the lion's part. I hope there is a play fitted.

SNUG. Have you the lion's part written? Pray you, if it be, give it me, for I am slow of study.

50 QUINCE. You may do it extempore, for it is nothing but roaring.

BOTTOM. Let me play the lion too. I will roar that I will do any man's heart good to hear me. I will roar that I will make the Duke say, "Let him roar again; let him roar again."

QUINCE. If you should to it too terribly, you would fright the Dutchess and the ladies, that they would shriek, and that were enough to hang us all.

ALL. That would hang us every mother's son.

BOTTOM. I grant you, friends, if you should fright the ladies out of their wits, they would have no more discretion but to hang us; but
60 I will aggravate my voice so that I will roar you as gently as any sucking dove; I will roar you an 'twere any nightingale.

QUINCE. You can play no part but Pyramus, for Pyramus is a sweet-faced man, a proper man as one shall see in a summer's day, a most lovely gentleman-like man. Therefore you must needs play Pyramus.

BOTTOM. Well, I will undertake it. What beard were I best to play it in?

QUINCE. Why, what you will.

BOTTOM. I will discharge it in either your straw-color beard, your orange-tawney beard, your purple-in-grain beard, your perfect yellow.

70 QUINCE. But masters, here are your parts, and I am to entreat you, request you, and desire you to con them by tomorrow night; and meet me in the palace-wood, a mile without the town, by moonlight. There we will rehearse; for if we meet in the city, we shall be dogged

---

68. grain beard] *G* omits the following: "or your French crown-colour'd beard."

70. But masters] *G* omits the preceding sentence, "Some of your French crowns have no hair at all, and then you will play barefac'd."

with company and our devices known. In the meantime I will draw a bill of properties such as our play wants. I pray you fail me not.

BOTTOM. We will meet, and there we may rehearse more obscenely and courageously. Take pains; be perfect. Adieu.

QUINCE. At the Duke's oak we meet.

BOTTOM. Enough. Hold, or cut bowstrings.

[SONG—*for Epilogue.*]

[*By* Quince, Bottom, Snug, Flute, Starveling, Snout.]

80 [QUINCE. Most noble Duke, to us be kind;
Be you and all your courtiers blind,
That you may not our errors find,
But smile upon our sport.
For we are simple actors all,
Some fat, some lean, some short, some tall;
Our pride is great, our merit small;
Will that, pray, do at court?

II.

STARVELING. The writer too of this same piece,
Like other poets here of Greece,
90 May think all swans that are but geese
And spoil your princely sport.
Six honest folks we are, no doubt,
But scarce know what we've been about,
And tho' we're honest, if we're out,
That will not do at court.

III.

BOTTOM. Shall tinkers, weavers, tailors dare
To strut and bounce like any player.
And show you all what fools we are,
And that way make you sport?
100 Our lofty parts we could not hit,
For what we undertook unfit;
Much noise indeed, but little wit,
That will not do at court.

79.1. SONG] *G* lists "Comic characters Epilogue" on his manuscript sheet of songs as his sixth. It is given here as printed in the 1763 Colman text. He places the number at Bottom's next-to-last speech in the scene, perhaps intending to have the epilogue sung before the final speeches of Quince and Bottom.

A Midsummer Night's Dream, II, iii
Folger Shakespeare Library

IV.

FLUTE. O would the Duke and Dutchess smile,
The court would do the same a while,
But call us after, low and vile,
And that way make their sport.
Nay, would you still more pastime make,
And at poor we your purses shake,
110 What'er you give, we'll gladly take,
For that will do at court.]

Exeunt.

ACT II.

[SCENE I. *Wood near* Athens.]

Enter a Fairy *at one door, and* Puck *at another.*

PUCK. Now now, spirit? Whither wander you?
FAIRY. Over hill, over dale,
Through bush, through briar.
Over park, over pale,
Through flood, through fire,
I do wander everywhere
Swifter than the moon's sphere;
And I serve the Fairy Queen
To dew her orbs upon the green.
10 The cowslips tall her pensioners be;
In their gold coats spots you see,
Those be rubies, fairy savors;
In those freckles live their favors.
I must go seek some dew-drops here,
And hang a pearl in every cowslip's ear.

[SONG.]

[Where the bee sucks, there lurk I.
In a cowslip's bell I lie;

---

0. *Wood near* Athens] added by *G*; "or Robin-goodfellow" in *S* eliminated after "Puck."

15.1. SONG] *G*'s seventh is Ariel's lyric in *The Tempest* (V, i, 88 ff.) as set by Arne, which is also in *The Fairies*. Again the word "suck" in the first line is changed to "lurk," following Theobald.

There I couch when owls do cry.
On the bat's back I do fly
20 After sunset merrily.
Merrily, merrily shall I live now,
Under the blossom that hangs on the bough.]

Farewell, thou lob of spirits; I'll be gone.
Our Queen and all her elves come here anon.
PUCK. The King doth keep his revels here tonight.
Take heed the Queen come not within his sight,
For Oberon is passing fell and wrath,
Because that she, as her attendant, hath
A lovely boy stolen from an Indian king;
30 She never had so sweet a changeling.
And jealous Oberon would have the child
Knight of his train, to trace the forests wild;
But she perforce withholds the loved boy,
Crowns him with flowers, and makes him all her joy.
And now they never meet in grove or green,
By fountain clear or spangled starlight sheen,
But they do square, that all their elves for fear
Creep into acorn cups and hide them there.
FAIRY. Or I mistake your shape and making quite,
40 Or else you are that shrewd and knavish sprite
Called Robin Goodfellow.
PUCK. Thou speak'st aright;
I am that merry wanderer of the night.
I jest to Oberon and make him smile
When I a fat and bean-fed horse beguile,
Neighing in likeness of a silly foal.
And sometimes lurk I in a gossip's bowl
In very likeness of a roasted crab,
And when she drinks, against her lips I bob

---

41. Goodfellow] the remainder of the *S* line and eight following lines are cut:

Are you not he
That frights the maidens of the villagery;
Skim milk, and sometimes labor in the quern,
And bootless made the breathless huswife churn;
And sometimes made the drink to bear no barm;
Mislead night-wanderers, laughing at their harm?
Those that Hobgoblin call you, and sweet Puck,
You do their work, and they shall have good luck.
Are you not he?

The emendation, made with his characteristic thin line, may be Colman's.

50 And on her withered dewlap pour the ale.
The wisest aunt, telling the saddest tale,
Sometime for three-foot stool mistaketh me;
Then slip I from her bum, down topples she,
And rails or cries, and falls into a cough,
And then the whole quire hold their hips and loffe,
And waxen in their mirth, and neeze, and swear
A merrier hour was never wasted there.
But make room, fairy, here comes Oberon.
FAIRY. And here my mistress. Would that he were gone.

Enter Oberon, King of Fairies, *at one door with his train, and the* Queen *at another with hers.*

60 OBERON. Ill met by moonlight, proud Titania.
QUEEN. What, jealous Oberon? Fairy, skip hence.
I have forsworn his bed and company.
OBERON. Tarry, rash wanton. Am not I thy Lord?
QUEEN. Then I must be thy lady. Why art thou here,
Come from the farthest step of India?
But that, forsooth, the bouncing Amazon,
Your buskined mistress and your warrior love,
To Theseus must be wedded, and you come
To give their bed joy and prosperity.
70 OBERON. How can'st thou thus for shame, Titania,
Glance at my credit with Hippolita,
Knowing I know thy love to Theseus?
Didst thou not lead him through the glimmering night
From Perigune, whom he ravished,
And make him with fair Egle break his faith,
With Ariadne, and Antiopa?
QUEEN. These are the forgeries of jealousy;
And never since that middle summer's spring
Met we on hill, in dale, forest, or mead,
80 By paved fountain or by rushy brook,
Or on the beached margent of the sea,
To dance our ringlets to the whistling wind,

---

54. rails or] tailor *S.*
64. thy lady] approximately four following lines are omitted: "but I know / When thou hast stol'n away from fairyland / And in the shape of Corin sat all day, / Playing on pipes of corn, and versing love / To am'rous Phillida."
65. step] steep *S.*
78. that] the *S.*

But with thy brawls thou hast disturbed our sport.
The spring, the summer,
The chiding autumn, angry winter, change
Their wonted liveries; and th' amazed world
By their increase now knows not which is which.
And this same progeny of evil comes
From our debate, from our dissention.
90 We are their parents and original.

OBERON. Do you amend it then; it lies in you.
Why should Titania cross her Oberon?
I do but beg a little changeling boy
To be my henchman.

QUEEN. Set your heart at rest;
The fairyland buys not the child of me.
His mother was a votress of my order,
And in the spiced Indian air by night
Full often she hath gossipped by my side
100 And sat with me on Neptune's yellow sands,
Marking th' embarked traders of the flood,
When we have laughed to see the sails conceive
And grow big-bellied with the wanton wind,

---

83. our sport] *G* omits twenty-three and a half following lines:

Therefore the winds, piping to us in vain,
As in revenge, have suck'd up from the sea
Contagious fogs; which, falling in the land,
Hath every pelting river made so proud
That they have overborne their continents.
The ox hath therefore stretch'd his yoke in vain,
The plowman lost his sweat, and the green corn
Hath rotted ere his youth attain'd a beard;
The fold stands empty in the drowned field,
And crows are fatten'd with the murrion flock;
The nine-men's morris is fill'd with mud;
And the queint mazes in the wanton green
For lack of tread are undistinguishable.
The human mortals want their winter cheer;
No night is now with hymn or carol blest.
Therefore the moon, the governess of floods,
Pale in her anger, washes all the air,
That rheumatic diseases do abound.
And thorough this distemperature we see
The seasons alter. Hoary-headed frosts
Fall in the fresh lap of the crimson rose;
And on old Hyem's chin and icy crown
An ordorous chaplet of sweet summer buds
Is, as a mockery, set.

Which she with pretty and with swimming gate
Would imitate, and sail upon the land
To fetch me trifles, and return again
As from a voyage, rich with merchandise.
But she, being mortal, of that boy did die,
And for her sake I do rear up her boy;
110 And for her sake I will not part with him.

OBERON. How long within this wood intend you stay?

QUEEN. Perchance 'till after Theseus' wedding day.
If you will patiently dance in our round,
And see our moonlight revels, go with us;
If not, shun me, and I shall spare your haunts.

OBERON. Give me that boy, and I will go with thee.

QUEEN. Not for thy fairy kingdom. Elves, away.
We shall chide downright if I longer stay.

Exeunt.

[SONG.]

[QUEEN. Away, away,
120 I will not stay,
But fly from rage and thee.

KING. Begone, begone,
You'll feel anon
What 'tis to injure me.

QUEEN. Away, false man!
Do all you can,
I scorn your jealous rage!

KING. We will not part;
Take you my heart!
130 Give me your favorite page.

QUEEN. I'll keep my page!

KING. And I my rage!
Nor shall you injure me.

QUEEN. Away, away!
I will not stay,
But fly from rage and thee.

BOTH. Away, away, &c.]

Exeunt.

---

104. swimming gate] the next line, "Following (her womb then rich with my young squire)," is omitted.

118.1. SONG] *G* lists this as his eighth song in the manuscript notes.

OBERON. Well, go thy way; thou shalt not from this grove
'Till I torment thee for this injury—
140 My gentle Puck, come hither. Thou rememberest
Since once I sat upon a promontory,
And heard a mermaid on a dolphin's back
Uttering such dulcet and harmonious breath,
That the rude sea grew civil at her song,
And certain stars shot madly from their spheres,
To hear the sea-maid's music.

PUCK. I remember.

OBERON. That very time I saw, but thou could'st not,
Flying between the cold moon and the earth,
150 Cupid all armed; a certain aim he took
At a fair vestal, throned by the west,
And loosed his love-shaft smartly from his bow,
As it should pierce a hundred thousand hearts;
But I might see young Cupid's fiery shaft
Quenched in the chaste beams of the wat'ry moon.
And the Imperial votress passed on,
In maiden meditation, fancy-free.
Yet, marked I where the bolt of Cupid fell.
It fell upon a little western flower;
160 Before, milk-white, now purple with love's wound,
And maidens call it love-in-idleness.
Fetch me that flower, the herb I showed thee once;
The juice of it on sleeping eyelids laid
Will make a man or woman madly dote
Upon the next live creature that it sees.
Fetch me this herb, and be thou here again
Ere the Leviathan can swim a league.

PUCK. I'll put a girdle round about the earth
In forty minutes.

Exit.

170 OBERON. Having once this juice,
I'll watch Titania when she is asleep
And drop the liquor of it in her eyes.
The next thing which she, waking, looks upon
(Be it on lion, bear, or wolf, or bull,
Or medling monkey, or on busy ape)

---

140. rememberest] a tentative excision of the next twenty-one lines is indicated but not carried out. Again, this may be an example of Colman's "crochets."

She shall pursue it with the soul of love.
And ere I take this charm off from her sight
(As I can take it with another herb)
I'll make her render up her page to me.
180 But who comes here? I am invisible,
And I will overhear their conference.

Enter Demetrius, Helena *following him.*

DEMETRIUS. I love thee not; therefore pursue me not.
Where is Lysander and fair Hermia?
Thou told'st me they were stolen into this wood.
Hence get thee gone, and follow me no more.
HELENA. You draw me on; I cannot help but follow.
Leave you your power to draw, Demetrius,
And I shall have no power to follow you.
DEMETRIUS. Do I entice you? Do I speak you fair?
190 Or rather do I not in plainest truth
Tell you I do not and I cannot love you?
HELENA. For that do I love thee more.
Spurn me, scorn me,
Neglect me, lose me; only give me leave,
Unworthy as I am, to follow you.
DEMETRIUS. Tempt not too much the hatred of my spirit,
For I am sick when I do look on thee.
HELENA. And I am sick when I look not on you.
DEMETRIUS. You do impeach your modesty too much
200 To leave the city and commit yourself
Into the hands of one that loves you not,
To trust the opportunity of night

183. fair Hermia] the next line in *S*, "This one I'll slay, the other slayeth me," is omitted.

184. this wood] the next two lines of *S* are omitted: "And here am I, and wode within this wood / Because I cannot meet my Hermia."

186. on; I cannot . . .] you hard-hearted adamant! *S*.
The next line and a half of *S* are cancelled: "But yet you draw not iron, for my heart / Is true as steel." The remainder of the line is emended by adding "Demetrius" at the end.

192. For that] *G* omits the opening words, "And even," and "the" before "more." Then two and a half lines are cancelled: "I am your spaniel; and, Demetrius, / The more you beat me, I will fawn on you. / Use me but as your spaniel."

193. scorn me] strike me *S*.

195. follow you] three following lines are omitted: "What worser place can I beg in your love / (And yet a place of high respect with me) / Than to be used as you use your dog?"

And the ill counsel of a desert place
With the rich worth of your virginity.
HELENA. Your virtue is my privilege; for that
It is not night when I do see your face.
Therefore I think I am not in the night,
Nor doth this wood lack worlds of company,
For you in my respect are all the world.
210 DEMETRIUS. I'll run from thee and hide me in the brakes,
And leave thee to the mercy of wild beasts.
HELENA. The wildest hath not such a heart as you;
Run when you will, the story shall be changed.
Apollo flies, and Daphne holds the chase;
The dove pursues the griffin; the mild hind
Makes speed to catch the tiger.
DEMETRIUS. I will not stay thy questions; let me go.
Or if you follow me, do not believe
But I shall do thee mischief in the wood.

Exit Demetrius.

220 HELENA. Ay, in the temple, in the town and field
You do me mischief. Fie, Demetrius!
Your wrongs do set a scandal on my sex.

[SONG.]

[Our softer sex can't fight for love,
As rougher men may do;
In gentle sighs our passion move,
We should be wooed, not woo.]

Exit.

OBERON. Fare thee well, nymph; ere he doth leave this grove
Thou shalt fly him, and he shalt seek thy love.
Hast thou the flower there? Welcome, wanderer.

Enter Puck.

---

209. the world] two following lines are omitted: "Then how can it be said I am alone, / When all the world is here to look on me?"

216. tiger] the remainder of the line and the one following are omitted: "Bootless speed, / When cowardice pursues, and valour flies."

222.1. SONG] *G* labels the ninth song "New." It is based on the first two of four *S* lines here omitted: "We cannot fight for love, as men may do; / We shou'd be woo'd, and were not made to woo. / I'll follow thee, and make a heaven of hell / To die upon the hand I love so well."

230 PUCK. Ay, there it is.

OBERON. I pray thee give it me;
I know a bank whereon the wild thyme blows,
Where oxslip and the nodding violet grows,
O'er canopied with luscious woodbine,
With sweet musk-roses and with eglantine.
There sleeps Titania sometime of the night,
Lulled in these flowers, with dances and delight;
And there the snake throws her enameled skin,
Weed wide enough to wrap a fairy in.
240 And with the juice of this I'll streak her eyes,
And make her full of hateful fantasies.
Take thou some of it and seek through this grove;
A sweet Athenian lady is in love
With a disdainful youth. Anoint his eyes,
But do it when the next thing he espies
May be the lady. Thou shalt know the man
By the Athenian garments he hath on.
Effect it with some care, that he may prove
More fond of her than she upon her love;
250 And look you meet me ere the first cock crow.

PUCK. Fear not, my lord; your servant shall do so.

[SONG.]

[Come, follow, follow me,
Ye fairy elves that be;
O'er tops of dewy grass,
So nimbly do we pass;
The young and tender stalk
Ne'er bends where we do walk.]

Exit.

[ACT III. SCENE I.]

Enter Queen *of fairies, with her train.*

QUEEN. Come, now a roundel, and a fairy song.
Then for the third part of a minute hence,

251.1. SONG] for his tenth song *G* notes, "May sing or not." Colman's printed version precedes this song with the notation, "*Enter* Second Fairy, *with a troop of Fairies.*" The song is in *The Fairies.*

Some to kill cankers in the musk-rose buds,
Some war with rearmice for their leathern wings
To make my small elves' coats, and some keep back
The clamorous owl, that nightly hoots and wonders
At our queint spirits. Sing me now asleep.
Then to your offices, and let me rest.

FAIRIES (*sing*). You spotted snakes with double tongue,
10 Thorny hedgehogs, be not seen,
Newts and blindworms, do no wrong,
Come not near our fairy Queen.
Philomel with melody
Sing in your sweet lullaby,
Lulla, lulla, lullaby; lulla, lulla, lullaby:
Never harm nor spell nor charm
Come our lovely lady nigh.
So good night with lullaby.

FAIRY II (*sings*). Weaving spiders come not here;
20 Hence you long-legged spinners, hence.
Beetles black approach not near;
Worm nor snail do no offence.
Philomel with melody, &c.

FAIRY I (*sings*). Hence away; now all is well.
One aloof stand sentinel.

Exeunt Fairies.

Enter Oberon.

OBERON. What thou seest when thou dost wake,
Do it for thy true love take;
Love and languish for his sake.
Be it ounce or cat or bear,
30 Pard or boar with bristled hair,
In thy eye what shall appear,
When thou wak'st, it is thy dear.
Wake when some vile thing is near.

Exit Oberon.

Enter Lysander *and* Hermia.

LYSANDER. Fair love, you faint with wand'ring in the wood;
And to speak truth, I have forgot our way.

9. You spotted . . .] for this eleventh song *G* again indicates, "May sing." It is in *S*.

We'll rest us, Hermia, if thou think it good,
And tarry for the comfort of the day.

HERMIA. Be't so, Lysander; find you out a bed,
For I upon this bank will rest my head.

40 LYSANDER. One turf shall serve as pillow for us both,
One heart, one bed, two bosoms, and one troth.

[DUET.]

[Not the silver doves that fly,
Yoked in Cytherea's car,
Are so beauteous to the eye
Are so choicely matched by far.

Not the wings that bear aloft
The gay sportive god of love
Are so lovely bright and soft,
Or with more consent do move.]

50 [HERMIA. My gentle friend, for love and courtesy
Permit me this one boon: let my faint limbs
Recruit their weariness 'till dawn appears,
And thou, Lysander, on that bank repose,

41.1. DUET] in his manuscript notes *G* lists this twelfth song as a duet for Lysander and Hermia. It was set by Smith. Following it, twenty-one and a half lines are rewritten and condensed by *G* into ten lines (4–59). *S* has:

HER. Nay, good Lysander. For my sake, my dear,
Lie further off yet; do not lie so near.
LYS. O take the sense, sweet, of my innocence!
Love takes the meaning in love's conference.
I mean that my heart unto yours is knit,
So that but one heart we can make of it;
Two bosoms interchained with an oath—
So then two bosoms and a single troth.
Then by your side no bed-room me deny;
For lying so, Hermia, I do not lie.
HER. Lysander riddles very prettily.
Now much beshrew my manners and my pride
If Hermia meant to say Lysander lied!
But, gentle friend, for love and courtesy
Lie further off, in humane modesty;
Such separation, as may well be said,
Becomes a virtuous bachelor and a maid.
So far be distant; and good night, sweet friend.
Thy love ne'er alter till thy sweet life end!
LYS. Amen, amen, to that fair prayer say I,
And then end life when I end loyalty.
Here is my bed.

For if perchance my woman's fears should seek
Protection in thy love and bravery,
I may not call on love and thee in vain.

LYSANDER. My honor is the best security for thine.
Repose thee, love; I'll watch thee thro' the night,
Nor harm shall reach the–
60 Sleep give thee all his rest.]

HERMIA. With half that wish, the wisher's eyes be prest!

They sleep.

Enter Puck.

PUCK. Through the forest have I gone,
But Athenian find I none
On whose eyes I might approve
This flower's force in stirring love.
Night and silence! who is here?
Weeds of Athens he doth wear.
This is he my master said
Despised the fair Athenian maid?
70 And there the maiden sleeping sound
On the dank and dirty ground.
Pretty soul! she durst not lie
Near to this kill-curtesie.
[But first I'll throw this youth into a trance
That fairy sprites may round him dance.
Melting sounds your power impart
That I may pierce his hardened heart.

Music.

LYSANDER. Whence is this sweet enchanting harmony?
A thicker shade o'erspreads the night! My senses
80 Some secret unknown influence feels–
I cannot shake it off; chains invisible
Already bind my limbs, and all my powers enthrall. (Lysander *sinks down.*)]

[PUCK. 'Tis done, 'tis done; and now my skill
His breast with other love shall fill.
Churl, upon thy eyes I throw

---

69. fair] added by *G.*
70. there] here *S.*
73. Near to . . .] *G* omits the following "this lack-love" of *S.* *G* then adds eleven lines, 73–83.

All the power this charm doth owe.
When thou wak'st, let love forbid
Sleep his seat on thy eyelid.
So awake when I am gone,
90 For I must now to Oberon.

Exit.]

Enter Demetrius *and* Helena *running.*

HELENA. Stay, tho' thou kill me, sweet Demetrius!
DEMETRIUS. I charge thee hence, and do not haunt me thus.
HELENA. O wilt thou, my love, leave me? Do not so.
DEMETRIUS. Stay on thy peril. I alone will go.

Exit Demetrius.

HELENA. O I am out of breath in this fond chase;
The more my prayer, the lesser is my favor.
Happy is Hermia, wheresoe'er she bides.
She hath attractive and bewitching eyes.
What wicked and dissembling glass of mine
100 Made me compare with Hermia's sphery eyes?
But who is here? Lysander on the ground!
Dead or asleep? I see no wound, no blood.
Lysander, if you live, good sir, awake.
LYSANDER. And run thro' fire for thee, sweet Helena. (*Waking.*)
Where is Demetrius? Oh, how fit a word
Is that vile name to perish on my sword!
HELENA. Do not say so, Lysander, say not so;
What tho' he loves your Hermia? What of that?

---

93. my love] darkling *S.*
96. favor] grace *S.*
98. She hath . . .] For she hath blessed and attractive eyes *S.* The next six lines are omitted:

> How came her eyes so bright? Not with salt tears.
> If so, my eyes are oft'ner wash'd than hers.
> No, no, I am as ugly as a bear;
> For beasts that meet me run away for fear.
> Therefore no marvel though Demetrius
> Do, as a monster, fly my presence thus.

The passage is lightly encircled, possibly by Colman.
100. eyes] eyne *S.* The change avoids a rhyme.
102. no blood] no blood, no wound *S.* The change avoids a rhyme.
104. for thee] I will for thy sweet sake *S.* Again the change eliminates a rhyme. Two following lines are omitted: "Transparent Helen, Nature here shows art / That through thy bosom makes me see thy heart."
108. What of that] Lord, what though? *S.*

Yet Hermia still loves you; be satisfied.

110 LYSANDER. Content with Hermia? No! I do repent
The tedious minutes I with her have lost.
Not Hermia, but Helena I love:
Who will not change a raven for a dove?
The will of man is by his reason swayed,
And reason says you are the worthier maid.
Reason becomes the marshal to my will
And leads me to your eyes, where I can read
Love's stories written in love's richest book.

HELENA. But wherefore this?

120 When at your hands did I deserve this scorn?
Is't not enough, is't not enough, Lysander,
That I did never, no, nor ever can
Deserve a sweet look from Demetrius
But you must flout my insufficiency?
Good troth, you do me wrong; good sooth, you do,
To woo one in such disdainful terms.
But fare you well.
I thought you lord of more true gentleness.

Exit.

LYSANDER. She sees not Hermia. Hermia, sleep thou there,

130 And never may'st thou come Lysander near.
For as a surfeit of the sweetest things
The deepest loathing to a stomach brings,
Or as the heresies that men do leave
Are hated most of those they did deceive,
So thou, my surfeit and my heresie,
Of all be hated, but the most of me.

---

109. be satisfied] then be content *S.*

111. lost] spent *S.* The change avoids the rhyme.

115. worthier maid] three following lines are omitted: "Things growing are not ripe until their season; / So I, being young, till now ripe not to reason, / And touching now the point of human skill."

117. can read] o'erlook *S.*

119. But wherefore this?] Wherefore was I to this keen mockery born? *S.*

121. Lysander] young man *S.*

122. ever] never *S.*

123. Demetrius] Demetrius' eye *S.* The alteration avoids a rhyme.

126. To woo . . .] in such disdainful manner me to woo *S.* Again a rhyme is avoided.

128. gentleness] two following lines of Helena are omitted: "Oh, that a lady, of one man refus'd, / Should of another therefore be abus'd!"

HERMIA. Help me, Lysander, help me. Do thy best
To pluck this crawling serpent from my breast.
Ay me, for pity, what a dream was here?
140 Lysander, look how I do quake with fear.
Methought a serpent eat my heart away,
And you sat smiling at his cruel prey.
Lysander! What, removed? Lysander, lord!
What, out of hearing? Gone? No sound, no word?
Alack, where are you? Speak, and if you hear,
Speak of all loves. I swoon almost with fear.

[SONG.]

[Sweet soothing hope, whose magic art
Transforms our night to day,
Dispel the clouds that wrap my heart
150 With thy enliv'ning ray.
Thus when the sky with noxious steams,
Has been obscured awhile,
The sun darts forth his piercing beams
And makes all nature smile.]

Exit.

[SCENE II.]

Enter Quince, Snug, Bottom, Flute, Snout, *and* Starveling.

The Queen of Fairies lying asleep.

BOTTOM. Are we all met?

QUINCE. Pat, pat; and here's a marvellous convenient place for our rehearsal. This green plot shall be our stage, this hawthorn our tiring house, and we will do it in action as we will do before the Duke.

BOTTOM. Peter Quince!

QUINCE. What say'st thou, bully Bottom?

BOTTOM. There are things in this comedy of *Pyramus and Thisby* that

146. with fear] two lines are marked for excision, perhaps tentatively and by Colman: "No? Then I well perceive you are not nigh. / Either death or you I'll find immediately." The rhyme would have bothered Colman.

146.1. SONG] *G* adds a marginal note that the thirteenth song is to be "Sweet soothing hope &c." In his manuscript notes he lists this as "Sweet Tooth[d] hope," set by Smith.

will never please. First, Pyramus must draw a sword and kill himself, which the ladies cannot abide. How answer you that?

10 SNOUT. By'r lakin, a parlous fear!

STARVELING. I believe we must leave the killing out, when all is done.

BOTTOM. Not a whit; I have a device to make all well. Write me a prologue, and let the prologue seem to say, we will do no harm with our swords, and that Pyramus is not killed indeed; and for more better assurance tell them that I, Pyramus, am not Pyramus, but Bottom the weaver. This will put them out of fear.

QUINCE. Well, we will have such a prologue, and it shall be written in eight and six.

BOTTOM. No, make it two more; let it be written in eight and eight.

20 SNOUT. Will not the ladies be afraid of the lion?

STARVELING. I fear it, I promise you.

BOTTOM. Masters, you ought to consider with yourselves. To bring in, God shield us, a lion among ladies is a most dreadful thing; for there is not a more fearful wildfowl than your lion living, and we ought to look to it.

SNOUT. Therefore another prologue must tell he is not a lion.

BOTTOM. Nay, you must name his name, and half his face must be seen through the lion's neck, and he himself must speak through, saying thus or to the same defect: "Ladies,"—or "Fair ladies,—I would 30 wish you"—or "I would request you"—or "I would entreat you—not to fear, not to tremble. My life for yours! If you think I come hither as a lion, it were pity of my life. No, I am no such thing. I am a man as other men are." And there indeed let him name his name and tell them plainly he is Snug the joiner.

QUINCE. Well, it shall be so. But there is two hard things, that is, to bring the moonlight into a chamber; for, you know, Pyramus and Thisby meet by moonlight.

SNUG. Doth the moon shine that night we play our play?

BOTTOM. A calendar, a calendar! Look in the almanac. Find out moon- 40 shine, find out moonshine.

QUINCE. Yes, it doth shine that night.

BOTTOM. Why then may you leave a casement of the great chamber window where we play open and the moon may shine in at the casement.

QUINCE. Ay, or else one must come in with a bush of thorns and a lanthorn and say he comes to disfigure or to present the person of Moonshine. Then there is another thing. We must have a wall in the great chamber, for Pyramus and Thisby (says the story) did talk through the chink of a wall.

50 SNUG. You can never bring in a wall. What say you, Bottom?

BOTTOM. Some man or other must present Wall; and let him have some plaster, or some loam, or some roughcast about him, to signify wall. Or let him hold his fingers thus; and through the cranny shall Pyramus and Thisby whisper.

QUINCE. If that may be, then all is well. Come, sit down every mother's son and rehearse your parts. Pyramus, you begin. When you have spoken your speech, enter into that brake, and so every one according to his cue.

SCENE [III].

Enter Puck.

PUCK. What hempen homespuns have we swaggering here,
So near the cradle of the Fairy Queen?
What, a play toward? I'll be an auditor—
An actor too perhaps, if I see cause.

QUINCE. Speak, Pyramus. Thisby, stand forth.

PYRAMUS. Thisby, the flower of odious savors sweet—

QUINCE. Odors, odors!

PYRAMUS. Odors savors sweet;
So doth thy breath, my dearest Thisby dear.
10 But hark, a voice! Stay thou but here a while,
And by and by I will to thee appear.

Exit Pyramus.

PUCK (*aside*). A stranger Pyramus than e'er played here.

THISBY. Must I speak now?

QUINCE. Ay, marry must you, for you must understand he goes but to see a noise that he heard and is to come again.

THISBY. Most radiant Pyramus, most lily white of hue;
Of color like the red rose on triumphant brier,
Most brisky juvenile, and eke most lovely Jew,
As true as truest horse that yet would never tire,
20 I'll meet thee, Pyramus, at Ninny's tomb.

QUINCE. Ninus' tomb, man! Why, you must not speak that yet; that you answer to Pyramus. You speak all your part at once, cues and all. Pyramus enter. Your cue is past; it is *never tire.*

Enter [Bottom (*with an*) *ass's head*].

23.1. *Enter* Bottom . . .] *Enter* Pyramus *S*.

THISBY. O as true as truest horse, that yet would never tire.
PYRAMUS. If I were fair, Thisby, I were only thine.
QUINCE. O monstrous! O strange! We are haunted. Pray masters, fly masters, help.

The Clowns exeunt.

PUCK. I'll follow you; I'll lead you about a round,
Through bog, through bush, through brake, through brier.
30 Sometimes a horse I'll be, sometimes a hound,
A hog, a headless bear, sometimes a fire.
And neigh, and bark, and grunt, and roar, and burn,
Like horse, hound, hog, bear, fire, at every turn.

Exit.

BOTTOM. Why do they run away? This is a knavery of them to make me afeard.

Enter Snout.

SNOUT. O Bottom, thou art changed. What do I see on thee?

Exit Snout.

BOTTOM. What do you see? You see an ass-head of your own, do you?

Enter Quince.

QUINCE. Bless thee, Bottom, bless thee, thou art translated.

Exit.

BOTTOM. I see their knavery. This is to make an ass of me, to fright me
40 if they could; but I will not stir from this place, do what they can. I will walk up and down here, and I will sing, that they shall hear I am not afraid. (*Sings.*)

The ousel-cock, so black of hue,
With orange-tawny bill,
The throstle with his note so true,
The wren with little quill,

QUEEN (*awaking*). What angel wakes me from my flow'ry bed?

BOTTOM (*sings*). The finch, the sparrow, and the lark
The plain-song cuckow gray,
50 Whose note full many a man doth mark.
And dares not answer nay.

34. BOTTOM] *Enter* Bottom *with an Ass-head S.*

For indeed, who would set his wit to so foolish a bird? Who would give a bird the lie, tho he cry cuckow never so?

QUEEN. I pray thee, gentle mortal, sing again;
Mine ear is much enamored of thy note.
So is mine eye enthralled to thy shape,
On the first view to say, to swear, I love thee.

BOTTOM. Methinks, mistress, you should have little reason for that. And yet, to say the truth, reason and love keep little company together
60 now-a-days. The more the pity that some honest neighbors will not make them friends. Nay, I can gleek upon occasion.

QUEEN. Thou art as wise as thou art beautiful.

BOTTOM. Not so neither. But if I had wit enough to get out of this wood, I have enough to serve mine own turn.

QUEEN. Out of this wood do not desire to go;
Thou shalt remain here whether thou wilt or no.
I am a spirit of no common rate;
The summer still doth tend upon my state,
And I do love thee. Therefore go with me.
70 I'll give thee fairies to attend on thee,
And they shall fetch thee jewels from the deep
And sing while thou on pressed flowers dost sleep.
And I will purge thy mortal grossness so
That thou shalt like an airy spirit go.

SCENE [IV].

Enter Peaseblossom, Cobweb, Moth, Mustardseed, *and four* Fairies.

FAIRY I. Ready.

FAIRY II. And I.

FAIRY III. And I.

FAIRY IV. And I. Where shall we go?

QUEEN. Be kind and courteous to this gentleman.
Hop in his walks and gambol in his eyes;
Feed him with apricocks and dewberries,
With purple grapes, green figs and mulberries;

---

56. So is . . .] *G* restores the proper Shakespeare reading, the lines being confused in the Tonson text. Tonson has, "On the first view . . . / So is mine yey . . . / And thy fair virtue's force (perforce) doth move me." *G* indicates the proper sequence by numbering the three lines 3, 1, and 2. He then cancels the last line (marked 2).

The honey-bags steal from the humblebees,
10 And for night-tapers crop their waxen thighs
And light them at the fiery glowworm's eyes,
To have my love to bed and to arise;
And pluck the wings from painted butterflies
To fan the moonbeams from his sleeping eyes.
Nod to him elves, and do him courtesies.

FAIRY I. Hail, mortal, hail!

FAIRY II. Hail!

FAIRY III. Hail!

BOTTOM. I cry your worship's mercy heartily; I beseech your worship's
20 name.

COBWEB. Cobweb.

BOTTOM. I shall desire of you more acquaintance, good Master Cobweb. If I cut my finger, I shall make bold with you. Your name, honest gentleman?

PEASEBLOSSOM. Peaseblossom.

BOTTOM. I pray you commend me to Mistress Squash, your mother, and to Master Peasecod, your father. Good Master Peaseblossom, I shall desire of you more acquaintance too. Your name I beseech you, sir?

MUSTARDSEED. Mustardseed.

30 BOTTOM. Good Master Mustardseed, I know your patience well. That same cowardly, giant-like Ox-beef hath devoured many a gentleman of your house. I promise you your kindred hath made my eyes water ere now. I desire more of your acquaintance, good Master Mustardseed.

QUEEN. Come wait upon him; lead him to my bower.
The moon, methinks, looks with a watery eye,
And when she weeps, weep every little flower,
Lamenting some enforced chastity.
Tie up my love's tongue; bring him silently.

Exeunt.

SCENE [V. *Another wood*].

Enter King of Fairies *solus.*

OBERON. I wonder if Titania be awaked;
Then what it was that next came in her eye

---

39. silently] *G* had considered adding a song here, having written in his manuscript list "Fai. Queen—Sweetest creature" and then having crossed it out.

Which she must dote on in extremity?

Enter Puck.

Here comes my messenger! How now, mad sprite.
What night-rule now about this haunted grove?

PUCK. My mistress with a monster is in love.
Near to her close and consecrated bower,
While she was in her dull and sleeping hour,
A crew of patches, rude mechanicals
10 That work for bread upon Athenian stalls,
Were met together to rehearse a play
Intended for great Theseus' nuptial day.
The shallow'st thickskin of that barren sort,
Who Pyramus presented in their sport,
Forsook his scene and entered in a brake;
When I did him at this advantage take,
An ass's nole I fixed on his head;
When they him spy,
As wild geese that the creeping fowler eye
20 Sever themselves and madly sweep the sky,
So at his sight away his fellows fly,
And at our stamp here o'er and o'er one falls;
He murder cries, and help from Athens calls.
I led them on in this distracted fear,
And left sweet Pyramus translated there;
When in that moment (so it came to pass)
Titania waked, and straitway loved an ass.

OBERON. This falls out better than I could devise.
But hast thou yet latched the Athenian's eyes
30 With the love-juice, as I did bid thee do?

PUCK. I took him sleeping (that is finished too),
And the Athenian woman by his side,
That when he wakes of force she must be eyed.

---

17. his head] G omits the line and a half following: "Anon his Thisby must be answered, / And forth my minnock comes."

19. fowler eye] two following lines are omitted: "Or russet-pated choughs, many in sort, / Rising and cawing at the gun's report."

23. Athens calls] four following lines are cancelled: "Their sense thus weak, lost with their fears thus strong, / Made senseless things begin to do them wrong. / For briars and thorns at their apparel snatch; / Some sleeves, some hats—from yielders all things catch."

SCENE [VI].

Enter Demetrius and Hermia.

OBERON. Stand close. This is the same Athenian.
PUCK. This is the woman, but not this the man.
DEMETRIUS. O why rebuke you him that loves you so?
HERMIA. Now I but chide, but I should use thee worse,
For thou, I fear, hast given me cause to curse thee.
If thou hast slain Lysander in his sleep,
Oh, kill me too.
The sun was not so true unto the day
As he to me. Would he have stol'n from hence
10 From sleeping Hermia?
It cannot be but thou hast murdered him.
DEMETRIUS. Why, gentle Hermia, will you still persist
To pierce me thro' the heart with your contempt?

[SONG.]

[How calm my soul in this blest hour,
How undisturbed my breast;
True love at length resumes his power,
And brings me peace and rest.

My faith and truth now stand confessed,
I now no longer roam.

3. you so] the next line of *S* is omitted: "Lay breath so bitter on your bitter foe."
10. sleeping Hermia] the remainder of the *S* line and three following are marked for omission:
"I'll believe as soon / This whole earth may be bor'd, and that the moon / May through the center creep, and so displease / Her brother's noontide with th' Antipodes."
11. murdered him] five lines are here omitted:

So should a murtherer look, so dread, so grim.
DEM. So should the murthered look, and so should I,
Pierc'd through the heart with your stern cruelty.
Yet you, the murtherer, look as bright, as clear
As yonder Venus in her glimmering sphere.

G then adds a two-line speech for Demetrius (12–13).
13.1. SONG] *G* indicates on his manuscript list that Demetrius here "may sing. How calm the Sky," a song he had included in *The Fairies* for Hermia. It is the fourteenth song on his list and differs from Colman's in the 1763 edition.

20 My heart with Hermia was a guest;
With Helen 'tis at home.]

HERMIA. What's this to my Lysander? Where is he?
Ah good Demetrius, give him my wishes!
DEMETRIUS. I'ad rather give his carcass to the dogs.
HERMIA. Thou drivest me past the bounds
Of maiden's patience. Hast thou slain him then?
And hast thou killed him sleeping?
Henceforth be never numbered among men.
Thou serpent!
30 DEMETRIUS. I am not guilty of Lysander's blood,
Nor is he dead for ought that I can tell.
HERMIA. Then from thy hated presence will I go
In search of my Lysander, come what may.

[SONG.]

[I'll range all around 'till I find out my love,
O'er mountains, in valleys, thro' deserts I'll rove;
Nor distance, nor danger, nor death can affright,
For love gives me courage, and wings for my flight.]

Exit.

DEMETRIUS. There is no following her in this fierce vein.
Upon this bank I will a while repose me.

---

23. give . . . wishes] wilt thou give him me *S.*
24. the dogs] my hounds *S.* The change avoids a rhyme.
25. Thou drivest] the first half line of *S*, "Out, dog! out, cur!" is omitted.
27. And hast . . .] the line is added by *G.*
28. among men] *G* here cancels seven lines, retaining only "Thou serpent!" (line 21) from the sixth:

O! once tell true, and even for my sake
Durst thou have look'd upon him, being awake?
And hast thou kill'd him sleeping? O brave touch!
Could not a worm, an adder do as much?
An adder did it; for with double[r] tongue
Than thine, thou serpent, never adder stung.
DEM. You spend your passion on a mispris'd mood.

31. can tell] three following lines are omitted: "HER. I pray thee tell me then that he is well. / DEM. And if I could, what would I get therefore? / HER. A privilege never to see me more."
32. Then] And *S.* will I go] part I so *S.*
33. In search . . .] See me no more, whether he be dead or no *S.*
33.1. SONG] on his manuscript list *G* labels this fifteenth song as "New."
39. Upon this bank . . .] Here therefore for a while I will remain *S.*

40 Sorrow's heaviness doth heavier grow
For debt that bankrupt sleep doth owe,
Which now is some slight measure it will pay. (*Lies down.*)

SCENE [VII].

OBERON. What hast thou done? Thou hast mistaken quite
And laid thy love-juice on some true-love's sight!
About the wood go swifter than the wind,
And Helena of Athens see thou find.
By some illusion see thou bring her here;
I'll charm his eyes against she doth appear.
PUCK. I go, I go! Look how I go,
Swifter than arrow from the Tartar's bow.

[SONG.]

OBERON. Flower of this purple die,
10 Hit with Cupid's archery,
Sink in apple of his eye!
When his love he doth espy
Let her shine as gloriously
As the Venus of the sky.
When thou wak'st, if she be by,
Beg of her for remedy.

Enter Puck.

PUCK. Captain of our fairy band,
Helena is here at hand,

---

41. doth owe] doth sorrow owe *S*.
42. will pay] *G* omits the last line of the scene, "If for his tender here I make some stay."
2. love's sight] four lines following are cancelled:

Of thy misprison must perforce ensue
Some true-love turn'd, not a false turn'd true.
PUCK. The fate o'errules, that, one man holding troth,
A million fail, confounding oath on oath."

4. thou find] two lines following are cancelled:
"All fancy-sick she is, and pale of cheer, / With sighs of love that costs the fresh blood dear."
8.1. SONG] *G* first wrote "Song 16" at this point in the prompt copy, then marked out the word "Song." In the opposite margin he wrote "stet." Since he numbers the next song 17, we judge that he meant to restore Oberon's spoken lines in *S* as a song.

And the youth mistook by me
20 Pleading for a lover's fee.
Shall we their fond pageant see?
Lord, what fools these mortals be!

OBERON. Stand aside. The noise they make
Will cause Demetrius to awake.

PUCK. Then will two at once woo one;
That must needs be sport alone.
And those things do best please me
That befall prepost'rously.

SCENE [VIII].

Enter Lysander and Helena.

LYSANDER. Why should you think that I should woo in scorn?
Scorn and derision never come in tears.
Look, when I vow I weep, and vows so born
In their nativity all truth appears.

[SONG.]

[How can these sighs and tears seem scorn to you?
They are the signs of love—O think 'em true!]

HELENA. You do advance your cunning more and more.
These vows are Hermia's; give 'em not to me.

LYSANDER. I had no judgment when to her I swore.

10 HELENA. Nor none, in my mind, now you swear to me.

LYSANDER. Demetrius loves her, and he loves not you.

DEMETRIUS (*awaking*). Oh, Helen, goddess, nymph, perfect, divine,
To what, my love, shall I compare thine eyes?
Crystal is muddy. Oh, how ripe in show

4.1. SONG] numbered 17 in the prompt copy, this is an alteration of two Shakespeare lines at the same point in the text: "How can these things in me seem scorn to you, / Bearing the badge of faith to prove them true?"

7. and more] *G* deletes the next line, "When truth kills truth, O devilish-holy fray," revises the next from "These vows are Hermia's. Will you give her o'er?" and deletes the next three lines: "Weigh oath with oath, and you will nothing weigh. / Your vows to her and me, put in two scales, / Will even weigh, and both as light as tales."

10. swear to me] give her o'er *S*. The alteration eliminates the rhyme.

13. eyes] eyne *S*. Again, a rhyme is eliminated.

Thy lips, those kissing cherries, tempting grow!
HELENA. O spite, O hell! I see you all are bent
To set against me for your mirth—poor me!
If you are men, as men you are in show,
You would not use a simple woman thus?
20 You both are rivals and love Hermia,
And now both rivals to mock Helena,
A trim exploit, a manly enterprise.
In my poor eyes to conjure up the tears
With your derision; 'tis unkindly done.
LYSANDER. You are unkind, Demetrius; O forbear,
For you love Hermia; this you know I know.
And here with all good will, with all my heart,
In Hermia's love I yield you up my pretentions.
And yours of Helena to me bequeath,
30 Whom I do love, to death, to death, Demetrius.
HELENA. What cruel mocking of a simple maid!
DEMETRIUS. Lysander, keep thy Hermia, I will none;
If e'er I loved her, all that love is past.
My heart to Hermia was but as a guest,
And now to Helen it is home returned,

---

15. tempting grow] the remaining omissions in this scene are made with what we consider to be Colman's thin and rather hesitant line. The revised lines, on the other hand, are Garrick's autograph. Here four lines are circled for possible (?) omission: "That pure congealed white, high Taurus' snow, / Fann'd with the eastern wind, turns to a crow / When thou hold'st up thy hand. O let me kiss / This princess of pure white, this seal of bliss!" The same lines are omitted in *The Fairies*.
17. mirth—poor me] merriment *S*. A rhyme is avoided by the change. Then four lines are circled for omission: "If you were civil and knew courtesy, / You would not do me thus much injury. / Can you not hate me, as I know you do, / But you must join in souls to mock me too?"
19. simple woman thus] gentle lady so *S*. The change avoids a rhyme. The two following lines are circled for omission: "To vow and swear and superpraise my parts, / When I am sure you hate me with your hearts."
23. In my poor . . .] To conjure tears up in a poor maid's eyes *S*. The change eliminates the rhyme.
24. 'tis unkindly done] none of noble sort *S*. Then two lines are circled for omission: "Would so offend a virgin and extort / A poor soul's patience, all to make you sport."
28. pretentions] part *S*. Again, a rhyme is eliminated.
30. to death . . . Demetrius] and will do to my death *S*. *S* makes a rhyme.
31. What cruel . . .] Never did mockers waste more idle breath *S*.
33. past] gone *S*. The change avoids the rhyme.
34. Hermia was but as a guest] her but as guestwise sojurn'd *S*. A rhyme is avoided by the alteration.

There ever to remain.

LYSANDER. Helen, it is not so.

DEMETRIUS. Disparage not the faith thou dost not know,
Lest to thy peril thou repent, Lysander.
40 Look where thy love comes. Yonder is thy dear.

SCENE [IX].

Enter Hermia.

HERMIA. Dark night, that from the eye his function takes,
Has made my ear more quick of apprehension.
Thou art not by mine eye found, Lysander.
My faithful ear, I thank it, brought me to thee.
But why unkindly didst thou leave me, love?

LYSANDER. Why should he stay, whom love doth press to go?

HERMIA. What love could press Lysander from my side?

LYSANDER. Lysander's love, his love for Helena,
Fair Helena, who more engilds the night
10 Than all yon fiery stars. Why seek'st thou me?
Why seek'st thou me?

HERMIA. You speak not as you think, Lysander!

HELENA. Lo, she is one of this confed'racy.
Injurious Hermia, most ungrateful maid,
Have you conspired, have you with these contrived

---

37. Helen] Tonson omits the opening word of *S* in this line; *G* restores it.
39. repent, Lysander] abide it dear *S*.
2. Has made . . .] The ear more quick of apprehension makes *S*. The change avoids a rhyme. Two following lines are cancelled: "Wherein it doth impair the seeing sense, / It pays the hearing double recompense."
3. found, Lysander] Lysander, found *S*. The change avoids the rhyme.
4. faithful] not in *S*.
thee] thy sound *S*. A rhyme is avoided.
5. love] so *S*. A rhyme is avoided.
8. his love for Helena] that would not let him bide *S*. Again, a rhyme is avoided.
10. stars. Why seek'st thou me?] oes and eyes of light *S*. The question at the end of the line in *G* is a marginal addition; it is not clear if the intention was to eliminate the next line, which repeats the question.
11. thou me] the remainder of the line in *S* and the next line are omitted: "Could not this make thee know / The hate I bare thee made me leave thee so?"
12. Lysander] it cannot be *S*. A rhyme is avoided.
13. confed'racy] the next two lines are circled for omission: "Now I perceive they have conjoin'd all three / To fashion this false sport in spite of me."

To bait me with this foul derision?
Is all the counsel that we two have shared,
The sisters' vows, the hours that we have spent
When we have chid the hasty-footed time
20 For parting us. O and is all forgot?
All schooldays' friendship, childhood innocence?
We, Hermia, like two artificial gods,
Created with our needles both one flower,
Both on one sampler, sitting on one cushion,
Both warbling of one song, both in one key,
As if our hands, our sides, voices and minds
Had been incorp'rate. So we grew together
Like a double cherry, seeming parted,
But yet an union in partition,
30 Two lovely berries molded on one stem,
So, with two seeming bodies, but one heart,
Two of the first, like coats in heraldry,
Due but to one, and crowned with one crest.
And will you rend our ancient love asunder,
To join with men in scorning your poor friend?
It is not friendly, 'tis not maidenly;
Our sex as well as I may chide you for it,
Though I alone do feel the injury.
HERMIA. Helen, I am amazed at your words.
40 I scorn you not; it seems that you scorn me.
HELENA. Have you not set Lysander as in scorn
To follow me and praise me in derision?
And made your other love, Demetrius
(Who even but now did spurn me with his foot),
To call me goddess, nymph, divine and rare,
Precious, celestial? Wherefore speaks he this
To her he hates? And wherefore doth Lysander
Deny your love, so rich within his soul,
And tender me, forsooth, affection,
50 But by your setting on, by your consent?

---

29. partition] the next four lines are bracketed for possible omission, pretty clearly by Colman, as have lines 35–37; but there is a large "stet" in Garrick's hand in the margin.

42. in derision] my eyes and face *S.*

44. (Who even . . .] this line, the last part of the next, and the first part of the following have been crossed out in the prompt, as have lines 56–57 and 59–60, but again Garrick has a large "stet" in the margin. Likewise, lines 61–62 have been bracketed but "stet" appears in the margin.

What though I be not so in grace as you,
So hung upon with love, so fortunate,
But miserable most, to love unloved?
This you should pity rather than despise.

HERMIA. I understand not what you mean by this.

HELENA. Ay, persevere in counterfeit sad looks.
Make mouths upon me when I turn my back;
Wink each at other; hold the sweet jest up.
This sport, well carried, shall be chronicled.
60 If you have any pity, grace, or manners,
You would not make me such an argument.
But fare ye well, 'tis partly mine own fault,
Which death or absence soon shall remedy.

LYSANDER. Stay, gentle Helena, hear my vows, my prayers.
My love, my life, my soul, fair Helena!

HELENA. O excellent!

LYSANDER. Helen, I love thee; by my life I do.
I swear by that which I will lose for thee
To prove him false that says I love thee not.

[SONG.]

70 [Let him come; let him come. I'll prove to his face
My passion no rival can bear.
Let him fly, let him fly, for he's sure of disgrace;
For my love feels the rage of despair.]

DEMETRIUS. I say, I love thee more than he can do.

LYSANDER. If thou say so, withdraw and prove it, traitor!

---

56. Ay, persevere . . .] Ay, do! Persever, counterfeit sad looks *S*.
64. vows, my prayers] excuse *S*.
66. excellent] the four following lines are omitted:

HER. Sweet, do not scorn her so.
DEM. If she cannot entreat, I can compel.
LYS. Thou canst compel no more than she entreat.
Thy threats have no more strength than her weak praise.

69.1. SONG] listed as "New" in Garrick's manuscript notes.
75. traitor] too *S*. Most of the remainder of the scene (about two and a half pages in the Tonson edition) has been cancelled (*S* lines 256–335). Then Helena's speech beginning "Good Hermia, do not be so bitter with me," is restored in part (*G* lines 65–70), omitting six *S* lines (309–13); and the exchange between the two girls beginning with Hermia's "O me, you juggler, you, you canker-blossom" is shifted from *S* lines 282–88 to near the end of the scene, following the exit of Lysander and Demetrius (*S* line 338). Because of the length of the omission, the *S* text is not reproduced here.

HELENA. Good Hermia, do not be so bitter with me;
I evermore did love you, Hermia,
Did ever keep your counsels, never wronged you.
And how, so you will let me quiet go,
80 To Athens will I bear my folly back
And follow you no further.

LYSANDER. Now follow if thou darest, to try whose right,
Of thine or mine, is most in Helena.

DEMETRIUS. Follow? Nay, I'll go with thee.

Exit Lysander *and* Demetrius.

HERMIA. Oh, me, you juggler, you, you canker-blossom,
You thief of love; what, have you come by night
And stolen my love's heart from him?

HELENA. Fine, i'faith!
Have you no modesty, no maiden shame,
90 No touch of bashfulness? What, will you tear
Impatient answers from my gentle tongue?
Fie, fie, you counterfeit, you puppet, you.

[DUET.]

[HELENA. With various griefs my mind is torn.
HERMIA. And mine with rage, and love, and scorn.
BOTH. My griefs can have no end.
HELENA. What greater ills can woman prove?
HERMIA. For friendship has betrayed my love.
HELENA. And love destroys the friend.]

HERMIA. You, mistress, all this coil is long of you.
100 Nay, go not back.

HELENA. I will not trust you, I,
Nor longer stay in your cursed company.
Your hands than mine are quicker for a fray;
My legs are longer, though, to run away.

HERMIA. I am amazed and know not what to say.

Exeunt.

---

85. you, you canker] the Tonson edition has "on, you canker," but the standard Shakespeare reading is simply "you canker." When *G* takes out "on" and adds "you" he may have unintentionally repeated "you" in attempting to restore Shakespeare's reading.

92.1. DUET] *G* indicates this as the nineteenth song but does not give it in his manuscript list.

[ACT IV. SCENE I.]

Enter Oberon *and* Puck.

OBERON. This is thy negligence. Still thou mistak'st,
Or else committ'st thy knaveries willingly.
PUCK. Believe me, king of shadows, I mistook.
Did not you tell me I should know the man
By the Athenian garments he hath on?
And so far blameless proves my enterprise
That I have 'nointed an Athenian's eyes;
And so far am I glad it did so sort,
As this their jangling I esteem a sport.
10 OBERON. Thou seest these lovers seek a place to fight;
Hie therefore, Robin; overcast the night.
I'll lead these testy rivals so astray
As one come not within another's way.
Like to Lysander sometime frame my tongue,
Then stir Demetrius up with bitter wrong;
And sometime like Demetrius will I rail
'Till o'er their brows death-counterfeiting sleep
With leaden legs and batty wings doth creep.
Then crush this herb into Lysander's eye,
20 Whose liquor hath this virtuous property
To take from thence all error with its might
And make his eyeballs rowl with wonted sight.
When they next wake, all this derision
Shall seem a dream and fruitless vision;
And back to Athens shall the lovers wend.
Then to my queen and beg her Indian boy;
And then I will her charmed eye release
From monster's view, and all things shall be peace.
PUCK. My fairy lord, this must be done with haste,

---

0. ACT IV] begins at III, ix, in Tonson and at III, ii, 345, in modern versions.
11. the night] two lines are omitted: "The starry welkin cover thou anon / With drooping fog as black as Acheron."
12. I'll] And *S.*
14. my] thy *S.*
16. like . . . rail] rail thou like Demetrius *S.* The change would have eliminated a rhyme with the next line; but that line is marked out: "And from each other look thou lead them thus."
25. lovers wend] the next two lines are omitted: "With league whose date till death shall never end / Whiles I in this affair do thee employ."
26. Then] I'll *S.*

30 For night's swift dragons cut the clouds full fast,
And yonder shines Aurora's harbinger.
OBERON. But we are spirits of another sort;
I with the morning light have oft made sport.

[SONG.]

Away, away, make no delay,
We must effect this business yet ere day.

Exit Oberon.

PUCK. Up and down, up and down,
I will lead them up and down.
I am feared in field and town.
I will lead them up and down.
40 Here comes one.

Enter Lysander.

LYSANDER. Where art thou, proud Demetrius? Speak, where art thou?
PUCK. Here, villain, drawn and ready. Where art thou?
LYSANDER. I will be with thee straight.
PUCK. Follow me then to plainer ground.

Enter Demetrius.

DEMETRIUS. Lysander, speak again;
Thou runaway, thou coward, art thou fled?

---

31. harbinger] seven lines are here marked for possible omission, probably by Colman:

At whose approach ghosts, wandering here and there,
Troop home to churchyards, damned spirits all,
That in crossways and floods have burial,
Already to their wormy beds are gone.
For fear lest day should look their shames upon,
They wilfully themselves exile from light
And must for aye consort with black-brow'd night.

33. made sport] four and a half lines are outlined for omission: "And like a forester the groves may tread / Even till the eastern gate, all fiery red, / Opening on Neptune, with fair blessed beams / Turns into yellow gold his salt-green streams. / But notwithstanding, haste."

33.1. SONG] *G* makes a song of the last two lines of Oberon's speech, adding "Away, away" in place of Shakespeare's "But notwithstanding, haste." *G*'s manuscript list indicates that the song was set by Smith.

36. Up and down . . .] Puck's lines, made into a song in *The Fairies*, are here marked first as "Sung," then changed to "Said."

39. I will] Goblin *S*.

41. where art thou] thou now *S*.

Speak! In some bush? Where dost thou hide thy head?
PUCK. Thou coward, art thou bragging to the wind,
Telling the bushes that thou look'st for wars,
50 And wilt not come? Come, recreant, come, thou boy.
I'll whip thee with a rod; he is defiled
That draws a sword on thee.
DEMETRIUS. Yea, art thou there?
PUCK. Follow my voice; we'll try one manhood now.
Here, recreant, here.

Exeunt.

LYSANDER. He goes before me, dares me to the fight.
When I come where he calls me, then he's gone.
The villain is much lighter-heeled than I.
I followed fast, but faster he did run. (*Shifting places.*)
60 Now tired and fallen in a dark uneven way,
Here will I rest me. Come thou gentle morning. (*Lies down.*)
For if but once thou show thy twilight gray,
I'll find Demetrius and revenge my wrongs.

Enter Puck *and* Demetrius.

PUCK. Ho, ho, ho, coward, why com'st thou not?
DEMETRIUS. Abide me, if thou dar'st; for well I wot
Thou runn'st before me, shifting every place,
And dar'st not stand. Recreant, speak.
Where art thou?
PUCK. Come thou hither. I am here.
70 DEMETRIUS. Then thou mock'st me; thou shalt buy this dear.
By day's approach, look to be visited.

---

48. wind] stars *S*. The change avoids a rhyme.
50. boy] child *S*. The change avoids a rhyme.
54. our manhood now] no manhood here *S*.
55. Here . . .] the line is added to the play.
56. dares . . . fight] and still dares me on *S*.
59. run] fly *S*. The change avoids a rhyme.
60. Now tired . . .] That fall'n am I in dark, uneven way *S*.
61. Here will . . .] And here will rest me. Come, thou gentle day *S*. The change eliminates a rhyme.
62. thy twilight gray] me thy gray light *S*. The change avoids the rhyme.
63. my wrongs] this spite *S*, thus avoiding a rhyme.
67. Recreant, speak] nor look me in the face *S*, again avoiding a rhyme.
71. By day's approach . . .] last line of *S* scene here transposed, with the normal line eliminated: "If ever I thy face by daylight see."

Now go thy way. Faintness constraineth me
To measure out my length on this cold bed. (*Lies down.*)

[SCENE II.]

Enter Helena.

HELENA. O weary night, O long and tedious night,
Abate thy hours; shine comforts from the East
That I may back to Athens by daylight
From these that my poor company detest;
And sleep, that sometimes shuts up sorrow's eye,
Steal me a while from mine own company. (*Sleeps.*)
PUCK. Yet but three? Come one more.
Two of both kinds make up four.
Here she comes, curst and sad;
10 Cupid is a knavish lad
Thus to make poor females mad.

Enter Hermia.

HERMIA. Never so weary, never so in woe,
Bedabbled with the dew and torn with briars,
I can no further crawl, no further go;
My legs can keep no pace with my desires.
Here will I rest me 'till the break of day.
Heav'ns shield Lysander, if they mean a fray. (*Lies down.*)
PUCK. On the ground, sleep thou sound.
I'll apply to your eye, gentle lover, remedy. (*Squeezing the juice on Lysander's eyes.*)
20 When thou wak'st, next thou tak'st
True delight in the sight of thy former lady's eye,
And the country proverb known,
That every man should take his own,
In your waking shall be shown.
Jack shall have Jill, nought shall go ill;
The man shall have his mare again, and all be well.

Exit Puck.

They sleep.

---

12. Never so weary] a marginal note indicates, "This may be sung."
18. sleep thou] sleep *S.*
20. next thou] Thou *S.*

[SCENE III.] *The wood.*

Enter Queen of Fairies, Bottom, Fairies *attending,*
and the King *behind them.*

QUEEN. Come, sit thee down upon this flowery bed,
While I thy amiable cheeks do coy
And stick musk roses in thy sleek-smoothed head,
And kiss thy fair large ears, my gentle joy.

[SONG.]

[Sweetest creature,
Pride of nature,
Loved as soon as seen,
Hear me sighing,
See me dying,
10 Alas, poor Queen!

II.

Never, slander,
Knew me wander
From our fairy ring.
But you charm me,
And so warm me,
Alas, poor King!]

BOTTOM. Where's Peaseblossom?
PEASEBLOSSOM. Ready.
BOTTOM. Scratch my head, Peaseblossom. Where's Monsieur Cobweb?
20 COBWEB. Ready.
BOTTOM. Monsieur Cobweb, good monsieur, get your weapons in your hand and kill me a red-hipped humblebee on the top of a thistle; and, good monsieur, bring me the honey-bag. Do not fret yourself too much in the action, monsieur; and good monsieur have a care the honey-bag break not. I should be loth to have you overflown with a honey-bag, signior. Where's Monsieur Mustardseed?
MUSTARDSEED. Ready.

---

0. SCENE III] the designation for IV, i, is marked out and "Scene 10" is added in the margin. But with Garrick's indication of act IV in place of the Tonson III, ix, it is clear that the intention is for this to be the third scene of the new act. The heading for the previous scene, marked "x" in Tonson, was not changed.

4.1. SONG] marked "20" by *G*, this is actually song 21, as *G* had changed Puck's spoken lines in scene i to a song. Garrick identifies the song in his manuscript list.

BOTTOM. Give me thy neaf, Monsieur Mustardseed. Pray you leave your courtesy, good monsieur.

30 MUSTARDSEED. What's your will?

BOTTOM. Nothing, good monsieur, but to help Cavalero Cobweb to scratch. I must to the barber's, monsieur, for methinks I am marvellous hairy about the face. And I am such a tender ass, if my hair doth but tickle me I must scratch.

QUEEN. What, wilt thou hear some music, my sweet love?

BOTTOM. I have a reasonable good ear in music. Let us have the tongs and the bones.

Music. Tongs, rural music.

QUEEN. Or say, sweet love, what thou desirest to eat.

BOTTOM. Truly, a peck of provender; I could munch your good dry
40 oats. Methinks I have a great desire to a bottle of hay: good hay, sweet hay hath no fellow.

QUEEN. I have a venturous fairy that shall seek the squirrel's hoard and fetch thee new nuts.

BOTTOM. I had rather have a handful or two of dried peas. But, I pray you, let none of your people stir me; I have an exposition of sleep come upon me.

QUEEN. Sleep thou, and I will wind thee in my arms:
Fairies, be gone, and be always away.
So doth the woodbine the sweet honeysuckle
50 Gently entwist; the female ivy so
Enrings the barky fingers of the elm.
Oh, how I love thee! How I dote on thee! [*Sleep.*]

Enter Puck.

OBERON. Welcome, good Robin. Seest thou this sweet sight?
Her dotage now I do begin to pity;
In seeking sweet favors for this hateful fool
I did upbraid her and fall out with her.

29. courtesy] courtsy *S.*
52. *Sleep*] added in margin in *G.*
54. to pity] the next line in *S*, "For meeting her of late behind the wood," is omitted.
55. In seeking] Seeking *S.*
56. with her] six following lines are marked for omission:

For she his hairy temples then had rounded
With coronet of fresh and fragrant flowers;
And that same dew which sometimes on the buds
Was wont to swell like round and orient pearls,
Stood now within the pretty flouriets' eyes,
Like tears that did their own disgrace bewail.

When I had at my pleasure taunted her
And she in mild terms begged my patience,
I then did ask of her her changeling child,
60 Which straight she gave me, and her fairy sent
To bear him to my bower in fairy land.
And now I have the boy, I will undo
This hateful imperfection of her eyes.
And, gentle Puck, take this transformed scalp
From off the head of this Athenian swain,
That he, awaking when the others do,
May all to Athens back again repair
And think no more of this night's accidents
But as the fierce vexation of a dream.
70 But first I will release the Fairy Queen.

[SONG.]

Be as thou wast wont to be;
See as thou wast wont to see;
Dian's bud or Cupid's flower
Hath such force and blessed power.

Now, my Titania, wake you, my sweet Queen.
QUEEN. My Oberon! What visions have I seen!
Methought I was enamored of an ass.
OBERON. There lies your love.
QUEEN. How came these things to pass?
80 Oh, how mine eyes do loathe this visage now!
OBERON. Silence a while. Robin, take off his head.
Titania, music call and strike more dead
Than common sleep of all these five the sense.
QUEEN. Music, ho, music, such as charmeth sleep.

Music still.

PUCK. When thou awak'st, with thine own fool's eyes peep.
OBERON. Sound music! Come, my queen, take hand with me
And rock the ground whereon these sleepers be.
Now thou and I are new in amity
And will tomorrow midnight solemnly

70.1. SONG] song 22, which G has marked "21," is indicated on the manuscript list. The lines are from Shakespeare. On the prompt he has the marginal note, "Set."

73. or] misprint for o'er?

83. five] Shakespeare's reading, restored by Garrick from "fine" in Tonson.

90 Dance in Duke Theseus' house triumphantly
And bless it to all fair posterity.
There shall the pairs of faithful lovers be
Wedded with Theseus all in jollity.
PUCK. Fairy King, attend and mark.
I do hear the morning lark.
OBERON. Then my Queen, in silence sad,
Trip we after the night's shade.
We the globe can compass soon,
Swifter than the wand'ring moon. (*Dance.*)
100 QUEEN. Come, my lord, and in our flight
Tell me how it came this night
That I sleeping here was found, (*Sleepers lie still.*)
With these mortals on the ground. (*Wind horns.*)

Exeunt.

[SCENE IV.]

Enter Theseus, Egeus, Hippolita, *and all his train.*

THESEUS. Go, one of you, find out the forester,
For now our observation is performed;
And since we have the vaward of the day,
My love shall hear the music of my hounds.
Uncouple in the western valley; go.
Dispatch, I say, and find the forester.
We will, fair Queen, up to the mountain's top
And mark the musical confusion
Of hounds and echo in conjunction.
10 HIPPOLITA. I was with Hercules and Cadmus once,
When in a wood of Crete they bayed the bear
With hounds of Sparta; never did I hear
Such gallant chiding. For besides the groves,
The skies, the fountains, every region near
Seemed all one mutual cry. I never heard
So musical a discord, such sweet thunder.
THESEUS. My hounds are bred out of the Spartan kind,

---

94. Fairy King . . .] ten lines, beginning with this one, are marked for possible excision, undoubtedly by Colman. Garrick has written "stet" opposite them.

99. wand'ring moon] Garrick indicates a dance at this point, and in his manuscript notes he has written "a Dance of Fairies."

So flewed, so sanded, and their heads are hung
With ears that sweep away the morning dew;
20 Crook-kneed and dewlapped like Thessalian bulls;
Slow in pursuit, but matched in mouth like bells,
Each under each. A cry more tuneable
Was never hollowed to, nor cheered with horn,
In Crete, in Sparta, nor in Thessaly.
Judge when you hear. But soft, what nymphs are these?

EGEUS. My lord, this is my daughter here asleep,
And this Lysander, this Demetrius is,
This Helena, old Nedar's Helena.
I wonder at their being here together.

30 THESEUS. No doubt they rose up early to observe
The rite of May, and, hearing our intent,
Came here in grace of our solemnity.
But speak, Egeus. Is not this the day
That Hermia should give answer of her choice?

EGEUS. It is, my lord.

THESEUS. Go bid the huntsmen wake them with their horns.

Horns, and they wake. Shout within. They all start up.
[*Horn Duet of Hunters.*]

THESEUS. Good morrow, friends; Saint Valentine is past.
Begin these wood-birds but to couple now?

LYSANDER. Pardon, my lord.

40 THESEUS. I pray you all stand up.
I know you two are rival enemies.
How comes this gentle concord in the world,
That hatred is so far from jealousy
To sleep by hate and fear no enmity?

---

36. their horns] here *G* indicates song 23 (22 by his markings). On his manuscript list Garrick noted, "Horn Duet of Hunters—Smith." A note (by Colman?) in the Tonson prompt at this point says, "here might be introduc'd a Hunting Song." Colman in his comments on Garrick's alteration had indicated, "Here as they are supposed to be in the wood to observe the Rite of May, it w[d] have a very good effect to awaken the sleepers with soft musick accompanied with a song in honour of May Morning—or rather, as the Poet seems to have intended, with the noise of the *Horns* accompanied with a *Hunting Song*—a song however, of some sort or or [*sic*] other, by all means!" In his 1763 edition Colman has here a song by Lysander: "Hark, hark, how the hounds and horn / Cherely rouse the slumb'ring morn / From the side of yon hoar hill, / Thro' the high wood echoing shrill."

LYSANDER. My lord, I shall reply amazedly,
Half sleep, half waking. But as yet I swear
I cannot truly say how I came here.
But as I think—for truly would I speak,
And now I do methink me, so it is—
50 I came with Hermia hither. Our intent
Was to be gone from Athens, where we might be
Without the peril of th' Athenian law.

EGEUS. Enough, enough, my lord; you have enough.
I beg the law, the law upon his head.
They would have stolen away, they would, Demetrius,
Thereby to have defeated you and me:
You of your wife, and me of my consent,
Of my consent that she should be your wife.

DEMETRIUS. My lord, fair Helen told me of their stealth,
60 Of this their purpose hither to this wood;
And I in fury hither followed them.
Fair Helena in fancy followed me.
But, my good lord, I wot not by what power
(But by some power it is) my love to Hermia
Is melted as the snow, seems to me now
As the remembrance of an idle gaude
Which in my childhood I did dote upon.
And all the faith, the virtue of my heart,
The object and the pleasure of mine eye,
70 Is only Helena. To her, my lord,
Was I betrothed ere I Hermia saw;
But like a sickness did I loathe this food;
But, as in health, come to my natural taste,
Now do I wish it, love it, long for it,
And will for evermore be true to it.

THESEUS. Fair lovers, you are fortunately met.
Of this discourse we shall hear more anon.
Egeus, I will overbear your will;
For in the temple, by and by, with us
80 These couples shall eternally be knit.
And, for the morning now is something worn,
Our purposed hunting shall be set aside.
Away with us to Athens! Three and three,
We'll hold a feast in great solemnity.
Come, Hippolita.

Exit Duke *and* Lords.

DEMETRIUS. These things seem small and undistinguishable,
Like far-off mountains turned into clouds.
HERMIA. Methinks I see these things with parted eye,
When every thing seems double.
90 HELENA. So methinks;
And I have found Demetrius like a jewel,
Mine own, and not mine own.
DEMETRIUS. It seems to me
That yet we sleep, we dream. Do not you think
The Duke was here and bid us follow him?
HERMIA. Yea, and my father.
HELENA. And Hippolita.
LYSANDER. And he bids us to follow to the temple.
DEMETRIUS. Why, then we are awake; let's follow him,
100 And by the way let us recount our dreams.

[*Here a song of joy and love among the four characters.*]

[SONG.]

[Pierce the air with sounds of joy;
Come Hymen with the winged boy,
Bring song and dance and revelry
From this our great solemnity.
Drive care and sorrow far away,
Let all be mirth and holiday.

CHORUS.

Hail to love! and welcome joy!
Hail to the delicious boy!
See the sun from love returning,
110 Love's the flame in which he's burning.]

Exeunt.

Bottom *wakes.*

100.1. SONG] *G* now numbers the twenty-fourth song correctly on both the prompt and notes, "Here a song of joy & love among y[e] four Characters." On his manuscript list of songs he has noted only, "Demet. may sing + *Loves -a Tempest.*" As he later indicated that Lysander would sing "*Tempest*" in the next act, the requirement of a "song of joy and love" is met here by that with which Colman ends the scene—and the play—in the 1763 edition.

SCENE [V].

BOTTOM. When my cue comes, call me, and I will answer. My next is, "Most fair Pyramus"—hey ho, Peter Quince! Flute the bellows-mender! Snout the tinker! Starveling! God's my life! Stol'n hence, and left me asleep! I have had a most rare vision. I had a dream past the wit of man to say what dream it was. Man is but an ass if he go about to expound this dream. Methought I was—there is no man can tell what. Methought I was, and methought I had. But man is but a patched fool if he will offer to say what methought I had. The eye of man hath not heard, the ear of man hath not seen; man's hand
10 is not able to taste, his tongue to conceive, nor his heart to report what my dream was. I will get Peter Quince to write a ballad of this dream. It shall be called "Bottom's Dream" because it hath no bottom; and I will sing it in the latter end of a play before the Duke. Peradventure, to make it the more gracious, I shall sing it at her death.

Exit.

SCENE [VI].

Enter Quince, Flute, Snout, *and* Starveling.

QUINCE. Have you sent to Bottom's house? Is he come home yet?

STARVELING. He cannot be heard of. Out of doubt he is transported.

FLUTE. If he be come not, then the play is marred. It goes not forward, doth it?

QUINCE. It is not possible. You have not a man in all Athens able to discharge Pyramus but he.

FLUTE. No, he hath simply the best wit of any handy-craft man in Athens.

QUINCE. Yea, and the best person too; and he is a very paramour for a
10 sweet voice.

FLUTE. You must say "paragon." A paramour is (God bless us) a thing of nought.

Enter Snug.

SNUG. Masters, the Duke is coming from the temple, and there is two or three lords and ladies more married. If our sport had gone forward, we had all been made men.

FLUTE. O sweet bully Bottom, thus hath he lost sixpence a day during his life; he could not have 'scaped sixpence a day. And the Duke had not given him sixpence a day for playing Pyramus, I'll be hanged. He would have deserved it. Sixpence a day in Pyramus, or nothing.

Enter Bottom.

20 BOTTOM. Where are these lads? Where are these hearts?

QUINCE. Bottom! O most courageous day! O most happy hour!

BOTTOM. Masters, I am to discourse wonders, but ask me not what; for if I tell you, I am no true Athenian. I will tell you everything as it fell out.

QUINCE. Let us hear, sweet Bottom.

BOTTOM. Not a word of me; all I will tell you is that the Duke hath dined. Get your apparel together, good strings to your beards, new ribbons to your pumps; meet presently at the palace; every man look o'er his part; for the short and the long is, our play is preferred.
30 In any case, let Thisby have clean linen, and let him that plays the lion pare his nails, for they shall hang out for the lion's claws, and, most dear actors, eat no onions nor garlic, for we are to utter sweet breath; and I do not doubt to hear them say it is a sweet comedy. No more words. Away, go, away!

Exeunt.

ACT V. SCENE I.

Enter Theseus, Hippolita, Egeus *and his* Lords.

HIPPOLITA. 'Tis strange, my Theseus, what these lovers speak of.

THESEUS. More strange than true. I never may believe
These antic fables, nor these fairy toys.
Lovers and madmen have such seething brains,
Such shaping fantasies, that apprehend more
Than cooler reason ever comprehends.
The lunatic, the lover, and the poet
Are of imagination all compact.
One sees more devils than vast hell can hold:
10 The madman. While the lover, all as frantic,
Sees Helen's beauty in a brow of Egypt.
The poets' eye, in a fine frenzy rolling,
Doth glance from heaven to earth, from earth to heaven;
And as imagination bodies forth
The forms of things unknown, the poet's pen
Turns them to shape[s] and gives to airy nothing

A local habitation and a name.
Such tricks hath strong imagination
That if he would but apprehend some joy,
20 It comprehends some bringer of that joy;
Or in the night, imagining some fear,
How easy is a bush supposed a bear?

HIPPOLITA. But all the story of the night told over,
And all their minds transfigured so together,
More witnesseth than fancy's images
And grows to something of great constancy;
But howsoever, strange and admirable.

Enter Lysander, Demetrius, Hermia *and* Helena.

THESEUS. Here come the lovers, full of joy and mirth.
Joy, gentle friends, joy and fresh days of love
30 Accompany your hearts.

LYSANDER. More than to us
Wait on your royal walks, your board, your bed.

[SONG.]

[Love's a tempest, life's the ocean,
Passion crossed, the deep deform;
Rude and raging tho' the motion,
Virtue, fearless, braves the storm.
Storms and tempests may blow over
And subside to gentle gales;
So the poor despairing lover,
40 When least hoping, oft prevails.]

THESEUS. Come now; what masks, what dances shall we have
To wear away this long age of three hours
Between our after-supper and bedtime?
Where is our usual manager of mirth?
What revels are in hand? Is there no play
To ease the anguish of a torturing hour?
Call Philostrate.

Enter Philostrate.

PHILOSTRATE. Here, mighty Theseus.

THESEUS. Say, what abridgment have you for this evening?
50 What mask? what music? How shall we beguile

The lazy time, if not with some delight?
PHILOSTRATE. There is a brief how many sports are rife;
Make choice of which your highness will see first.
LYSANDER. "The battle with the Centaurs, to be sung
By an Athenian eunuch to the harp."
THESEUS. We'll none of that. That have I told my love
In glory of my kinsman Hercules.
LYSANDER. "The riot of the tipsy Bacchanals,
Tearing the Thracian singer in their rage."
60 THESEUS. That is an old device, and it was played
When I from Thebes came last a conqueror.
LYSANDER. "The thrice three Muses mourning for the death
Of learning, late deceased in beggary."
THESEUS. That is some satire, keen and critical,
Not sorting with a nuptial ceremony.
LYSANDER. "A tedious brief scene of young Pyramus
And his love Thisbe; very tragical mirth."
THESEUS. Merry and tragical? tedious and brief?
How shall we find the concord of this discord?
70 PHILOSTRATE. A play there is, my lord, some ten words long,
Which is as brief as I have known a play;
But by ten words, my lord it is too long,
Which makes it tedious; for in all the play
There is not one word apt, one player fitted.
And tragical, my noble lord, it is;
For Pyramus therein doth kill himself,
Which when I saw rehearsed, I must confess
Made mine eyes water; but more merry tears
The passion of loud laughter never shed.
80 THESEUS. What are they that do play it?
PHILOSTRATE. Hard-handed men that work in Athens here,
Which never labored in their minds 'till now;
And now have toiled their unbreathed memories
With this same play against your nuptials.
THESEUS. And we will hear it.
PHILOSTRATE. No, my noble lord,
It is not for you. I have heard it over,
And it is nothing, nothing in the world
Unless you can find sport in their intents,
90 Extremely stretched and conned with cruel pain,
To do you service.
THESEUS. I will hear that play;
For never any thing can be amiss

When simpleness and duty tender it.
Go bring them in, and take your places, ladies.

Exit Philostrate.

HIPPOLITA. I love not to see wretchedness o'ercharged,
And duty in his service perishing.
THESEUS. Why, gentle sweet, you shall see no such thing.
HIPPOLITA. He says they can do nothing in this kind.
100 THESEUS. The kinder we, to give them thanks for nothing.
Our sport shall be to take what they mistake;
And what poor duty cannot do, noble respect
Takes it in might, not merit.
Where I have come, great clerks have purposed
To greet me with premeditated welcomes;
Where I have seen them shiver and look pale,
Make periods in the midst of sentences,
Throttle their practiced accent in their fears,
And in conclusion dumbly have broke off,
110 Not paying me a welcome. Trust me, sweet;
Out of this silence yet I picked a welcome.
And in the modesty of fearful duty
I read as much as from the rattling tongue
Of saucy and audacious eloquence.
Love, therefore, and tongue-tied simplicity
In least speak most, to my capacity.

Enter Philomon.

PHILOMON. So please your Grace, the prologue is addressed.
THESEUS. Let him approach.

Flourish of trumpet.

SCENE II.

Enter Vaughan *for the prologue.*

PROLOGUE. If we offend, it is with our good will,
That you should think we come not to offend,
But with good will. To show our simple skill,
That is the true beginning of our end.

4. our end] four following lines are indicated for possible omission, probably by Colman: "Consider then, we come but in despite. / We do not come as minding to content you. / Our true intent is all for your delight; / We are not here that you should here repent you."

The actors are at hand, and, by their show,
You shall know all that you are like to know.

THESEUS. This fellow doth not stand upon points.

LYSANDER. He hath rid his prologue like a rough colt; he knows not the stop. A good moral, my lord. It is not enough to speak, but to speak
10 true.

HIPPOLITA. Indeed he hath played on his prologue like a child on the recorder—a sound, but not in government.

THESEUS. His speech was like a tangled chain: nothing impaired, but all disordered. Who is the next?

Enter Pyramus, *and* Thisbe, Wall, Moonshine, *and* Lion.

PROLOGUE. Gentles, perchance you wonder at this show,
But wonder on, 'till truth make all things plain.
This man is Pyramus, if you would know;
This beauteous lady Thisby is certain.
This man with lime and roughcast doth present
20 Wall, the vile wall, which did these lovers sunder;
And through wall's chink, poor souls, they are content
To whisper. At the which, let no man wonder.
This man with lanthorn, dog, and bush of thorn
Presenteth Moonshine. For if you will know,
By moonshine did these lovers think no scorn
To meet at Ninus' tomb, there, there to woo.
This grizly beast, which Lion hight by name,
The trusty Thisby, coming first by night,
Did scare away, or rather did affright.
30 And as she fled, her mantle she let fall,
Which Lion vile with bloody mouth did stain.
Anon comes Pyramus, sweet youth and tall,
And finds his trusty Thisby's mantle slain;
Whereat, with blade, with bloody blameful blade,
He bravely broached his boiling bloody breast.
And Thisby, tarrying in the mulberry shade,
His dagger drew, and died. For all the rest,
Let Lion, Moonshine, Wall, and lovers twain
At large discourse, while there they do remain.

Exeunt all but Wall.

40 THESEUS. I wonder if the lion be to speak.

DEMETRIUS. No wonder, my lord; one lion may, when many asses do.

WALL. In this same interlude it doth befall,

That I, one Snout by name, present a wall,
And such a wall, as I would have you think,
That had in it a crannied hole or chink
Through which the lovers, Pyramus and Thisby,
Did whisper often very secretly.
This loam, this roughcast, and this stone doth show
That I am that same wall; the truth is so.
50 And this the cranny is, right and sinister,
Through which the fearful lovers are to whisper.

THESEUS. Would you desire lime and hair to speak better?

DEMETRIUS. It is the wittiest partition that ever I heard discourse, my lord.

THESEUS. Pyramus draws near the wall. Silence!

Enter Bottom *as* Pyramus.

PYRAMUS. O grim-looked night! O night with hue so black!
O night, which ever art when day is not!
O night, O night, alack, alack, alack,
I fear my Thisby's promise is forgot.
60 And thou, O wall, O sweet and lovely wall,
That stands between her father's ground and mine,
Thou wall, O wall, O sweet and lovely wall,
Show me thy chink, to blink through with my eyne.

[Wall *makes a chink with his fingers.*]

Thanks, courteous wall. Jove shield thee well for this.
But what see I? No Thisby do I see.
O wicked wall, through whom I see no bliss,
Curst be thy stones for thus deceiving me.

THESEUS. The wall, methinks, being sensible, should curse again.

PYRAMUS. No, in truth, sir, he should not. "Deceiving me" is Thisby's
70 cue. She is to enter, and I am to spy her through the wall. You shall see it will fall pat as I told you. Yonder she comes.

Enter Thisby.

THISBY. O wall, full often hast thou heard my moans,
For parting my fair Pyramus and me.
My cherry lips have often kissed thy stones,

---

43. Snout] a correction by Garrick to restore Shakespeare's reading. Tonson has "Flute."

55.1. *Enter . . .* Pyramus] "Bottom as" is added by *G.*

Thy stones with lime and hair knit up in thee.
PYRAMUS. I see a voice; now will I to the chink
To spy as I can hear my Thisby's face.
Thisby!
THISBY. My love! Thou art my love, I think.
80 PYRAMUS. Think what thou wilt, I am thy lover's grace.
And, like Limander, am I trusty still.
THISBY. And I like Helen, 'till the fates me kill.
PYRAMUS. Not Shafalus to Procrus was so true.
THISBY. As Shafalus to Procrus, I to you.
PYRAMUS. Oh kiss me through the hole of this vile wall.
THISBY. I kiss the wall's hole, not your lips at all.
PYRAMUS. Wilt thou at Ninny's tomb meet me straightway?
THISBY. 'Tide life, 'tide death, I come without delay.
WALL. Thus have I, Wall, my part discharged so,
90 And being done, thus Wall away doth go.

Exit.

HIPPOLITA. This is the silliest stuff that e'er I heard.
THESEUS. The best in this kind are but shadows, and the worst are no worse if imagination amend them.
HIPPOLITA. It must be your imagination, then, and not theirs.
THESEUS. If we imagine no worse of them than they of themselves, they may pass for excellent men. Here come two noble beasts in, a man and a lion.

Enter Lion *and* Moonshine.

LION. You ladies, you whose gentle hearts do fear
The smallest monstrous mouse that creeps on floor,
100 May now perchance both quake and tremble here,
When lion rough in wildest rage doth roar.
Then know that I one Snug the joiner am,
No lion fell, nor else no lion's dam;
For if I should, as lion, come in strife
Into this place, 'twere pity of my life.
THESEUS. A very gentle beast, and of a good conscience.
DEMETRIUS. The very best at a beast, my lord, that e'er I saw.
LYSANDER. This lion is a very fox for his valor.

---

90. doth go] The following exchange between Theseus and Demetrius is omitted: "THES. Now is the mural down between the two neighbours. / DEM. No remedy, my lord, when walls are so wilful to hear without warning."

THESEUS. True, and a goose for his discretion.

10 MOONSHINE. This lanthorn doth the horned moon present—

DEMETRIUS. He should have worn the horns on his head.

THESEUS. He is no crescent, and his horns are invisible within the circumference.

MOONSHINE. This lanthorn doth the horned moon present;
Myself the man i'th' moon doth seem to be.

THESEUS. This is the greatest error of all the rest; the man should be put into the lanthorn. How is it else the man i'th' moon?

DEMETRIUS. He dares not come here for the candle; for you see it is already in snuff.

20 HIPPOLITA. I am weary of this moon; would he would change.

THESEUS. It appears, by this small light of discretion, that he is [in] the wane; but yet, in courtesy, in all reason, we must stay the time.

LYSANDER. Proceed, Moon.

MOONSHINE. All that I have to say is to tell you that the lanthorn is the moon, I the man in the moon; this thornbush my thornbush, and this dog my dog.

DEMETRIUS. Why, all these should be in the lanthorn; for they are in the moon. But silence! There comes Thisby.

Enter Thisby.

THISBY. This is old Ninny's tomb. Where is my love?

30 LION. Oh. (*The* Lion *roars.* Thisby *runs off.*)

DEMETRIUS. Well roared, Lion.

THESEUS. Well run, Thisby.

HIPPOLITA. Well shone, Moon. Truly the moon shines with a good grace.

THESEUS. Well mouthed, Lion.

DEMETRIUS. And then came Pyramus.

[*Exit* Lion.]

LYSANDER. And so the lion vanished.

Enter Pyramus.

PYRAMUS. Sweet Moon, I thank thee for thy sunny beams;
I thank thee, Moon, for shining now so bright;
40 For by thy gracious, golden, glittering streams

109. his discretion] another exchange between Theseus and Demetrius is cancelled: "DEM. Not so, my lord, for his valour cannot carry his discretion, and the fox carries the goose. / THES. His discretion, I am sure, cannot carry his valour; for the goose carries not the fox. It is well. Leave it to his discretion, and let us listen to the moon."

I trust to taste of truest Thisby's sight.
But stay. O spight!
But mark, poor knight,
What dreadful dole is here?
Eyes, do you see?
How can it be?
O dainty duck! O dear!
Thy mantle good,
What, stained with blood!
150 Approach, you Furies fell!
O fates! come, come.
Cut thread and thrum,
Quail, crush, conclude, and quell.

THESEUS. This passion and the death of a dear friend
Would go near to make a man look sad.
HIPPOLITA. Beshrew my heart, but I pity the man.

PYRAMUS. O wherefore, nature, didst thou lions frame?
Since lion vile hath here deflowered my dear,
Which is—no, no—which was the fairest dame
160 That lived, that loved, that liked, that looked with cheer.
Come tears, confound! Out sword, and wound
The pap of Pyramus.
Ay, that left pap, where heart doth hop. [*Stabs himself.*]
Thus die I, thus, thus, thus.
Now am I dead, now am I fled; my soul is in the sky.
Tongue, lose thy light; moon, take thy flight.
Now die, die, die, die, die.

DEMETRIUS. No die, but an ace, for him; for he is but one.
LYSANDER. Less than an ace, man; for he is dead; he is nothing.
170 THESEUS. With the help of a surgeon he might yet recover and prove an ass.
HIPPOLITA. How chance the Moonshine is gone before Thisby comes back and finds her lover?

Enter Thisby.

THESEUS. She will find him by starlight.
Here she comes; and her passion ends the play.
HIPPOLITA. Methinks she should not use a long one for such a Pyramus. I hope she will be brief.
DEMETRIUS. A moth will turn the balance, which Pyramus, which

178. moth] for *mote*?

Thisby is the better.

180 LYSANDER. She hath spied him already with those sweet eyes.

DEMETRIUS. And thus she means, *videlicet*—

THISBY. Asleep, my love?
What, dead, my dove?
O Pyramus, arise!
Speak, speak! Quite dumb?
Dead, dead? A tomb
Must cover thy sweet eyes.
These lily lips, this cherry nose,
These yellow cowslip cheeks
190 Are gone, are gone.
Lovers, make moan;
His eyes were green as leeks.
O Sisters Three,
Come, come to me,
With hands as pale as milk;
Lay them in gore,
Since you have shore
With shears this thread of silk.
Tongue, not a word!
200 Come, trusty sword;
Come blade, my breast imbrue.
And farewell friends;
Thus Thisby ends.
Adieu, adieu, adieu.

THESEUS. Moonshine and Lion are left to bury the dead.

DEMETRIUS. Ay, and Wall too.

BOTTOM. No, I assure you, the wall is down that parted their fathers. Will it please you to see the epilogue, or to hear a Bergomask dance between two of our company?

210 THESEUS. No epilogue, I pray you; for your play needs no excuse. Never excuse; for when the players are all dead, there need none to be blamed. Marry, if he that writ it had played Pyramus and hung himself in Thisby's garter, it would have been a fine tragedy. And so it is truly, and very notably discharged. But come, your Bergomask; let your epilogue alone.

Here a dance of clowns.

179. the better] the remainder of the usual Shakespeare speech is omitted in the Tonson text: "he for a man, God warr'nt us; she for a woman, God bless us."

The iron tongue of midnight hath told twelve.
Lovers, to bed; 'tis almost fairy time.
I fear we shall outsleep the coming morn
As much as we this night have overwatched.
220 This palpable gross play hath well beguiled
The heavy gait of night. Sweet friends, to bed.
A fortnight hold we this solemnity
In nightly revel and new jollity.

Exeunt.

[CHORUS.]

[Hail to love! and welcome joy!
Hail to the delicious boy!
See the sun from love returning,
Love's the flame in which he's burning.]

Finis.

223.1. CHORUS] *G* notes a closing chorus in the prompt and has in his manuscript list, "Finishing piece for all." The chorus given here is that used by Colman to close his version. *G.* omits the *S* scene iii entirely.

Hamlet,
Prince of Denmark

A Tragedy

1772

That Father lost, lost his, and the Survivor bound
In filial Obligation for some Term
To do obsequious Sorrow. But to persevere
In obstinate Condolement, does express
An impious Stubbornness; 'tis unmanly Grief.
It shews a Will most incorrect to Heaven:
'A Heart unfortify'd, a Mind impatient,
' An Understanding simple and unschool'd:
' For what we know must be, and is as common
' As any the most vulgar thing to Sense,
' Why should we in our peevish Opposition,
' Take it to Heart? Fie! 'tis a Fault to Heav'n
' A fault against the Dead, a Fault to Nature,
' To Reason most absurd, whose common Theme
' Is Death of Fathers, and who still hath cry'd
' From the first Course, till he that died to-day,
' This must be so.' We pray you, throw to Earth
This unprevailing Woe, and think of us
As of a Father; and let the World take Note,
You are the most immediate to our Throne:
' And with no less Nobility of Love,
' Than that which dearest Father bears his Son,
Do I impart towards you: For your Intent,
In going back to school to *Wittenberg*,
It is most retrograde to our Desire:
And we beseech you, bend you to remain
Here in the Chear and Comfort of our Eye,
' Our chiefest Courtier, Cousin, and our Son.'

Queen. Let not thy Mother lose her Prayers, *Hamlet*;
I pray thee stay with us, go not to *Wittenberg*.

Ham. I shall in all my best obey you, Madam.

King. Why, 'tis a loving and a fair Reply,
Be as Ourself in *Denmark*. Madam, come,
This gentle and unforc'd Accord of *Hamlet*
Sits smiling to my Heart; in Grace whereof,
No jocund Health that *Denmark* drinks to day,
But the great Cannon to the Clouds shall tell,
' And the King's Rouse, the Heav'n shall bruit again,
' Re-speaking earthly Thunder. Come away.' [*Exeunt*.

Manet Hamlet.

Ham. O that this too, too solid Flesh would melt,
Thaw, and resolve itself into a Dew;
Or that the Everlasting had not fix'd
His Canon 'gainst Self-Murder!

How

How weary, stale, flat, and unprofitable
Seem to me all the Uses of this World!
Fie on't! O fie! 'tis an unweeded Garden,
That grows to Seed; Things rank and gross in Nature
Possess it meerly. That it should come to this!
But two Months dead! nay, not so much, not two ——
So excellent a King, 'that was to this,
' *Hyperion* to a Satyr!' So loving to my Mother,
That he permitted not the Winds of Heav'n
Visit her Face too roughly! ' Heaven and Earth!
' Must I remember?' —— why she would hang on him,
As if Increase of Appetite had grown
By what it fed on; and yet within a Month! ——
Let me not think on't — Frailty, thy Name is Woman:
A little Month! —— or ere those Shoes were old,
With which she follow'd my poor Father's Body,
' Like *Niobe*, all Tears —— Why she, ev'n she ——
' O Heav'n! A Beast that wants Discourse of Reason,
' Would have mourn'd longer' — married with mine Uncle,
My Father's Brother; but, no more like my Father,
Than I to *Hercules*. ' Within a Month!
' Ere yet the Salt of most unrighteous Tears
' Had left the Flushing in her galled Eyes,
' She marry'd. O most wicked Speed! to post
' With such Dexterity t'incestuous Sheets:
' It is not, nor it cannot come to good.
' But break, my Heart, for I must hold my Tongue.'

Enter Horatio, Bernardo, *and* Marcellus.

Hor. Hail to your Lordship.

Ham. I'm glad to see you well:
Horatio? or I forget myself.

Hor. The same, my Lord, and your poor Servant ever.

Ham. Sir, my good Friend; I'll change that Name with you:
And what makes you from *Wittenberg*, *Horatio*?
Marcellus! ——

Mar. My good Lord! ——

Ham. I'm very glad to see you; good Ev'n, Sir.
But what, in faith, makes you from *Wittenberg*?

Hor. A truant Disposition, good my Lord.

Ham. I would not have your Enemy say so;
Nor shall you do mine Ear that Violence,
To be a Witness of your own Report
Against yourself. I know you are no Truant;

But

Facsimile pages from Garrick's preparation copy
Folger Shakespeare Library

Dramatis Personae

		[*Cast of alteration*, 1772]
Claudius, *King of* Denmark,	*Mr.* Bickerstaff.	[Jefferson]
Fortinbras, *King of* Norway,		
Hamlet, *Son of the former King*,	Mr. Wilkes.	[Garrick]
Polonius, *Lord Chamberlain*,	Mr. Cross.	[Baddeley]
Horatio, *Friend to* Hamlet,	Mr. Mills.	[Packer]
Laertes, *Son to* Polonius,	Mr. Ryan.	[J. Aicken]
Rosencrans, } *Courtiers*,	Mr. Wilkes, *Jun.*	[Davies]
Guildenstern, }	Mr. Quin.	[Fawcett]
' Voltimand.		
' Cornelius.		
Ostrick, *a Fop*,	Mr. Bowen.	
Marcellus, *an Officer*,	Mr. Shepherd.	[Ackman]
Bernardo, } *Two Centinels.*		[Wrighten]
Francisco, }		[Griffith]
' Reynaldo, *Servant to* Polonius.		
Ghost of Hamlet's *Father*,	Mr. Booth.	[Bransby]
Lucianus,	Mr. Norris.	[Parsons]
Two Grave-diggers,	Mr. Johnson. Mr. Leigh.	
[Player-King.]		[Keen]
[Player-Queen.]		[Mrs. Johnston]
[Messenger]		[Wright]

Gertrude, *Queen of* Denmark, *and Mother to* Hamlet,	Mrs. Porter.	[Mrs. Hopkins]
Ophelia, *Daughter to* Polonius, *in love with* Hamlet,	Mrs. Santlow.	[Mrs. Smith]
Ladies attending on the Queen.		

SCENE ELSINOOR.

This Play being too long to be acted upon the Stage, such Lines as are left out in the Acting, are marked thus ' .

Hamlet, Prince of Denmark

ACT I.

SCENE I. *An open place before the palace.*

Enter Bernardo *and* Francisco, *two Centinels.*

BERNARDO. Who's there?
FRANCISCO. Nay, answer me. Stand and unfold yourself.
BERNARDO. Long live the King!
FRANCISCO. Bernardo?
BERNARDO. He.
FRANCISCO. You come most carefully upon your hour.
BERNARDO. 'Tis now struck twelve. Get thee to bed, Francisco.
FRANCISCO. For this relief much thanks. 'Tis bitter cold,
And I am sick at heart.
10 BERNARDO. Have you had quiet guard?
FRANCISCO. Not a mouse stirring.
BERNARDO. Well, good night.
If you do meet Horatio and Marcellus,
The rivals of my watch, bid them make haste.

Enter Horatio *and* Marcellus.

FRANCISCO. I think I hear them. Stand ho, who's there?
HORATIO. Friends to this ground.
MARCELLUS. And liegemen to the Dane.
FRANCISCO. Good night.
MARCELLUS. Farewell, honest soldier: who hath relieved you?
20 FRANCISCO. Bernardo has my place. Good night.

Exit Francisco.

MARCELLUS. Holla, Bernardo!
BERNARDO. Say, what, is Horatio there?
HORATIO. A piece of him.
BERNARDO. Welcome, Horatio. Welcome, good Marcellus.
MARCELLUS. What, has this thing appeared again tonight?
BERNARDO. I have seen nothing.
MARCELLUS. Horatio says 'tis but a fantasy,
And will not let belief take hold of him
Touching the dreadful sight, twice seen of us.
30 Therefore I have entreated him along
With us to watch the minutes of this night,
That, if again this apparition come,
He may approve our eyes and speak to it.
HORATIO. 'Twill not appear.
BERNARDO. ' Sit down awhile,
And ' let us once again assail your ears,
That are so fortified against our story,
What we have two nights seen.
HORATIO. Well, ' sit we down,
40 And ' let us hear Bernardo speak of this.
BERNARDO. Last night of all,
When yon same star that's westward from the pole
Had made his course t'enlighten that part of heaven
Where it now burns, Marcellus and myself,
The bell then beating one–

Enter Ghost.

MARCELLUS. Peace! break thee off! Look where it comes again!
BERNARDO. In the same figure, like the King that's dead.
MARCELLUS. ' Thou art a scholar; ' speak to it Horatio.
BERNARDO. ' Looks it not like the King? Mark it, Horatio.
50 HORATIO. Most like. ' It startles me with fear and wonder.
BERNARDO. It would be spoke to.
MARCELLUS. Speak to it, Horatio.
HORATIO. What art thou that usurp'st this time of night
Together with that fair and warlike form
In which the majesty of buried Denmark
Did sometimes march? I charge thee speak!
MARCELLUS. It is offended.
BERNARDO. See, it stalks away.
HORATIO. Stay! Speak, speak! I charge thee speak.

Exit Ghost.

60 MARCELLUS. 'Tis gone and will not answer.
BERNARDO. How now, Horatio? You tremble and look pale:
Is not this something more than fantasy?
What think you of it?
HORATIO. I could not this believe
Without the sensible and true avouch
Of mine own eyes.
MARCELLUS. Is it not like the King?
HORATIO. As thou art to thyself.
Such was the very armor he had on
70 When th' ambitious Norway he combated;
' So frowned he once when, in an angry parle,
' He smote the sledded Pole-ax on the ice.
' 'Tis strange–'
MARCELLUS. Thus twice before, and just at the same hour,
With martial stalk hath he gone by our watch.
HORATIO. In what particular thought to work I know not;
But, in the scope of mine opinion,
This bodes some strange eruption to our state.
MARCELLUS. Pray tell me, he that knows,
80 Why this same strict and most observant watch
So nightly toils the subject of the land,
' And why such daily cost of brazen cannon
' And foreign mart for implements of war;
' Why such impress of shipwrights, whose sore task
' Does not divide the Sunday from the week;
' What might be toward, that this sweaty haste '
Doth make the night joint-laborer with the day?
' Who is't that can inform me? '
HORATIO. That can I;
90 ' At least the whisper goes so. ' Our last king,
Whose image ev'n but now appeared to us,
Was, as you know, by Fortinbras of Norway,
' Thereto pricked on by a most emulent pride, '
Dared to the combat; in which our valiant Hamlet
' (For so this side of our known world esteemed him) '
Did slay this Fortinbras; who, by a sealed compact,
Well ratified by law and heraldry,
Did forfeit, with his life, all these his lands
' Which he stood seized on, to the conqueror;
100 ' Against the which a moiety competent
' Was gaged by our king; which had returned

' To the inheritance of Fortinbras,
' Had he been vanquisher, as, by the same compact
' And carriage of the article's design
' His fell to Hamlet. ' Now, sir, young Fortinbras,
' Of unimproved mettle hot and full, '
Hath in the skirts of Norway, here and there,
Sharked up a list of lawless resolutes,
' For food and diet to some enterprise
110 ' That hath a stomach in't; which is no other,
' As it doth well appear unto our state,
' But ' to recover ' of us by strong hand
' And terms compulsive, ' those aforesaid lands
So by his father lost; and this, I take it,
Is the main motive of our preparations,
' The source of this our watch, and the chief head
' Of this post-haste and romage in the land. '

BERNARDO. I think it is no other but even so.
Well may it sort that this portentous figure
120 Comes armed through our watch so like the King
That was and is the question of the wars.

HORATIO. ' A mote it is to trouble the mind's eye.
' In the most high and flourishing state of Rome,
' A little ere the mightiest Julius fell,
' The grave stood tenantless, and the sheeted dead
' Did squeak and gibber in the Roman streets;
' Stars shone with trains of fire, dews of blood fell,
' Disasters veiled the sun; and the moist star
' Upon whose influence Neptune's empire stands
130 ' Was sick almost to doomsday with eclipse.
' And ev'n the like precurse of fierce events,
' As harbingers preceding still the fates
' And prologue to the omen coming on,
' Have heaven and earth together demonstrated
' Unto our climatures and countrymen. '

Enter Ghost.

But soft! behold! Lo, where it comes again!
I'll cross it, though it blast me.—Stay, illusion! (*Spreading his arms.*)
If thou hast any sound, or use of voice,
Speak to me—
140 If there be any good thing to be done,
That may to thee do ease and grace to me,
Speak to me.

If thou art privy to thy country's fate,
Which happily foreknowing may avoid
O, speak!–
Or if thou hast uphoarded in thy life
Extorted treasure in the womb of earth
(For which, they say, you spirits oft walk in death),

Cock crows.

Speak of it! Stay, and speak!–Stop it, Marcellus!
150 MARCELLUS. Shall I strike it with my partisan?
HORATIO. Do, if it will not stand.
BERNARDO. 'Tis here!
HORATIO. 'Tis here!
MARCELLUS. 'Tis gone.–
We do it wrong, being so majestical,
To offer it the show of violence;
It is ever, as the air, invulnerable,
And our vain blows malicious mockery.
BERNARDO. It was about to speak, when the cock crew.
160 HORATIO. And then it started, like a guilty thing
Upon a fearful summons. I have heard
The cock, that is the trumpet to the morn,
Doth with his lofty and shrill-sounding throat
Awake the god of day; and at his warning,
Whether in sea or fire, in earth or air,
Th' extravagant and erring spirit hies
To his confine. ' And of the truth herein
' This present object made probation.
MARCELLUS. ' It faded at the crowing of the cock.
170 ' Some say that ever 'gainst that season comes
' Wherein our Savior's birth is celebrated,
' This bird of dawning singeth all night long;
' And then, they say, no spirit dares stir abroad,
' The nights are wholesome, then no planets strike,
' No fairy takes, no witch hath power to charm,
' So hallowed and so gracious is the time.
HORATIO. ' So have I heard and do in part believe it. '
But look, the morn, in russet mantle clad,
Walks o'er the dew of yon high eastern hill.
180 Break we our watch up; and by my advice
Let us impart what we have seen tonight
Unto young Hamlet. Perhaps
This spirit, dumb to us, will speak to him.

' Do you consent we shall acquaint him with it,
' As needful in our loves, fitting our duty? '

MARCELLUS. Let's do't, I pray; and I this morning know
Where we shall find him most conveniently.

Exeunt.

SCENE II. *The palace.*

Enter King, *Queen*, Hamlet, Polonius, Laertes, ' Voltimand, Cornelius, ' *Gentlemen and Guards.*

KING. Though yet of Hamlet our dear brother's death
The memory be green, and that it us befitted
To bear our hearts in grief, and our whole kingdom
To be contracted in one brow of woe,
Yet so far hath discretion fought with nature
That we with wisest sorrow think on him
Together with remembrance of ourselves.
Therefore our sometimes sister, now our queen,
Th' imperial jointress to this warlike state,
10 Have we, as 'twere with a defeated joy,
' With one auspicious, and one dropping eye,
' With mirth in funeral, and with dirge in marriage,
' In equal scale weighing delight and dole, '
Taken to wife. Nor have we herein barred
Your better wisdoms, which have freely gone
With this affair along. ' For all, our thanks.
' Now follows, that you know, young Fortinbras,
' Holding a weak supposal of our worth,
' Or thinking by our late dear brother's death
20 ' Our state to be disjoint and out of frame,
' Colleagued with this dream of his advantage,
' He hath not failed to pester us with message
' Importing the surrender of those lands
' Lost by his father, with all bonds of law,
' To our most valiant brother. So much for him.
' Now for ourself and for this time of meeting.
' Thus much the business is: we have here writ
' To Norway, uncle of young Fortinbras,
' Who, impotent and bedrid, scarcely hears
30 ' Of this his nephew's purpose, to suppress

'His further gait herein, in that the levies,
' The lists, and full proportions are all made
' Out of his subjects; ' and we now dispatch
' You, good Cornelius, and you Voltimand, '
Ambassadors to Norway,
' Giving to you no further personal power
' Of treaty with the King, more than the scope
' Of these dilated articles allow.
' Farewell, and let your haste commend your duty.

40 ' CORNELIUS, VOLTIMAND. In that, and all things, will we show our duty.

' KING. We doubt it nothing. Heartily farewell.

' *Exeunt* Voltimand *and* Cornelius.

' And now, Laertes, what's the news with you?
' You told us of some suit. What is't, Laertes?
' You cannot speak of reason to the Dane
' And lose your voice. What wouldst thou beg, Laertes,
' That shall not be my offer, not thy asking?
' The head is not more native to the heart,
' The hand more instrumental to the mouth,
' Than is the throne of Denmark to thy father.
50 ' What wouldst thou have, Laertes? '

LAERTES. My dear lord,
Your leave and favor to return to France;
From whence though willingly I came to Denmark
To show my duty in your coronation,
Yet now, I must confess, that duty done,
My thoughts and wishes bend again toward France
' And bow them to your gracious leave and favor. '

KING. Have you your father's leave? What says Polonius?

POLONIUS. He hath, my lord, by laborsome petition,
60 Wrong [*sic*] from me my slow leave; and at the last,
Upon his will I sealed my hard consent.
' I do beseech you give him leave to go. '

KING. Take thy fair hour, Laertes. Time be thine,
' And thy best graces ' spend it at thy will!
But now, my cousin Hamlet, and my son—

HAMLET. A little more than kin, and less than kind.

KING. How is it that the clouds still hang on you?

HAMLET. Not so, my lord. I am too much i' th' sun.

QUEEN. Good Hamlet, cast thy nightly color off,
70 And let thine eye look like a friend on Denmark.
Do not for ever with thy veiled lids

Seek for thy noble father in the dust.
Thou know'st 'tis common, all that live must die,
Passing through nature to eternity.

HAMLET. Ay, madam, it is common.

QUEEN. If it be,
Why seems it so particular with thee?

HAMLET. Seems, madam! Nay, it is. I know not "seems."
'Tis not alone this mourning suit, good mother,[1]
80 Together with all forms, modes, shapes of grief
That can denote me truly. These indeed seem,
' For they are actions that a man might play; '
But I have that within which passeth show—
These but the trappings and the suits of woe.

KING. 'Tis sweet and commendable in your nature, Hamlet,
To give these mourning duties to your father;
But you must know, your father lost a father;
That father lost, lost his, and the survivor bound
In filial obligation for some term
90 To do obsequious sorrow. But to persevere
In obstinate condolment does express
An impious stubbornness[2] to Heaven.[3]
We pray you, throw to earth
This unprevailing woe, and think of us
As of a father; and let the world take note,

---

1. Garrick cut four lines: "Nor customary suits of solemn black, / Nor windy suspiration of forc'd breath, / No nor the fruitful river in the eye, / Nor the dejected haviour of the visage."
2. Garrick cut these partial lines: "'tis unmanly grief. / It shows a will most incorrect . . ."
3. Garrick cut ten and a half lines:

    A heart unfortified, a mind impatient,
    An understanding simple and unschooled.
    For what we know must be, and is as common
    As any the most vulgar thing to sense,
    Why should we in our peevish opposition,
    Take it to heart? Fie! 'tis a fault to Heav'n
    A fault against the dead, a fault to nature,
    To reason most absurd, whose common theme
    Is death of fathers, and who still hath cry'd
    From the first course, till he that died to-day,
    This must be so.

4. Garrick cut seven lines:

    And with no less nobility of love,

You are the most immediate to our throne:[4]
' Our chiefest courtier, cousin, and our son. '
QUEEN. Let not thy mother lose her prayers, Hamlet:
I pray thee stay with us, go not to Wittenberg.
100 HAMLET. I shall in all my best obey you, madam.
KING. Why, 'tis a loving and a fair reply.
Be as ourself in Denmark. Madam, come.
This gentle and unforced accord of Hamlet
Sits smiling to my heart: in grace whereof,
No jocund health that Denmark drinks today
But the great cannon to the clouds shall tell.[5]

Exeunt.

Manet Hamlet.

HAMLET. O that this too, too solid flesh would melt,
Thaw, and resolve itself into a dew!
Or that the Everlasting had not fixed
110 His canon 'gainst self-murder!
How weary, stale, flat, and unprofitable
Seem to me all the uses of this world!
Fie on't! O fie! 'tis an unweeded garden
That grows to seed; things rank and gross in nature
Possess it merely. That it should come to this!
But two months dead! nay, not so much, not two!
So excellent a king.[6] So loving to my mother
That he permitted not the winds of heaven
Visit her face too roughly![7] Why, she would hang on him
120 As if increase of appetite had grown
By what it fed on; and yet, within a month—
Let me not think on't! Frailty, thy name is woman!—
A little month![8]—married with mine uncle,

Than that which dearest father bears his son,
Do impart towards you: For your intent,
In going back to school to *Wittenberg*,
It is most retrograde to our desire:
And we beseech you, bend you to remain
Here in the chear and comfort of our eye,

5. Garrick cut two lines: "And the King's rouse, the Heav'n shall bruit again, / Re-speaking earthly thunder. Come away."
6. Garrick cut two half-lines: "that was to this, / *Hyperion* to a satyr!"
7. Garrick cut two half-lines: "Heaven and Earth! / Must I remember?"
8. Garrick cut five lines: "or ere those shoes were old, / With which she follow'd

My father's brother, but no more like my father
Than I to Hercules.[9]
It is not, nor it cannot come to good.
' But break, my heart, for I must hold my tongue! '

Enter Horatio, Bernardo, *and* Marcellus.

HORATIO. Hail to your lordship!
HAMLET. I am glad to see you well:
130 Horatio? or I forget myself.
HORATIO. The same, my lord, and your poor servant ever.
HAMLET. Sir, my good friend—I'll change that name with you.
And what makes you from Wittenberg, Horatio?
Marcellus!
MARCELLUS. My good lord!
HAMLET. I'm very glad to see you. Good ev'n, sir.
But what, faith, makes you from Wittenberg?
HORATIO. A truant disposition, good my lord.
HAMLET. I would not have your enemy say so,
140 Nor shall you do mine ear that violence
To be a witness of your own report
Against yourself. I know you are no truant.
But what is your affair in Elsinoor?
We'll teach you to drink deep ere you depart.
HORATIO. My lord, I came to see your father's funeral.
HAMLET. I prithee do not mock me, fellow student,
I think it was to see my mother's wedding.
HORATIO. Indeed, my lord, it followed hard upon.
HAMLET. Thrift, thrift, Horatio! The funeral baked meats
150 Did coldly furnish forth the marriage tables.
Would I had met my dearest foe in heaven
Ere I had seen that day, Horatio.
My father—methinks I see my father.
HORATIO. Where, my lord?
HAMLET. In my mind's eye, Horatio.
HORATIO. I saw him once. He was a goodly king.

---

my poor father's body, / Like *Niobe*, all tears—Why she, ev'n she—/ O Heav'n! A beast that wants discourse of reason, / Would have mourn'd longer—."

9. Garrick cut four and a half lines: "Within a month! / Ere yet the salt of most unrighteous tears / Had left the flushing in her galled eyes, / She marry'd. O most wicked speed! to post / With such dexterity t'incestuous sheets."

Garrick as Hamlet
Folger Shakespeare Library

HAMLET. He was a man, take him for all in all.
I shall not look upon his like again.
HORATIO. My lord, I think I saw him yesternight.
160 HAMLET. Saw? who?
HOTATIO. My lord, the king your father.
HAMLET. The king, my father?
HORATIO. Defer your admiration for a while
With an attentive ear, till I deliver,
Upon the witness of these gentlemen,
This wonder to you.
HAMLET. Pray, let me hear.
HORATIO. Two nights together had these gentlemen
(Marcellus and Bernardo) on their watch
170 In the dead waste and middle of the night
Been thus encountered. A figure like your father,
And armed exactly *cap-à-pie*,
Appears before them, and with solemn march
Goes slowly and stately by them. Thrice he walked
' By their oppressed and fear-surprised eyes '
Within my rapier's length; whilst they, bestilled
Almost to jelly with their fear,
Stand dumb and speak not to him. This to me
In dreadful secrecy impart they did,
180 And I with them the third night kept the watch;
Where, as they had delivered, both in time,
Form of the thing, each word made true and good,
The apparition comes.
HAMLET. But where was this?
MARCELLUS. My lord, upon the platform where we watched.
HAMLET. Did you not speak to it?
HORATIO. My lord, I did;
But answer made it none. Yet once methought
It lifted up its head and did address
190 Itself to motion, like as it would speak;
But even then the morning cock crew loud,
And at the sound it shrunk in haste away
And vanished from our sight.
HAMLET. 'Tis very strange.
HORATIO. As I do live, my honored lord, 'tis true;
And we did think it then our duty
To let you know it.
HAMLET. Indeed, sirs, but this troubles me.
Hold you the watch tonight?

200 BOTH. We do, my lord.
HAMLET. Armed, say you?
BOTH. Armed, my lord.
HAMLET. From top to toe?
BOTH. From head to foot.
HAMLET. Then saw you not his face?
HORATIO. O, yes, my lord! He wore his beaver up.
HAMLET. What, look'd he frowningly?
HORATIO. A countenance more in sorrow than in anger.
HAMLET. Pale or red?
210 HORATIO. Nay, very pale.
HAMLET. And fixed his eyes upon you?
HORATIO. Most constantly.
HAMLET. I would I had been there.
HORATIO. It would have much amazed you.
HAMLET. Very like. Stayed it long?
HORATIO. While one with moderate haste might tell a hundred.
ALL. Longer, longer.
HORATIO. Not when I saw't.
HAMLET. His beard was grizzled?
220 HORATIO. It was, as I have seen it in his life,
A sable silvered.
HAMLET. I'll watch tonight. Perchance 'twill walk again.
HORATIO. I warrant, my lord, it will.
HAMLET. If it assumes my noble father's person,
I'll speak to it, though hell itself should gape
And bid me hold my peace. I pray you all,
If you have hitherto concealed this sight,
Let it require your silence still;
And whatsoever else shall hap tonight,
230 Give it an understanding but no tongue.
I will requite your loves. So, fare ye well.
Upon the platform, 'twixt eleven and twelve,
I'll visit you.
ALL. Our duty to your honor.

Exeunt.

HAMLET. Your loves, as mine to you. Farewell.
My father's spirit in arms! All is not well.
I doubt some foul play. Would the night were come!
Till then sit still, my soul. Foul deeds will rise,
Though all the earth o'erwhelm them from men's eyes.

Ex[*it*].

[ACT II.][1]

SCENE [I. Polonius' *house*].

Enter Laertes *and* Ophelia.

LAERTES. My necessaries are embarked, farewell.
And, sister, as the winds permit
And convoy is assistant, do not sleep,
But let me hear from you
OPHELIA. Do not doubt that.
LAERTES. For Hamlet and the trifling of his favor,
Hold it a fashion and a toy in blood,
A violet in the youth and prime of nature,
Forward, not permanent, tho' sweet, not lasting,
10 The perfume of a minute.
OPHELIA. No more but so?
LAERTES. Think it no more.
' For nature crescent does not grow alone
' In thews and bulk, but as this temple waxes,
' The inward service of the mind and soul
' Grows wide withal. Perhaps he loves thee now,
' And now no soil nor cautel doth besmirch
' The virtue of his will; but you must fear,
' His greatness weighed, his will is not his own;
20 ' For he himself is subject to his birth. '
He may not, as inferior persons do,
Carve for himself; for on his choice depends
The sanctity and health of this whole state.
' And therefore must his choice be circumscribed
' Unto the voice and yielding of that body
' Whereof he is the head. Then if he says he loves you,
' It fits your wisdom so far to believe it
' As he in his peculiar act and place
' May give this saying deed, which is no further
30 ' Than the main voice of Denmark goes withal. '
Then weigh what loss your honor may sustain,
If with your credulous ear you hear his passion,
' Or lose your heart, or your chaste treasure open
' To his unmastered importunity. '
Fear it, Ophelia, fear it, my dear sister,
' And keep within the rear of your affection,
' Out of the shot and danger of desire. '

---

1. Garrick here divides Shakespeare's act I and begins his own II, i.

The chariest maid is prodigal enough
If she unmask her beauty to the moon:
40 ' Virtue itself scapes not calumnious strokes:
' The canker galls the infant of the spring
' Too oft before the buttons be disclosed,
' And in the morn and liquid dew of youth
' Contagious blastments are most imminent.
' Be wary then; best safety lies in fear;
' Youth to itself rebels, though none else near. '

OPHELIA. I shall the effect of this good lesson keep
About my heart. But, good brother,
Do not, as some ungracious pastors do,
50 Show me the steep and thorny way to heaven;
Whilst, like a libertine,
Himself the primrose path of dalliance treads
' And reaks not his own reed. '

LAERTES. O, fear me not!
I stay too long: but here my father comes.

Enter Polonius.

' A double blessing is a double grace;
' Occasion smiles upon a second leave. '

POLONIUS. Yet here, Laertes? Aboard, aboard, for shame!
Though late, very late, the moon is up
60 *And in full beauty lights you to your vessel.*
' The wind sits in the shoulder of your sail,
' And you are stayed for there. My blessing with you,
' And these few precepts in thy memory
' See thou character: Give thy thoughts no tongue,
' Nor any unproportioned thought his act.
' Be thou familiar, but by no means vulgar:
' The friends thou hast, and their adoption tried,
' Grapple them to thy soul with hoops of steel;
' But do not dull thy palm with entertainment
70 ' Of each new-hatched, unfledged comrade. Beware
' Of entrance to a quarrel, but being in,
' Bear't that th' opposer may beware of thee.
' Give every man thine ear, but few thy voice;
' Take each man's censure, but reserve thy judgment.[2]

---

2. Garrick cut eleven lines:

Costly thy habit as thy purse can buy,
But not express'd in fancy; rich, nor gaudy:

' Farewell, my blessing season this in thee! '
LAERTES. Most humbly do I take my leave, my lord.
POLONIUS. The time invites you; go; your servants tend.
LAERTES. Farewell, Ophelia, and remember well
What I have said to you.
80 OPHELIA. 'Tis in my memory lock'd,
And you yourself shall keep the key of it.
LAERTES. Farewell.

Exit Laertes.

POLONIUS. What is't, Ophelia, he has said to you?
OPHELIA. So please you, something touching the Lord *Hamlet.*
POLONIUS. Marry, well bethought!
'Tis told me he hath very oft of late
Given private time to you, and you yourself
Have of your audience been most free and bounteous.
If it be so, as so it seems to be,
90 And that in way of caution—I must tell you
You do not understand yourself so clearly
As it behooves my daughter and your honor.
What is between you? Give me up the truth.
OPHELIA. He hath, my lord, of late made many tenders
Of his affection to me.
POLONIUS. Affection! Pooh! You speak like a green girl,
Unsifted in such perilous circumstance.
Do you believe his tenders, as he calls them?
OPHELIA. I do not know, my lord, what I should think.
100 POLONIUS. Marry, I'll teach you: think yourself a baby,
That you have ta'en these tenders for true pay,
Which are not sterling. Tender yourself more dearly;
' Or (not to crack the wind of this poor phrase,
' Wringing it thus) ' you'll tender me a fool.
OPHELIA. My lord, he hath importuned me with love
In honorable fashion.

For the apparel oft proclaims the man.
And they in France, of the best rank and station,
Are most select and gen'rous, chief in that.
Neither a borrower nor a lender be;
For loan oft loses both itself and friend:
And borrowing dulls the edge of husbandry.
This above all, to thine own self be true;
And it must follow, as the night the day,
Thou can'st not then be false to any man.

POLONIUS. Ay, fashion you may call it: go to, go to.
OPHELIA. And hath given countenance to his speech, my lord,
With almost all the holy vows of heaven.
110 POLONIUS. Ay, springes to catch woodcocks. I do know,
When the blood burns, how prodigal the soul
Lends the tongue vows. ' These blazes, daughter,
' Giving more light than heat, extinct in both,
' Even in their promise, as it is a-making,
' You must not take for fire. From this time, daughter,
' Be somewhat scanter of your maiden presence.
' Set your entreatments at a higher rate
' Than a command to parley. For Lord Hamlet,
' Believe so much in him, that he is young,
120 ' And with a larger tether may he walk
' Than may be given you. In few, Ophelia,
' Do not believe his vows; for they are brokers,
' Not of that dye which their investment show,
' But mere implorers of unholy suits,
' Breathing like sanctified and pious bawds,
' The better to beguile. ' This is for all:
I would not, in plain terms, from this time forth
Have you so slander any moment's leisure
As to give words or talk with the Lord Hamlet.
130 Look to't, I charge you. Come your way.
OPHELIA. I shall obey, my lord.

Exeunt.

SCENE II. *The platform before the palace.*[1]

Enter Hamlet, Horatio, *and* Marcellus.

HAMLET. The air bites shrewdly; it is very cold.
HORATIO. It is a nipping and an eager air.
HAMLET. What hour now?
HORATIO. I think it lacks of twelve.
MARCELLUS. No, it has struck.
HORATIO. I heard it not. Then it draws near the season
Wherein the spirit held his wont to walk.

1. This is I, iii, in the 1747 Hughes-Wilkes edition which Garrick used. This edition will be referred to by the letters H. W.

Noise of warlike music within.

What does this mean, my lord?

HAMLET. The King doth wake tonight and takes his rouse,[2]

10 And, as he takes his draughts of Rhenish down,
The kettledrum and trumpet thus proclaim
The triumph of his pledge.

HORATIO. Is it a custom?

HAMLET. Ah, marry is't:
But to my mind, though I am native here
And to the manner born, it is a custom
More honored in the breach than the observance.[3]

Enter Ghost.

HORATIO. Look, my lord, where it comes!

HAMLET. Angels and ministers of grace defend us!

20 Be thou a spirit of health or goblin damn'd,
Bring with thee airs from heaven or blasts from hell,
Be thy intents wicked or charitable,
Thou com'st in such a questionable shape
That I will speak to thee. I'll call thee Hamlet,
King, Father, royal Dane. Oh, answer me!

---

2. Garrick cut one line: "Keeps wassel, and the swagg'ring upspring reels."
3. Garrick cut twenty-one and a half lines:

This heavy-handed revel, East and West,
Makes us traduc'd and tax'd of other nations:
They clepe us drunkards, and with swinish praise
Soil our addition; and indeed it takes
From our achievements, tho' perform'd at height,
The pith and marrow of our attribute.
So oft it changes in partic'lar men,
That for some vitious mole of nature in them
As in their birth, wherein they are not guilty,
(Since nature cannot chuse his origin)
By their o'er-growth of some complexion
Oft breaking down the pales and forts of reason;
Or by some habit that too much o'er-levens
The form of plausive manners, that these men
Carrying, I say, the stamp of one defect,
Being nature's livery, or fortune's star,
His virtues else, be they as pure as grace,
As infinite as man may undergo
Shall in the general censure take corruption.
From that partic'lar fault: The dram of ease
Doth all the noble substance of a doubt
To his own scandal.

Let me not burst in ignorance, but tell
Why thy canonized bones, hearsed in death,
Have burst their cerements; why the sepulchre,
Wherein we saw thee quietly interred,
30 Hath oped his ponderous and marble jaws
To cast thee up again. What may this mean
That thou, dead corse, again in complete steel,
Revisits thus the glimpses of the moon,
Making night hideous? And we fools of nature
So horridly to shake our disposition
With thoughts beyond the reaches of our souls?
Say, why is this? wherefore? what should we do?

Ghost *beckons* Hamlet.

HORATIO. It beckons you to go away with it,
As if it some impartment did desire
40 To you alone.
MARCELLUS. Look with what courteous action
It waves you to a more removed ground.
But do not go with it!
HORATIO. No, by no means! (*Holding* Hamlet.)
HAMLET. It will not speak; then I will follow it.
HORATIO. Do not, my lord.
HAMLET. Why, what should be the fear?
I value not my life;
And for my soul, what can it do to that,
50 Being a thing immortal as itself?
It waves me forth again: I'll follow it.
HORATIO. What if it tempts you towards the flood, my lord,
Or to the dreadful border of the cliff,[4]
And there assume some other horrible form
' Which might deprive your sovereignty of reason '
And draw you into madness.[5]
HAMLET. It waves me still.
Go on; I'll follow thee.
MARCELLUS. You shall not go, my lord.
60 HAMLET. Hold off your hands!
HORATIO. Be ruled; you shall not go.

---

4. Garrick cut one line: "That bettels o'er his base into the sea."
5. Garrick cut four lines: "Think of it, / The very place puts toys of desperation, / Without more motive, into every brain, / That looks so many fathoms to the sea, / And hears it roar beneath."

HAMLET. My fate cries out
And makes each petty artery in this body
As hardy as the Nemean lion's nerve.
Still I am call'd. Unhand me, gentleman!
By heav'n, I'll make a ghost of him that lets me!
I say, away! Go on; I'll follow thee.

Exeunt Ghost *and* Hamlet.

HORATIO. He grows desperate with imagination.
MARCELLUS. Let's follow; 'tis not fit thus to obey him.
70 HORATIO. To what issue will this come?
MARCELLUS. Something is rotten in the state of Denmark.
HORATIO. Heaven will discover it.
MARCELLUS. Nay, let's follow him.

Exeunt.

Enter Ghost *and* Hamlet.

HAMLET. Whither wilt thou lead me? Speak; I'll go no further.
GHOST. Mark me.
HAMLET. I will.
GHOST. My hour is almost come,
When I to sulph'rous and tormenting flames
Must render up myself.
80 HAMLET. Alas, poor ghost!
GHOST. Pity me not, but lend thy serious hearing
To what I shall unfold.
HAMLET. Speak; I am bound to hear.
GHOST. So art thou to revenge what thou shalt hear.
HAMLET. What?
GHOST. I am thy father's spirit,
Doom'd for a certain term to walk the night,
And for the day confined to fast in fires,
Till the foul crimes done in my days of nature
90 Are burnt and purged away. But that I am forbid
To tell the secrets of my prison house,
I could a tale unfold whose lightest word
Would harrow up thy soul, freeze thy young blood,
Make thy two eyes, like stars, start from their spheres,
Thy knotted and combined locks to part,
And each particular hair to stand an end
Like quills upon the fretful porcupine.
But this eternal blazon must not be

To ears of flesh and blood. List, list, O list!
100 If thou didst ever thy dear father love—
HAMLET. O Heaven!
GHOST. Revenge his foul and most unnatural murder.
HAMLET. Murder?
GHOST. Murder most foul, as in the best it is;
But this most foul, strange, and unnatural.
HAMLET. Haste me to know't, that I, with wings as swift
As meditation or the thoughts of love,
May fly to my revenge.
GHOST. I find thee apt;
110 ' And duller shouldst thou be than the fat weed
' That roots itself in ease on Lethe's wharf,
' Wouldst thou not stir in this. ' Now, Hamlet, hear:
'Tis given out that, sleeping in my garden,
A serpent stung me; so the whole ear of Denmark
Is by a forged process of my death
Rankly abused; but know, thou noble youth,
The serpent that did sting thy father's heart
Now wears his crown.
HAMLET. O my prophetic soul!
120 My uncle?
GHOST. Ay, that incestuous, that adult'rate beast,
' With witchcraft of his wits, with trait'rous gifts—
' O wicked wits and gifts, that have the power
' So to seduce! ' won to his shameful lust
The will of my most seeming virtuous queen.
' O Hamlet, what a falling-off was there,
' From me, whose love was of that dignity
' That it went hand in hand even with the vow
' I made to her in marriage, and to decline
130 ' Upon a wretch whose natural gifts were poor
' To those of mine!
' But virtue, as it never will be moved,
' Though lewdness court it in a shape of heaven,
' So vice, though to a radiant angel linked,
' Will sort itself in a celestial bed
' And prey on garbage. '
But soft! methinks I scent the morning air;
Brief let me be. Sleeping within my garden,
My custom always of the afternoon,
140 Upon my secure hour thy uncle stole,
With juice of cursed hebona in a vial,

And in the porches of my ears did pour
The leprous distilment, whose effects
Hold such an enmity with blood of man
That swift as quicksilver it courses through
The natural gates and alleys of the body,
And with sudden vigor does possess
' And curd, like eager droppings into milk, '
The thin and wholesome blood; so did it mine,
150 And a most instant tetter barked about,
Most lazar-like, with vile and loathsome crust
All my smooth body.
Thus was I, sleeping, by a brother's hand
Of life, of crown, of queen at once bereft;
Cut off even in the blossoms of my sin,
' Unhouseled, unappointed, unaneal'd, '
No reckoning made, but sent to my account
With all my imperfections on my head.

HAMLET. O, horrible! O horrible! most horrible!

160 GHOST. If thou hast nature in thee, bear it not.
Let not the royal bed of Denmark be
A couch for luxury and damned incest.
But, howsoever thou pursuest this act,
Taint not thy mind, nor let thy soul design
Against thy mother aught. Leave her to heaven,
And to those thorns that in her bosom lodge
To gord and sting her. Fare thee well at once!
The glow-worm shows the morning to be near
And gins to pale his uneffectual fire.
170 Farewell; remember me!

Exit.

HAMLET. ' O all you host of heaven! '[6] Hold, hold, my heart!
And you, my sinews, grow not instant old,
But bear me strongly up. Remember thee?
Ay, thou poor ghost, while memory holds a seat
In this distracted globe. Remember thee?
Yes, from the table of my memory
I'll wipe away all trivial fond records,
All registers of books, all forms and pressures past
That youth and observation copied there,

6. Garrick cut two half-lines: "O Earth! what else? / And shall I couple hell? O fie!"

180 And thy commandment all alone shall live
Within the book and volume of my brain.[7]
O most pernicious woman!
O villain, villain, smiling, damned villain!
My tables! meet it is I should set down
That one may smile, and smile, and be a villain;
At least I'm sure he may be so in Denmark. (*Writing.*)
So, Uncle, there you are. Now to my word:
It is "Farewell, remember me."
I have sworn't.

190 HORATIO (*within*). My lord, my lord!
MARCELLUS (*within*). Lord Hamlet!
HORATIO (*within*). Heaven secure him!
HAMLET. So be it!
HORATIO (*within*). [H] Illo, ho, ho, my lord!
HAMLET. Hillo, ho, ho, boy! Come, boy, come.

Enter Horatio *and* Marcellus.

MARCELLUS. How is't, my noble lord?
HAMLET. O, wonderful!
HORATIO. Good my lord, tell it.
HAMLET. No, you'll reveal it.
200 HORATIO. Not I, my lord.
MARCELLUS. Not I, my lord.
HAMLET. How say you then? Would heart of man once think it?
But you'll be secret.
BOTH. As death, my lord.
HAMLET. There's ne'er a villain dwelling in all Denmark
But he's an arrant knave.
HORATIO. There needs no ghost, my lord, come from the grave
To tell us this.
HAMLET. Why, right! You're in the right!
210 And so, without more circumstance at all,
I hold it fit that we shake hands and part;
You as your business and desire shall point you:
For every man hath business and desire,
Such as it is; and for my poor part,
I will go pray.
HORATIO. These are but wild and windy words, my lord.
HAMLET. I'm sorry they offend you, heartily;
' Yes, faith, heartily. '
HORATIO. There's no offence, my lord.

7. Garrick cut one line: "Unmixed with baser matter; yes, by Heaven."

220 HAMLET. Yes, by Saint Patrick, but there is, Horatio,
And much offence too. Touching this vision here,
It is an honest ghost, that let me tell you.
For your desire to know what is between us,
O'ermaster't as you may. And now, good friends,
As you are friends, scholars, and soldiers,
Grant me one poor request.

HORATIO. What is't, my lord? We will.

HAMLET. Never make known what you have seen tonight.

BOTH. My lord, we will not.

230 HAMLET. Nay, but swear't.

HORATIO. In faith,
My lord, not I.

MARCELLUS. Nor I, my lord, in faith.

HAMLET. Upon my sword.[8]

GHOST. Swear. (Ghost *cries under the stage.*)[9]

HORATIO. O day and night, but this is wondrous strange!

HAMLET. And therefore as a stranger give it welcome.
There are more things in heaven and earth, Horatio,
Than are dreamt of in your philosophy. But come!
240 Here, as before, never, so help your mercy,
How strange or odd so'er I bear myself
(As I perchance hereafter shall think meet
To put an antic disposition on),
That you at such times seeing me, ne'er shall,
With arms encumber'd thus, or head thus shak'd,
Or by pronouncing of some doubtful phrase,

---

8. Two lines cut: Garrick cut two lines: "MAR. We have sworn, my lord, already. / "HAM. Indeed upon my sword, indeed."

9. Garrick cut fifteen lines:

HAM. Ha, ha, Boy, say'st thou so? art thou there, old True-penny?
Come on, you hear this fellow in the cellarage;
Consent to swear.

HOR. Propose the oath, my lord.

HAM. Never to speak of this that you have seen,
Swear by my sword.

GHOST (*below*). Swear.

HAM. Then we'll shift our ground;
Come hither, hither, Gentlemen,
And lay your hands again upon my sword.
Swear by my sword,
Never to speak of this that you have heard.

GHOSTS (*below*). Swear.

HAM. Well said, old mole, can'st work i'th' ground, so fast?
A worthy pioneer! once more remove, good friends.

As "Well, well, we know," or "We could, and if we would,"[10]
Or such ambiguous giving out, to note
That you know aught of me—this you must swear.[11]

250 GHOST. Swear.

HAMLET. Rest, rest, perturbed spirit! So, gentlemen,
With all my love I do commend me to you;
And what so poor a man as Hamlet is
May do t'express his love and friendship to you
Shall never fail. Let us go in together;
And still your fingers on your lips, I pray.
The time is out of joint. O cursed spite
That ever I was born to set it right![12]

Exeunt.

ACT III.[1]

SCENE I. *An apartment in* Polonius's *house.*

Enter Polonius, ' *with his Man.*

' POLONIUS. Give him this money and these two notes, Reynaldo.

' REYNALDO. I will, my lord.

' POLONIUS. You shall do marvelous wisely, good Reynaldo,
' Before you visit him, to make inquiry
' Of his behavior.

' REYNALDO. My lord, I did intend it.

' POLONIUS. Marry, well said, very well said. Look you, sir,
' Enquire me first what Danskers are in Paris;
' And how, and who, what means, and where they keep,
10 ' What company, at what expense; and finding
' By this encompassment and drift of question
' That they do know my son, come you more near;
' Then your particular demands will touch it.
' Take you, as 'twere, some distant knowledge of him;
' As thus, "I know his father and his friends,
' And in part him." Do you mark this, Reynaldo?

' REYNALDO. Ay, very well, my lord.

---

10. Garrick cut one line: "Or, if we list to speak; or there be, or if there might."
11. Garrick cut one line: "So grace and mercy at your most need help you."
12. Garrick cut one line: "Nay come, let's go together."
1. This is II, i, in H. W.

' POLONIUS. "And in part him, but," you may say, "not well
' But if it be he I mean, he's very wild,
20 ' Addicted so and so;" and there put on him
' What forgeries you please; marry, none so rank
' As may dishonor him—take heed of that;
' But, sir, such wanton, wild and usual slips
' As are companions noted and most known
' To youth and liberty.
' REYNALDO. As gaming, my lord.
' POLONIUS. Ay, or drinking, fencing, swearing,
' Quarreling, drabbing. You may go so far.
' REYNALDO. My lord, that will dishonor him.
30 ' POLONIUS. Faith, no, as you may season it i' th' charge.
' You must not put another scandal on him,
' That he is open in incontinency.
' That's not my meaning. But breathe his faults so quaintly
' That they may seem the taints of liberty,
' The flash and outbreak of a fiery mind,
' A savageness in unreclaimed blood,
' Of general assault.
' REYNALDO. But, my good lord—
' POLONIUS. Wherefore should you do this?
40 ' REYNALDO. Ay, my lord,
' I would know that.
' POLONIUS. Marry, sir, here's my drift;
' And I believe it is a fetch of wit:
' You laying these slight sullies on my son,
' As 'twere a thing a little soiled with working,
' Mark you,
' Your party in converse, he you would sound,
' Having ever seen in the prenominate crimes
' The youth you breathe of guilty, be assured
50 ' He closes with you in this consequence:
' "Good sir," or so, a "friend," or "gentleman"—
' According to the phrase or the addition
' Of man and country—
' REYNALDO. Very good, my lord.
' POLONIUS. And then, sir, does he this?—he does—What was I about to say? By the mass, I was about to say something! Where did I leave?
' REYNALDO. At "closes in the consequence."
' POLONIUS. At "closes in the consequence"—Ay, marry!
60 ' He closes thus: "I know the gentleman.

' I saw him yesterday, or th' other day,
' Or then, or then, with such and such, and, as you say,
' There was he gaming; there o'ertook in's rouse;
' There falling out at tennis, or perchance,
' I saw him enter such and such a house of sale,"
' *Videlicet*, a brothel, or so forth. See you now,
' Your bait of falsehood takes this carp of truth;
' And thus do we of wisdom and of reach,
' With windlasses and with assays of bias,
70 ' By indirection find directions out.
' So, by my former lecture and advice,
' Shall you my son. You have me, have you not?
' REYNALDO. My lord, I have.
' POLONIUS. Good be t'ye, fare ye well.
' REYNALDO. Good, my lord.
' POLONIUS. Observe his inclination in yourself.
' REYNALDO. I shall, my lord.
' POLONIUS. And let him ply his music.
' REYNALDO. Well, my lord.

' *Exit Reynaldo.* '

Enter Ophelia.

80 POLONIUS. ' Farewell. ' How now, Ophelia, what's the matter?
OPHELIA. O, my lord, my lord, I have been so affrighted!
POLONIUS. With what?
OPHELIA. My lord, as I was reading in my closet,
Prince Hamlet, ' with his doublet, ' all unbraced,
' No hat upon his head, his stockings loose,
' Ungart'red, and down-gyved to his ankle; '
Pale as his shirt, his knees knocking each other,
And with a look so piteous,
As if he had been sent from hell
90 To speak of horrors—he comes before me.
POLONIUS. Mad for thy love?
OPHELIA. My lord, I do not know,
But truly I do fear it.
POLONIUS. What said he?
OPHELIA. He took me by the wrist and held me hard;
Then he goes to the length of all his arm,
And, with his other hand thus o'er his brow,
He falls to such perusal of my face
As he would draw it. Long stayed he so.

100 At last, a little shaking of my arm,
And thrice his head thus waving up and down,
He raised a sigh so piteous and profound
As it did seem to shatter all his bulk
And end his being. That done, he lets me go,
And with his head over his shoulders turned
He seemed to find his way without his eyes,
For out of doors he went without their helps,
And to the last bended their light on me.

POLONIUS. Come, go with me. I will go seek the King.
110 This is the very ecstasy of love,
' Whose violent property forgoes itself
' And leads the will to desperate undertakings
' As oft as any passion under heaven
' That does afflict our natures. I am sorry.
' What, ' have you given him any hard words of late?

OPHELIA. No, my good lord; but, as you did command,
I did repel his letters and denied
His access to me.

POLONIUS. That hath made him mad.
120 ' I'm sorry that with better heed and judgment
' I had not quoted him. I feared he did but trifle
' And meant to wreck thee; but beshrew my jealousy!
' It seems it is as proper to our age
' To cast beyond ourselves in our opinions
' As it is common for the younger sort
' To lack discretion. ' Come, go with me to the King.
This must be known, which, being kept close, might move
More grief to hide than hate to utter love.
Come.

Exeunt.

SCENE II. *The palace.*

Enter King, Queen, Rosencrans, *and* Guildenstern.

KING. Welcome, good Rosencrans and Guildenstern.
Besides that we did long to see you,
The need we have to use you did provoke
Our hasty sending. Something you have heard
Of Hamlet's transformations. ' So I call it,
' Sith nor th' exterior nor the inward man
' Resembles that it was. ' What it should be

More than his father's death, ' that thus hath put him
' So much from th' understanding of himself, '
10 I cannot dream of. I entreat you both
' That, being of so young days brought up with him,
' And sith so neighbor'd to his youth and havior, '
That you vouchsafe your rest here in our court
Some little time; so by your companies
To draw him on to pleasures, and to ' gather
' So much as from occasion you may ' glean,
Whether aught to us unknown afflicts him thus
That lies within our remedy.

QUEEN. Good gentlemen, he hath much talked of you,
20 And sure I am two men are not living
To whom he more adheres. If it will please you
To show us so much gentleness and good will
As to employ your time with us a while,
For the supply and profit of our hope,
Your visitation shall receive such thanks
As fits a king's remembrance.

ROSENCRANS. Both your Majesties
Might, by the sovereign power you have over us,
Put your dread pleasure more into command
30 Than to entreaty.

GUILDENSTERN. But we both obey,
And here give up ourselves in the full bent,
To lay our service freely at your feet.

KING. Thanks, Rosencrans, and gentle Guildenstern.

QUEEN. ' Thanks, Guildenstern, and gentle Rosencrans. '
And I beseech you instantly to visit
My too much changed son.—Go, some of you,
And bring these gentlemen where *Hamlet* is.

GUILDENSTERN. Heaven make our presence and our practices
40 Pleasant and helpful to him!

QUEEN. Amen!

Exeunt Rosencrans and Guildenstern.

Enter Polonius.

' POLONIUS. Th' ambassadors from Norway, my good lord,
' Are joyfully return'd.

' KING. Thou still hast been the father of good news.

' POLONIUS. Have I, my lord? I assure my good liege
' I hold my duty as I hold my soul,

' Both to my God and to my gracious king;
' And ' I do think—or else this brain of mine
Hunts not the trail of policy or sure
50 As it has used to do—that I have found
The very cause of Hamlet's lunacy.

KING. O, speak of that! That I do long to hear.

' POLONIUS. Give first admittance to the ambassadors,
' My news shall be the fruit to that great feast.

' KING. Thyself do grace to them, and bring them in.

' *Exit* Polonius.

' He tells me, my dear Gertrude, he hath found
' The head and source of all your son's distemper.

' QUEEN. I doubt it is no other but the main,
' His father's death and our o'erhasty marriage.

' *Enter* Polonius *and* Ambassadors.

60 ' KING. Well, we shall sift him.—Welcome, my good friends.
' Say, Voltimand, what from our brother Norway?

' VOLTIMAND. Most fair return of greetings and desires.
' Upon our first, he sent out to suppress
' His nephew's levies, which to him appeared
' To be a preparation 'gainst the Pollack,
' But better looked into, he truly found
' It was against your Highness; whereat grieved,
' That so his sickness, age, and impotence
' Was falsely borne in hand, sends out arrests
70 ' On Fortinbras; which he, in brief, obeys,
' Receives rebuke from Norway, and, in fine,
' Makes vow before his uncle never more
' To give the assay of arms against your Majesty.
' Whereon old Norway, overcome with joy,
' Gives him three thousand crowns in annual fee
' And his commission to employ those soldiers,
' So levied as before, against the Pollack;
' With an entreaty, herein further shown,
' That it might please you to give quiet pass
80 ' Through your dominions for this enterprise,
' On such regards of safety and allowance
' As herein are set down.

' KING. It likes us well;
' And at our more considered time we'll read,
' Answer, and think upon this business.

' Meantime we thank you for your well-took labor.
' Go to your rest; at night we'll feast together.
' Most welcome home!

' *Exeunt* Ambassadors.

POLONIUS. ' This business is well ended. '
90 My liege, and madam, to expostulate
What majesty should be, what duty is,
Why day is day, night night, and time is time,
Were nothing but to waste night, day, and time.
Therefore, brevity is the soul of wit,
And tediousness the limbs and outward flourishes.
I will be brief. Your noble son is mad.
Mad call I it; for, to define true madness,
What is't but to be nothing else but mad?
But let that go.
100 QUEEN. More matter, with less art.
POLONIUS. Madam, I swear I use no art at all.
That he is mad, 'tis true: 'Tis true 'tis pity;
And pity 'tis 'tis true. A foolish figure!
But farewell it, for I will use no art.
Mad let us grant him then. And now remains
That we find out the cause of this effect—
Or rather say, the cause of this defect,
For this effect defective comes by cause.
Thus it remains, and the remainder thus. Consider:
110 I have a daughter (have while she is mine),
Who in her duty and obedience, mark,
Hath given me this. Now gather, and surmise. (*Reads.*)
To the celestial, and my soul's idol, the most beautified Ophelia:—
That's an ill phrase, a vile phrase; *beautified* is a vile phrase. But you shall hear—*Thus in her excellent white bosom, these, &c.*
QUEEN. Came this from Hamlet to her?
POLONIUS. Good madam, stay awhile. I will be faithful.

Doubt that the stars are fire;
Doubt that the sun doth move;
120 *Doubt truth to be a liar;*
But never doubt I love.

O dear Ophelia, *I am ill at these numbers; I have not art to reckon my groans; but that I love thee best, O most best, believe it. Adieu. Thine evermore, most dear lady, while this machine is to him,* Hamlet.

This, in obedience, hath my daughter shown me;
And more concerning his solicitings,
As they fell out by time, by means, and place,
' All given to mine ear. '

130 KING. But how hath she
Received his love?

POLONIUS. What do you think of me?

KING. As of a man faithful and honorable.

POLONIUS. I would fain prove so. But what might you think,
' When I had seen this hot love on the wing
' (As I perceived it, I must tell you that,
' Before my daughter told me), what might you '
Or my dear Majesty your queen here, think,
If I had ' played the desk or table book,
140 ' Or given my heart a winking mute and dumb, '
Or looked upon this love with idle sight?
' What might you think? ' No, I went round to work,
And my young mistress thus I charged:
"Lord Hamlet is a prince above thy sphere.
This must not be." And then I precepts gave her,
That she should lock herself from his resort,
Admit no messengers, receive no tokens.
Which done, she took the fruits of my advice,
And he, repelled, a short tale to make,
150 Fell into a sadness, then into a fast,
' Thence to a watch, thence into a weakness, '
Thence to a lightness, and, by this declension,
Into the madness wherein he now raves,
And all we wail for.

KING. Do you think 'tis this?

QUEEN. It may be, very likely.

POLONIUS. Hath there been such a time—I would fain know that—
That I have positively said " 'Tis so."
When it proved otherwise?

160 KING. Not that I know.

POLONIUS. Take this from this, if this be otherwise.
If circumstances lead me, I will find
Where truth is hid, though it were hid indeed
Within the centre.

KING. How may we try it farther?

POLONIUS. Sometimes he walks four hours together
Here in the lobby.

QUEEN. So he does indeed.

POLONIUS. At such time I'll loose my daughter to him.

170 So please your Majesty to hide yourself
Behind the arras then.
Mark the encounter. If he love her not,
And be not from his reason fall'n thereon,
Let me be no assistant for a state,
But keep farm and carters.

KING. We will try it.

Enter Hamlet *reading*.

QUEEN. But look where sadly the poor wretch comes reading.

POLONIUS. Away, I do beseech you, both away!

Exeunt King *and* Queen.

I'll board him presently. ' O give me leave, '
180 How does my good lord Hamlet?

' HAMLET. Excellent well.

' POLONIUS. Do you know me, my lord? '

HAMLET. Excellent well. You are a fishmonger.

POLONIUS. Not I, my lord.

HAMLET. Then I would you were so honest a man.

POLONIUS. Honest, my lord?

HAMLET. Ay, sir. To be honest, as this world goes, is to be one man picked out of ten thousand.

POLONIUS. That is very true, my lord.

190 HAMLET. For if the sun breed maggots in a dead dog, being a good kissing carrion—Have you a daughter?

POLONIUS. I have, my lord.

HAMLET. Let her not walk i' th' sun. Conception is a blessing, but as your daughter may conceive, Friend, look to't.

POLONIUS (*aside*). ' How say you by that? ' Still harping on my daughter. Yet he knew me not at first, but said I was a fishmonger. He is far gone! And truly in my youth I suffered much extremity for love —very near this. I'll speak to him again.—What do you read, my lord?

HAMLET. Words, words, words.

200 POLONIUS. What is the matter, my lord?

HAMLET. Between who?

POLONIUS. I mean the matter that you read, my lord.

HAMLET. Slanders, sir; for the satirical rogue says here that old men have grey beards; that their faces are wrinkled; their eyes purging thick amber and plum-tree gum; and that they have a plentiful lack of wit, together with most weak hams. All which, sir, though I most potently believe, yet I hold it not honesty to have it thus set down; for you yourself, sir, shall grow old as I am if, like a crab, you could go backward.

210 POLONIUS. Though this be madness, yet there's method in't.—Will you walk out of the air, my lord?

HAMLET. Into my grave?

POLONIUS. Marry, that's out of the air indeed. How pregnant his replies are! a happiness that often madness hits on, ' which reason and sanity could not so happily be delivered of. I will leave him and my daughter. ' My lord, I will take my leave of you.

HAMLET. You cannot take from me anything that I will not more willingly part withal, except my life.

POLONIUS. Fare you well, my lord.

220 HAMLET. These tedious old fools!

Enter Guildenstern *and* Rosencrans.

POLONIUS. You go to seek Lord Hamlet; there he is.

Exit.

ROSENCRANS. Save you, sir.

GUILDENSTERN. My honored lord!

ROSENCRANS. My most dear lord!

HAMLET. My excellent good friends! How dost thou, Guildenstern? Ah, Rosencrans! Good lads, how do you both? [1] Well, what news?

ROSENCRANS. None, my lord, but that the world's grown honest.

HAMLET. Then is doomsday near! Sure your news is not true.[2] But in the beaten way of friendship, what makes you at Elsinoor?

---

1. Garrick cut nine and a half lines:

ROS. As the indiff'rent children of the earth.

GUIL. Happy in that we are not over-happy; on tun's cap we're not the very button.

HAM. Nor the soles of her shoe.

GUIL. Neither, my lord.

HAM. Then you live about her waist, or in the middle of her favour.

GUIL. Faith, in her privates we.

HAM. In the secret parts of fortune; Oh most true! She is a strumpet.

2. Garrick cut thirty and a half lines:

Let me question more in particular: What have you, my good friends, deserv'd at the hands of fortune, that she sends you to prison hither?

GUIL. Prison, my lord?

HAM. *Denmark's* a prison.

ROS. Then is the world one.

HAM. A goodly one, in which there are many confines, wards and dungeons; *Denmark* being one o'th' worst.

30 ROSENCRANS. To visit you, my lord; no other occasion.

HAMLET. Beggar that I am, I am even poor in thanks; but I thank you. Were you not sent for? Is it your own inclining? Is it a free visitation? Come, come, deal justly with me! Nay, speak.

GUILDENSTERN. What should we say, my lord?

HAMLET. Anything, but to the purpose you were sent for. There is a kind of confession in your looks, which your modesties have not craft enough to color. I know the good King and Queen have sent for you.

ROSENCRANS. To what end, my lord?

40 HAMLET. Nay, that you must teach me. But let me conjure you by the rights of our fellowships, by the consonancy of our youth, by the obligation of our love, and by what more dear a better proposer could charge you withal, be even and direct with me, whether you were sent for or no.

ROSENCRANS. What say you?

HAMLET. Nay then, I have an eye of you. If you love me, hold not off.

GUILDENSTERN. My lord, we were sent for.

HAMLET. I will tell you why; so shall my anticipation prevent your discovery, and your secrecy to the King and Queen moult no feather.
50 I have of late—but wherefore I know not—lost all my mirth, forgone all custom of exercises, ' and indeed it goes so heavily with my disposition, ' that this goodly frame, the earth, seems to me a sterile promontory; this most excellent canopy, the air, this majestical roof fretted with golden fire—why, it appears nothing to me but a foul and pestilent congregation of vapors. What a piece of work is man! how noble in reason! how infinite in faculties! in form and moving how express and admirable! in action how like an angel! in appre-

---

ROS. We think not so, my lord.

HAM. Why then 'tis none to you; for there is nothing either good or bad, but thinking makes it so: To me it is a prison.

ROS. Why then your ambition makes it one: 'Tis too narrow for your mind.

HAM. O God! I could be bound in a nut-shell, and count myself a king of infinite space, were it not that I have bad dreams.

GUIL. Which dreams indeed are ambitious, for the very substance of the ambitious is merely the shadow of a dream.

HAM. A dream itself is but a shadow.

ROS. Truly, and I hold ambition of so airy and light quality, that it is but a shadow's shadow.

HAM. Then are our beggars bodies, and our monarchs and out-stetch'd heroes, the beggars shadows. Shall we to th' court? for by my fey I cannot reason.

BOTH. We'll wait upon you.

HAM. No such matter. I will not sort you with the rest of my servants; for to speak to you like an honest man, I am most dreadfully attended.

hension the beauty of the world, the paragon of animals! And yet to me what is quintessence of dust? Man delights not me, nor woman
260 neither, though by your smiling you seem to say so.

ROSENCRANS. My lord, there was no such stuff in my thoughts.

HAMLET. Why did ye laugh then, when I said "Man delights not me"?

ROSENCRANS. To think, my lord, if you delight not in man, what Lenten entertainment the players shall receive from you. We met them on the way, and hither are they coming to offer you service.

HAMLET. He that plays the king shall be welcome—his Majesty shall have tribute of me; the adventurous knight shall use his foil and target; the lover shall not sigh gratis; the humorous man shall end his part in peace; and the lady shall speak her mind freely, or the blank
270 verse shall halt for't. What players are they?

ROSENCRANS. Even those you were wont to take such delight in, the tragedians of the city.[3]

HAMLET. Do they hold the same estimation they did when I was in the city? Are they so followed?

ROSENCRANS. No indeed they are not.[4]

HAMLET. It is not very strange; for my uncle is King of Denmark, and those that would make mouths at him while my father lived, now give twenty, forty, fifty, nay, a hundred ducats apiece for his picture in little. There is something in this more than natural, if philosophy
280 could find it out. (*A flourish.*)

---

3. Garrick cut four lines: "HAM. How chances it they travel? their residence both in reputation and profit was better both ways. / ROS. I think their inhibition comes by the means of the late innovation."

4. Garrick cut twenty-six lines:

HAM. How comes it? do they grow rusty?

ROS. Nay, their endeavour keeps in the wonted pace; but there is, Sir, an airy of children, little yases, that cry out on the top of question, and are most tyrannically clapp'd for't: these are now the faction, and so be-rattled the common stages (so they call them) that many wearing rapiers, are afraid of goose-quills, and dare scarce come thither.

HAM. What, are they children? Who maintains 'em? How are they escorted? will they pursue the quality no longer than they can sing? Will they not say afterwards, if they should grow themselves to common players, as it is most like, if their means are no better, their writers do them wrong to make them exclaim against their own succession?

ROS. Faith, there has been much to do on both sides; and the nation holds it no sin to tarre them on to controversy. There was for a while no money bid for argument, unless the poet and the player went to cuffs in the question.

HAM. Is't possible?

GUIL. Oh there has been much throwing about of brains!

HAM. Do the boys carry it away?

ROS. Ay, that they do, my lord, *Hercules* and his load too.

GUILDENSTERN. Shall we call the players?

HAMLET. Gentlemen, you are welcome to Elsinoor. Your hands, come![5] The appurtenance of welcome is fashion and ceremony.[6] But my uncle-father and aunt-mother are deceived.

GUILDENSTERN. In what, my dear lord?

HAMLET. I am but mad north-north-west. When the wind is southerly I know a hawk from a handsaw.

Enter Polonius.

POLONIUS. Well be with you, gentlemen!

HAMLET. Hark you, Guildenstern and Rosencrans—that great baby that
90 you see there is not yet out of his swaddling clouts.

ROSENCRANS. Haply he is the second time come to them; for they say an old man is twice a child.

HAMLET. I prophesy that he comes to tell me of the players. Mark it.—You say right, sir; a Monday morning; 'twas then indeed.

POLONIUS. My lord, I have news to tell you.

HAMLET. My lord, I have news to tell you; when Roscius was an actor in Rome—

POLONIUS. The actors are come hither, my lord.

HAMLET. Buzz, buzz!

00 POLONIUS. Upon mine honor.

HAMLET. Then came each actor on his ass—

POLONIUS. The best actors in the world, either for tragedy, comedy, history, pastoral, pastoral-comical, historical-pastoral; ' scene undividable, or poem unlimited. ' Seneca cannot be too heavy, nor Plautus too light, for the law of wit and liberty. These are the only men.

HAMLET. O Jephtha, judge of Israel, what a treasure hadst thou!

POLONIUS. What a treasure had he, my lord?

HAMLET. Why one fair daughter and no more, the which he loved pass-
10 ing well.

POLONIUS (*aside*). Still on my daughter.

' HAMLET. Am I not i' th' right, old Jephtha?

' POLONIUS. If you call me Jephtha, my lord, I have a
' Daughter that I love passing well. '

HAMLET. Nay, that follows not.

POLONIUS. Nay, what follows then, my lord?

---

5. Words cut by Garrick in Hamlet's speech: "come then."
6. Garrick cut four lines: "let me comply with you in / this garb, lest my extent to the players, which I / tell you must shew fairly outwards, should more appear / like entertainment than yours; you are welcome."

HAMLET. 'Why, as by lot, God wot, and then you know it came to pass as most like it was.' The first row of the rubric will show you more, for look where my abridgement comes.

Enter Players.

320 HAMLET. 'You are welcome, masters, welcome all,[7] my old friend! Why thy face is valanced since I saw thee last. Com'st thou to beard me in Denmark? What, my young lady and mistress! marry, your ladyship is grown nearer to heaven than when I saw you last by the altitude of a chopine. I wish your voice, like a piece of uncurrent gold, be not cracked within the ring.–Masters, you are all welcome. We'll e'en to't like friendly falconers, fly at anything we see. We'll have a speech straight. Come, give us a taste of your quality. Come, a passionate speech.

PLAYERS. What speech, my good lord?

330 HAMLET. I heard thee speak me a speech once, but it was never acted; or if it was, not above once; for the play, I remember, pleased not the million, 'twas caviar to the multitude.[8] One speech in't I chiefly loved. 'Twas Aeneas's talk to Dido, and thereabout of it especially where he speaks of Priam's slaughter. If it live in your memory, begin at this line–let me see, let me see–"The rugged Pyrrhus, like th' Hyrcanian beast"–"Beast!" no, that's not it, yet it begins with Pyrrhus.
The rugged Pyrrhus, he whose sable arms,
Black as his purpose, did the night resemble,[9]

---

7. Garrick cut part of one line: "I am glad to see thee well; welcome, good friends. Oh."
8. Garrick cut eight lines: "but it was, as I receiv'd it and others, whose judgments in such matters cried in the top of mine, an excellent play, well digested in the scenes, set down with as much modesty as cunning. I remember one said there were no salt in the lines to make the matter savory, nor no matter in the phrase that might indite the author of affection, but call'd it an honest method, as wholesome as sweet, and by very much more handsome than fine."
9. Garrick cut ten lines:

When he lay couched in the om'nous Horse,
Hath now his beard and black complexion smear'd
With heraldry more dismal; head to foot
Now is he total gules; horribly trick'd
With blood of fathers, mothers, daughters, sons,
Bak'd and impasted with the parching streets,
That lend a tyrannous and a damned light
To their lord's murder; roasted in wrath and fire,
And thus o'er-cised with coagulate gore,
With eyes like carbuncles, the hellish *Pyrrhus*

340 ' Old gransire Priam seeks. '
So proceed you.

POLONIUS. My lord, well-spoken, with good accent and good discretion.

HAMLET. So proceed you.

PLAYER. Anon he finds him,
Striking too short at Greeks, his antic sword
Rebellious to his arm, lies where it falls,
Repugnant to command. Unequal matched,
Pyrrhus at Priam drives, in rage strikes wide;
But with the whiff and wind of his fell sword
350 Th' unnerved father falls. Then senseless Ilium,
' Seeming to feel his blow, with flaming top
' Stoops to his base, and with a hideous crash
' Takes prisoner Pyrrhus' ear. For lo! his sword,
' Which was declining on the milky head
' Of reverend Priam, seemed i' th' air to stick.
' So, as a painted tyrant, Pyrrhus stood,
' And like a neutral to his will and matter,
' Did nothing. '
But as we often see against some storm,
360 A silence in the heaven, the rack stand still,
The bold wind speechless, and the orb below
As hush as death—anon the dreadful thunder
Doth rend the region; so, after Pyrrhus' pause,
Aroused vengeance sets him new awork;
And never did the Cyclops' hammers fall
On Mars his armor, forged for proof eterne,
With less remorse than Pyrrhus' bleeding sword
Now falls on Priam.
Out, out, thou strumpet fortune! ' All you gods,
370 ' In general synod take away her power;
' Break all the spokes and felloes from her wheel,
' And bowl the round nave down the hill of heaven,
' As low as to the fiends! '

POLONIUS. This is too long.

HAMLET. It shall to the barber's, with your beard.—Prithee, say on. He's for a jig or a tale of bawdry, or he sleeps. Say on, and come to Hecuba.

PLAYER. But who, alas, had seen the mobled queen—

HAMLET. The mobled queen!

380 POLONIUS. That's good.

PLAYER. Run barefoot up and down, threat'ning the flames;
A clout upon that head

Where late the diadem stood, and for a robe,
' About her lank and all o'erteemed loins, '
A blanket, in th' alarm of fear caught up—
Who this had seen, with tongue in venom steeped,
'Gainst fortune's state would treason have pronounced.
' But if the gods themselves did see her then,
' When she saw Pyrrhus make malicious sport
390 ' In mincing with his sword her husband's limbs,
' The instant burst of clamor that she made
' Unless things mortal move them not at all,
' Would have made milch the burning eyes of heaven
' And passion in the gods. '

POLONIUS. Look whether he has not turned his color, and has tears in's eyes. Prithee, no more!

HAMLET. 'Tis well. I'll have thee speak out the rest of this soon. Good my lord, will you see the players well bestowed? Do you hear? Let them be well used; for they are the abstract and brief chronicles of 400 the time. After your death you were better have a bad epitaph than their ill report while you live.

POLONIUS. My lord, I will use them according to their desert.

HAMLET. Much better! Use every man, sir, according to his desert, and who should 'scape whipping? Use 'em after your own honor and dignity. The less they deserve, the more merit is in your bounty. Take them in.

POLONIUS. Come, sirs.

HAMLET. Follow him, friends.[10] Dost thou hear me, old friend? Can you play "The Murder of Gonzago"?

410 PLAYER. Ay, my lord.

HAMLET. We'll have it tomorrow night. You could for need study a speech of some dozen lines which I would set down and insert, could you not?

PLAYER. Ay, my lord.

HAMLET. Very well. Follow that lord—and look you mock him not. My good friends, I'll leave you till night. You are welcome to Elsinoor.[11]

Exeunt all but Hamlet.

HAMLET. O what a wretch and pleasant slave am I!
Is it not monstrous that this player here,
But in a fiction, in a dream of passion,
420 Could force his soul so to his own conceit

---

10. Garrick cut this line: "we'll have a play tomorrow."
11. Garrick cut two lines: "ROS. Farewell, my lord. / HAM. "I so, good by t'ye."

That, from her working, all the visage warmed,
Tears in his eyes, distraction in his aspect,
A broken voice, and his whole function suiting
With forms to his conceit? and all for nothing,
For Hecuba?
What's Hecuba to him, or he to Hecuba,
That he should weep for her? What would he do,
Had he the motive and that ground for passion
That I have? He would drown the stage with tears,[12]
30 Make mad the guilty and appal the free,
Confound the ignorant, and amaze indeed
The very faculties of eyes and ears.[13]
For it cannot be. *Am I a coward*?
But I am pigeon-livered and lack gall
To make oppression bitter, or ere this
I should have fatted all the region kites
With this slave's offal.[14] I have heard
That guilty creatures, sitting at a play,
Have by the very cunning of the scene
40 Been struck so to the soul that presently
They have proclaimed their malefactions;
For murder, though it have no tongue, will speak
' With most miraculous organ. ' I'll have these players
Play something like the murder of my father
Before my uncle. I'll observe his looks.
I'll tent him to the quick; if he look pale,
I know my course. The spirit that I have seen
May be a devil, and the devil may have power

---

12. Garrick cut one line: "and cleave the gen'ral ear with horrid speech,"
13. Garrick cut ten lines:

yet I,
A dull and muddy-mettled rascal, peak
Like *John-a-dreams*, unpregnant of my cause,
And can say nothing; no, not for a King,
Upon whose property, and most dear life,
A damn'd defeat was made. Am I a coward?
Who calls me villain, breaks my pate across,
Plucks off my beard, and blows it in my face,
Tweeks me by the nose, gives me the lye i'th' throat
As deep as to the lungs; Who does me thus?
Ha! why I should take it;

14. Garrick cut eight lines:

Bloody, bawdy villain!
Remorseless, treacherous, leach'rous, kindless villain!

T'assume a pleasing shape;[15] I'll have grounds
450 More relative than this. The play's the thing
Wherein I'll catch the conscience of the King.

Exit.

ACT IV.[1]

SCENE I. [*The palace.*]

Enter King, Queen, Polonius, Ophelia, Rosencrans, Guildenstern, *gentlemen and guards.*

KING. And can you by no drift of conference
Get from him why he puts on this confusion,
' Grating so harshly all his days of quiet
' With turbulent and dangerous lunacy?
ROSENCRANS. He does confess he feels himself distracted,
But from what cause he will by no means speak.
' GUILDENSTERN. Nor do we find him forward to be sounded,
' But with a crafty madness keeps aloof
' When we would bring him on to some confession
10 ' Of his true state. '
QUEEN. Did he receive you well?
ROSENCRANS. Most civilly.
GUILDENSTERN. But with much forcing of his disposition.
ROSENCRANS. Unapt to question, but of our demands
Most free in his reply.
QUEEN. Did you invite him to any pastime?
ROSENCRANS. Madam, it so fell out that certain players
We o'ertook on the way; of these we told him,
And there did seem in him a kind of joy

What what an ass am I? This is most brave,
That I, the son of a dear father murder'd,
Prompted to my revenge by Heav'n and Hell,
Must, like a whore, unpack my heart with words,
And fall a cursing like a very drab, a scullion; fie upon't! foh!
About my brain: hum.

15. Garrick cut three lines: "yes, and perhaps / Out of my weakness, and my melancholy, / As he is very potent with such spirits, / Abuses me to damn me."

1. This is III, i, in H. W.

20 To hear of it. They're here about the court,
And, as I think, they have already order
This night to play before him.

POLONIUS. 'Tis most true;
And he beseeched me to entreat your Majesties
To hear and see the matter.

KING. With all my heart. And it doth much content me
To hear him so inclined.
Good gentlemen, give him a further edge
And urge him to these delights.

30 ROSENCRANS. We shall, my lord.

Exeunt Rosencrans *and* Guildenstern.

KING. Sweet Gertrude, leave us too;
For we have closely sent for Hamlet hither,
That he, as 'twere by accident, may meet
Ophelia here. Her father and myself
Will so bestow ourselves that, seeing and unseen,
We may of their encounter judge,
' And gather by him as he is behaved, '
If it be the affliction of love or no,
' That thus he suffers for. '

40 QUEEN. I shall obey you;
And for my part, Ophelia, I do wish
That your good beauties be the happy cause
Of Hamlet's wildness. So shall I hope your virtues
Will bring him to his wonted way again,
' To both your honors. '

Exit Queen.

OPHELIA. Madam, I wish it may.

POLONIUS. Ophelia, walk you here, whilst we
(If so your Majesty shall please) retire concealed.
' Read on this book,
50 ' That show of such an exercise may color
' Your loneliness. We're oft to blame in this,
' 'Tis too much proved, that with devotion's visage
' And pious action, we do sugar o'er
' The devil himself.

' KING (*aside*). O, 'tis too true!
' How smart a lash that speech doth give my conscience!
' The harlot's cheek, beautied with plast'ring art,
' Is not more ugly to the thing that helps it

' Than is my deed to my most painted word.
60 ' O heavy burden! '

POLONIUS. I hear him coming. Retire, my lord.

Exeunt King *and* Polonius.

Enter Hamlet.

HAMLET. To be, or not to be, that is the question:
Whether 'tis nobler in the mind to suffer
The slings and arrows of outrageous fortune
Or to take arms against a sea of troubles,
And by opposing end them. To die—to sleep
No more; and by a sleep to say we end
The heartache, and the thousand natural shocks
That flesh is heir to. 'Tis a consummation
70 Devoutly to be wished, to die, to sleep;—
To sleep—perchance to dream: ay, there's the rub!
For in that sleep of death what dreams may come
When we have shuffled off this mortal coil,
Must give us pause. There's the respect
That makes calamity of so long life:
For who would bear the whips and scorns of time,
The oppressor's wrong, the proud man's contumely,
The pangs of despised love, the law's delay,
The insolence of office, and the spurns
80 That patient merit of th' unworthy takes,
When he himself might his *quietus* make
With a bare bodkin? Who would fardels bear,
To groan and sweat under a weary life,
But that the dread of something after death—
The undiscovered country, from whose bourn
No traveler returns—puzzles the will,
And makes us rather bear those ills we have,
Than fly to others that we know not of?
Thus conscience does make cowards of us all,
90 And thus the healthful face of resolution
Is sicklied o'er with the pale cast of thought,
And enterprises of great pith and moment
With this regard their currents turn away
And lose the name of action.— ' Soft you now! '
The fair Ophelia!—Nymph, in thy orisons
Be all my sins remembered.

OPHELIA. Good my lord, how do ye?

HAMLET. I humbly thank you; well.

OPHELIA. My lord, I have remembrances of yours
100 That I have longed to re-deliver.
Pray you now receive them.

HAMLET. No, not I. I never gave you aught.

OPHELIA. My honored lord, you know right well you did,
And with them words of so sweet breath composed
As made these things more rich. Their perfume lost,
Take these again; for to the noble mind
Rich gifts wax poor when givers prove unkind.
There, my lord.

HAMLET. Ha, ha! Are you honest?

110 OPHELIA. My lord!

HAMLET. Are you fair?

OPHELIA. What means your lordship?

HAMLET. That if you be honest and fair, you should admit no discourse to your beauty.

OPHELIA. Could beauty, my lord, have better commerce than with honesty?

HAMLET. Ay, truly; for the power of beauty will sooner transform honesty from what it is to a bawd than the force of honesty can translate beauty to his likeness. This was sometime a paradox, but
120 now the time gives it proof. I did love you once.

OPHELIA. Indeed, my lord, you make me believe so.

HAMLET. You should not have believed me; for virtue cannot so evacuate our old stock but we shall relish of it. I loved you not.

OPHELIA. I was the more deceived.

HAMLET. Get thee to a nunnery! Why wouldst thou be a breeder of sinners? I am myself indifferent honest, but yet I could accuse me of such things that it were better my mother had not bore me. I am very proud, revengeful ambitious; with more offenses at my back than I have thoughts to put them in, imagination to give them shape,
130 or time to act them in. What should such fellows as I do, crawling between earth and heaven? We are arrant knaves; believe none of us. Go thy ways to a nunnery. Where's your father?

OPHELIA. At home, my lord.

HAMLET. Let the doors be shut upon him, that he may play the fool nowhere but in's own house. Farewell.

OPHELIA. O help him, you sweet heavens!

HAMLET. If thou dost marry, I'll give thee this plague for thy dowry: be thou as chaste as ice, as pure as snow, thou shalt not 'scape calumny. Get thee to a nunnery. Or if thou wilt needs marry, marry
140 a fool; for wise men know well enough what monsters you make of them. To a nunnery go; ' and quickly too. Farewell. '

OPHELIA. Heavenly pow'rs, restore him!

HAMLET. I have heard of your paintings well enough. Nature hath given you one face, and you make yourselves another. You jig and amble, and you lisp; you nickname heaven's creatures and make your wantonness your ignorance. Go to, I'll no more on't! it hath made me mad. I say, we will have no more marriages. Those that are married already—all but one—shall live; the rest shall keep as they are. To a nunnery, go.

Exit.

150 OPHELIA. O what a noble mind is here o'erthrown!
' The courtier's, soldier's, scholar's, eye, tongue, sword, '
The expectation and rose of the fair state,
' The glass of fashion and the mould of form, '
Th' observed of all observers, quite, quite down!
And I, of ladies most deject and wretched,
' That sucked the honey of his music vows, '
Now see that noble and most sovereign reason,
Like sweet bells jangled, out of tune and harsh;
' That unmatched form and stature of blown youth
160 ' Blasted with ecstasy. ' O, woe is me
T' have seen what I have seen, seeing what I see!

Exit.

Enter King *and* Polonius.

KING. Love! his affections do not that way tend;
For what he spake, though it lack form a little,
Was not like madness. ' There's something in his soul,
' O'er which his melancholy sits on brood,
' And I do doubt the hatch and the disclose
' Will be some danger, which to prevent
' I have a quick determination.
' Thus set down. ' He shall with speed to England,
170 For the demand of our neglected tribute.
Haply the seas, and countries different,
With variable objects, shall expel
This something-settled matter in his heart,
Whereon his brains still beating puts him thus
From fashion of himself. What think you on't?

Enter Ophelia.

POLONIUS. It shall do well. ' But yet I do believe
' Th' origin and commencement of it

’ Sprung from neglected love. ’ How now, Ophelia?
You need not tell us what Lord Hamlet said;
80 We heard it all.—My lord, do as you please;
But if you hold it fit, after the play
Let his queen mother all alone entreat him
To show his grief. Let her be round with him;
And I’ll be placed, so please you, in the ear
Of all their conference. If she find him not,
To England send him; or confine him where
Your wisdom best shall think.

KING. It shall be so.
Madness in great ones must not unwatched go.

Exeunt.

Enter Hamlet *and three Players.*

90 HAMLET. Speak the speech, I pray you, as I pronounced it to you, smoothly from the tongue. But if you mouth it, as many of our players do, I had as lief the town-crier spoke my lines. And do not saw the air too much with your hand, thus, but use all gently; for in the very torrent, tempest, and (as I may say) whirlwind of passion, you must acquire and beget a temperance that may give it smoothness. O, it offends me to the soul to hear a robustious periwigpated fellow tear a passion to very rags to split the ears of the groundlings, who (for the most part) are capable of nothing but inexplicable dumb shows and noise. I would have such a fellow whipped for
00 o’erdoing Termagant; it out-Herod’s Herod. Pray you avoid it.

PLAYER. I warrant your honor.

HAMLET. Be not too tame neither; but let your own discretion be your tutor. Suit the action to the word, the word to the action; with this special observance, that you o’erstep not the modesty of nature: for anything so o’erdone is from the purpose of playing, whose end, both at first and now, was and is, to hold, as ’twere, the mirror up to nature; to show virtue her feature, scorn her own image, and the very age and body of the time his form and pressure. O, there be players that I have seen play, and heard others praise, and that
10 highly (not to speak it profanely), that, neither having the accent of Christians, nor the gait of Christian, pagan, nor man, have so strutted and bellowed that I have thought some of nature’s journeymen had made men, and not made them well, they imitated humanity so abominably.

PLAYER. I hope we have reformed that indifferently with us.

HAMLET. O, reform it altogether! And let those that play your clowns

speak no more than is set down for them. For there be of them that will themselves laugh, to set on some quantity of barren spectators to laugh too, though in the meantime some necessary question of
220 the play be then to be considered. That's villainous and shows a most pitiful ambition in the fool that uses it. Go make you ready. ' How now, my lord, will the King hear this piece of work? '

Enter Polonius, Guildenstern *and* Rosencrans.

' POLONIUS. And the Queen too, and that presently. '
HAMLET. Bid the players make haste. Will you two help to hasten them?
ROSENCRANS. Ay, my lord.

Exeunt those three.

Enter Horatio.

HAMLET. What ho, Horatio!
HORATIO. Here, my lord, at your service.
HAMLET. Horatio, thou art e'en as just a man
As e'er my conversation met withal.
230 HORATIO. O, my dear lord!
HAMLET. Nay, do not think I flatter;
For what advancement may I hope from thee,
That hast no revenue but thy good spirits
To feed and clothe thee? Why should the poor be flatter'd? [2]
Since my dear soul was mistress of her choice
And could of men distinguish her election,
Sh' hath sealed thee for herself. For thou hast been
As one in suffering all, hast suffered nothing.[3]
Give me the man
240 That is not passion's slave, and I will wear him
In my heart's core, ay, in my heart of hearts,
As I do thee. Something too much of this!
There is a play tonight before the King.
One scene of it comes near the circumstance,
Which I have told thee, of my father's death.
I prithee, when thou seest that act on foot,

2. Garrick cut three lines: "No, let the candy'd tongue lick absurd pomp, / And crook the pregnant hinges of the knee, / Where thrift may follow fawning. Dost thou hear?"

3. Garrick cut five lines: "A man that fortune's buffets and rewards / Hath ta'en with equal thanks: and blest are those / Whose blood and judgment are so well commingled, / That they are not a pipe for fortune's finger, / To sound what stop she please."

Even with the very comment of thy soul
Observe my uncle.[4] Give him heedful note;
For I mine eyes will rivet to his face,
250 And after we will both our judgments join
In censure of his seeming.

HORATIO. I will, my lord.[5]

Enter King, Queen, Polonius, Ophelia, *gentlemen.*

HAMLET. They're coming to the play. I must be idle.
Get you a place.

KING. How fares our cousin Hamlet?

HAMLET. Excellent, i' faith, of the chameleon's dish: I eat the air, promise-crammed. You cannot feed capons so.

KING. I have nothing with this answer, Hamlet. These words are not mine.

260 HAMLET. No, nor mine now, my lord. (*To* Polonius.) You played once in the university, you say?

POLONIUS. That I did, my lord, and was accounted a very good actor.

HAMLET. What did you enact?

POLONIUS. I did enact Julius Caesar. I was killed i' th' Capitol; Brutus killed me.

HAMLET. It was a brute part of him to kill so capital a calf there. Be the players ready?

ROSENCRANS. Ay, my lord. They wait upon your patience.

QUEEN. Come hither, my dear Hamlet, sit by me.

270 HAMLET. No, good mother, here's metal more attractive.

POLONIUS. O, ho! do you mark that?

HAMLET. Lady, shall I lie in your lap?

OPHELIA. No, my lord.

HAMLET. Do you think I mean country matters?[6]

OPHELIA. You are merry, my lord.

HAMLET. 'Who, I?'[7] Your only jig-maker! What should a man do but be merry? For look how cheerfully my mother looks, and my father died within's two hours.

---

4. Garrick cut four lines: "if then his hidden guilt, / Do not itself discover in one speech, / It is a damned ghost that we have seen, / And my imaginations are as foul / As *Vulcan's* stithy."

5. Garrick cut two lines: "If he steal aught the whilst the play is playing, / And 'scape detection, I will pay the theft."

6. Garrick cut four lines: "OPH. I think nothing, my lord. / HAM. That's a fair thought, to lie between maids legs. / OPH. What is, my lord? / HAM. Nothing."

7. Garrick cut one line: "OPH. Ay, my lord."

OPHELIA. Nay, 'tis twice two month, my lord.

280 HAMLET. So long? Nay then, let the devil wear black, for I'll have a suit of sables. ' O heavens! ' die two months ago, and not forgotten yet? Then there's hope a great man's memory may outlive his life half a year. But he must build churches then.[8]

OPHELIA. What means the play, my lord?

HAMLET. It is munching *Mallico*. It means mischief.

OPHELIA. But what's the argument?

Enter Prologue.

HAMLET. We shall know by this fellow. The players cannot keep secret; they'll show all.

OPHELIA. Are they so good at show, my lord?

290 HAMLET. Ay, at any show that you will show them. Be not you ashamed to show, and they'll not blush to tell you what it means.

OPHELIA. You are naught, you are naught! I'll mark the play.

PROLOGUE. *For us, and for our tragedy,*
Here stooping to your clemency,
We beg your hearing patiently.

HAMLET. Is this a prologue, or the posy of a ring?

OPHELIA. 'Tis brief, my lord.

HAMLET. As woman's love.

Enter Player-King *and* Queen.

PLAYER-KING. Full thirty times hath Phoebus' car gone round
300 ' Neptune's salt wash and Tellus orbed the ground,
' And thirty dozen moons with borrowed sheen
' About the world have twelve times thirty been, '
Since love our hearts, and Hymen did our hands,
Unite, enfolding them in sacred bands.

PLAYER-QUEEN. So many journeys may the sun and moon
Make us again count o'er, ere love be done!
But woe is me! you are so sick of late,
And so far different from your former state,
That I distrust you. Yet, tho' I distrust,
310 Discomfort you, my lord, it nothing must;
For women fear too much, ev'n as they love,
' Now women's fear and love hold quantity

8. Garrick cut two and a half lines: "or else shall he suffer not thinking on, with the hobby-horse, whose epitaph is, for O, for O, the hobby-horse is forgot."

'In neither ought, or in extremity.'
Now what my love has been, proof makes you know;
And as my love is great, my fear is so.
Where love is great, the smallest doubts are fear;
Where little fear grows great, great love grows there.

PLAYER-KING. I must leave thee, love, and shortly too;
My working powers their functions leave to do.
320 But thou shalt live in this fair world behind,
Honored, beloved, and haply one as kind
For husband shalt thou—

PLAYER-QUEEN. O, confound the rest!
Such love must needs be treason in my breast.
In second husband let me be accurst!
None wed the second but who killed the first.

HAMLET. That's wormwood.

' PLAYER-QUEEN. The instances that second marriage move
'Are base respects of thrift, but none of love.
330 'A second time I kill my husband dead
'When second husband kisses me in bed.'

PLAYER-KING. I do believe you think what now you speak;
But what we do determine oft we break.
'Purpose is but the slave of memory,
'Of violent birth, but poor validity;
'Which now, like fruits unripe, sticks on the tree,
'But fall unshaken when they mellow be.
'Most necessary 'tis that we forget
'To pay ourselves what to ourselves is debt.
340 'What to ourselves in passion we propose,
'The passion ending, doth the purpose lose.
'The violence of either grief or joy
'Their own enactures with themselves destroy.
'Where joy must revels, grief doth most lament;
'Grief joys, joy grieves, on slender accident.
'This world is not for aye, nor 'tis not strange
'That even our loves should with our fortunes change;
'For 'tis a question left us yet to prove,
'Whether love lead fortune, or else fortune love.
350 'The great man down, you mark his favorite flies,
'The poor advanced makes friends of enemies.
'And hitherto doth love our fortune tend,
'For who not needs shall never lack a friend,
'And who in want a hollow friend doth try,
'Directly seasons him his enemy.

' But, orderly to end where I begun,
' Our wills and fates do so contrary run
' That our devices still are overthrown;
' Our thoughts are ours, their ends none of our own.'
360 Think still thou wilt no second husband wed;
But thy thoughts die when thy first lord is dead.

PLAYER-QUEEN. Nor earth to give me food, nor heaven light,
Sport and respose lock from me day and night,
' To desperation turn my trust and hope,
' An anchor's cheer in prison be my scope,
' Each opposite that blanks the face of joy,
' Meet what I would have well, and it destroy,'
Both here and hence pursue me lasting strife,
If once I widow be, and then a wife.

370 HAMLET. If she should break it now!

PLAYER-KING. 'Tis deeply sworn. Sweet, leave me here awhile.
My spirits grow dull, and fain I would beguile
The tedious day with sleep.

PLAYER-QUEEN. Sleep rock thy brain,
And never come mischance between us twain!

Exeunt.

HAMLET. Madam, how like you the play?

QUEEN. The lady doth protest too much, methinks.

HAMLET. O, but she'll keep her word.

KING. Have you heard the argument? Is there no offense in't?

380 HAMLET. No, no! They do but jest, poison in jest; no offense.

KING. What do they call the play?

HAMLET. "The Mousetrap." Marry, how? Tropically. This play is the image of a murder done in Vienna. Gonzago is the duke's name: his wife, Baptista. You shall see anon. 'Tis a knavish piece of work; but what of that? Your Majesty and we shall have free souls; it touches us not. Let the galled jade winch; our withers are unwrung. This is one Lucianus, nephew to the King.

Enter Lucianus.

OPHELIA. You are as good as a chorus, my lord.

HAMLET. I could interpret between you and your love,
390 If I could see the puppets dallying.[9]

9. Garrick cut four lines: "OPH. You are keen, my lord, you are keen. / HAM. It would cost you a groaning to take off mine edge. / OPH. Still worse and worse. / HAM. So you mistake your husbands."

Begin, murderer. Leave thy damnable faces and begin!
Come, this croaking raven doth bellow forth revenge.

LUCIANUS. Thoughts black, hands apt, drugs fit, and time agreeing;
Confederate season, and no creature seeing;
Thou mixture rank, of midnight weeds collected,
With Hecate's bane thrice blasted, thrice infected,
Thy natural magic and dire property
On wholesome life usurps immediately.

HAMLET. He poisons him i' th' garden for his estate; his name's Gonzago. The story is extant, and written in very choice Italian. You shall see anon how the murderer gets the love of Gonzago's wife.

400

OPHELIA. The King rises.

' HAMLET. What, frighted with false fire? '

QUEEN. How fares my lord?

POLONIUS. Give o'er the play.

KING. Give me some lights! Away!

POLONIUS. Lights, lights, lights!

Exeunt all but Hamlet *and* Horatio.

HAMLET. Why, let the strucken deer go weep,
The hart ungalled go play;
For some must watch, whilst some must sleep:
Thus runs the world away.[10]

410

O good Horatio, I'll take the ghost's word for a thousand pounds. Didst perceive?

HORATIO. Very well, my lord.

HAMLET. Upon the talk of poisoning?

HORATIO. I did very well note him.

HAMLET. Ah, ah, come, some music! Come, the recorders! [11]

[*Exit* Horatio.]

---

10. Garrick cut eleven lines:
Would not this, sir, and a forest of feathers, if the rest of my fortunes turn *Turk* with me, with provincial roses on my raz'd shoes, get me a fellowship in a city of players?

HOR. Half a share.

HAM. A whole one, I.

For thou dost know, O *Damon* dear,
This realm dismantled was
Of *Jove* himself, and now reigns here
A very very—peacock.

HOR. You might have rhym'd.

11. Garrick cut two and a half lines: "For the King likes not the comedy, / Why then perhaps he likes it not perdie. / Come, some music."

Enter Rosencrans *and* Guildenstern.

GUILDENSTERN. Good my lord, vouchsafe me a word with you.

HAMLET. Sir, a whole history.

420 GUILDENSTERN. The King, sir.–

HAMLET. Ay, sir, what of him?

GUILDENSTERN. Is in his retirement marvellous distempered.

HAMLET. With drink, sir?

GUILDENSTERN. No, my lord, with choler.

HAMLET. Your wisdom would show itself richer to signify this to the doctor; for me to put him to his purgation would perhaps plunge him into more choler.

GUILDENSTERN. Good my lord, put your discourse into some frame, and start not so wildly from my business.

430 HAMLET. I am tame, sir; pronounce.

GUILDENSTERN. The Queen, your mother, in most great affliction of spirit hath sent me to you.

HAMLET. You are welcome.

GUILDENSTERN. Nay, my good lord, this courtesy is not of the right breed. If it shall please you to make me a wholesome answer, I will do your mother's commandment; if not, your pardon and my return shall be the end of the business.

HAMLET. Sir, I cannot.

ROSENCRANS. What, my lord?

440 HAMLET. Make you a wholesome answer; my wit's diseased. But, sir, such answer as I can make, you shall command, or rather, as you say, my mother.[12]

ROSENCRANS. Then thus she says: your behavior of late hath struck her into amazement and admiration.

HAMLET. O wonderful son, that can thus astonish a mother! But is there no sequel at the heels of this mother's admiration? Impart.

ROSENCRANS. She desires to speak with you in her closet ere you go to bed.

HAMLET. We shall obey, were she ten times our mother. Have you any

450 further trade with us?

ROSENCRANS. My lord, you once did love me.

HAMLET. And do still, by these pickers and stealers.

ROSENCRANS. Good my lord, what is the cause of your distemper? You do surely bar the door upon your own liberty, if you deny your griefs to your friend.

HAMLET. Sir, I lack advancement.

---

12. Garrick cut one line: "therefore no more, but to the matter: my mother, you say."

ROSENCRANS. How can that be, when you have the voice of the King himself for your succession in Denmark?

Enter Horatio *with recorders.*

HAMLET. Ay, sir, but "while the grass grows"—the proverb is something musty. Oh, the recorders! Let me see one. To withdraw with you—why do you go about to recover the wind of me, as if you would drive me into a toil?

460

GUILDENSTERN. Oh, my lord, if my duty be too bold, my love is too unmannerly.

HAMLET. I do not well understand that. Will you play upon this pipe?

GUILDENSTERN. My lord, I cannot.

HAMLET. I pray you.

GUILDENSTERN. Believe me, I cannot.

HAMLET. I beseech you.

470 GUILDENSTERN. I know no touch of it, my lord.

HAMLET. 'Tis as easy as lying. Govern these vantages with your fingers and the thumb, give it breath with your mouth, and it will discourse most excellent music. Look you, these are the stops.

GUILDENSTERN. But these cannot I command to any utterance of harmony. I have not the skill.

HAMLET. Why, look ye now, how unworthy a thing you make of me! You would play upon me; you would seem to know my stops; you would pluck out the heart of my mystery; you would sound me from my lowest note to the top of my compass; and there is much music, excellent voice, in this little organ, yet cannot you make it speak. 'Sdeath, do you think I'm easier to be played on than a pipe? Call me what instrument you will, though you can fret me, you cannot play upon me.

480

Enter Polonius.

POLONIUS. My lord, the Queen would speak with you, and presently.

HAMLET. Do you see yonder cloud that's almost in shape of a camel?

POLONIUS. 'Tis like a camel, indeed.

HAMLET. Methinks 'tis like a weasel.

POLONIUS. It is black like a weasel.

HAMLET. Or like a whale.

490 POLONIUS. Very like a whale.

HAMLET. Then I will come to my mother by-and-by.
They fool me to the top of my bent. 'I will come by-and-by.'[13]

Exeunt [Polonius, Rosencrans, Guildenstern].

---

13. Garrick cut two lines: "POL. I will say so. / HAM. By and by is easily said. Leave me, friends."

'Tis now the very witching time of night,
When churchyards yawn, and hell itself breathes out
Contagion to the world. Now could I drink hot blood
And do such deeds as day itself
Would quake to look on. Soft! now to my mother!
O heart, lose not thy nature; let not ever
The soul of Nero enter this firm bosom!
500 Let me be cruel, not unnatural;
I will speak daggers to her, but use none.[14]

Exit.

Enter King, Rosencrans, *and* Guildenstern.

KING. I like him not, nor stands it safe with us
To let his madness range. Therefore prepare you.
' I your commission will forthwith dispatch,
' And he to England shall along with you.
' The terms of our estate may not endure
' Hazards so near us as do hourly grow
' Out of his lunacies.
' GUILDENSTERN. We will ourselves provide.
510 ' Most holy and religious fear it is
' To keep those many bodies safe
' That live and feed upon your Majesty.
' ROSENCRANS. The single and peculiar life is bound
' With all the strength and armor of the mind
' To keep itself from noyance; but much more
' That spirit upon whose weal depend and rest
' The lives of many. The cease of majesty
' Dies not alone, but like a gulf doth draw
' What's near it with it; or it's a massy wheel,
520 ' Fixed on the summit of the highest mount,
' To whose huge spokes ten thousand lesser things
' Are mortised and adjoined; which when it falls,
' Each small annexment, petty consequence,
' Attends the boist'rous ruin. Ne'er alone
' Did the king sigh, but with a general groan. '
KING. Arm then, I pray you, to this speedy voyage;
For we will fetters put about this fear,
Which now goes to free-footed.
ROSENCRANS. We will make haste.

14. Garrick cut three lines: "My tongue and soul, in this be hypocrites. / How in my words soever be she shent, / To give them seals never my soul consent."

Exeunt Rosencrans *and* Guildenstern.

Enter Polonius.

530 POLONIUS. Sir, he is going to his mother's closet.
Behind the arras I'll convey myself
To hear the process. I'll warrant she'll tax him home;
And as you said, and wisely was it said,
'Tis meet that some more audience than a mother,
Since nature makes them partial, should o'erhear
Their speech. Fare you well, my liege.
I'll call upon you ere you go to bed
And tell you what I hear.

Exit.

KING. Thanks, dear my lord.
540 O, my offense is rank, it smells to heaven!
It hath the eldest curse upon't,
A brother's murder! Pray I cannot,
Though inclination be as sharp as will.
My stronger guilt defeats my strong intent,
And, like a man to double business bound,
I stand in pause where I shall first begin,
And both neglect. What if this cursed hand
Were thicker than itself with brother's blood,
Is there not rain enough in the sweet heavens
550 To wash it white as snow? Whereto serves mercy
But to confront the visage of offense?
' And what's in prayer but this twofold force,
' To be forestalled ere we come to fall,
' Or pardoned being down? ' Then I'll look up.
' My fault is past; but oh! what form of prayer
' Can serve my turn? "Forgive me my foul murder"? '
That cannot be; since I am still possessed
Of those effects for which I did the murder—
My crown, mine own ambition, and my queen.
560 May one be pardoned and retain the offense?
In the corrupted currents of this world
Offense's gilded hand may shove by justice,
And oft 'tis seen the wicked prize itself
Buys out the law; but 'tis not so above.
There is no shuffling; there the action lies
In its true nature, and we ourselves compelled,
Even to the teeth and forehead of our faults,

To give in evidence. What then? What rests?
Try what repentance can: what can it not?
570 Yet what can it, when one cannot repent?
O wretched state! O bosom black as death!
O limed soul, that, struggling to be free,
Art more engaged! ' Help, angels! Make assay! '
Bow, stubborn knees; and heart with strings of steel
Be soft as sinews of the new-born babe!
All may be well. (*The* King *kneels.*)

Enter Hamlet.

HAMLET. Where is this murderer? He kneels and prays;
And now I'll do't. And so he goes to heaven,
And so I am revenged. That would be scanned.
580 He killed my father; and for that,
I, his sole son, send him to heaven.
Why this is reward—not revenge!
He took my father grossly, ' full of bread, '
With all his crimes broad blown, as flush as May;
And how his audit stands, who knows save heaven?
But in our circumstance and course of thought,
'Tis heavy with him; and am I then revenged,
To take him in the purging of his soul,
When he is fit and seasoned for his passage? No.
590 Up, sword, and know thou a more horrid time.
When he is drunk, asleep, or in a rage,
Or in th' incestuous pleasures of his bed;
' At gaming, swearing, ' or about some act
That has no relish of salvation in't—
Then trip him, that his heels may kick at heaven,
' And that his soul may be as damned and black
' As hell whereto it goes. ' My mother stays.
This physic but prolongs thy sickly days.

Exit.

KING. My words fly up, my thoughts remain below;
600 Words without thoughts never to heaven go.

Exit.

Enter Queen *and* Polonius.

POLONIUS. He will come straight. Look you lay home to him.
Tell him his pranks have been too broad to bear with,

And that your Grace hath stood between
Much heat and him. I'll here conceal myself.
Pray you be round with him.
HAMLET (*within*). Mother, mother, mother!
QUEEN. I warrant you,
Fear me not. Withdraw; I hear him coming.

Enter Hamlet.

HAMLET. Now, mother, what's the matter?
610 QUEEN. Hamlet, thou hast thy father much offended.
HAMLET. Mother, you have my father much offended.
QUEEN. Come, come, you answer with an idle tongue.
HAMLET. Go, go, you question with a wicked tongue.
QUEEN. Why, how now, Hamlet?
HAMLET. What's the matter now?
QUEEN. Have you forgot me?
HAMLET. No, ' by the rood, not so. '
You are the Queen, your husband's brother's wife,
And—would it were not so—you are my mother.
620 QUEEN. Nay, then I'll set those to you that can speak.
HAMLET. Come, come, and sit you down; you shall not budge!
You go not till I set you up a glass
Where you may see the utmost part of you.
QUEEN. What wilt thou do? Thou wilt not murder me?
Help, ho!
POLONIUS (*behind the arras*). What ho, help!
HAMLET. How now, a rat? dead for a ducket, dead. (*Kills* Polonius.)
POLONIUS. O, I am slain!
QUEEN. O me, what hast thou done?
630 HAMLET. Nay, I know not. Is it the King?
QUEEN. O, what a rash and bloody deed is this!
HAMLET. A bloody deed—almost as bad, good mother,
As kill a king and marry with his brother.
QUEEN. As kill a king?
HAMLET. Ay, lady, 'twas my word.
Thou wretched, rash, intruding fool, farewell!
I took thee for thy better. Take thy fortune.
Thou find'st to be too busy is some danger.—
Leave wringing of your hands. Peace! sit you down
640 And let me wring your heart; for so I shall
If it be made of penetrable stuff;
' If damned custom have not brazed it so
' That it be proof and bulwark against sense. '

QUEEN. What have I done that thou dar'st wag thy tongue
In noise so rude against me?
HAMLET. Such an act
That blurs the grace and blush of modesty;
Calls virtue hypocrite; takes off the rose
From the fair forehead of an innocent love,
650 And sets a blister there; make marriage vows
As false as dicer's oath. Oh, such a deed
As from the body of contraction plucks
The very soul, and sweet religion makes
A rhapsody of words! [15] Ah me! that act!
QUEEN. Ah me, what act? [16]
HAMLET. Look here upon this picture, and on this,
The counterfeit presentment of two brothers.
See what grace was seated on this brow;
Hyperion's curls; the front of Jove himself;
660 An eye like Mars, to threaten and command;
' A station like the herald Mercury
' New-lighted on a heaven-kissing hill; '
A combination and a form indeed
Where every god did seem to set his seal
To give the world assurance of a man.
This was your husband. Look you now what follows.
Here is your husband, like a mildewed ear
Blasting his wholesome brother. Have you eyes?
Could you on this fair mountain leave to feed
670 And batten on the moor? Ha! have you eyes?
You cannot call it love; for at your age
The heyday of the blood is tame, it's humble,
And waits upon the judgment; and what judgment
Would step from this to this? Sense sure you have,
Else could you not have motion; but sure that sense
Is apoplexed; for madness would not err,
Nor sense to ecstasy was never yet so thralled
But it reserved some quantity of choice
To serve in such a difference. ' What devil was't
680 ' That thus has cozened you at hoodman-blind?

---

15. Garrick cut three lines: "Heav'n's face does glow; / Yes, this solidity and compound mass, / With heated visage, as against the doom, / Is thought-sick at the Act."
16. Garrick cut one line: "That roars so loud, and thunders in the index."

' Eyes without feeling, feeling without sight,
' Ears without hands or eyes, smelling sans all,
' Or but a sickly part of one true sense
' Could not so mope. ' Oh shame! where is thy blush?
Rebellious hell,
If thou canst mutiny in a matron's bones,
To flaming youth let virtue be as wax
And melt in her own fire. ' Proclaim no shame '
When the compulsive ardor gives the charge,
690 Since frost itself as actively doth burn
As reason panders will.

QUEEN. O Hamlet, speak no more!
Thou turn'st my very eyes into my soul.

HAMLET. Nay, but to live
In the rank sweat of an incestuous bed,
Stewed in corruption, ' honeying and making love
' Over the nasty sty! '

QUEEN. O speak no more, sweet Hamlet!

HAMLET. A murderer and a villain!
700 A slave that's not the twentieth part the tithe
Of your precedent lord; a vice of kings;
A cutpurse of the empire and the rule,
That from a shelf the precious diadem stole
And put it in his pocket!
A king of shreds and patches.

Enter Ghost.

Save me and hover o'er me with your wings,
You heavenly guards! What would your gracious figure?

QUEEN. Alas, he's mad!

HAMLET. Do you not come your tardy son to chide,
710 That, lapsed in time and passion, lets go by
Th' important acting of your dread command: O say!

GHOST. Do not forget. This visitation
Is but to whet thy almost blunted purpose.
But look, amazement on thy mother sits.
O step between her and her fighting soul!
Conceit in weakest bodies strongest works.
Speak to her, Hamlet.

HAMLET. How is it with you, madam?

QUEEN. Alas, how is't with you,
720 That you do bend your eye on vacancy,

And with the incorporeal air do hold discourse?
Forth at your eyes your spirits wildly peep;
And, as the sleeping soldiers in the alarm,
Your hair starts up and stands on end. O gentle son,
Upon the heat and flame of thy distemper
Sprinkle cool patience! Whereon do you look?

HAMLET. On him, on him! Look you how pale he glares!
His form and cause conjoined, preaching to stones,
Would make them capable.—Don't look upon me,
730 Lest with this piteous action you convert
My stern effects. Then what I have to do
Will want true color—tears perchance for blood.

QUEEN. To whom do you speak this?

HAMLET. Do you see nothing there?

QUEEN. Nothing at all; yet all that's here I see.

HAMLET. Nor did you nothing hear?

QUEEN. No, nothing but ourselves.

HAMLET. Why, look you there! Look how it stalks away!
My father, in his habit as he lived!
740 Look where he goes ev'n now out at the portal!

Exit Ghost.

QUEEN. This is the very coinage of your brain.
This bodiless creation ecstasy is very cunning in.

HAMLET. My pulse as yours doth temperately keep time
And makes as healthful music. 'Tis not madness
That I have uttered. Bring me to the test,
And I the matter will reword; which madness
Cannot do. Mother, for the love of grace,
Lay not that flattering unction to your soul,
That not your trespass but your madness speaks.
750 It will but skin and film the ulcerous place,
While rank corruption, mining all within,
Infects unseen. Confess yourself to heaven;
Repent what's past; avoid what is to come.[17]

QUEEN. O Hamlet, thou hast cleft my heart.

HAMLET. Then throw away the worser part of it,
And live the purer with the other half.
Goodnight—but go not to my uncle's bed.

---

17. Garrick cut five lines: "And do not spread the compost on the weeds, / To make them ranker. Forgive me this my virtue; / For in the fatness of these pursy times, / Virtue itself of vice must pardon beg. / Yea, curb and woo for leave to do him good."

Assume a virtue, if you have it not.[18]
Once more, goodnight,
60 ' And when you are desirous to be blest,
' I'll blessing beg of you. ' For this same lord, (*Pointing to* Polonius.)
I do repent; but heaven hath pleased it so,
To punish me with this, and this with me,
That I must be their scourge and minister.
I will bestow him, and will answer well
The death I gave him. So again, goodnight.
I must be cruel, only to be kind;
Thus bad begins, and worse remains behind.
One word more.

70 QUEEN. What shall I do?[19]

HAMLET. Let not the King tempt you to bed again,[20]
Make you to ravel all this matter out,
That I essentially am not in madness,
But mad in craft.[21]

QUEEN. Be thou assured, if words be made of breath,
And breath of life, I have no life to breathe
What thou hast said to me.

---

18. Garrick cut nine and a half lines:

> That monster custom, who all sense doth eat,
> Of habits dev'l, is angel yet in this,
> That to the use of actions fair and good
> He likewise gives a frock or livery,
> That aptly is put on: refrain tonight,
> And that shall lend a kind of easiness
> To the next abstinence, the next more easy;
> For use almost can change the stamp of nature,
> And master the devil, or throw him out
> With wondrous potency.

19. Garrick cut one line: "Not this by no means that I bid you do."
20. Garrick cut three lines: "Pinch wanton on your cheek, call you his mouse; / And let him not for a pair of reechy kisses, / Or paddling in your neck with his damn'd fingers."
21. Garrick cut eight and a half lines:

> 'twere good you let him know,
> For who that's but a queen, fair, sober, wise,
> Would from a paddock, from a bat, a gib,
> Such dear concernings hide? who would do so?
> So, in despite of sense and secrecy
> Unpeg the basket on the house's top,
> Let the birds fly, and like the famous ape,
> To try conclusions, in the basket creep,
> And break your own neck down.

HAMLET. I must to England; you know that?
QUEEN. Alack,
780 I had forgot. 'Tis so concluded on.[22]
HAMLET. ' My two schoolfellows delve one yard below their mines,
' And blow them at the moon. O, 'tis most sweet
' When in one line two crafts directly meet. '
This man will set me packing.
I'll lug the guts into the neighb'ring room.–
Mother, goodnight.–This counsellor
Is now most still, most secret, and most grave,
Who was in's life a foolish prating knave.
Come, sir, to draw toward an end with you.
790 Goodnight, mother.

Exit Hamlet, *dragging in* Polonius.

ACT V.[1]

SCENE I. *A royal apartment.*

Enter King *and* Queen, *with* Rosencrans *and* Guildenstern.

KING. There's matter in these sighs; ' these profound heaves; '
You must *translate*; *'tis fit we understand them.*[2]
Where is your son?
QUEEN. Bestow this place on us a little while.

Exeunt Rosencrans *and* Guildenstern.

Ah, my lord, what have I seen tonight!
KING. What, Gertrude? How does Hamlet?

---

22. Six lines cut: Garrick cut six lines:

> There's letters seal'd, . . .
> Whom I will trust as I will adders fang'd,
> They bear the mandate; they must sweep my way,
> And marshal me to knavery: let it work,
> For 'tis the sport to have the engineer
> Hoist with his own petard, and 'tshall go hard
> But I will . . .

1. This is IV, i, in H. W.
2. Garrick replaces H. W.'s "Your must expound them" with Shakespeare's text.

QUEEN. Mad as the seas[3] and wind when both contend
Which is mightier. In his lawless fit,
Behind the arras hearing something stir,
10 *He* whips his rapier *out and* cries a Rat! [4]
And in his brainish apprehension kills
The unseen good old man.
KING. O heavy deed!
It had been so with us, had we been there.
' His liberty is full of threats to all,
' To you yourself, to us, to every one.
' Alas, how shall this bloody deed be answered?
' It will be laid to us, whose providence
' Should have *kept short*, *restrained and out of haunt*[5]
20 ' This mad young man. But so much was our love,
' We would not understand what was most fit;
' But like the owner of a *dire*[6] disease
' To keep it from divulging, let it feed
' Even on the pith of life. ' Where is he gone?
QUEEN. To draw apart the body he hath killed,
' O'er whom his *very*[7] madness like some ore
Among a mineral of *metals*[8] base,
' Shows itself poor; he weeps for what is done. '
KING. O[9] Gertrude, come away!
30 The sun no sooner shall the mountains touch
But we will ship him hence; and this vile deed
We must with all our majesty and skill
Both count'nance and excuse.—Ho, Guildenstern!

Enter Rosencrans *and* Guildenstern.[10]

Friends both, go join you with some further aid.
Hamlet in madness hath Polonius slain,
And from his mother's closet he has dragged him.
Go seek him out; speak fair, and bring the body

3. Garrick restored Shakespeare's "seas" for "Sea" in H. W.
4. Garrick's alteration of the H. W.: "Whips out his Rapier cries a Rat, a Rat."
5. Shakespeare's line restored in place of H. W.: "Should have restrain'd this mad young man"
6. H. W. has "foul."
7. This Shakespearean word omitted in H. W.
8. H. W. has "metal."
9. Garrick restored Shakespeare's "O," omitted in H. W.
10. H. W. places this entrance earlier, after line 31.

Into the chapel;[11] pray you haste in this.
Come, Gertrude, we'll call up our wisest friends
40 And let them know both what we mean to do
And what's untimely done. *For sland'rous malice*[12]
' (Whose whisper o'er the world's diameter,
' As level as the cannon to his blank,
' Transports his poisoned shot)–may miss our name
' And hit the woundless air.–O, come away!
' My soul is full of discord and dismay. '

Exeunt.

Enter Hamlet.

HAMLET. Safely stowed.

Within: Hamlet! *Lord* Hamlet!

What noise? who calls *on*[13] Hamlet?
O here they come.

[*Enter* Rosencrans *and* Guildenstern.]

50 ROSENCRANS. What have you done, my lord, with the dead body?
HAMLET. Compounded it with dust, whereto *'tis*[14] kin.
ROSENCRANS. Tell us where 'tis, that we may take it thence
And bear it to the chapel.
HAMLET. Do not believe it.
ROSENCRANS. Believe what?
HAMLET. That I can keep your counsel, and not my own. Besides, to be demanded of a sponge, what replication should be made by the son of a king?
ROSENCRANS. Take you me for a sponge, my lord?
60 HAMLET. Ay, sir, that soaks up the King's countenance, his rewards, his authorities. But such officers do the King best service in the end. He keeps them, like an apple, in the corner of his jaw; first mouthed to be the last swallowed. When he needs what you have gleaned, it is but squeezing you and, sponge, you shall be dry again.
ROSENCRANS. I understand you not, my lord.
HAMLET. I am glad of it: a knavish speech sleeps in a foolish ear.
ROSENCRANS. My lord, you must tell me where the body is and go with us to the King.

---

11. H. W.: "I pray you haste in this."
12. Garrick's phrase supplies the omission in the Folio. H. W. followed the Second Quarto.
13. Shakespeare's word "on" restored by Garrick. H. W. omits the word.
14. H. W.: "whereto it is akin."

' HAMLET.[15] The King is a thing.

70 ' GUILDENSTERN. A thing, my lord!

HAMLET. ' Of nothing. ' Bring me to him.

Exeunt.

Enter King *and* Gentlemen.

KING. I've sent to seek him and to find the body.
How dang'rous is it that this man goes loose!
Yet must we not put the strong law upon him.
He's loved of the distracted multitude,
Who like not in their judgment, but their eyes;
And where 'tis so, th' offender's scourge is weighed,
But never the offense. To bear all smooth and even,
This sudden sending him away must seem
80 Deliberate pause. Diseases desperate grown
By desperate appliance are reliev'd,
Or not at all.

Enter Rosencrans *and* Guildenstern.

How now? What hath befallen?

ROSENCRANS. Where the dead body is bestowed, my lord,
We cannot get from him.

KING. But where is he?

ROSENCRANS. Without, my lord; guarded, to know your pleasure.

KING. Bring him before us.

ROSENCRANS. Ho, Guildenstern! Bring in *my* lord.[16]

Enter Hamlet *and* Guards.

90 KING. Now, Hamlet, where's Polonius?

HAMLET. At supper.

KING. At supper? Where?

HAMLET. Not where he eats, but where he is eaten. A certain convocation of politic worms are e'en at him.[17]

---

15. Garrick cut one and a half lines: "The Body is with the King, but the King is / Not with the Body."

16. Garrick restored Shakespeare. H. W.: "Ho, bring in the Lord *Hamlet*."

17. Garrick cut eleven lines:

Your worm is your only emperor for diet. We fat all creatures else to fat us, and we fat ourselves for maggots: your fat king and you lean beggar is but variable service; two dishes but to one table, that's the end.

KING. Alas! Alas!

HAM. A man may fish with the worm that hath eat of a king, eat of the fish that hath fed of that worm.

KING. Where is Polonius?

HAMLET. In heaven. Send thither to see. If your messenger find him not there, seek him i' th' other place yourself. But indeed, if you find him not within this month, you shall nose him as you go upstairs into the lobby.

100 KING. Go seek him there.

HAMLET. He will stay till you come.

KING. Hamlet, this deed, for thine especial safety,–
(Which we do tender as we dearly grieve
' For that which thou hast done,) ' –must send thee hence
With fiery quickness.[18] Therefore prepare thyself.
The bark is ready and the wind *at help.*[19]
' Th' associates tend, and everything is bent '
For England.

HAMLET. For England?

110 KING. Ay, Hamlet.

HAMLET. Good.

KING. So is it, if thou knew'st our purposes.

HAMLET. I see a cherub that sees them. But come; for England! Farewell, dear mother.

KING. Thy loving father, Hamlet.

HAMLET. My mother! Father and mother is man and wife; man and wife is one flesh; and so, my mother. Farewell, mother. Come, for England!

Exit.

KING. Follow him *at foot;*[20] tempt him with speed aboard;
120 ' Delay it not, ' I'll have him hence tonight.
Away! Everything is sealed and done
' That else leans on the affair. Pray make you haste. '

Exeunt Guildenstern, Rosencrans.[21]

And England, if my present love thou hold'st at aught,[22]

KING. What dost thou mean by this?

HAM. Nothing, but to show you how a king may go a progress thro' the guts of a beggar.

18. Garrick restores Shakespeare. Omitted in H. W.
19. Shakespeare's expression restored. H. W. has "sits Fair."
20. Garrick's restoration. H. W. omits this.
21. Garrick's stage direction.
22. Garrick cut ten lines:

As my great power therefore may give thee sense
Since yet thy Cicatrice looks raw and red

Let it be testified in Hamlet's death.[23]
O do it, England—for like a hectic in my blood he rages
And thou must cure me.[24]

Exit.

SCENE [II]. *A wood.*[1]

Trumpets and drums at a distance.

Enter Hamlet and Rosencrans meeting Guildenstern.

' HAMLET. *Well, the news! Have you learnt whence are those powers?*[2]
' GUILDENSTERN. They are of Norway, sir—
' And claim conveyance of a promised march
' Over this kingdom.
' HAMLET. How purposed, sir, I pray you?
' GUILDENSTERN. Against some part of Poland.
' HAMLET. Who commands them, *pray*?[3]
' GUILDENSTERN. The nephew of old Norway, Fortinbras.
10 ' HAMLET. Goes it against the main of Poland, sir,
' Or against some frontier?
' GUILDENSTERN. Truly to speak, and with no addition,
' *They*[4] go to gain a little patch of ground
' That hath in it no profit but the name.
' To pay five ducats, five, I would not farm it;
' Nor will it yield to Norway or the Pole

After the *Danish* Sword, and thy free Awe
Pays Homage to us, thou may'st not coldly set
Our Sov'reign Process, which import as full
By letters conjuring to that Effect,
The present death of *Hamlet*; do it *England*,
For like a Hectic in my Blood he rages,
And thou must cure me; till I know 'tis done;
Howe'er my haps, my joys were ne'er begun. [*Ex.*

23. Line from Garrick's 1763 edition.
24. Garrick's alteration of the last lines in the King's speech.
1. This scene is Shakespeare's IV, iv. Garrick restored it without Fortinbras and gave the Captain's lines to Guildenstern. In the scene Garick added two lines and altered another.
2. Garrick's line.
3. H. W. has "Sir?"
4. H. W. has "We."

' A ranker rate, should it be sold in fee.
' HAMLET. Why, then the Pollack never will defend it.
' GUILDENSTERN. Nay, it is already garrisoned.
20 ' HAMLET. Two thousand souls and twenty thousand ducats
' Will not debate the question of this straw.
' This is th' imposthume of much wealth and peace,
' That inward breaks, and shows no cause without
' Why the man dies.[5]
' ROSENCRANS. Wilt please you go, my lord?
' HAMLET. I'll be with you straight. Go a little before.

' [*Exeunt* Rosencrans *and* Guildenstern.]

' How all occasions do inform against me
' And spur my dull revenge! What is a man,
' If his chief good and market of his time
30 ' Be but to sleep and feed? A beast, no more.
' Sure he that made us with such large discourse,
' Looking before and after, gave us not
' That capability and godlike reason
' To rust in us unused. Now, whether it be
' Bestial oblivion, or some craven scruple
' Of thinking too precisely on th' event,–
' A thought which, quartered, hath but one part wisdom
' And ever three parts coward,–I do not know
' Why yet I live to say "This thing's to do,"
40 ' Sith I have cause, and will, and strength, and means
' To do't. Examples gross as earth exhort me.
' Witness this army of such mass and charge,
' Led by a delicate and tender prince,
' Whose spirit with divine ambition puffed,
' Makes mouths at the invincible event,
' Exposing what is mortal and unsure
' To all that fortune, death, and danger dare,
' Ev'n for an eggshell. Rightly to be great
' Is not to stir without great argument,
50 ' But greatly to find quarrel in a straw
' When honor's at the stake. How stand I then,
' That have a father killed, a mother stained,
' Excitements of my reason and my blood,
' And let all sleep, while to my shame I see

---

5. One line cut: Garrick cut one line: "I humbly thank you, Sir. [CAPT. God be w'ye, Sir"

' The imminent death of twenty thousand men
' That for a fantasy and trick of fame
' Go to their graves like beds, fight for a plot
' Whereon the numbers cannot try the cause,
' Which is not tomb enough and continent
60 ' To hide the slain? O, from this time forth,
' My thoughts be bloody ' *all! the hour is come—*
' *I'll fly my keepers—sweep to my revenge.*[6]

Exit.

Enter Queen, Horatio, *and a Gentleman.*

QUEEN. I will not speak with her.
GENTLEMAN. She is importunate, indeed *distract;*[7]
Her mood needs be pitied.[8]
QUEEN. What would she have?
GENTLEMAN. She speaks much of her father, says she hears
There's tricks i' th' world, and hems, and beats her heart;
Spurns enviously at straws; speaks things in doubt,
70 That carry but half sense. Her speech is nothing,
Yet the unshaped use of it doth move
The hearers to collection; ' they aim at it, '
' And botch the words up fit to their own thoughts; '
Which, as her winks and nods and gestures yield them,
' Indeed would make one think there might be thoughts, '
Though nothing sure, yet much unhappily.
HORATIO. 'Twere good she were spoken with; for she may strew
Dangerous conjectures in ill-breeding minds.
QUEEN. Let her come in.[9]

Enter Ophelia.

80 OPHELIA. Where is the beauteous Majesty of Denmark?
QUEEN. How now, Ophelia?

OPHELIA (*sings*). *How should I your true-love know*
From another one?
By his cockle hat and staff
And his sandal shoon.

---

6. Garrick's alteration.
7. H. W.: "distracted."
8. H. W.: and deserves your pity."
9. Garrick restored this speech to the Queen and then cut the next four lines: "QUEEN. To my sick Soul, as Sin's true Nature is, / Each Toy seems Prologue to some great Amiss: / So full of artless Jealousy is Guilt, / It spills itself, in fearing to be spilt."

QUEEN. Alas, sweet lady, what imports this song?
OPHELIA. Say you? Nay, pray you mark. (*Sings.*)

He is dead and gone, lady,
He is dead and gone;
90 *At his head a grass-green turf,*
At his heels a stone.
O, ho!

QUEEN. Nay, but Ophelia—
OPHELIA. Pray you mark. (*Sings.*)

White his shroud as the mountain snow,
Larded all with sweet flowers;
Which beweept to the ground did not go
With true love-showers.

Enter King.

' QUEEN. Alas! look here, my lord. '
100 KING. How do you, pretty lady?
OPHELIA. Well, good dil'd you! They say the owl was a baker's daughter. We know what we are, but know not what we may be.
KING. Conceit upon her father.
OPHELIA. Pray let's have no words of this; but when they ask you what it means, say this: (*Sings.*)

Tomorrow is St. Valentine's Day,
All in the morning betime;
And I a maid at your window,
To be your valentine.

110 KING. Pretty Ophelia!
OPHELIA. Indeed, without an oath, I'll make an end on't!

Then up he rose and donned his clothes
And ope'd his chamber door;
Let in the maid, that out a maid
Never departed more.
By Gis and by St. Charity,
' *Alack, and fie for shame!*
' *Young men will do't if they come to't.*
' *By cock, they are to blame.*
120 ' *Quoth she, "Before you tumbled me,*
' *You promised me to wed."*
' (He answers) *So should I have done, by yonder sun,*
' *And thou hadst not come to my bed.* '

KING. How long hath she been thus?

OPHELIA. I hope all will be well. We must be patient; but I cannot choose but weep to think they would lay him i' th' cold ground. My brother shall know of it; and so I thank you for your good counsel. Come, my coach! Goodnight, ladies. Goodnight, sweet ladies, goodnight, goodnight.

Exit.

130 KING. Follow her close; give her good watch, I pray you.
O, this is the poison of deep grief; it springs
All from her father's death. ' O Gertrude, Gertrude,
' When sorrows come, they come not single spies,
' But in battalions! First, her father slain;
' Next, your son gone, and he most *frantic*[10] author
' Of his own just remove; the people muddied,
' Thick and unwholesome in their thoughts and whispers
' For good Polonius' death, and we have done but greenly,
' Obscurely to inter him; poor Ophelia
140 ' Divided from herself and her fair judgment,
' Without which we're but pictures or mere beasts.
' Last, and as much containing as all these,
' Her brother, *tempest-beaten back to Denmark.*[11]
' Feeds on this wonder, keeps himself in clouds,
' And wants not whispers to infect his ear
' With pestilent speeches of his father's death.[12]

A noise within.

Enter Gentleman.

QUEEN. Alack, what noise is this?

KING. ' Where are my *Swissers?* Let 'em guard the door. '
What is the matter?

150 GENTLEMAN. ' Save yourself, my lord.
' The ocean, over-piercing of his list,
' Eats not the flats with more impetuous haste
' Than ' young Laertes in a riotous head,
O'erbears your officers. The rabble call him lord;
' And, as the world were now but to begin,

10. H. W.: "violent."

11. H. W.: "is in secret come from France."

12. Garrick cut five lines: "Wherein Necessity of Matter baggar'd, / Will nothing stick our Persons to arraign / In Ear and Ear. O my dear *Gertude*, this, / Like to a murd'ring Piece, in many Places / Gives me superfluous Death."

' Antiquity forgot, custom not known,[13]
' They cry "Choose we Laertes for our king!" '
Caps, hands, and tongues applaud it to the clouds,
"Laertes shall be king! Laertes king!"[14]

A noise within.

160 ' KING. The doors are broke! '
LAERTES (*within*). Where is the King? Sirs, stand you all without.
ALL. No, let's come in.
LAERTES. I pray you give me leave.
ALL. We will, we will!
LAERTES. I thank you. Keep the door.

Enter Laertes.

O thou vile King, give me my father.
QUEEN. Calmly, good Laertes.
LAERTES. That drop of blood that's calm proclaims me bastard;
Cries cuckold to my father, brands the harlot
170 Ev'n here between the chaste unsmitched brows
Of my true mother.
KING. What is the cause, Laertes,
That thy rebellion looks so giantlike?
Let him go, Gertrude. Do not fear our person.
There's such divinity doth hedge a king
That treason dares not reach at what it would.[15]
' Tell me, ' Laertes,
' Why thou art thus incensed? Let him go, Gertrude. '
LAERTES. Where is my father?
180 KING. Dead.
QUEEN. But not by him.
KING. Let him demand his fill.
LAERTES. How came he dead? I'll not be juggled with:
To hell, allegiance! vows, to the blackest devil![16]
To this point I stand,
That both the worlds I give to negligence,
Let come what *comes*; *only*[17] I'll be revenged
Most thoroughly for my father.

---

13. One line cut: Garrick cut one line: "The Ratifiers and Props of ev'ry Word,"
14. Garrick cut two lines—Queen's speech: "How chearfully on the false Trail they cry! [*A Noise within* / O this is counter, you false *Danish* Dogs!"
15. Garrick cut a half line: "Acts little of his Will."
16. Garrick cut one and a half lines: "Conscience and Grace to the profoundest Pit, / I dare Damnation."
17. Restoration for H. W.: "Let come what will, I'll be reveng'd,"

KING. Who shall stay you?

190 LAERTES. My will, not all the world!
And for my means, I'll husband them so well
They shall go far with little.

KING. Will you in revenge of your
Dear father's death destroy both friend and foe?

LAERTES. None but his enemies.

KING. Will you know them then?

LAERTES. To his good friends thus wide I'll ope my arms
And, like the kind life-rend'ring pelican,
Repast[18] them with my blood.

200 KING. Why, now you speak
Like a good child and a true gentleman.
That I am guiltless of your father's death,
And am most sensible in grief for it,
It shall as level to your judgment *pierce*[19]
As day does to your eye. //[20] Go but apart,
Make choice of whom your wisest friends you will,
And they shall hear and judge 'twixt you and me.
If by direct or by collateral hand
They find us touched, we will our kingdom give
210 To you in satisfaction; but if not,
Be you content to lend your patience to us,
And we shall jointly labor with your soul
To give it due content.

LAERTES. Let this be so.
His means of death, his obscure funeral—
No trophy sword, or hatchment o'er his bones,
No noble rite nor formal ostentation,—
Cry to be heard, as 'twere from earth to heaven,
That I must call't in question.

220 KING. So you shall;
And where th' offense is let the great ax fall.
I pray you go with me. //

---

18. H. W.: "Relieve."
19. H. W.: "lie."
20. George Winchester Stone's note reads: "The section between //–// in the original comes after the entrance and exit of Ophelia. Garrick has clipped this portion from another printing of his 1763 text: printed London for H. Woodfall (and others) 1767, p. 55, and has pasted it into this his 1772 alteration." All textual notes quoting Professor George Winchester Stone, Jr., are reprinted by permission of the Modern Language Association from the article "Garrick's Long Lost Alteration of *Hamlet*," *PMLA*, 49 (1934), 890–921.

Noise within.[21] *As they are going they see* Ophelia.[22]

//[23] LAERTES (*within*). O *my* poor Ophelia!—*Let her come in.*[24]

Enter Ophelia.[25]

By heaven, thy madness shall be paid with weight
Till our scale turn the beam. O rose of May!
Dear maid, kind sister, sweet Ophelia!
O heavens! is't possible a young maid's wits
Should be as mortal as a sick man's life?

OPHELIA (*sings*). *They bore him barefaced on the bier,*
230 *And in his grave rained many a tear;*
Fare you well, my love.

LAETRES. Hadst thou thy wits, and didst persuade revenge,
It could not move thus.

OPHELIA. You must sing "Down a-down," and you, "Call him a-down-a." O how the wheel becomes it! It is the false steward that stole his master's daughter.

LAERTES. This nothing is much more than matter.

OPHELIA. There's rosemary, that's for remembrance. Pray you, love, remember. And there's pansies, that's for thoughts.

240 LAERTES. A document in madness! Thoughts and remembrance fitted.

OPHELIA. There's fennel for you, and columbines. There's rue for you, and here's some for me. We may call it herb of grace o' Sundays. O, you may wear your rue with a difference. There's a daisy. I would give you some violets, but they all withered when my father died. They say he made a good end. // (*Sings.*)
//*For bonny sweet Robin is all my joy.*

LAERTES. Thought and affliction, passion, hell itself,
She turns to favor and to prettiness.

OPHELIA. *And will he not come again?*
250 *And will he not come again?*

---

21. Garrick's stage direction.
22. Garrick's stage direction.
23. Stone's note reads: "The material in this and the next section as indicated //–// are clippings pasted over page 73 of the H. W. . . . These clippings were cut from H. Woodfall 1767, pp. 54 and 55 respectively. In the original they precede the lines // Go but apart, etc."
24. The original line of Horatio is given to Laertes, with the alteration "my" and added "*Let her come in.*"
25. Garrick cut three lines: "How now? What Noise is that? / O Heat, dry up my Brains; Tears sev'n times salt, / Burn out the sense and Virtue of mine Eye."

No, no, he is dead;
Go to thy deathbed;
He never will come again.

His beard as white as snow,
All flaxen was his poll.
He is gone, he is gone,
And we cast away moan;
And peace be with his soul,
And with all lovers' souls.

Exit. //

260 // LAERTES. O treble woe
Fall ten times double on that cursed head
Whose wicked deed deprived thee of
Thy most ingenious sense! [26] *Let me but see him* heaven! [27]
'Twould warm the very sickness of my heart,
That I should live and tell him to his teeth
"Thus didst thou!" [28]

[*Enter* Hamlet.]

HAMLET. What is he whose griefs
Bear such an emphasis? whose phrase of sorrow
Conjures the wand'ring stars, and makes them stand
270 Like wonder-wounded hearers? *This*[29] is I,
Hamlet the Dane!
LAERTES. *Then my revenge is come.*[30] (*Draws his sword.*)[31]
HAMLET.[32] I prithee take thy fingers from *thy sword*,[33]

26. Garrick cut six and a half lines:

Hold off the Earth awhile,
'Till I have caught her once more in my Arms:
[*Leaps into the Grave.*
Now pile your Dust upon the Quick and Dead,
'Till of this Flat a Mountain you have made,
T' o'er-top old *Pelion*, or the skyish Head
Of blue *Olympus.*

27. Garrick's alteration for H. W.: "Hold off the Earth awhile."
28. Stone's note reads: "This is brought forward in Garrick's autograph from Act IV, Sc. 7 and is part of Laertes' reply to the King who has just received and read aloud Hamlet's letter. The tense of the verbs only has been changed." H. W.: "It warms . . . That I shall . . ."
29. H. W.: "It is I."
30. H. W.: "LAER. Perdition catch thee! "
31. Garrick's stage direction.
32. Garrick cut one line: "Thou pray'st not well."
33. H. W. "my throat."

For, though I am not splenetive and rash,
Yet have I in me something dangerous,
Which let thy wisdom fear.[34]

KING. *Keep*[35] them asunder.

HAMLET. Why, I'll fight with him upon this theme
Until my eyelids will no longer wag.

280 QUEEN. O my son, what theme?

HAMLET. I loved Ophelia. Forty thousand brothers
Could not (with all their quantity of love)
Make up my sum. What wilt thou do for her?

KING. O, he is mad, Laertes.

HAMLET. Show me what thou wilt do.
Wilt weep? wilt fight? wilt fast? wilt tear thyself?
Wilt drink up eisell? eat a crocodile? //[36]
I'll do't! and more[37]*—nay,*[38] *and you'll mouth it, sir,*
I'll rant as well as thou—

290 QUEEN. O Hamlet—Hamlet—[39]
For love of heav'n forbear him![40]—(*To* Laertes.)

KING.[41] *We will not bear this insult to our presence.*
Hamlet, I did command you hence to England.
Affection hitherto has curbed my power,
But you have trampled on allegiance,
And now shall feel my wrath.—Guards!

HAMLET. *First feel mine!*—(*Stabs him.*)

---

34. Garrick cut a half line: "Hold off thy Hand."
35. H. W. "Pluck."
36. Stone's note reads: "This portion between the marks / / LAER. O treble . . . Crocodile? // is a clipping from the burial scene of Ophelia, Act V, Sc. I, slightly changed. It is pasted over page 74 of the H. W. which Garrick used as a basis for his alteration and was cut from H. Woodfall, 1767, p. 66."
37. Stone's note reads: "The last four lines are in Garrick's autograph but are Shakespeare's words with the exception of *and More*, *Sir*, and *O*, which are Garrick's insertions."
38. Garrick cut six and a half lines between "I'll do it . . ." and "nay":

    Dost thou come hither here to whine?
    To out-face me with leaping in her Grave?
    Be bury'd quick with her, and so will I.
    And if you prate of Mountains, let them throw
    Millions of Acres on us, till our Ground
    Singeing his Pate against the burning Zone
    Make *Ossa* like a Wart:

39. This line in Shakespeare's text follows "KING. Pluck them asunder."
40. H. W.: "Forbear him."
41. From this point to the end of the drama Garrick has composed the lines italicized. Other lines are taken from the Shakespearean text V, v.

Here, thou incestuous, murd'rous, damned Dane.
There's for thy treachery, lust, and usurpation!

300 KING. O yet defend me, friends; I am but hurt—(*Falls and dies.*)

QUEEN. *O mercy, heaven!—Save me from my son—*(*Runs out*).

LAERTES. *What treason, ho! Thus then do I revenge*
My father, sister, and my King—

Hamlet *runs upon* Laertes's *sword and falls.*

HORATIO. *And I, my prince and friend—*(*Draws.*)

HAMLET. *Hold, good Horatio! 'Tis the hand of heav'n*
Administers by him this precious balm
For all my wounds. Where is the wretched Queen?

Enter Messenger·

MESSENGER. *Struck with the horror of the scene, she fled.*
But 'ere she reached her chamber door she fell
310 *Entranced and motionless—unable to sustain the load*
Of agony and sorrow—

HAMLET. *O, my Horatio—watch the wretched Queen,*
When from this trance she wakes—O, may she breathe
An hour of penitence 'ere madness ends her.
Exchange forgiveness with me, brave Laertes,
Thy sister's, father's death, come not on me,
Nor mine on thee!

LAERTES. *Heaven make us free of 'em.*

HAMLET. O, I die, Horatio!—*But one thing more.*
320 *O take this hand from me—unite your virtues—*(*Joins* Horatio's *hand to* Laertes'.)
To calm this troubled land. I am no more;
Nor have I more to ask but mercy, heav'n! (*Dies.*)

HORATIO. Now cracks a noble heart. Goodnight, sweet prince,
And flights of angels sing thee to thy rest.[42]
Take up the body; such a sight as this
Becomes the field, but here shows much amiss.

End.

42. Stone's note reads: "Forty-one lines omitted between rest . . . and, . . . Take up, in which Fortinbras returns and takes over the kingdom, and in which the deaths of Rosencrantz and Guildenstern are reported. Inasmuch as Fortinbras does not return in Garrick's Alteration, Hamlet commends his kingdom to the care of Horatio and Laertes, the latter of whom does not die as Davies supposes. See *Dramatic Miscellanies*, III, 145 ff."

The Tempest

A Comedy

1773

THE

TEMPEST

A COMEDY, by SHAKESPEARE.

AS PERFORMED AT THE

THEATRE-ROYAL, DRURY-LANE,

Regulated from the PROMPT-BOOK,

With PERMISSION of the MANAGERS,

By Mr. HOPKINS, Prompter.

An INTRODUCTION, and NOTES
CRITICAL and ILLUSTRATIVE,

ARE ADDED BY THE

AUTHORS of the DRAMATIC CENSOR.

LONDON:
Printed for JOHN BELL, near Exeter-Exchange, in the Strand
And C. ETHERINGTON, at York.
MDCCLXXIII.

Facsimile title page of the First Edition
Folger Shakespeare Library

Introduction

The following dramatic romance, for so it should certainly be titled, is an odd, improbable, yet agreeable mixture, though sense attacks it with severe strictures. Some fine sentiments scattered up and down through high-finished characters, Prospero, Miranda, and Caliban, with the occasional aid of music and machinery, render it pleasing. Of Shakespeare's original we may say, it is more nervous and chaste, but not so well supplied with humour or business, as Dryden's; making the sailors get drunk, instead of the landmen, is highly characteristic, as the former must be supposed much less affected by a shipwreck than the latter, therefore more ready to indulge in excess. At the conclusion of the alteration there is a masque very well introduced; and upon the whole, we are of opinion that by properly blending, as in Lear, a better piece than either might be produced.

[By Francis Gentleman]

0. Introduction] *D1*; not in *D2*.

Dramatis Personae

Drury-Lane.

Alonso.	Mr. Bransby.
Sebastian.	Mr. Keen.
Prospero.	Mr. Packer.
Anthonio.	Mr. Hurst.
Ferdinand.	Mr. Vernon.
Gonzalo.	Mr. J. Aickin.
Francisco.	Mr. Griffith.
Caliban.	Mr. Ackman.
Trinculo.	Mr. Baddeley.
10 Stephano.	Mr. Love.
Boatswain.	Mr. Wrighten.
Miranda.	Mrs. *Smith.*
Ariel.	Mrs. *Scot*[*t*].
Hymen } Spirits.	Mr. *Kear.*
Ceres. } Spirits.	Mrs. *Wrighten.*
Reapers.	

Other Spirits, attending on Prospero.

SCENE, *an uninhabited island.*

4. Anthonio. Mr. *Hurst*] *D*1; omitted *D*2.
7. Mr. Griffith] *D*1; Mr. Norris *D*2.
8. Mr. Ackman] *D*1; Mr. Wright *D*2.
10. Mr. Love] *D*1; Mr. Moody *D*2.
11. Mr. Wrighten] *D*1; Mr. Griffiths *D*2.
16. Reapers] *D*1; omitted *D*2.
17–18. Other Spirits... *island*] *D*1; omitted *D*2.

The Tempest

ACT I.

SCENE [I], *On a ship at sea.*

A tempestuous noise of thunder and lightning heard.
Shipmaster *and a* Boatswain.

MASTER. Boatswain—

BOATSWAIN. Here, Master. What cheer?

MASTER. Good, speak to th' mariners! Fall to't yarely, or we run ourselves aground. Bestir, bestir!

Exit.

Enter Mariners.

BOATSWAIN. Hey, my hearts; cheerly, my hearts. Yare, yare, take in the topsail! Tend to th' master's whistle! Blow till thou burst thy wind, if room enough.

Enter Alonso, Sebastian, Anthonio, Ferdinand, *and* Gonzalo.

ALONSO. Good Boatswain, have care. Where's the master? Play the men.

BOATSWAIN. I pray now, keep below.

10 ANTHONIO. Where is the master, Boatswain?

BOATSWAIN. Do you not hear him? You mar our labor; keep your cabins. You do assist the storm.

GONZALO. Nay, good, be patient.

---

0. The Tempest] "The name and first material incident of this piece are exceedingly contrastic to comedy; however, there is a good opportunity afforded for pleasing scenery and curious mechanism" (F. G. [Francis Gentleman's notes are identified by "F. G." following the note]).

7.1. Ferdinand, *and* Gonzalo] *D*1; Ferdinand, 'Gonzalo *and others,*' indicating omission of those in single quotes *D*2.

BOATSWAIN. When the sea is. Hence—what care these roarers for the name of King? To cabin! Silence! Trouble us not.

GONZALO. Good, yet remember whom thou hast aboard.

BOATSWAIN. None that I more love than myself. You are a counsellor; if you can command these elements to silence and work the peace o'the present, we will not hand a rope more. Use your authority.
20 If you cannot, give thanks you have lived so long, and make yourself ready in your cabin for the mischance of the hour, if it so hap. Cheerly, good hearts. Out of our way, I say.

Exit.

GONZALO. I have great comfort from this fellow. Methinks he hath no drowning mark upon him; his complexion is perfect gallows. Stand fast, good Fate, to his hanging; make the rope of his destiny our cable, for our own doth little advantage. If he be not born to be hanged, our case is miserable.

Exeunt.

Re-enter Boatswain.

BOATSWAIN. Down with the top-mast. Yare, lower, lower; bring her to try with main-course! (*A cry within.*) A plague upon this howling!

Re-enter Sebastian, Anthonio, *and* Gonzalo.

30 SEBASTIAN. A pox o'your throat, you bawling, blasphemous, uncharitable dog.

BOATSWAIN. Work you, then.

ANTHONIO. Hang, cur, hang, you whoreson, insolent, noisemaker; we are less afraid to be drowned than thou art.

GONZALO. I'll warrant him from drowning, though the ship were no stronger than a nutshell and as leaky as an unstanched wench.

BOATSWAIN. Lay her ahold, ahold; set her two courses off to sea again! Lay her off!

Enter Mariners *wet.*

MARINERS. All lost! To prayers, to prayers! All lost!

Exeunt.

---

29. this howling] *D*1, *D*2 omit three following lines for the Boatswain: "They are louder than the weather, or our office. Yet again? What do you here? Shall we give o'er and drown? Have you a mind to sink?" "This scene we think very ill written; in Dryden's alteration, which seems to us a better acting play than that before us, it is mended; but the sea terms, in both, to be characteristic want much to be modernized" (F. G.).

39. prayers! All lost] *D*1, *D*2 omit the remainder of the scene, twenty lines.

SCENE [II] *changes to a part of the enchanted island, near the cell of* Prospero.

Enter Prospero *and* Miranda.

MIRANDA. If by your art, my dearest father, you have
Put the wild waters in this roar, allay them.
The sky, it seems, would pour down stinking pitch
But that the sea, mounting to the welkin's cheek,
Dashes the fire out. Oh, I have suffered
With those that I saw suffer: a brave vessel
(Who had, no doubt, some noble creatures in her)
Dashed all to pieces. Oh, the cry did knock
Against my very heart. Poor souls, they perished!
10 Had I been any god of power, I should
Have sunk the sea within the earth or ere
It should the good ship so have swallowed, and
The fraighting souls within her.
PROSPERO. Be collected.
No more amazement. Tell your piteous heart
There's no harm done.
MIRANDA. Oh, woe the day!
PROSPERO. No harm.
I have done nothing but in care of thee
20 (Of thee, my dear one, thee, my daughter) who
Art ignorant of what thou art, nought knowing
Of whence I am; nor that I am more better
Than Prospero, master of a full poor cell,
And thy no greater father.
MIRANDA. More to know
Did never meddle with my thoughts.
PROSPERO. 'Tis time
I should inform thee farther. Lend thy hand

0.3. *Enter* Prospero . . .] "Being professed foes to all sentiments and characters which inculcate ideas of enchantment, conjuration, or supernatural appearances, we necessarily declare ourselves against the very foundation of this play; however, as what Prospero utters in point of sentiment is, all through, both nervous and sensible, he requires a performer of oratorical ability to support him. Venerable appearance is likewise requisite. Miranda should describe an elegant simplicity" (F. G.)

10. should] *D1*, *D2*; would *S*.

13. within her] "There is something enchantingly humane in the ideas of this speech" (F. G.)

22. more better] "More better is a very strange degree of comparison" (F. G.)

And pluck my magic garment from me; so! (*Lays down his mantle.*)
30 Lie there, my art. Wipe thou thine eyes; have comfort.
The direful spectacle of the wreck, which touched
The real virtue of compassion in thee,
I have with such provision in mine art
So safely ordered that there is no soul lost,
No, not so much perdition as an hair
Betid to any creature in the vessel
Which thou heard'st cry, which thou saw'st sink. Attend;
For thou must now know farther.

MIRANDA. You have often
40 Begun to tell me what I am, but stopped
And left me to a bootless inquisition,
Concluding, "Stay, not yet."

PROSPERO. The hour's now come,
The very minute bids thee ope thine ear;
Obey, and be attentive. Canst thou remember
A time before we came unto this cell?
I do not think thou canst, for then thou wast not
Out three years old.

MIRANDA. Certainly, sir, I can.

50 PROSPERO. By what? By any other house or person?
Of anything the image tell me that
Hath kept in thy remembrance.

MIRANDA. 'Tis far off,
And rather like a dream than an assurance
That my remembrance warrants. Had I not
Four or five women, once, that tended me?

PROSPERO. Thou hadst, and more, Miranda. But how is it
That this lives in thy mind? What seest thou else
In the dark backward and abysm of time?

---

32. real] *D1*; very *D2*, *S*.

34. soul lost] *D1*; foyle *D2*; soul *S*. Theobald's note in *D2* identifies his term as meaning "no damage, loss, detriment. The two old folios read—*is no soul*, which will not agree in grammar with the following part of the sentence. R. Rowe first substituted—*no soul left*, which does not much mend the matter, taking the context together. *Foyle* is a word familiar with our poet, and in some degree synonymous to *perdition* in the next line."

37. Attend] *D1*; Sit down *D2*, *S*.

52. thy remembrance] "There is a pleasing natural ease in the manner of Prospero's sifting his daughter's recollection; it leads on the scene agreeably" (F. G.).

60 If thou remember'st aught ere thou cam'st here,
How thou cam'st here thou may'st.

MIRANDA. But that I do not.

PROSPERO. 'Tis twelve years since, Miranda, twelve years since.
Thy father was the Duke of Milan and
A Prince of power.

MIRANDA. Sir, are not you my father?

PROSPERO. Thy mother was a piece of virtue, and
She said thou wast my daughter; and thy father
Was Duke of Milan, and thou his only heir
70 A Princess, no worse issued.

MIRANDA. O the heavens!
What foul play had we that we came from thence?
Or blessed was't we did?

PROSPERO. Both, both, my girl.
By foul play (as thou say'st) were we heaved thence,
But blessedly helped hither.

MIRANDA. O my heart bleeds
To think o'the' teen that I have turned you to,
Which is from my remembrance. Please you, farther.

80 PROSPERO. My brother, and thy uncle, called Anthonio—
I pray thee, mark me—that a brother should
Be so perfidious!—he whom next thyself
Of all the world I loved, and to him put
The manage of my state, as, at that time,
Through all the signiories it was the first,
And Prospero the prime Duke, being so reputed
In dignity, and for the liberal arts
Without a parallel, those being all my study.
The government I cast upon my brother
90 And to my state grew stranger, being transported
And rapt in secret studies. Thy false uncle—
Dost thou attend me?

MIRANDA. Sir, most heedfully.

PROSPERO. I pray thee, mark me, then.

---

76. helped] *D1*, *D2*; holp *S*.

93. most heedfully] *D1*, *D2* omit ten following lines. (Note: Shakespeare's reading is given in the notes only when they amount to fewer than ten lines.)

94. me, then] *D1*, *D2*; me S. *D1*, *D2* then omit eight and a half lines:

I thus neglecting worldly ends, all dedicated
To closeness, and the bettering of my mind
With that which, but by being so retir'd,

He being thus lorded,
Not only with what my revenue yielded
But what my power might else exact, like one
Who having unto truth, by telling oft,
Made such a sinner of his memory
100 To credit his own lie, he did believe
He was indeed the Duke, from substitution,
And executing the outward face of royalty
With all prerogative. Hence his ambition growing—
Dost thou hear?

MIRANDA. Your tale, sir, would cure deafness.

PROSPERO. To have no screen between this part he played
And him he played it for, he needs will be
Absolute Milan. Me—poor man!—my library
Was Dukedom large enough; of temporal royalties
110 He thinks me now incapable, confederates
(So dry he was for sway) with the King of Naples
To give him annual tribute, do him homage,
Subject his coronet to his crown, and bend
The Dukedom, yet unbowed (alas, poor Milan!)
To most ignoble stooping.

MIRANDA. O the heavens!

PROSPERO. Mark his condition, and the event; then tell me
If this might be a brother.

MIRANDA. I should sin
120 To think but nobly of my grandmother.

PROSPERO. Now the condition:
This King of Naples, being an enemy
To me inveterate, hearks my brother's suit,
Which was, that he, in lieu of the premises,

O'er priz'd all popular rate, in my false brother
Awak'd an evil nature, and my trust,
Like a good parent, did beget of him
A falsehood in its contrary as great
As my trust was, which had indeed no limit,
A confidence sans bound.

98. oft] *D*1; of it *D*2, *S*.
101. from substitution] *D*1, *D*2; out o' th' substitution *S*.
111. So dry . . . sway] "We think this very impoverished phraseology; a change in our apprehension might mend it—he *thirsted* so for sway" (F. G.)
120. my grandmother] *D*1 *D*2 omit the following line, "Good wombs have borne bad sons."
123. hearks] *D*1, *D*2; hearkens *S*.

Of homage and I know not how much tribute,
Should presently extirpate me and mine
Out of the Dukedom and confer fair Milan,
With all the honors, on my brother. Whereon
A treacherous army levied, one midnight
130 Fated to the purpose, did Anthonio open
The gates of Milan; and, in the dead of darkness,
The ministers for the purpose hurried thence
Me and thy crying self.

MIRANDA. Alack, for pity!
I, not remembering how I cried out then,
Will cry it o'er again; it is a hint
That wrings mine eyes to't.

PROSPERO. Hear a little further,
And then I'll bring thee to the present business
140 Which now's upon's, without the which this story
Were most impertinent.

MIRANDA. Why did they not
That hour destroy us?

PROSPERO. Well demanded, wench;
My tale provokes that question. Dear, they durst not,
So dear the love my people bore me, set
A mark so bloody on the business, but
With colors fairer painted their foul ends.
In few, they hurried us aboard a bark,
150 Bore us some leagues to sea, where they prepared
A rotten carcase of a boat, not rigged,
Nor tackle, sail, nor mast; the very rats
Instinctively had quit it. There they hoist us,
To cry to the sea that roared to us; to sigh
To the winds, whose pity, sighing back again,
Did us but loving wrong.

MIRANDA. Alack! What trouble
Was I then to you!

PROSPERO. O, a cherubim

---

130. Fated] "Fated is rather an exaggerated term here" (F. G.).

142. Why] *D*1, *D*2; Wherefore *S*.

146. set] *D*1, *D*2; nor set *S*.

151. boat] *D*1, *D*2; butt *S*.

156. loving wrong] "Prospero describes the treatment himself and his infant daughter met, with the deplorable situation they were turned adrift in, in strong terms" (F. G.).

159. a cherubim] "There is much paternal tenderness and delicacy in this very affectionate remark" (F. G.).

160 Thou wast, that did preserve me. Thou didst smile,
Infused with a fortitude from heaven,
When I have decked the sea with drops full salt,
Under my burden groaned, which raised in me
An undergoing stomach, to bear up
Against what should ensue.

MIRANDA. How came we ashore?

PROSPERO. By providence divine.
Some food we had, and some fresh water, that
A noble Neapolitan, Gonzalo,
170 Out of his charity (being then appointed
Master of this design) did give us, with
Rich garments, linens, stuffs, and necessaries,
Which since have steaded much. So of his gentleness,
Knowing I loved my books, he furnished me
From my own library with volumes that
I prize above my dukedom.

MIRANDA. Would I might
But ever see that man!

PROSPERO. Now attend
180 And hear the last of our sea-sorrow.
Here in this island we arrived, and here
Have I, thy school-master, made thee more profit
Than other princes can, that have more time
For vainer hours, and tutors not so careful.

MIRANDA. Heavens thank you for it! And now, I pray you, sir,—
For still 'tis beating in my mind—your reason
For raising this sea-storm?

PROSPERO. Know thus far forth,
By accident most strange, bountiful fortune
190 (Now my dear lady) hath mine enemies
Brought to this shore, and by my prescience
I find my zenith doth depend upon
A most auspicious star, whose influence
If now I court not, but omit, my fortunes
Will ever after droop.—Here cease more questions;
Thou art inclined to sleep. 'Tis a good dulness,
And give it way. (*Aside.*) I know thou canst not choose—

---

170. being] *D1*, *D2*; who being *S*.
179. Now attend] *D1*, *D2*; Now I arise. / Sit still *S*.
191. my prescience] "This foreknowledge, joined with magic, we by no means like; they are ticklish ideas for young or weak minds, therefore ill calculated for public utterance or private perusal" (F. G.).

Miranda *sleeps.*

Come away, servant, come; I'm ready now.
Approach, my Ariel, come!

Enter Ariel.

200 ARIEL. All hail, great master! Grave sir, hail! I come
To answer thy best pleasure, be't to fly,
To swim, to dive into the fire, to ride
On the curled clouds. To thy strong bidding task
Ariel and all his qualities.
PROSPERO. Hast thou, spirit,
Performed to point the tempest that I bade thee?
ARIEL. To every article.
I boarded the King's ship; now on the beak,
Now in the waste, the deck, in every cabin,
210 I flamed amazement. Sometimes, I'd divide,
And burn in many places: on the top mast,
The yards, and bolt-sprit,
Then meet and join. Jove's lightnings, the precursers
Of dreadful thunderclaps, more momentary
And sight out-running were not; the fire and cracks
Of sulphurous roaring the most mighty Neptune
Seemed to besiege and make his bold waves tremble,
Yea, his dread trident shake.
PROSPERO. My brave, brave spirit!
220 Who was so firm, so constant, that this coil
Would not infect his reason?
ARIEL. Not a soul
But felt a fever of the mind and played
Some tricks of desperation. All but mariners
Plunged in the foaming brine and quit the vessel,
Then all afire with me. The King's son Ferdinand,
With hair up-staring (then like reeds, not hair)
Was the first man that leaped; cried, "Hell is empty;
And all the devils are here."
230 PROSPERO. Why, that's my spirit!

199.1. *Enter* Ariel] "Ariel should be remarkably delicate in appearance and expression, with a good musical voice; the description of his operation upon the ship is remarkably animated and poetical" (F. G.).

210. I'd] *D1*, *D2*; I'ld *S.*

212. bolt-sprit] *D1*, *D2*; boresprit *S.*

219. brave, brave] *D1*, *D2*; brave *S.*

223. mind] *D1*, *D2*; mad *S.*

But was not this nigh shore?

ARIEL. Close by, my master.

PROSPERO. But are they, Ariel, safe?

ARIEL. Not a hair perished.
On their sustaining garments not a blemish,
But fresher than before. And as thou badst me,
In troops I have dispersed them 'bout the isle.
The King's son have I landed by himself,
Whom I left cooling of the air with sighs
240 In an odd angle of the isle, and sitting,
His arms in this sad knot.

PROSPERO. Of the King's ship
The mariners, say, how thou hast disposed,
And all the rest o'th' fleet?

ARIEL. Safely in harbor
Is the King's ship; in the deep nook where once
Thou called me up at midnight to fetch dew
From the still-vexed Bermudas, there she's hid,
The mariners all under hatches stowed,
250 Who, with a charm joined to their suffered labor,
I've left asleep; and for the rest o'th' fleet,
(Which I dispersed) they all have met again
And are upon the Mediterranean flote,
Bound sadly home for Naples,
Supposing that they saw the King's ship wrecked
And his great person perish.

PROSPERO. Ariel, thy charge
Exactly is performed; but there's more work.
What is the time o'th' day?

260 ARIEL. Past the mid season.

PROSPERO. At least two glasses; the time 'twixt six and now
Must by us both be spent most preciously.

ARIEL. Is there more toil? Since thou dost give me pains,
Let me remember thee what thou hast promised,
Which is not yet performed me.

PROSPERO. How now! moody?
What is't thou canst demand?

ARIEL. My liberty.

PROSPERO. Before the time be out? No more.

270 ARIEL. I pr'y thee,
Remember, I have done thee worthy service,

---

251. I've] *D1*, *D2*; I have *S*.

Told thee no lies, made no mistakings, served
Without or grudge or grumblings. Thou didst promise
To bate me a full year.

PROSPERO. Dost thou forget
From what a torment I did free thee?

ARIEL. No.

PROSPERO. Thou liest, malignant thing! Hast thou forgot
The foul witch Sycorax, who with age and envy
80 Was grown into a hoop? Hast thou forgot her?

ARIEL. No, sir.

PROSPERO. Thou hast. Where was she born? Speak! Tell me.

ARIEL. Sir, in Argier.

PROSPERO. Oh, was she so? I must
Once in a month recount what thou hast been,
Which thou forget'st. This damned witch Sycorax,
For mischiefs manifold and sorceries terrible
To enter human hearing, from Argier,
Thou know'st, was banished. For one thing she did
90 They would not take her life. Is not this true?

ARIEL. Ay, sir.

PROSPERO. This blue-eyed hag was hither brought with child
And here was left by the sailors; thou, my slave,
As thou report'st thyself, was then her servant,
And, for thou wast a spirit too delicate
To act her earthy and abhorred commands,
Refusing her grand hests, she did confine thee,
By help of her more potent ministers,
And in her most unmitigable rage,
100 Into a cloven pine; within which rift
Imprisoned thou didst painfully remain
A dozen years, within which space she died
And left thee there, where thou didst vent thy groans
As fast as millwheels strike. Then was this island

---

274. full year] "The spirit's squabbling here with Prospero shows too much of the sulky mortal servant; a being of this kind, and of such power, must previously know that such resistance could be of no effect, therefore superfluous" (F. G.).

277. No] *D*1, *D*2 omit five following lines:

> PROS. Thou dost; and think'st it much to tread the ooze
> Of the salt deep,
> To run upon the sharp wind of the North,
> To do me business in the veins o' th' earth
> When it is bak'd with frost.
> ARI. I do not, sir.

(Save for the son that she did litter here,
A freckled whelp, hag-born) not honored with
A human shape.

ARIEL. Yes, Caliban, her son.

PROSPERO. Dull thing, I say so: he, that Caliban,
310 Whom now I keep in service. Thou best know'st
What torment I did find thee in; thy groans
Did make wolves howl and penetrate the breasts
Of ever-angry bears; it was a torment
To lay upon the damned, which Sycorax
Could not again undo. It was mine art,
When I arrived and heard thee, that made gape
The pine and let thee out.

ARIEL. I thank thee, master.

PROSPERO. If thou more murmur'st, I will rend an oak
320 And peg thee in his knotty entrails 'till
Thou'st howled away twelve winters.

ARIEL. Pardon, master.
I will be correspondent to command
And do my sp'riting gently.

PROSPERO. Do so, and after two days
I will discharge thee.

ARIEL. That's my noble master!
What shall I do? Say what! What shall I do?

PROSPERO. Go make thyself like to a nymph o'th' sea.
330 Be subject to no sight but mine; invisible
To every eye-ball else. Go take this shape
And hither come in it. Go hence with diligence.

Exit Ariel.

Awake, dear heart, awake! Thou hast slept well; awake—

MIRANDA. The strangeness of your story put
Heaviness in me.

PROSPERO. Shake it off. Come on;
I'll visit Caliban, my slave, who never
Yields us kind answer.

MIRANDA. 'Tis a villain, sir,
340 I do not love to look on—

PROSPERO. But, as 'tis,
We cannot miss him. He does make our fire,

307. human shape] "The only use we see in this quarrel between master and attendant is to eke out a scene rather too long before, and to make mention of Sycorax, which might have been done as well elsewhere" (F. G.).

Fetch in our wood, and serves in offices
That profit us.

Exit Miranda.

What ho, slave! Caliban!
Thou earth thou! Speak.

CALIBAN (*within*). There's wood enough within.

PROSPERO. Come forth, I say; there's other business for thee.
Come, thou tortoise! When?—

Enter Ariel, *like a water nymph.*

350 Fine apparition! My quaint Ariel,
Hark in thine ear.

ARIEL. My Lord, it shall be done.

Exit Ariel.

PROSPERO. Thou poisonous slave, got by the devil himself
Upon thy wicked dam, come forth.

Enter Caliban.

CALIBAN. As wicked dew as e'er my mother brushed
With raven's feather from unwholesome fen
Drop on you both! A southwest blow on you
And blister you all o'er!

PROSPERO. For this, be sure, tonight thou shalt have cramps,
360 Side-stitches that shall pen thy breath up; urchins
Shall, for that vast of night that they may work,
All exercise on thee; thou shalt be pinched
As thick as honeycombs, each pinch more stinging
That bees that made 'em.

CALIBAN. I must eat my dinner.
This island's mine by Sycorax, my mother,
Which thou tak'st from me. When thou camest first,
Thou stroak'd'st me and mad'st much of me, and would'st give me
Water with berries in't' and teach me how
370 To name the bigger light, and how the less,
That burn by day and night; and then I loved thee,
And showed thee all the qualities o'th' isle,
The fresh springs, brine pits, barren place and fertile.

354.1. *Enter* Caliban] "The figure of Caliban is totally made; his language, which is most admirably adapted, would be uttered with a rough, malignant costiveness of expression" (F. G.).

368. and would'st] *D1*, *D2*; would'st *S*.

Cursed be I that I did so! All the charms
Of Sycorax, toads, beetles, bats light on you!
For I am all the subjects that you have,
Who first was mine own king; and here you sty me,
In this hard rock, whiles you do keep from me
The rest of the island.

380 PROSPERO. Thou most lying slave,
Whom stripes may move, not kindness, I have used thee
(Filth as thou art) with humane care, and lodged
In mine own cell, 'till thou didst seek to violate
The honor of my child.

CALIBAN. Oh ho, oh ho!—I would it had been done!
Thou didst prevent me; I had peopled else
This isle with Calibans.

PROSPERO. Abhorred slave,
Which any print of goodness wilt not take,
390 Being capable of all ill! I pitied thee,
Took pains to make thee speak, taught thee, each hour,
One thing or other. When thou didst not, savage,
Know thine own meaning, but wouldst gabble like
A thing most brutish, I endowed thy purposes
With words that made them known.

CALIBAN. You taught me language, and my profit on't
Is, I know how to curse. The red plague rid you
For learning me your language!

PROSPERO. Hag-seed, hence!
400 Fetch us in fuel, and be quick (thou wert best)
To answer other business. Shrug'st thou, malice?
If thou neglect it, or dost unwillingly
What I command, I'll rack thee with old cramps,
Fill all thy bones with aches, make thee roar
That beasts shall tremble at thy din.

CALIBAN. No, pray thee.
[*Aside.*] I must obey; his art is of such power
It would control my dam's god, Setebos,

---

388. Abhorred slave] "As ingratitude is a very deep mark of a bad, unprincipled heart, and which is never found among the brute creation when kindly used, fixing a positive charge of it on Caliban heightens his gloomy character much" (F. G.).

395. known] *D1*, *D2* omit four following lines: "But thy vile race, / Though thou didst learn, had that in't which good natures / Could not abide to be with. Therefore wast thou / Deservedly confin'd into this rock, who hadst / Deserv'd more than a prison."

402. neglect it] *D1*; neglect'st *D2*; neglect *S*.

And make a vassal of him.

410 PROSPERO. So, slave, hence!

Exit Caliban.

Enter Ferdinand, *and* Ariel, *invisible*, *playing and singing.*

ARIEL'S SONG.

[ARIEL.] Come unto these yellow sands,
And then take hands:
Curtsied when you have, and kist,
The wild waves whist;
Foot it featly here and there,
And, sweet spirits, the burden bear.

BURDEN (*dispersedly*). Hark, hark! Bough-waugh! The watchdogs bark, Bough waugh.

[ARIEL.] Hark, hark, I hear
420 The strain of strutting chanticleer
Cry, Cock-a-doodle-do.

A dance of spirits.

FERDINAND. Where should this music be, i'th' air or earth?—
It sounds no more; and sure it waits upon
Some god o'th' island. Sitting on a bank,
Weeping again the King my father's wreck,
This music crept by me upon the waters,
Allaying both their fury and my passion
With its sweet air; thence I have followed it,
Or it hath drawn me rather—but 'tis gone.

Music plays.

430 No, it begins again.

ARIEL'S SONG.

[ARIEL.] Full fatham five thy father lies;
Of his bones are coral made;
Those are pearls that were his eyes;
Nothing of him that doth fade
But doth suffer a sea-change
Into something rich and strange.

---

422. earth] *D*1, *D*2; th' earth *S*.
425. wreck] *D*1, *D*2; wrack *S*.

The Tempest, I, vi
Folger Shakespeare Library

Sea-nymphs hourly ring his knell:
Hark, now I hear them, ding-dong bell.

BURDEN. Ding dong.

440 FERDINAND. The ditty does remember my drowned father,
This is no mortal business, nor no sound
That the earth owns. (*Music again.*) I hear it now above me.

Exit Ferdinand *and* Ariel.

SCENE [III], *another part of the island.*

Enter Ariel *and* Ferdinand *on one side, and* Prospero
and Miranda *on the other.*

PROSPERO. The fringed curtains of thine eyes advance
And say what thou see'st yond.

MIRANDA. What is't, a spirit?
Lord, how it looks about! Believe me, sir,
It carries a brave form. But is't a spirit?

PROSPERO. No, wench, it eats, and sleeps, and hath such senses
As we have, such. This gallant which thou seest
Was in the wreck; and, but he's something stained
With grief (that's beauty's canker), thou might'st call him
10 A goodly person. He hath lost his fellows
And strays about to find them.

MIRANDA. I might call him
A thing divine, for nothing natural
I ever saw so noble.

PROSPERO (*aside*). It goes on, I see,
As my soul prompts it. Spirit, fine spirit, I'll free thee
Within two days for this.

FERDINAND. Most sure, the goddess
On whom these airs attend! vouchsafe my prayer
20 May know if you remain upon this island,
And that you will some good instruction give
How I may bear me here. My prime request,
Which I do last pronounce, is (O you wonder!)
If you be maid or no?

MIRANDA. No wonder, sir,
But certainly a maid.

---

442. owns] *D1*, *D2*; owes *S*.

1. PROSPERO] continuation of I, ii, in *S*.

5. a spirit] "Miranda's simplicity of surprise at seeing Ferdinand for the first time is natural and finely imagined" (F. G.).

FERDINAND. My language! Heavens!
I am the best of them that speak this speech,
Were I but where 'tis spoken.

30 PROSPERO. How? the best?
What wert thou if the King of Naples heard thee?

FERDINAND. A single thing, as I am now, that wonders
To hear thee speak of Naples. He does hear me;
And that he does I weep. Myself am Naples,
Who with mine eyes (ne'er since at ebb) beheld
The King my father wrecked.

MIRANDA. Alack, for mercy!

FERDINAND. Yes, faith, and all his lords, the Duke of Milan
And his brave son being twain.

40 PROSPERO [*aside*]. The Duke of Milan
And his more brave daughter could control thee,
If now 'twere fit to do't. (*To* Ariel.) At the first sight
They have changed eyes.—
A word, good sir.
I fear you've done yourself some wrong. A word—

MIRANDA. Why speaks my father so urgently? This
Is the third man that I e'er saw, the first
That e'er I sighed for. Pity move my father
To be inclined my way!

50 FERDINAND. O if a virgin,
And your affection not gone forth, I'll make you
The Queen of Naples.

PROSPERO. Soft, sir; one word more.
(*Aside.*) They're both in either's power. But this swift business
I must uneasy make, lest too light winning
Make the prize light.—Sir, one word more. I charge thee
That thou attend me. Thou dost here usurp
The name thou ow'st not, and hast put thyself
Upon this island as a spy to win it
60 From me, the lord on't.

---

36. wrecked] *D*1; wreckt *D*2; wrack'd *S*.

43. eyes] *D*1, *D*2 omit two following half lines:

"Delicate Ariel, / I'll set thee free for this!"

49. my way] "The young lady, we think, is rather forward in declaring her inclination, especially considering the abstracted, lonely state she has been brought up in. Nature has sudden feelings, but sense and delicacy check them" (F. G.).

54. power] *D*1, *D*2; pow'rs *S*.

56. Sir] *D*1, *D*2; not in *S*.

FERDINAND. No, as I'm a man.
MIRANDA. There's nothing ill can dwell in such a temple.
If the ill spirit have so fair an house,
Good things will strive to dwell with't.
PROSPERO. Follow me.–
Speak not you for him: he's a traitor. Come,
I'll manacle thy neck and feet together;
Sea-water shalt thou drink; thy food shall be
The fresh-brook mussels, withered root, and husks
70 Wherein the acorn cradled. Follow.
FERDINAND. No,
I will resist such entertainment 'till
Mine enemy has more power. (*He draws and is charmed from moving.*)
MIRANDA. Oh, dear father,
Make not too rash a trial of him, for
He's gentle, and not fearful.
PROSPERO. What, I say,
My foot my tutor? Put thy sword up, traitor,
Who mak'st a show but dar'st not strike, thy conscience
80 Is so possessed with guilt. Come from thy ward,
For I can here disarm thee with this stick
And make thy weapon drop.
MIRANDA. Beseech you, father. (*Kneels.*)
PROSPERO. Hence! Hang not on my garment.
MIRANDA. Sir, have pity;
I'll be his surety.
PROSPERO. Silence! One word more
Shall make me chide thee, if not hate thee. What!
An advocate for an impostor? Hush!
90 Thou think'st there are no more such shapes as he,
Having seen but him and Caliban. Foolish wench!
To th' most of men this is a Caliban,
And they to him are angels.
MIRANDA. My affections
Are then most humble. I have no ambition
To see a goodlier man.
PROSPERO. Come on, obey;
Thy nerves are in their infancy again

---

63. an] *D*1, *D*2; a *S*.
93. are angels] "The stern behavior of Prospero is well conceived to check for a time, though it, in reality, increases the precipitate affection for each other entertained by the young pair" (F. G.).

And have no vigor in them.

100 FERDINAND. So they are.

My spirits, as in a dream, are all bound up.
My father's loss, the weakness which I feel,
The wreck of all my friends, and this man's threats,
To whom I am subdued, were but light to me,
Might I but through my prison once a day
Behold this maid. All corners else o'th' earth
Let liberty make use of; space enough
Have I in such a prison.

PROSPERO. [*aside.*] It works. [*To* Ferdinand.] Come on.

110 [*To* Ariel.] Thou hast done well, fine Ariel. [*To* Ferdinand.] Follow me.

(*To* Ariel.) Hark what thou else shalt do me.

MIRANDA. Be of comfort.

My father's of a better nature, sir,
Than he appears by speech. This is unwonted
Which now came from him.

PROSPERO. Thou shalt be as free

As mountain winds; but then exactly do
All points of my command.

120 ARIEL. To th' syllable.

PROSPERO. Come, follow. Speak not for him.

Exeunt.

ACT II.

SCENE I, *another part of the island.*

Enter Alonso, Sebastian, Anthonio, Gonzalo, *and* Francisco.

GONZALO. Beseech you, sir, be merry. You have cause

(So have we all) of joy, for our escape

---

103. wreck] *D*1, *D*2; wrack *S.* and] *D*1, *D*2; nor *S.*

104. were] *D*1, *D*2; are *S.*

121.1. *Exeunt*] "The first act, exclusive of the bustling first scene and two agreeable songs, we deem exceedingly heavy, though Caliban must be admitted a very original object and well worthy particular notice. The sentiments and language are good, but spirit and variation are wanting" (F. G.).

0.1. *Enter* . . . Gonzalo, *and* Francisco] *D*1, *D*2; . . . Gonzalo, Adrian, Francisco, *and others S.* "If this half-drowned king and his sea-soused attendants are decent figures and decent speakers, they walk through well enough" (F. G.).

Is much beyond our loss. Our hint of woe
Is common. Every day some sailor's wife,
The master of some merchant, and the merchant
Have just our theme of woe; but for the miracle—
I mean our preservation—few in millions
Can speak like us. Then wisely, good sir, weigh
Our sorrow with our comfort.

10 ALONSO. Pr'ythee, peace.

GONZALO. Methinks our garments are now as fresh as
When we put them on first in Africk, at the marriage of
The King's fair daughter Claribel to the King of Tunis.

ALONSO. You cram these words into mine ears against
The stomach of my sense. Would I had never
Married my daughter there! For, coming thence,
My son is lost.

FRANCISCO. Sir, he may live.
I saw him beat the surges under him
20 And ride upon their backs; his bold head
'Bove the contentious waves he kept, and oared
Himself with his good arms in lusty strokes
To the shore. I not doubt
He came alive to land.

ALONSO. No, no, he's gone.

SEBASTIAN. Sir, you may thank yourself for this great loss,
That would not bless our Europe with your daughter,
But rather lose her to an African,
Where she, at least, is banished from your eye,
30 Who hath cause to wet the grief on't.

ALONSO. Pr'ythee, peace.

SEBASTIAN. You were kneeled to and importuned otherwise

---

10. peace] *D1*, *D2* omit fifty-six following lines. "There are near three pages of the scene succeeding this speech in the original very properly left out, as they are strangely trifling and therefore not worthy either utterance or perusal" (F. G.).
13. Tunis] *D1*, *D2* omit thirty-three lines following.
17. lost] *D1*, *D2* omit four and a half lines: "and, in my rate, she too, / Who is so far from Italy remov'd / I ne'er again shall see her. O thou mine heir / Of Naples and of Milan, what strange fish / Hath made his meal on thee?"
20. backs] *D1*, *D2* omit about three lines here: "He trod the water, / Whose enmity he flung aside, and breasted / The surge most swol'n that met him."
22. strokes] *D1*, *D2*; stroke *S.*
23. shore] *D1*, *D2* omit part of two lines: "that o'er his wave-worn basis bow'd, / As stooping to relieve him."

By all of us; and the fair soul herself
Weighed, between loathness and obedience, at
Which end the beam should bow. We've lost your son,
I fear, for ever. Milan and Naples have
More widows in them of this business' making
Than we bring men to comfort them.
The fault's your own.

40 ALONSO. So is the dearest o'th' loss.

GONZALO. My Lord Sebastian,
The truth you speak doth lack some gentleness,
And time to speak it in. You rub the sore
When you should bring the plaster.

ALONSO. Still let me hope. Good Francisco, look
Out again, scout round the rocks, and bring my
Heart some comfort with my son.

Exit Francisco.

GONZALO. Had I the plantation of this isle, my lord,
And were a king on't, what would I do?
50 I would with such perfection govern, sir,
T' excel the golden age.

ALONSO. Pr'ythee, no more. Thou dost talk
Nothing to me. Let us sit down upon
This bank and rest our sorrows.

GONZALO. I will, my Lord, for I am very heavy.

---

44. plaster] "This rebuff Gonzalo gives Sebastian for remarks monstrously ill timed and most indecently cruel" (F. G.).

45. ALONSO] *D*1, *D*2 add this three-line speech. Slightly more than three lines are omitted:
SEB. Very well.
ANT. And most chirurgeonly.
GON. It is foul weather in us all, good sir,
When you are cloudy.
SEB. Foul weather?
ANT. Very foul.

48. my lord] *D*1, *D*2 (silently) omit a one-line exchange here:
"ANT. He'd sow't with nettle seed. / SEB. Or docks, or mallows."

49. I do] *D*1, *D*2 (silently) omit twenty-one lines following.

51. age] *D*1, *D*2 (silently) omit a line and a half here: "SEB. Save his Majesty! / ANT. Long live Gonzalo! / GON. And—do you mark me, sir?"

53. to me] *D*1, *D*2 (silently) omit approximately twenty-four lines here and add the two and a half lines beginning "Let us sit."

They lie down upon the bank.

SEBASTIAN. Please you, sir,
Do not omit the heavy offer of it.
It seldom visits sorrow; when it doth,
It is a comforter.

60 ANTHONIO. We two, my Lord,
Will guard your person while you take your rest,
And watch your safety.

ALONSO. Thank you. Wond'rous heavy—

All sleep but Sebastian *and* Anthonio. *Soft music is played.*

SEBASTIAN. What a strange drowsiness possesses them!

ANTHONIO. It is the quality o'th' climate.

SEBASTIAN. Why
Doth it not then our eye-lids sink? I find not
Myself disposed to sleep.

ANTHONIO. Nor I. My spirits are nimble.
70 They fell together all, as by consent;
They dropped as by a thunderstroke. What might,
Worthy Sebastian—Oh what might—no more.
And yet methinks I see it in thy face
What thou should'st be. Th' occasion speaks thee, and
My strong imagination sees a crown
Dropping upon thy head.

SEBASTIAN. What, art thou waking?

ANTHONIO. Noble Sebastian,
Thou let'st thy fortune sleep.

80 SEBASTIAN. Pr'ythee, say on;
The setting of thine eye and cheek proclaim
A matter from thee, and a birth, indeed,
Which throes thee much to yield.

55.1. *They lie down*] "We think sleep is too often called upon; Miranda has had a nap in the first act to very little use, and here we are presented with another, to less" (F. G.).

77. waking] *D*1, *D*2 omit five and a half lines here:

ANT. Do you not hear me speak?
SEB. I do; and surely
It is a sleepy language, and thou speak'st
Out of thy sleep. What is it thou didst say?
This is a strange repose, to be asleep
With eyes wide open; standing, speaking, moving,
And yet so fast asleep.

79. sleep] *D*1, *D*2 omit twelve lines here.

ANTHONIO. Thus, sir:
Will you grant, with me,
That Ferdinand is drowned?
SEBASTIAN. He's gone.
ANTHONIO. Then tell me
Who's the next heir of Naples?
90 SEBASTIAN. What mean you?
ANTHONIO. Say this were death
That now hath seized them, why, they were no worse
Than now they are. There be that can rule Naples,
As well as he that sleeps;
Oh, that you bore
The mind that I do; what a sleep was this
For your advancement! Do you understand me?
SEBASTIAN. Methinks I do.
ANTHONIO. And how does your content
100 Tender your own good fortune?
SEBASTIAN. I remember
You did supplant your brother Prospero.
ANTHONIO. True.
And look how well my garments sit upon me:
Much feater than before. My brother's servants
Were then my fellows; now they are my men.
SEBASTIAN. But, for your conscience–
ANTHONIO. Ay, sir; where lies that?
Ten consciences that stand 'twixt me and Milan,
110 Candied be they, and melt, e'er they molest!
Here lies your brother–
No better than the earth he lies upon
If he were that which now he's like, that's dead;
Whom I with this obedient steel, three inches of it,
Can lay to bed forever. You doing thus,

---

84. Thus, sir] *D1*, *D2* omit eleven and a half lines here.
89. Naples] *D1*, *D2* (silently) omit fifteen lines here.
90. SEBASTIAN] *D1*, *D2* add this line.
94. sleeps] *D1*, *D2* omit three lines here: "lords that can prate / As amply and unnecessarily / As this Gonzalo. I myself could make / A clough of as deep chat."
102. Prospero] "There is above a page of this dull scene most necessarily sliced out; patience must otherwise cry out loudly" (F. G.).
108. lies that] *D1*, *D2* omit two lines: "If 'twere a kibe, / 'Twould put me to my slipper; but I feel not / This deity in my bosom."
109. Ten] *D1*, *D2*; Twenty *S*.
115. You] *D1*, *D2*; whiles you *S*.

To the perpetual wink for aye might put
This ancient morsel, this Sir Prudence, who
Should not upbraid our course. For all the rest,
They'll tell the clock to any business that
120 We say befits the hour.

SEBASTIAN. Thy case, dear friend,
Shall be my precedent. As thou got'st Milan,
I'll come by Naples. Draw thy sword; one stroke
Shall free thee from the tribute which thou pay'st,
And I the King shall love thee.

ANTHONIO. Draw together;
And when I rear my hand, do you the like,
To fall it on Gonzalo.

SEBASTIAN. Oh, but one word—

Enter Ariel.

130 ARIEL. My master through his art forsees the danger
That you, his friend, are in; and sends me forth,
(For else his project dies) to keep them living. (*Sings in* Gonzalo's *ear.*)

While you here do snoring lie,
Open-eyed conspiracy
His time doth take.
If of life you keep a care,
Shake off slumber and beware.
Awake! Awake!

ANTHONIO. Then let us both be sudden.

140 GONZALO. Now, good angels preserve the King!

They wake.

ALONSO. Why, how now? Ho, awake? Why are you drawn?
Wherefore this ghastly looking?

GONZALO. What's the matter?

SEBASTIAN. While we stood here securing your repose,
Even now we heard a hollow burst of bellowing,
Like bulls, or rather lions; did't not wake you?
It struck mine ear most terribly.

---

118. the rest] *D1*, *D2* omit one following line: "They'll take suggestion as a cat laps milk."

120. the hour] "This strange suggestion of murdering a king for dominions which they know not they shall ever see again, and by people so lately saved themselves, appears a strain of probability and is besides superfluous" (F. G.).

ALONSO. I heard nothing.

ANTHONIO. Oh, 'twas a din to fright a monster's ear,

150 To make an earthquake. Sure it was the roar
Of a whole herd of lions.

ALONSO. Heard you this?

GONZALO. Upon my honor, sir, I heard a humming,
And that a strange one too, which did awake me.
I shaked you, sir, and cried. As mine eyes opened,
I saw their weapons drawn; there was a noise,
That's verity. 'Tis best we stand on guard,
Or that we quit this place. Let's draw our weapons.

ALONSO. Lead off this ground, and let's make further search

160 For my poor son.

GONZALO. Heavens keep him from these beasts!
For he is, sure, i'th' island.

ALONSO. Lead away.

Exeunt.

SCENE [II] *changes to another part of the island.*

Enter Caliban *with a burden of wood; a noise of thunder heard.*

CALIBAN. All the infections that the sun sucks up
From bogs, fens, flats, on Prospero fall and make him
By inchmeal a disease! His spirits hear me,
And yet I needs must curse. But they'll not pinch,
Fright me with urchin shows, pitch me i'th' mire,
Nor lead me, like a firebrand in the dark,
Out of my way unless he bid'em'; but
For every trifle are they set upon me.
Sometimes like apes, that moe and chatter at me,

10 And after bite me; then like hedgehogs, which
Lie tumbling in my bare-foot way, and mount

152. you this?] *D1*, *D2*; you this, Gonzalo *S.*

157. verity] *D1*, *D2*; verily *S.*

163. Lead away] *D1*, *D2*, omit Ariel's final speech, two lines: "Prospero my lord shall know what I have done. / So, King, go safely on to seek thy son."

1. CALIBAN] "This speech is extremely and peculiarly picturesque; nothing could be better conceived or expressed for a mongrel monster. The ideas are abundantly rich, and happy in their kind" (F. G.).

4. not] *D1*, *D2*; nor *S.*

Their pricks at my footfall; sometime am I
All wound with adders, who with cloven tongues
Do hiss me into madness. Lo now! lo!

Enter Trinculo.

Here comes a spirit of his, and to torment me
For bringing wood in slowly. I'll fall flat;
Perchance he will not mind me.

TRINCULO. Here's neither bush nor shrub to bear off any weather at all, and another storm brewing; I hear it sing i'th' wind. Yon same
20 black cloud, yon huge one, looks like a foul bumbard that would shed his liquor. If it should thunder as it did before, I know not where to hide my head. Yon same cloud cannot choose but fall by pailfuls.—What have we here, a man or a fish? dead or alive? A fish; he smells like a fish, a very ancient and fish-like smell. A kind of, not of the newest, Poor John. A strange fish! Were I in England now, as once I was, and had but this fish painted, not an holiday fool there but would give a piece of silver. There would this monster make a man; any strange beast there makes a man. When they will not give a doit to relieve a lame beggar, they will
30 lay out ten to see a dead Indian. Legged like a man! and his fins like arms! Warm, o'my troth! I do now let loose my opinion, hold it no longer: this is no fish, but an islander that hath lately suffered by a thunder-bolt. Alas! the storm is come again. My best way is to creep under his gaberdine. There is no other shelter hereabout. Misery acquaints a man with strange bedfellows. I will here shroud 'till the dregs of the storm be past.

Enter Stephano, *singing.*

STEPHANO. I shall no more to sea, to sea;
Here shall I die ashore.

This is a very scurvy tune to sing at a man's funeral.
40 Well, here's my comfort. (*Drinks*; *than sings.*)

The master, the swabber, the boatswain, and I,
The gunner, and his mate,

---

19. yon] *D*1, *D*2; yond *S.*
20. bumbard] *D*1, *D*2; bombard *S.*
22. Yon] *D*1, *D*2; yond *S.*
36. be past] "There is considerable spirit and humor in this speech, which, as well as the rest of Trinculo, requires a good low comedian. His remark on the English taste for strange sights is tart, pleasant, and just. Stephano is nearly in the style of his companion" (F. G.).

Loved Mall, Meg, and Marian, and Margery,
But none of us cared for Kate;
For she had a tongue with a tang,
Would cry to a sailor, "Go hang!"
She loved not the savor of tar nor of pitch,
Yet a tailor might scratch her where'e'er she did itch.
Then to sea, boys, and let her go hang.

50 This is a scurvy tune, too; but here's my comfort. (*Drinks.*)

CALIBAN. Do not torment me, oh!

STEPHANO. What's the matter? Have we devils here? Do you put tricks upon's with savages and men of Inde, ha? I have not scaped drowning to be afraid now of your four legs; for it hath been said, "As proper a man as ever went upon four legs cannot make him give ground." And it shall be said so again, while Stephano breaths at his nostrils.

CALIBAN. The spirit torments me. Oh!

STEPHANO. This is some monster of the isle, with four legs, who has got, 60 as I take it, an ague. Where the devil should he learn our language? I will give him some relief, if it be but for that. If I can recover him, and keep him tame, and get to Naples with him, he's a present for any emperor that ever trod on neat's-leather.

CALIBAN. Do not torment me, pr'ythee; I'll bring my wood home faster.

STEPHANO. He's in his fit now and does not talk after the wisest. He shall taste of my bottle. If he never drunk wine afore, it will go near to remove his fit. If I can recover him and keep him tame, I will not take too much for him; he shall pay for him that hath him, and that soundly.

70 CALIBAN. Thou dost me yet but little hurt; thou wilt anon; I know it by thy trembling. Now Prosper works upon thee.

STEPHANO. Come on your ways; open your mouth. Here is that which will give language to you, cat. Open your mouth; this will shake your shaking, I can tell you, and that soundly. You cannot tell who's your friend. Open your chaps again.

TRINCULO. I should know that voice. It should be—but he is drowned; and these are devils. Oh! defend me—

STEPHANO. Four legs and two voices; a most delicate monster! His forward voice now is to speak well of his friend; his backward voice 80 is to spatter foul speeches and to detract. If all the wine in my bottle will recover him, I will help his ague. Come! Amen! I will pour some in thy other mouth.

TRINCULO. Stephano—

56.7. at his] *D1*, *D2*; at' *S*.

STEPHANO. Doth thy other mouth call me? Mercy! Mercy! This is a devil, and no monster. I will leave him; I have no long spoon.

TRINCULO. Stephano! If thou beest Stephano, touch me and speak to me; for I am Trinculo—be not afraid—thy good friend Trinculo.

STEPHANO. If thou beest Trinculo, come forth, I'll pull thee by the lesser legs. If any be Trinculo's legs, these are they. Thou art very

90 Trinculo, indeed. How cam'st thou to [be] the siege of this mooncalf? Can he vent Trinculos?

TRINCULO. I took him to be killed with a thunderstroke. And art thou living, Stephano? Oh, Stephano, two Neapolitans scaped!

STEPHANO. Pr'ythee, do not turn me about; my stomach is not constant.

CALIBAN [*aside*]. These be fine things, an if they be not sprites. That's a brave god and bears celestial liquor. I will kneel to him.

STEPHANO. How did'st thou scape? How cam'st thou hither? Swear by this bottle how thou cam'st hither. I escaped upon a butt of sack which the sailors heaved overboard, by this bottle, which I made

100 of the bark of a tree with mine own hands since I was cast ashore.

CALIBAN. I'll swear upon that bottle to be thy true subject, for the liquor is not earthly.

STEPHANO. Here. Swear then how escap'st thou?

TRINCULO. Swam ashore, man, like a duck; I can swim like a duck, I'll be sworn.

STEPHANO. Here, kiss the book. Though thou can'st swim like a duck, thou art made like a goose.

TRINCULO. Oh, Stephano, hast any more of this?

STEPHANO. The whole butt, man; my cellar is in a rock by the seaside,

110 where my wine is hid. How now, mooncalf, how does thine ague?

CALIBAN. Hast thou not dropped from heaven?

STEPHANO. Out o'th' moon, I do assure thee. I was the man in th' moon when time was.

CALIBAN. I have seen thee in her, and I do adore thee. My mistress showed me thee, and thy dog and thy bush.

STEPHANO. Come, swear to that; kiss the book. I will furnish it anon with new contents. Swear.

CALIBAN. I'll show thee every fertile inch o'th' isle, and I will kiss thy foot. I pr'ythee, be my god.

120 TRINCULO. By this light, a most perfidious and drunken monster; when

---

87. afraid] *D1*, *D2*; afeard *S*.

92. thunderstroke] *D1*, *D2* omit approximately four prose lines of Trinculo's speech here: "But art thou not drown'd, Stephano? I hope now thou art not drown'd. Is the storm overblown? I hid me under the dead moon-calf's gaberdine for fear of the storm."

104. Swam] *D1*; Swom *D2*; variously Swum, Swom in *S*.

his god's asleep he'll rob his bottle.

CALIBAN. I'll show thee the best springs; I'll pluck thee berries;
I'll fish for thee, and get thee wood enough.
A plague upon the tyrant that I serve!
I'll bear him no more sticks, but follow thee,
Thou wondrous man.

TRINCULO. A most ridiculous monster, to make a wonder of a poor drunkard!

CALIBAN. I pr'ythee, let me bring thee where crabs grow;
130 And I with my long nails will dig thee pignuts;
Show thee a jay's nest, and instruct thee how
To snare the nimble marmazet. I'll bring thee
To clust'ring filberts, and sometimes I'll get thee
Young shamois from the rock. Wilt thou go with me?

STEPHANO. I pr'thee now lead the way without any more talking. Trinculo, the King and all our company else being drowned, we will inherit here. Hear, bear my bottle. Fellow Trinculo, we'll fill him by-and-by again.

CALIBAN (*sings drunkenly*). Farewell, master; farewell, farewell.

140 TRINCULO. A howling monster! a drunken monster!

CALIBAN. No more dams I'll make for fish,
Nor fetch in firing at requiring,
Nor scrape trencher, nor wash dish,
Ban' Ban', Cacaliban
Has a new master. Get a new man.

Freedom, hey-day! Hey-day, freedom! Freedom, hey-day, freedom!

STEPHANO. O brave monster, lead the way.

Exeunt.

---

134. Swear] *D1*, *D2* omit Trincolo's next speech: "By this good light, this is a very shallow monster! I afeard of him? A very weak monster! The Man i' the Moon? A most poor credulous monster! Well drawn, monster, in good sooth."

121. his bottle] *D1*, *D2* omit a five-speech exchange of about seven prose lines among Caliban, Stephano, and Trinculo: "CAL. I'll kiss thy foot. I'll swear myself thy subject. / STE. Come on then, down, and swear! / TRIN. I shall laugh myself to death at this puppy-headed monster. A most scurvy monster! I could find in my heart to beat him—"

132. marmazet] *D1*, *D2*; marmoset *S*.

134. shamois] *D1*, *D2*; scamels *S*.

148.1. *Exeunt*] "Though this last scene has some humor, we cannot help thinking the second act more languid and inconsiderable than the first; the actors, in the grave part, have a most insipid load to sustain" (F. G.).

ACT III.

SCENE I, *before* Prospero's *cell.*
Ferdinand *discovered, bearing a log.*

FERDINAND. There be some sports are painful, but their labor
Delight in them sets off; some kinds of baseness
Are nobly undergone, and most poor matters
Point to rich ends. This my mean task would be
As heavy to me as 'tis odious; but
The mistress which I serve quickens what's dead
And makes my labors pleasure. Oh, she is
Ten times more gentle than her father's crabbed;
And he's composed of harshness. I must move
10 Some thousands of these logs and pile them up,
Upon a sore injunction. My sweet mistress
Weeps when she sees me work, and says such baseness
Had ne'er like executor. I forget;
But these sweet thoughts do even refresh my labor,
Most busyless when I do it.

Enter Miranda.

MIRANDA. Alas, now, pray you,
Work not so hard; I would the lightning had
Burnt up those logs that thou'rt enjoined to pile.
Pray, set it down and rest you; when this burns,
20 'Twill weep for having wearied you. My father
Is hard at study; pray now, rest yourself;
He's safe for these three hours.
FERDINAND. O most dear mistress,
The sun will set before I shall discharge
What I must strive to do.
MIRANDA. If you'll sit down,
I'll bear your logs the while. Pray, give me that;
I'll carry't to the pile.
FERDINAND. No, precious creature,
30 I'd rather crack my sinews, break my back,
Than you should such dishonor undergo

---

2. Delight] "This sentiment, though very well expressed here, is delivered more concisely in *Macbeth*: The labor we delight in physics pain" (F. G.).
9. move] *D1, D2*; remove *S.*
14. labor] *D1, D2*; labours *S.*

While I sit lazy by.

MIRANDA. It would become me
As well as it does you; and I should do it
With much more ease; for my good will is to it,
And yours it is against.
You look wearily.

FERDINAND. No, noble mistress; 'tis fresh morning with me
When you are by at night. I do beseech you
40 (Chiefly that I might set it in my prayers),
What is your name?

MIRANDA. Miranda. O my father,
I've broke your hest to say so.

FERDINAND. Admired Miranda!
Indeed, the top of admiration, worth
What's dearest to the world! Full many a lady
I've eyed with best regard, and many a time
Th' harmony of their tongues hath into bondage
Brought my too diligent ear; for several virtues
50 Have I liked several women; never any
With so full soul but some defect in her
Did quarrel with the noblest grace she owed
And put it to the foil. But you, O you,
So perfect and so peerless, are created
Of every creature's best.

MIRANDA. I do not know
One of my sex; no woman's face remember,
Save from my glass mine own; nor have I seen
More that I may call men than you, good friend,
60 And my dear father. How features are abroad
I'm skillless of; but, by my modesty
(The jewel in my dower), I would not wish
Any companion in the world but you;
Nor can imagination form a shape
Besides yourself to like of.

FERDINAND. I am, in my condition,
A prince, Miranda; I do think, a king
(I would not so!) and would no more endure
This wooden slavery than I would suffer
70 The flesh-fly blow my mouth. Hear my soul speak;

---

36. against] *D1*, *D2* omit a one- and a-half-line aside of Prospero: "Poor worm, thou art infected! / This visitation shows it."

65. like of] *D1*, *D2* omit two lines of Miranda's speech: "But I prattle / Something too wildly, and my father's precepts / I therein do forget."

The very instant that I saw you did
My heart fly to your service, there resides
To make me slave to it; and for your sake
Am I this patient log-man.

MIRANDA. Do you love me?

FERDINAND. O heaven, O earth, bear witness to this sound,
And crown what I profess with kind event
If I speak true; if hollowly, invert
What best is boded me to mischief! I,
80 Beyond all limit of what else i'th' world,
Do love, prize, honor you.

MIRANDA. I am a fool
To weep at what I'm glad of.

FERDINAND. Wherefore weep you?

MIRANDA. At mine unworthiness, that dare not offer
What I desire to give; and much less take
What I shall die to want. But this is trifling;
And all the more it seeks to hide itself,
The bigger bulk it shows. Hence, bashful cunning!
90 And prompt me, plain and holy innocence.
I am your wife, if you will marry me;
If not, I'll die your maid. To be your fellow
You may deny me; but I'll be your servant,
Whether you will or no.

FERDINAND. My mistress, dearest,
And I thus humble ever.

MIRANDA. My husband then?

FERDINAND. Ay, with a heart as willing
As bondage e'er of freedom; here's my hand.

100 MIRANDA. And mine, with my heart in't; and now, farewell
Till half an hour hence.

FERDINAND. A thousand thousand!

Exeunt.

---

81. honor you] "We know not a prettier or more delicate pattern of love than this scene exhibits; it is not quite so warm as that in the second act of *Romeo and Juliet* but, considering Miranda's sequestered education, has equal merit" (F. G.).

83. glad of] *D1*, *D2* omit the following two-line aside of Prospero: "Fair encounter / Of two most rare affections! Heavens rain grace / On that which breeds between 'em!"

102. thousand thousand] *D1*, *D2* omit Prospero's five-line speech which ends the scene: "So glad of this as they I cannot be, / Who are surpris'd withal; but my rejoicing / At nothing can be more. I'll to my book; / For yet ere supper time must I perform / Much business appertaining."

SCENE [II] *changes to another part of the island.*

Enter Caliban, Stephano, *and* Trinculo.

STEPHANO. Tell not me; when the butt is out, we will drink water, not a drop before. Therefore bear up and board 'em, servant monster; drink to me.

TRINCULO. Servant monster! The folly of this island! They say there's but five upon this isle. We are three of them. If the other two be brained like us, the state totters.

STEPHANO. Drink, servant monster, when I bid thee; thy eyes are almost set in thy head.

TRINCULO. Where should they be set else? He were a brave monster
10 indeed if they were set in his tail.

STEPHANO. My man-monster hath drowned his tongue in sack. For my part, the sea cannot drown me. I swam, ere I could recover the shore, five and thirty leagues, off and on; by this light, thou shalt be my lieutenant, monster, or my standard.

TRINCULO. Your lieutenant, if you list; he's no standard.

STEPHANO. We'll not run, Monsieur Monster.

TRINCULO. Nor go neither; but you'll lie like dogs, and yet say nothing neither.

STEPHANO. Mooncalf, speak once in thy life, if thou beest a good moon-
20 calf.

CALIBAN. How does thy honor? Let me lick thy shoe.
I'll not serve him; he is not valiant.

TRINCULO. Thou liest, most ignorant monster; I am in case to justle a constable; why, thou deboshed fish, thou, was there ever a man a coward that hath drunk so much sack as I, today? Wilt thou tell a monstrous lie, being but half a fish and half a monster?

CALIBAN. Lo, how he mocks me. Wilt thou let him, my lord?

TRINCULO. Lord, quoth he! That a monster should be such a natural!

CALIBAN. Lo, lo, again! Bite him to death, I pr'ythee.

30 STEPHANO. Trinculo, keep a good tongue in your head; if you prove a mutineer, the next tree! The poor monster's my subject, and he shall not suffer indignity.

CALIBAN. I thank my noble lord. Wilt thou be pleased
To hearken once again to the suit I made to thee?

STEPHANO. Marry, will I. Kneel and repeat it; I will stand, and so shall Trinculo.

Enter Ariel *invisible.*

---

24. a man] *D1*, *D2*; man *S.*

CALIBAN. As I told thee before, I am subject to a tyrant, a sorcerer, that by his cunning hath cheated me of the island.

ARIEL. Thou liest.

40 CALIBAN. Thou liest, thou jesting monkey, thou;
I would my valiant master would destroy thee.
I do not lie.

STEPHANO. Trinculo, if you trouble him any more in's tale, by this hand I will supplant some of your teeth.

TRINCULO. Why, I said nothing.

STEPHANO. Mum then, and no more. [*To* Caliban.] Proceed.

CALIBAN. I say, by sorcery he got this isle;
From me he got it. If thy greatness will
Revenge it on him (for I know thou dar'st,
50 But this thing dares not—)

STEPHANO. That's most certain.

CALIBAN. Thou shalt be lord of it, and I'll serve thee.

STEPHANO. How now shall this be compassed? Can'st thou bring me to the party?

CALIBAN. Yea, yea, my lord, I'll yield him thee asleep,
Where thou may'st knock a nail into his head.

ARIEL. Thou liest; thou canst not.

CALIBAN. What a pied ninny's this! Thou scurvy patch!
I do beseech thy greatness, give him blows,
60 And take this bottle from him; when that's gone,
He shall drink nought but brine, for I'll not show him
Where the quick freshes are.

STEPHANO. Trinculo, run into no further danger. Interrupt the monster one word further and, by this hand, I'll turn my mercy out of doors and make a stockfish of thee.

TRINCULO. Why, what did I? I did nothing. I'll go further off.

STEPHANO. Didst thou not say he lied?

ARIEL. Thou liest.

STEPHANO. Do I so? Take you that. (*Beats him.*)
70 As you like this, give me the lie another time.

TRINCULO. I did not give thee the lie; out o' your wits, and hearing too? A pox o' your bottle! This can sack and drinking do. A murrain on your monster, and the devil take your fingers!

CALIBAN. Ha, ha, ha.

STEPHANO. Now, forward with your tale.—Pr'ythee, stand further off.

---

68. Thou liest] "The invisibility of Ariel, with his interruptions, give a zest to this scene, which in other respects has considerable humor" (F. G.).

CALIBAN. Beat him enough; after a little time
I'll beat him too.

STEPHANO. Stand further.—Come, proceed.

CALIBAN. Why, as I told thee, 'tis a custom with him
80 I'th' afternoon to sleep; there thou may'st brain him,
Having first seized his books; or with a log
Batter his skull, or paunch him with a stake,
Or cut his weasand with thy knife. Remember
First to possess his books; for without them
He's but a sot, as I am, nor hath not
One spirit to command. They all do hate him
As rootedly as I. Burn but his books;
He has brave utensils (for so he calls them)
Which, when he has an house, he'll deck withal.
90 And that most deeply to consider is
The beauty of his daughter; he himself
Calls her a nonpareil. I ne'er saw woman
But only Sycorax my dam and she.
But she as far surpasses Sycorax
As greatest does the least.

STEPHANO. Is it so brave a lass?

CALIBAN. Ay, lord; she will become thy bed, I warrant,
And bring thee forth brave brood.

STEPHANO. Monster, I will kill this man. His daughter and I will be king
100 and queen, save our Graces! And Trinculo and thyself shall be viceroys. Dost thou like the plot, Trinculo?

TRINCULO. Excellent.

STEPHANO. Give me thy hand. I am sorry I beat thee; but, while thou liv'st, keep a good tongue in thy head.

CALIBAN. Within this half hour will he be asleep.
Wilt thou destroy him then?

STEPHANO. Ay, on my honor.

ARIEL. This will I tell my master.

CALIBAN. Thou mak'st me merry; I am full of pleasure.
110 Let us be jocund. Will you troll the catch
You taught me but whilere?

STEPHANO. At thy request, monster, I will do reason, any reason. Come on, Trinculo, let us sing. (*Sings.*) Flout 'em, and scout 'em, and scout 'em, and flout 'em; thought is free.

CALIBAN. That's not the tune.

Ariel *plays the tune on a tabor and pipe.*

---

110. be jocund] "Jocund is a very improper word for Caliban" (F. G.).

STEPHANO. What is this same?

TRINCULO. This is the tune of our catch, played by the picture of No-body.

STEPHANO. If thou be'st a man, show thyself in the likeness; if thou be'st
120 a devil, take't as thou list.

TRINCULO. Oh, forgive my sins!

STEPHANO. He that dies pays all debts. I defy thee. Mercy upon us!

CALIBAN. Art thou afraid?

STEPHANO. No, monster, not I.

CALIBAN. Be not afraid; the isle is full of noises,
Sounds and sweet airs that give delight and hurt not.
Sometimes a thousand twanging instruments
Will hum about mine ears, and sometimes voices
That, if I then had waked after long sleep,
130 Will make me sleep again; and then in dreaming
The clouds, methought, will open and show riches
Ready to drop upon me; then, when I waked,
I cried to dream again.

STEPHANO. This will prove a brave kingdom to me, where I shall have my music for nothing.

CALIBAN. When Prospero is destroyed.

STEPHANO. That shall be by and by. I remember the story.

TRINCULO. The sound is going away; let's follow it, and after do our work.

140 STEPHANO. Lead, monster; we'll follow. I would I could see this taborer. He lays it on.

TRINCULO. Wilt come? I'll follow, Stephano.

Exuent.

SCENE [III] *changes to another part of the island.*

Enter Alonso, Sebastian, Anthonio, Gonzalo, Francisco, *&c.*

GONZALO. By'r lakin, I can go no further, sir;
My bones ache. Here's a maze trod indeed,
Through forthrights and meanders! By your patience,
I needs must rest me.

ALONSO. Old lord, I cannot blame thee,
Who am myself attached with weariness

123. afraid] *D1*, *D2*; afeard *S*.
125. afraid] *D1*, *D2*; afeard *S*.

To th' dulling of my spirits. Sit down and rest.
Ev'n here I will put off my hope, and keep it
No longer for my flatterer. He is drowned
10 Whom thus we stray to find, and the sea mocks
Our frustrate search on land. Well, let him go.

ANTHONIO [*aside*]. I am right glad that he's so out of hope.
Do not for one repulse forego the purpose
That you resolved t'effect.

SEBASTIAN [*aside*]. The next advantage
Will we take throughly.

ANTHONIO [*aside*]. Let it be tonight;
For, now they are oppressed with travel, they
Will not, nor cannot, use such vigilance
20 As when they're fresh.

SEBASTIAN [*aside*]. I say tonight. No more.

Solemn and strange music.

ALONSO. What harmony is this? My good friends, hark!

GONZALO. Marvellous sweet music!

ALONSO. Give us kind keepers, heaven! What were these?

A dance of fantastic spirits.

SEBASTIAN. A living drollery. Now I will believe
That there are unicorns, that in Arabia
There is one tree, the phoenix' throne, one phoenix
At this hour reigning there.

ANTHONIO. I'll believe both;
30 And what does else want credit, come to me,
And I'll be sworn 'tis true. Travellers ne'er did lie,
Though fools at home condemn 'em.

GONZALO. If in Naples
I should report this now, would they believe me?
If I should say I saw such islanders
(For, certes, these are people of the island)
Who, tho' they are of monstrous shape, yet, note,
Their manners are more gentle kind than of
Our human generation you shall find
40 Many; nay, almost any.

ALONSO. I cannot too much muse
Such shapes, such gesture, and such sound, expressing

---

40. almost any] *D1*, *D2* omit Prospero's following two-line aside: "Honest lord, / Thou hast said well; for some of you there present / Are worse than devils."

(Although they want the use of tongue) a kind
Of excellent dumb discourse.

FRANCISCO. They vanished strangely.

Thunder. Two devils rise out of the stage, with a table decorated.

SEBASTIAN. No matter, since
They've left their viands behind; for we have stomachs.
Will't please you taste of what is here?

ALONSO. Not I.

50 GONZALO. Faith, sir, you need not fear.

ALONSO. I will stand to and feed,
Although my last, no matter, since I feel
The best is past. Brother, my Lord the Duke,
Stand to and do as we.

The devils vanish with the table. Thunder and lightning.

Enter Ariel.

ARIEL. You are three men of sin, whom destiny
The never-surfeited sea
Hath caused to belch up, and on this island,
Where man doth not inhabit, you 'mongst men
Being most unfit to live. I have made you mad;
60 And even with such like valor men hang and drown
Their proper selves. You fools! I and my fellows
Are ministers of fate; the elements,
Of whom your swords are tempered, may as well
Wound the loud winds, or with bemocked-at stabs
Kill the still-closing waters, as diminish
One down that's in my plume. My fellow ministers

---

44. discourse] *D1*, *D2* omit a half-line aside for Prospero: "Praise in departing."

50. not fear] *D1*, *D2* omit six lines of Gonzalo's speech:

When we were boys,
Who would believe that there were mountaineers
Dewlapp'd like bulls, whose throats had hanging at 'em
Wallets of flesh? or that there were such men
Whose heads stood in their breasts? which now we find
Each putter-out of five for one will bring us
Good warrant of.

55. whom destiny] *D1*, *D2* omit a line and a half here: "That hath to instrument this lower world / And what is in't—"

61. proper selves] at this point in *S*, Alonso, Sebastiano, etc., draw their swords.

66. down] *D1*, *D2*; dowle *S*.

Are like invulnerable. If you could hurt,
Your swords are now too massy for your strengths
And will not be uplifted. But remember
70 (For that's my business to you) that you three
From Milan did supplant good Prospero;
Exposed unto the sea (which hath requit it)
Him and his innocent child; for which foul deed
The powers, delaying, not forgetting, have
Incensed the seas and shores, yea, all the creatures,
Against your peace. Thee of thy son, Alonso,
They have bereft, and do pronounce by me
Ling'ring perdition, worse than any death
Can be at once, shall step by step attend
80 You and your ways, whose wrath to guard you from
(Which here in this most desolate isle else falls
Upon your heads) is nothing but heart's sorrow
And a clear life ensuing.

Exit Ariel.

GONZALO. I'th' name of something holy, sir, why stand you
In this strange stare?
ALONSO. Oh, it is monstrous! monstrous!
Methought the billows spoke and told me of it;
The winds did sing it to me; and the thunder,
That deep and dreadful organ-pipe, pronounced
90 The name of Prosper. It did base my trespass.
Therefore my son i'th' oooze is bedded; and
I'll seek him deeper than e'er plummet sounded,
And with him there lie mudded.

Exit.

SEBASTIAN. But one fiend at a time,
I'll fight their legions o'er.
ANTHONIO. I'll be thy second.

Exeunt.

GONZALO. All three of them are desperate; their great guilt,
Like poison given to work a great time after,

83. life ensuing] *D1*, *D2* omit here an eleven-line aside of Prospero. "This awful address and condemnation, with the preparative circumstances, are well framed to strike torment and terror deep into guilty breasts" (F. G.).

90. base] *D1*, *D2*; bass *S*.

Now gins to bite the spirits. I do beseech you
100 That are of suppler joints, follow them swiftly,
And hinder them from what this ecstasy
May now provoke them to.

Exeunt.

ACT IV.

SCENE I, Prospero's *cell.*

Enter Prospero, Ferdinand, *and* Miranda.

PROSPERO. If I have too austerely punished you,
Your compensation makes amends; for I
Have given you here a thread of mine own life,
Or that for which I live. All thy vexations
Were but my trials of thy love, and thou
Hast strangely stood the test. Here, afore heaven,
I ratify this my rich gift. Oh, Ferdinand,
Do not smile at me that I boast her off,
For thou shalt find she will outstrip all praise
10 And make it halt behind her.
FERDINAND. I believe it
Against an oracle.
PROSPERO. Then, as my gift, and thine own acquisition
Worthily purchased, take my daughter. But
If thou dost break her virgin-knot before
All sanctimonious ceremonies may
With full and holy rite be ministered,
No sweet aspersions shall the heavens let fall
To make this contract grow, but barren hate,
20 Sour-eyed disdain, and discord shall bestrew
The union of your bed with weeds so loathly
That you shall hate it both. Therefore take heed,
As Hymen's lamps shall light you.

---

102. them to] *D1*, *D2* omit one line, "Follow, I pray you," assigned to Adrian in the original; he has been dropped. "The third act has more life, humor, and entertaining matter than the two preceding ones; it performs far beyond them. As to perusal, there is little or no difference" (F. G.).

3. thread] *D1*, *D2*; third *S.*

23. light you] "There is something very fanciful and prudent in this precautionary intimation, but the third line seems to us rather indelicate" (F. G.).

FERDINAND. As I hope
For quiet days, fair issue, and long life,
With such love as 'tis now, the murkiest den,
The most opportune place, the strongest suggestion
Our worser genius can shall never melt
Mine honor into lust; to take away
30 The edge of that day's celebration,
When I shall think or Phoebus' steeds are foundered
Or night kept chained below.

PROSPERO. Fairly spoke.
Sit then, and talk with her; she is thine own.
What, Ariel! My industrious servant, Ariel!

Enter Ariel.

ARIEL. What would my potent master? Here I am.

PROSPERO. Thou and thy meaner fellows your last service
Did worthily perform, and I must use you
In such another trick. Go, bring the rabble,
40 O'er whom I give thee power, here to this place.
Incite them to quick motion, for I must
Bestow upon the eyes of this young couple
Some vanity of mine art. It is my promise,
And they expect it from me.

ARIEL. Presently?

PROSPERO. Ay, with a twink.

ARIEL (*sings*). Before you can say, "Come," and "Go,"
And breathe twice, and cry, "So, so,"
Each one, tripping on his toe,
50 Will be here with mop and mow,
Do you love me, master? No!

PROSPERO. Why, that's my delicate Ariel; do not approach
'Till thou dost hear me call.

Exit Ariel.

Look thou be true; do not give dalliance
Too much the rein; the strongest oaths are straw
To th' fire i'th' blood. Be more abstemious,
Or else goodnight your vow!

FERDINAND. I warrant you, sir;

52. Why, that's my] *D1*; Dearly, my *D2*, *S*.
53. call] *D1*, *D2* omit Ariel's next speech, a half line: "Well, I conceive."

The white, cold, virgin-snow upon my heart
60 Abates the ardor of my liver.

PROSPERO (*to* Ferdinand). Well.
No tongue; all eyes. Be silent.

MASQUE

Soft music. Enter Juno.

RECITATIVE.

Hither, Hymen, speed your way,
Celebrate this happy day;
Hither, Ceres, haste away,
Celebrate this happy day.
With blithsome look and jocund mien,
Come and tread this short grass green,
Leave behind your grief and care,
70 Come and bless this happy pair.

Enter Hymen *and* Ceres.

Honor, riches, marriage, blessing,
Long continuance and increasing,
Hourly joys be still upon ye.
Hymen sings his blessings on ye.

CERES. Earth's increase, foison plenty.
Barns and garners never empty;
Vines with clust'ring bunches growing,
Plants with goodly burdens bowing.

BOTH. Honor, riches, marriage, blessing,
80 Long continuance and increasing,
Hourly joys be still upon ye,
Hymen sings his blessings on ye.

---

61. Well] *D1*, *D2* omit Prospero's next two lines: "Now come, my Ariel! Bring a corollary / Rather than want a spirit. Appear, and pertly!"

62.2. *Enter* Juno] *D1*, *D2*; *Enter* Iris *S*. *D1*, *D2* omit *S* lines 60–105, the speeches of Iris, Ceres, and Juno. The recitative of Juno is not in *S*.

71. Honor, riches . . .] *D1*, *D2*; Hymen's song is by Juno in *S*, with her last line, "Juno sings her blessings on you," revised to indicate that Hymen is the singer.

78. bowing] *D1*, *D2* omit the next four lines of the song: "Spring come to you at the farthest / In the very end of harvest! / Scarcity and want shall shun you, / Ceres' blessing so is on you."

79. BOTH] *D1*, *D2*; not in *S*.

DUET.

CERES. Scarcity and want shall shun ye,
Ceres sings her blessings on ye.
HYMEN. Hourly joys be still upon ye,
Hymen sings his blessing on ye.

RECITATIVE.

You sun-burned sickle men, of August weary,
Come hither from the furrow, and be merry.

DUET.

HYMEN *and* CERES. Away, away, make holiday,
90 Your rye-straw hats put on;
Bring each his lass, and beat the grass,
Let toil and care be gone.

Enter certain Reapers, *properly habited; they join with the* Nymphs *in a graceful dance; towards the end whereof* Prospero *starts suddenly, and speaks.*

PROSPERO. Break off, break off,
I had forgot that foul conspiracy
Of the beast Caliban and his confed'rates
Against my life; the minute of their plot
Is almost come. Well done! Avoid; no more.

Exeunt Dancers, *&c.*

FERDINAND. This is most strange; your father's in some passion
That works him strongly.
100 MIRANDA. Never 'till this day
Saw I him touched with anger so distempered.
PROSPERO. You look, my son, in a moved sort,
As if you were dismayed. Be cheerful, sir.
Our revels now are ended. These our actors,
As I foretold you, were all spirits and
Are melted into air, into thin air;

82.1. DUET] *D1*, *D2*; not in *S*.
86.1. RECITATIVE] *D1*, *D2*; not in *S*.
92. be gone] *D1*, *D2* (silently) omit twenty-one lines of *S*, the discussion of Ferdinand and Prospero of the masque, and the further comment of Iris.
93. Break off . . .] *D1*, *D2*; the line is not in *S*.

And, like this unsubstantial pageant faded,
The cloud-capt towers, the gorgeous palaces,
The solemn temples, the great globe itself,
110 Yea, all which it inherit, shall dissolve,
And, like the baseless fabric of a vision,
Leave not a rack behind!—Sir, I am vexed,
Bear with my weakness; my old brain is troubled.
Be not disturbed with my infirmity;
If thou be pleased, retire into my cell
And there repose. A turn or two I'll walk
To still my beating mind.

FERDINAND *and* MIRANDA. We wish your peace.

Exit Ferdinand *and* Miranda.

PROSPERO. Come with a thought! I thank you—Ariel, come.

Prospero *comes forward*; *enter* Ariel *to him*.

120 ARIEL. Thy thoughts I cleave to; what's thy pleasure?
PROSPERO. Spirit,
We must prepare to meet with Caliban.
ARIEL. Ay, my commander. When I presented Ceres,
I thought to have told thee of it; but I feared
Lest I might anger thee.
PROSPERO. Say again, where didst thou leave these varlets?
ARIEL. I told you, sir, they were red hot with drinking;
So full of valor that they smote the air
For breathing in their faces, beat the ground
130 For kissing of their feet; yet always bending
Towards their project. Then I beat my tabor,
At which, like unbacked colts, they pricked their ears,

---

107. this unsubstantial pageant faded] *D1*, *D2*; the baseless fabric of this vision *S*.

108. The cloud-capt . . .] "Of this passage, so universally known and so justly admired, we may say that it possesses eastern magnificence of idea, clothed with the chastest eloquence. No author ever soared beyond, and Shakespeare himself but rarely comes up to it" (F. G.).

111. the baseless fabric of a vision] *D1*, *D2*; this insubstantial pageant faded *S*. Lines 106 and 110 are interchanged in the Garrick version, with the use of "a" for "this" and "unsubstantial" for "insubstantial."

112. rack behind] *D1*, *D2* omit Prospero's two best-known lines: "We are such stuff / As dreams are made on, and our little life / Is rounded with a sleep."

119. you] *D1*, *D2*; thee *S*.

Advanced their eyelids, lifted up their noses
As they smelt music; so I charmed their ears
That, calf-like, they my lowing followed through
Toothed briars, sharp furzes, pricking goss and thorns,
Which entered their frail shins; at last I left them
I'th' filthy mantled pool beyond your cell.

PROSPERO. This was well done, my bird.
140 Thy shape invisible retain thou still.
The trumpery in my house, go bring it hither
For stale to catch these thieves.

ARIEL. I go, I go.

Exit.

PROSPERO. A devil, a born devil, on whose nature
Nurture can never stick; on whom my pains,
Humanely taken, all, all lost, quite lost;
And, as with age his body uglier grows,
So his mind cankers. I will plague them all,
Even to roaring. Come, hang them on this line. (Prospero *remains invisible.*)

Enter Caliban, Stephano, *and* Trinculo, *all wet.*

150 CALIBAN. Pray you, tread softly, that the blind mole may not hear a footfall; we now are near his cell.

STEPHANO. Monster, your fairy, which you say is a harmless fairy, has done little better than played the Jack with us.

TRINCULO. Monster, I do smell all horse-piss, at which my nose is in great indignation.

STEPHANO. So is mine. Do you hear, monster? If I should take a displeasure against you, look you—

TRINCULO. Thou wert but a lost monster.

CALIBAN. Good my lord, give me thy favor still;
160 Be patient, for the prize I'll bring thee to
Shall hoodwink this mischance; therefore, speak softly.

---

134. smelt music] "The *smelling* of music is a very strange idea, or at least one of singular latitude to whatever objects it may be applied" (F. G.).

138. your cell] *D1*, *D2* omit the last line and a half of Ariel's speech: "There dancing up to th' chins, that the foul lake / O'erstunk their feet."

155. great indignation] "This speech of Trinculo is very indelicate and unnecessary, for it conveys a nauseous idea without a gleam of humor. Some passages, censurably gross, have a plea of pleasantry in their favor; this, having none, should certainly be omitted" (F. G.).

161. hoodwink] "*Hoodwink mischance*, which has an allusion to falconry, is certainly too fanciful an expression for such a brute" (F. G.).

All's hushed as midnight yet.

TRINCULO. Ay, but to lose our bottles in the pool—

STEPHANO. There is not only disgrace and dishonor in that, monster, but an infinite loss.

TRINCULO. That's more to me than my wetting; yet this is your harmless fairy, monster.

STEPHANO. I will fetch off my bottle, though I be o'er ears for my labor.

170 CALIBAN. Pr'ythee, my king, be quiet. Seest thou here?
This is the mouth o'th' cell; no noise, and enter.
Do that good mischief which may make this island
Thine own for ever; and I, thy Caliban,
For ay thy foot-licker.

STEPHANO. Give me thy hand. I do begin to have bloody thoughts.

TRINCULO. Oh, King Stephano! O, Peer! Oh, worthy Stephano!
Look, what a wardrobe here is for thee!

CALIBAN. Let it alone, thou fool; it is but trash.

TRINCULO. Oh, oh, monster; we know what belongs to a frippery.—Oh,
180 King Stephano!

STEPHANO. Put off that gown, Trinculo; by this hand, I'll have that gown.

TRINCULO. Thy Grace shall have it.

CALIBAN. The dropsy drown this fool! What do you mean,
To dote thus on such luggage? Let's along
And do the murder first. If he awake,
From toe to crown he'll fill our skins with pinches,
Make us strange stuff.

STEPHANO. Be you quiet, monster. Mistress line, is not this my jerkin?
190 Now is the jerkin under the line. Now, jerkin, you are like to lose your hair and prove a bald jerkin.

TRINCULO. Do, do; we steal by line and level, an't like your Grace.

STEPHANO. I thank thee for that jest; here's a garment for't. Wit shall not go unrewarded while I am king of this country. "Steal by line and level" is an excellent pass of pate; there's another garment for't.

TRINCULO. Monster, come, put some lime upon your fingers, and away with the rest.

CALIBAN. I will have none on't; we shall lose our time
And all be turned to barnacles, or apes
200 With foreheads villainous low.

STEPHANO. Monster, lay to your fingers; help to bear this away where

---

185. Let's along] *D*1, *D*2; Let't alone *S*.
199. or apes] *D*1, *D*2; or to apes *S*.

my hogshead of wine is, or I'll turn you out of my kingdom. Go to; carry this.

TRINCULO. And this.

STEPHANO. Ay, and this.

Thunder. Enter divers Spirits; Prospero *and* Ariel *setting them on.* Caliban, Stephano, *and* Trinculo *driven out, roaring.*

PROSPERO. Go, charge my goblins that they grind their joints
With dry convulsions; shorten up their sinews
With aged cramps; and more pinch-spotted make them
Than pard or cat o'mountain.

Roaring within.

210 ARIEL. Hark, they roar.

PROSPERO. Let them be hunted soundly. At this hour
Lie at my mercy all mine enemies.
Shortly shall all my labors end, and thou
Shalt have the air at freedom; for a little
Follow and do me service.

Exeunt

ACT V.

SCENE I, *before the cell.*

Enter Prospero, *in his magic robes, and* Ariel.

PROSPERO. Now does my project gather to a head;
My charms crack not, my spirits obey, and time
Goes upright with his carriage. How's the day?

ARIEL. On the sixth hour, at which time, my Lord,
You said our work should cease.

PROSPERO. I did say so
When first I raised the tempest; say, my spirit,

---

205. Ay, and this] *D1*, *D2* (silently) omit the three-line exchange between Prospero and Ariel which follows: "PROS. Hey, Mountain, hey! / ARI. Silver; there it goes, Silver! / PROS. Furry, furry! There, Tyrant, there! Hark, hark!"

215.1. *Exeunt*] "This act, though inferior to the third, yet has matter and spirit enough to please in representation. It is to be remarked in general of this play that it stands a good deal indebted for agreeable effects to music and dancing" (F. G.).

How fares the King and's followers?
ARIEL. Confined
10 In the same fashion as you gave in charge;
Just as you left them, all prisoners, sir,
In the lime grove which weather-fends your cell—
They cannot budge 'till your release. The King,
His brother, and yours abide all three distracted,
And the remainder mourning over them,
Brimfull of sorrow and dismay; but chiefly
Him that you termed the good old Lord Gonzalo.
His tears run down his beard like winter drops
From eaves of reeds. Your charm so strongly works 'em
20 That if you now beheld them, your affections
Would become tender.
PROSPERO. Do'st thou think so, spirit?
ARIEL. Mine would, sir, were I human.
PROSPERO. And mine shall.
Hast thou, which art but air, a touch, a feeling
Of their afflictions, and shall not myself,
One of their kind, that relish all as sharply
Passioned as they, be kindlier moved than thou art?
Tho' with their high wrongs I am struck to th' quick,
30 Yet with my nobler reason gainst my fury
Do I take part. The rarer action is
In virtue than in vengeance; they being penitent,
The sole drift of my purpose doth extend
Not a frown further. Go, release them, Ariel;
My charms I'll break, their senses I'll restore,
And they shall be themselves.
ARIEL. I'll fetch them, sir.

Exit.

PROSPERO. Ye elves of hills, brooks, standing lakes, and groves,
And ye that on the sands with printless foot
40 Do chase the ebbing Neptune, and do fly him
When he comes back; you demi-puppets that

---

9. Confined] *D*1, *D*2; Confined together *S*.

28. Passioned] *D*1, *D*2; Passion *S*.

32. In virtue] "There is here a signal elevation of sentiment, a peculiar fineness of feeling, which does the author great honor; but why Ariel, as a good spirit, should have no tender sensations we know not. He feels joy and pain for himself; why not a little for human beings distressed?" (F. G.).

By moonshine do the green sour ringlets make,
Whereof the ewe not bites; and you, whose pastime
Is to make midnight mushrooms, that rejoice
To hear the solemn curfew; by whose aid
(Weak masters tho' ye be) I have bedimmed
The noontide sun, called forth the mutinous winds,
And 'twixt the green sea and the azured vault
Set roaring war; to the dread rattling thunder
50 Have I given fire and rifted Jove's stout oak
With his own bolt; the strong-based promontory
Have I made shake, and by the spurs plucked up
The pine and cedar; graves, at my command,
Have waked their sleepers, oped, and let them forth
By my so potent art. But this rough magic
I here abjure; and when I have required
Some heavenly music, which even now I do
(To work mine end upon their senses, that
This airy charm is for), I'll break my staff,
60 Bury it certain fathoms in the earth,
And deeper than did ever plummet sound
I'll drown my book.

Solemn music.

Here enters Ariel *before*; *then* Alonso, Gonzalo, Sebastian, Anthonio, Francisco. *They all enter the circle which* Prospero *had made and stand charmed*; *which* Prospero *observing, speaks.*

There stand,
For you are spell-stopped.–
Holy Gonzalo, honorable man,
Mine eyes, even sociable to th' show of thine,
Fall fellow drops. The charm dissolves apace,

---

44. mushrooms] *D*1, *D*2; mushrumps *S.*

62. my book] "There is great poetical solemnity and richness of description in his speech, which concludes well with Prospero's determination to give up the pernicious power and study of magic" (F. G.).

63. There stand] *D*1, *D*2 (silently) omit nearly three lines immediately preceding this one: "A solemn air, and the best comforter / To an unsettled fancy, cure thy brains, / Now useless, boil'd within thy skull!"

65. honorable man] "This speech is also beautiful and humane; it almost teaches us to feel pity and forgiveness for those wretched characters we have hitherto justly despised" (F. G.).

And as the morning steals upon the night,
Melting the darkness, so their rising senses
70 Begin to chase the ign'rant fumes that mantle
Their clearer reason. Sir—most cruelly
Didst thou, Alonso, use me and my daughter.
Thy brother was a furtherer in the act;
Thou'rt pinched for't now, Sebastian, flesh and blood.
You, brother mine, that entertained ambition,
Expelled remorse and nature, I do forgive thee,
Unnat'ral though thou art. Their understanding
Begins to swell, and the approaching tide
Will shortly fill the reasonable shore,
80 That now lies foul and muddy. Not one of them
That yet looks on me or would know me.—Ariel,
Fetch me the hat and rapier in my cell;
I will discase me and myself present
As I was sometime Milan. Quickly, spirit;
Thou shalt ere long be free. (Prospero *goes in.*)

ARIEL (*sings*). Where the bee sucks, there lurk I
In a cowslip's bell I lie;
There I couch when owls do cry.
On the bat's back I do fly,
90 After sunset, merrily,
Merrily, merrily shall I live now,
Under the blossom that hangs on the bough.

Enter Prospero, *dressed.*

---

71. clearer reason] *D1*, *D2* omit three lines here: "O good Gonzalo, / My true preserver, and a loyal sir / To him thou follow'st! I will pay thy graces / Home both in word and deed."
Sir] *D1*; not in *D2*, *S*.

76. and nature] *D1*, *D2* omit two lines: "who, with Sebastian / (Whose inward pinches therefore are most strong), / Would here have kill'd your king."

86. lurk] *D1*, *D2*; suck *S*. The Garrick text follows Theobald, who notes in *D2*: "I have ventured to vary from the printed copies here. Could Ariel, a spirit of refined aetherial essence, be intended to want food? Besides, the sequent lines rather counterbalance *lurk*."

90. sunset] *D1*, *D2*; summer *S*. Theobald notes in *D2*: "Why *after* summer? unless we must suppose our author alluded to that mistaken notion of bats, swallows, &c. crossing the seas in pursuit of hot weather. I conjectured, in my *Shakespeare Restor'd*, that sunset was our author's word; and this conjecture Mr. Pope, in his last edition, thinks probably should be espoused. My reasons for the change were from the known nature of the bat."

PROSPERO. Why, that's my dainty Ariel! I shall miss thee;
But yet thou shalt have freedom.
To the King's ship, invisible as thou art.
There shalt thou find the mariners asleep
Under the hatches. The master and boatswain
Being awake, enforce them to this place,
And presently, I pr'ythee.

100 ARIEL. I drink the air before me and return
Or ere your pulse twice beat.

GONZALO. All torment, trouble, wonder, and amazement
Inhabit here; some heavenly power guide us
Out of this fearful country!

PROSPERO. Behold, Sir King,
The wronged Duke of Milan, Prospero.
For more assurance that a living prince
Does now speak to thee, I embrace thy body.

ALONSO. Be'st thou he or no,
110 Or some enchanted trifle to abuse me,
As late I have been, I not know; thy pulse
Beats as of flesh and blood; and since I saw thee,
Th' affliction of my mind amends, with which,
I fear, a madness held me; this must crave
(And if this be at all) a most strange story.
Thy dukedom I resign, and do intreat
Thou pardon me my wrongs; but how should Prospero
Be living, and be here?

PROSPERO [Gonzalo]. First, noble friend,
120 Let me embrace thine age, whose honor cannot
Be measured or confined.

GONZALO. Whether this be
Or be not, I'll not swear.

PROSPERO. You do yet taste
Some subtleties o' th' isle that will not let you
Believe things certain. Welcome, my friends all.

---

108. thy body] *D*1, *D*2 omit a line and a half here: "And to thee and thy company I bid / A hearty welcome."

109. Be'st thou he] *D*1, *D*2; whe'r thou be'st he *S*.

126. friends all] *D*1, *D*2 omit four lines here:

But you, my brace of lords, were I so minded,
I here could pluch his Highness' frown upon you
And justify you traitors. At this time
I will tell no tales.
SEB. (*aside*). The devil speaks in him.
PRO. No.

(*To* Alonso.) For you, most wicked sir, whom to call brother
Would even infect my mouth, I do forgive
Thy rankest faults, all of them, and require
30 My dukedom of thee, which perforce I know
Thou must restore.

ALONSO. If thou be'st Prospero,
Give us particulars of thy preservation,
How thou hast met us here, who, three hours since,
Were wrecked upon this shore; where I have lost
(How sharp the point of this remembrance is!)
My dear son Ferdinand.

PROSPERO. I'm woe for't, sir.

ALONSO. Irreparable is the loss, and Patience
40 Says it is past her cure.

PROSPERO. I rather think
You have not sought her help, of whose soft grace
For the like loss I have her sov'reign aid
And rest myself content.

ALONSO. You the like loss?

PROSPERO. As great to me, for I
Have lost my daughter.

ALONSO. A daughter?
Oh, heavens! that they were living both in Naples,
50 The King and Queen there! That they were, I wish
Myself were mudded in that oozy bed
Where my son lies. When did you lose your daughter?

PROSPERO. In this last tempest. I perceive these lords
At this encounter do so much admire
That they devour their reason and scarce think
Their eyes do offices of truth, their words
Are natural breath. But, howsoe'er you have
Been justled from your senses, know for certain
That I am Prospero and that very duke
160 Which was thrust forth of Milan; who most strangely
Upon this shore, where you were wrecked, was landed,
To be the lord on't. No more yet of this,
For 'tis a chronicle of day by day,
Not a relation for a breakfast, nor
Befitting this first meeting. Welcome, sir;

146. to me] *D1*, *D2* omit two lines: "as late; and, supportable / To make the dear loss, have I means much weaker / Than you may call to comfort you."

This cell's my court; here have I few attendants,
And subjects none abroad. Pray you, look in.
My dukedom since you've given me again,
I will requite you with as good a thing;
170 At least bring forth a wonder to content ye,
As much as me my dukedom.

SCENE [II] *opens to the entrance of the cell.*

Here Prospero *discovers* Ferdinand *and* Miranda *playing at chess.*

MIRANDA. Sweet Lord, you play me false.
FERDINAND. No, my dear love,
I would not for the world.
MIRANDA. Yes, for a score of kingdoms you should wrangle,
And I would call it fair play.
ALONSO. If this prove
A vision of the island, one dear son
Shall I twice lose.
SEBASTIAN. A most high miracle!
10 FERDINAND. Though the seas threaten, they are merciful.
I've cursed them without cause. (*Kneels.*)
ALONSO. Now all the blessings
Of a glad father compass thee about!
Arise, and say how thou cam'st here.
MIRANDA. O, wonder!
How many goodly creatures are there here!
How beauteous mankind is! O brave new world,
That has such people in't!
PROSPERO. 'Tis new to thee.
20 ALONSO. What is this maid with whom thou wast at play?
Your eld'st acquaintance cannot be three hours.
Is she the goddess that hath severed us
And brought us thus together?
FERDINAND. Sir, she's mortal;
But by immortal providence she's mine.
I chose her when I could not ask my father
For his advice, nor thought I had one. She
Is daughter to this famous Duke of Milan,

2. dear] *D1*, *D2*; dearest *S*.

Of whom so often I have heard renown
30 But never saw before; of whom I have
Received a second life, and second father
This lady makes him to me.

ALONSO. I am hers;
But, O, how oddly will it sound that I
Must ask my child forgiveness!

PROSPERO. There, sir, stop;
Let us not burden our remembrance with
An heaviness that's gone.

GONZALO. I've inly wept,
40 Or should have spoke ere this. Look down, you gods,
And on this couple drop a blessed crown;
For it is you that have chalked forth the way
Which brought us hither!

ALONSO. I say amen, Gonzalo!
Give me your hands.
Let grief and sorrow still embrace his heart
That doth not wish you joy!

GONZALO. Be't so! Amen!

Enter Ariel, *with the* Master *and* Boatswain *amazedly following.*

O, look, sir, look, sir, here are more of us!
50 I prophesied, if a gallows were on land
This fellow could not drown. Now, blasphemy,
Not an oath on shore?
Hast thou no mouth by land? What is the news?

BOATSWAIN. The best news is that we have safely found
Our king and company; the next, our ship,

---

38. that's gone] "It speaks exceeding delicacy of sense in Prospero to check the slings of self-reproch" (F. G.).

44. amen, Gonzalo] *D1*, *D2* omit a nine-line speech here:

> Was Milan thrust from Milan that his issue
> Should become kings of Naples? O, rejoice
> Beyond a common joy, and set it down
> With gold on lasting pillars: In one voyage
> Did Claribel her husband find at Tunis,
> And Ferdinand her brother found a wife
> Where he himself was lost; Prospero his dukedom
> In a poor isle; and all of us ourselves
> When no man was his own.

51. blasphemy] *D1*, *D2* omit a half line of Gonzalo's speech: "That swear'st grace o'erboard."

Which but three glasses since we gave out split,
Is tight and yare, and bravely rigged as when
We first put out to sea.

ARIEL [*aside to* Prospero]. Sir, all this service
60 Have I done since I went.

PROSPERO [*aside*]. My tricksey spirit!

ALONSO. These are not natural events; they strengthen
From stranger to stranger. Say how came you hither?

BOATSWAIN. If I did think, sir, I were well awake,
I'd strive to tell you. We were dead asleep
And, how we know not, all clapt under hatches,
Where but even now with strange and several noises
Of roaring, shrieking, howling, jingling chains,
And more diversity of sounds, all horrible,
70 We were awaked; straightway at liberty,
Where we, in all her trim, freshly beheld
Our royal, good, and gallant ship; our master
Cap'ring to eye her. On a trice, so please you,
Even in a dream, were we divided from them
And were brought moping hither.

ARIEL [*aside to* Prospero]. Was't well done?

PROSPERO [*aside*]. Bravely, my diligence; thou shalt be free.

ALONSO. This is as strange a maze as e'er men trod,
And there is in this business more than nature
80 Was ever conduct of; some oracle
Must rectify our knowledge.

PROSPERO. Sir, my liege,
Do not infest your mind with beating on
The strangeness of this business; at picked leisure
(Which shall be shortly) single I'll resolve you,
Which to you shall seem probable, of every
These happened accidents; till when be cheerful
And think of each thing well. [*Aside to* Ariel.] Come hither, spirit;
Set Caliban and his companions free.
90 Untie the spell. [*Exit* Ariel.] How fares my gracious sir?
There are yet missing of your company
Some few odd lads that you remember not.

Enter Ariel, *driving in* Caliban, Stephano, *and* Trinculo, *in their stolen apparel.*

STEPHANO. Every man shift for all the rest, and let no man take care for himself; for all is but fortune. Coragio, bully-monster, coragio!

TRINCULO. If these be true spies which I wear in my head, here's a goodly sight.

CALIBAN. O Setebos, these be brave spirits indeed!
How fine my master is! I am afraid,
He will chastise me.

100 PROSPERO. Mark but the badges of these men, my lords,
Then say if they be true. This misshaped knave,
His mother was a witch, and one so strong
That could control the moon, make flows and ebbs.
These three have robbed me; and this demi-devil
(For he's a bastard one) had plotted with them
To take my life. Two of these fellows you
Must know and own; this thing of darkness I
Acknowledge mine.

CALIBAN. I shall be pinched to death.

110 ALONSO. Is not this Stephano, my drunken butler?

SEBASTIAN. He's drunk now. Where had he wine?

ALONSO. And Trinculo is reeling ripe; where should they
Find this grand 'lixir that hath gilded 'em?
How cam'st thou in this pickle?

TRINCULO. I have been in such a pickle since I saw you last that I fear me will never out of my bones. I shall not fear fly-blowing.

SEBASTIAN. Why, how now, Stephano?

STEPHANO. Oh, touch me not! I am not Stephano, but a cramp.

PROSPERO. You'd be king o'th' isle, sirrah?

120 STEPHANO. I should have been a sore one then.

ALONSO. 'Tis a strange thing as e'er I looked on.

PROSPERO. He is as disproportioned in his manners
As in his shape. Go, sirrah, to my cell;
Take with you your companions. As you look
To have my pardon, trim it handsomely.

CALIBAN. Ay, that I will; and I'll be wise hereafter,

---

99. chastise me] *D1*, *D2* omit three and a half lines here:
Ha, ha!
What things are these, my Lord Antonio?
Will money buy 'em?
ANT. Very like. One of them
Is a plain fish and no doubt marketable.

101. misshaped] *D1*, *D2*; misshapen *S*.

103. and ebbs] *D1*, *D2* omit the following line: "And deal in her command without her power."

113. 'lixir] *D1*, *D2*; liquor *S*.

121. 'Tis a strange thing] *D1*, *D2*; This is a strange thing *S*.

And seek for grace. What a thrice-double ass
Was I to take this drunkard for a god
And worship this dull fool!

130 PROSPERO. Go to, away!

ALONSO. Hence, and bestow your luggage where you found it.

SEBASTIAN. Or stole it rather.

Exeunt Caliban, Stephano, *and* Trinculo.

PROSPERO. Sir, I invite your Highness and your train
To my poor cell, where you shall take your rest
For this one night, which (part of it) I'll waste
With such discourse as, I not doubt, shall make it
Go quick away—the story of my life
And the particular accidents gone by
Since I came to this isle; and in the morn
140 I'll bring you to your ship, and so to Naples,
Where I have hope to see the nuptials
Of these our dear-beloved solemnized;
And thence retire me to my Milan, where
Every third thought shall be my grave.

ALONSO. I long
To hear the story of your life, which must
Take the ear strangely.

PROSPERO. I'll deliver all
And promise you calm seas, auspicious gales,
150 And sail so expeditious that shall catch
Your royal fleet far off. My Ariel, chick,
That is thy charge. Then to the elements
Be free, and fare thou well! Please you, draw near.

[*Exeunt* omnes.]

---

141. nuptials] *D1*, *D2*; nuptial *S*.

153. draw near] "This last act has a considerable share of business, the incidents are pleasing, the writing nervous, the characters well disposed, and the catastrophe most pleasingly brought about" (F. G.).

Epilogue

Spoken by Prospero.

Now my charms are all o'erthrown,
And what strength I have's mine own,
Which is most faint. And now, 'tis true,
I must be here confined by you,
Or sent to Naples. Let me not,
Since I have my dukedom got
And pardoned the deceiver, dwell
In this bare island by your spell;
But release me from my bands
10 With the help of your good hands.
Gentle breath of yours my sails
Must fill, or else my project fails,
Which was to please. For now I want
Spirits t' enforce, art to enchant;

As you would pardoned wish to be,
Let your indulgence set me free!

The End of The Tempest.

3. And now] *D1, D2*; Now *S*.
14. to enchant] *D1, D2* omit the next four lines: "And my ending is despair / Unless I be reliev'd by prayer, / Which pierces so that it assaults / Mercy itself and frees all faults."
15. As you . . .] *D1, D2*; As you from crimes would pardon'd be *S*.

List of References
Commentary and Notes
Index to Commentary

List of References

In this edition references to works are given by short title only. This list of references does not include a listing of newspapers and periodicals of the time.

Baker, David Erskine. *The Companion to the Playhouse.* 2 vols. London, 1764.

———, Isaac Reed, and Stephen Jones. *Biographia Dramatica.* London, 1812.

Boaden, James, ed. *The Private Correspondence of David Garrick.* 2 vols. London, 1831–32.

Boswell, James. *The London Journal.* New York, 1950.

Branam, George C. *Eighteenth-Century Adaptations of Shakespearean Tragedy.* Berkeley, 1956.

Burney, Fanny. *The Early Diary of Frances Burney, 1768–1778.* Ed. Annie R. Ellis. 2 vols. London, 1889.

Carlisle, Carol Jones. *Shakespeare from the Greenroom.* Chapel Hill, 1969.

Cibber, Theophilus. *A Serio-Comic Apology.* Dublin, 1748.

———. *Two Dissertations on the Theatres.* London, 1756.

Colman, George. *A True State of the Differences Subsisting between the Proprietors of Covent-Garden Theatre; in Answer to a false, Scandalous, and Malicious manuscript Libel, exhibited on Saturday, Jan. 23, and the two following Days; and to a Printed Narrative signed by T. Harris and J. Rutherford.* London, 1768.

Cooke, William. *Memoirs of Charles Macklin.* London, 1804.

Cozens-Hardy, Basil, ed. *The Diary of Sylas Neville, 1767–1788.* Oxford, 1950.

———. Typescript of the Neville MS Microfilm. Folger Shakespeare Library, Washington, D.C.

Cross, Richard. MS Diaries, 1747–60, 1760–68. Folger Shakespeare Library.

Davies, Thomas. *Dramatic Miscellanies.* 3 vols. London, 1783.

———. *Memoirs of the Life of David Garrick.* 2 vols. London, 1808.

Doran, John. *Annals of the English Stage.* 3 vols. London, 1888.

Dryden, John. *The Tempest, or the Enchanted Island.* London, 1670.

Evans, Maurice. *Maurice Evans' G.I. Production of Hamlet.* New York, 1947.

Fiske, Roger. *English Theatre Music in the Eighteenth Century.* Oxford, 1973.

Fitzgerald, Percy. *The Life of David Garrick.* Rev. ed. (2 vols. in 1). London, 1899.

———. *A New History of the English Stage.* 2 vols. London, 1882.

Foot, Jesse. *Life of Arthur Murphy*. London, 1811.

Garrick, David. *An Essay on Acting: In which will be consider'd The Mimical Behaviour of a Certain fashionable faulty Actor . . . To which will be added A short Criticism on His acting Macbeth*. London, 1744.

Genest, John. *Some Account of the English Stage*. 10 vols. Bath, 1832.

Gentleman, Francis. *The Dramatic Censor*. London, 1770.

Gray, Charles H. *Theatrical Criticism in London to 1795*. New York, 1931.

Guffy, George Robert. *After the Tempest*. Los Angeles, 1969.

Harris, Arthur J. "Garrick, Colman, and *King Lear*." *Shakespeare Quarterly*, 22, No. 1 (Winter 1971), 57–66.

Haywood, Charles. "William Boyce's 'Solemn Dirge' in Garrick's *Romeo and Juliet* Production. *Shakespeare Quarterly*, 11 (Spring 1960), 173–88.

Hedgcock, Frank A. *A Cosmopolitan Actor: David Garrick and His French Friends*. London [1912].

Hogan, Charles Beecher. *Shakespeare in the Theatre, 1701–1800*. 2 vols. Oxford, 1952–57.

Hopkins, William. MS Diary, 1769–76. Folger Shakespeare Library.

Knapp, Mary E. *A Checklist of Verse by David Garrick*. Rev. ed. Charlottesville, Va., 1974.

Knight, Joseph. *David Garrick*. London, 1894.

Little, David Mason, George M. Kahrl, and Phoebe de K. Wilson. *The Letters of David Garrick*. 3 vols. Cambridge, Mass., 1963.

MacMillan, Dougald. *Catalogue of the Larpent Plays in the Huntington Library*. San Marino, 1939.

———. *Drury Lane Calendar, 1747–1776*. Oxford, 1938.

Montagu, Elizabeth. *Mrs. Montagu, "The Queen of the Bluestockings," Her Correspondence from 1720 to 1761*. Ed. Emily J. Climenson. 2 vols. London, 1906.

Murphy, Arthur. *The Works of Arthur Murphy, Esq.* 7 vols. London, 1786.

———. *The Life of David Garrick*. 2 vols. London, 1801.

Nicoll, Allardyce. *British Drama*. New York, 1925.

———. *A History of Early Eighteenth-Century Drama, 1700–1750*. Cambridge, 1925.

———. *A History of Late Eighteenth-Century Drama, 1750–1800*. Cambridge, 1927.

———. *A History of Restoration Drama, 1660–1700*. Cambridge, 1923.

Noverre, Jean Georges. *Letters on Dancing and Ballets*. Trans. C. W. Beaumont, London, 1951.

Odell, G. C. D. *Shakespeare from Betterton to Irving*. 2 vols. New York, 1920.

Oulton, W. C. *The History of the London Theatres*. 2 vols. London, 1796.

Page, E. R. *George Colman, the Elder*. New York, 1935.

Pedicord, Harry William. *The Theatrical Public in the Time of Garrick*. New York, 1954.

Scouten, Arthur H. "The Increase in Popularity of Shakespeare's Plays in the Eighteenth Century." *Shakespeare Quarterly*, 7 (Spring 1957), 189–202.

———. *The London Stage*. Part 3: *1729–1747*. 2 vols. Carbondale, Ill., 1961.

Shattuck, Charles H. "Shakespeare's Plays in Performance, from 1660 to the Present." *The Riverside Shakespeare.* Boston, 1974.

Spencer, Christopher, ed. *Davenant's Macbeth from the Yale Manuscript.* New Haven, 1961.

———. *Five Restoration Adaptations of Shakespeare.* Urbana, Ill., 1965.

Spencer, Hazelton. *Shakespeare Improved.* Cambridge, Mass., 1927.

Stein, Elizabeth P. *David Garrick, Dramatist.* New York, 1938.

Stone, George Winchester, Jr. "The Authorship of a Letter to Miss Nossiter." *Shakespeare Quarterly*, January 1952, pp. 69–70.

———. "A Century of *Cymbeline*; or Garrick's Magic Touch." *PQ*, 54, No. 1 (Winter 1975), 310–22.

———. "David Garrick's Significance in the History of Shakespearean Criticism." *PMLA*, 65 (March 1950), 183–97.

———. "Garrick and an Unknown Operatic Version of *Love's Labour's Lost.*" *Review of English Studies*, 15 (July 1939), 323–28.

——— "Garrick's Handling of *Macbeth.*" *Studies in Philology*, 38 (October 1941), 609–28.

———. "Garrick's Handling of Shakespeare's Plays and His Influence upon the Changed Attitude of Shakespearean Criticism during the Eighteenth Century." 2 vols. Diss. Harvard 1938.

———. "Garrick's Long Lost Alteration of *Hamlet.*" *PMLA*, 49 (September 1934), 890–921.

———. "Garrick's Presentation of *Antony and Cleopatra.*" *Review of English Studies*, 13 (January 1937), 20–38.

———. "Garrick's Production of *King Lear*: A Study in the Temper of the Eighteenth-Century Mind." *Studies in Philology*, 45 (January 1948), 89–103.

———. "The God of his Idolatry." *Joseph Quincy Adams Memorial Studies.* Ed. James G. MacManaway et al. Washington, D.C., 1948, pp. 115–28.

———. *The London Stage.* Part 4: *1747–1776.* 3 vols. Carbondale, Ill., 1962.

———. "*A Midsummer Night's Dream* in the Hands of Garrick and Colman." *PMLA*, 54 (June 1939), 467–82.

———. "*Romeo and Juliet*: The Source of Its Modern Stage Career." *Shakespeare Quarterly*, 15 (1964), 191–206.

———. "Shakespeare's *Tempest* at Drury Lane During Garrick's Management." *Shakespeare Quarterly*, 7 (Winter 1956), 1–7.

Summers, Montague. *Shakespeare Adaptations.* London, 1922.

Victor, Benjamin. *The History of the Theatres of London.* 3 vols. London, 1761, 1771.

Walpole, Horace. *The Letters of Horace Walpole.* Ed. Mrs. Paget Toynbee. 16 vols. Oxford, 1903–5.

Wilkes, Thomas. *A General View of the Stage.* London, 1959.

Wilkinson, Tate. *Memoirs of His Own Life.* 4 vols. York, 1790.

———. *The Wandering Patentee.* 4 vols. London, 1795.

Commentary and Notes

Antony and Cleopatra

Shakespeare's play of grand passion has a shadowy history. Thought to have been first produced in late 1606 or early 1607, it was entered in the Stationer's Register on 20 May 1608 but apparently remained unpublished until the appearance of the First Folio in 1623. There are no records of production in Shakespeare's time, but we may suppose that this, his second-longest play (3,095 lines after *Hamlet's* 3,929), underwent some cutting before it could have been presented on the Elizabethan stage, even considering the bare platform and the rapid entrances and exits of the players. And this must have been its story ever since, for modern productions do not attempt the play in its entirety.

"Must have been" tells the story of much of its theatrical history, for we do not hear about the play for a long time. With the reopening of the theatres after the Restoration *Antony and Cleopatra* was selected for production by the King's Company, though there is no record that it was performed at that time. On 24 April 1677 Sir Charles Sedley's *Antony and Cleopatra* was licensed and the next year appeared Dryden's version, *All for Love, or, The World Well Lost.* Apparently Sedley's play, written for the Duke's Company in prosaic couplets ("Good Asp bite deep and deadly in my Brest, / And give me sudden and Eternal Rest"), briefly took the place of Shakespeare's just as Dryden's, "Written in Imitation of Shakespeare's Stile," took the place of Sedley's. It was not, indeed until Garrick revived Shakespeare's play in 1759, "fitted for the Stage by abridging only," that Dryden's *All for Love* faced any competition. Even so, Garrick's production was not a success; the fashionable "love and honour" theme and the unified form of Dryden's effort kept that play alive, albeit barely, at Covent Garden as late as the 1790–91 season.

Garrick's grand production of the play, the first recorded performance ever, opened at Drury Lane on 3 January 1759, achieved six performances that season, and was never played again. Even though the box office was respectable each night,[1] one must conclude that the revival had but an indif-

1. Richard Cross's diary in the Folger Shakespeare Library indicates receipts

ferent success—in spite of the fact it had been given the most careful preparation, over a period of at least five months, and was dressed with new costumes and new scenes. Note Garrick's letter of 3 August 1758 to William Young, who had requested the loan of the Drury Lane Roman costumes for a private performance of *Julius Caesar*: "Our Roman Shapes at Drury Lane are so very bad, that We are now making New ones for ye Revival of Anthony [*sic*] and Cleopatra, & our false trimming will not be put upon 'Em till a little time before they are Wanted, as it is apt to tarnish wth lying by. I cannot therefore Accommodate You wth Dresses."[2] Yet, in spite of "all the advantages of new scenes, habits, and other decorations proper to the play," as Thomas Davies says, "it did not answer his [Garrick's] own and the public expectation."[3] Said Richard Cross after opening night, "This Play tho' all new dress'd & had Fine Scenes did not seem to give ye Audience any great plasure [*sic*] or draw any Applause."[4] A command performance of the Prince of Wales on 12 January attracted but £10 more than the previous three nights. The gross was, on the whole, respectable enough, and the play was presented each time without the necessity of an afterpiece; but the expense of mounting it and of keeping it on the stage was great, and in the end Garrick gave it up after that first season.

Part of the problem was Garrick's own role, one of his most demanding. Finally he was exhausted with playing Antony; as he wrote to Benjamin Wilson, the painter, following his last appearance as Antony: "I was so ill & Weak with a kind of bilious Colick, when I play'd Anthony [*sic*], that I was not in a condition the next morn^{g} to do half my Business, that I sh^{d} have done."[5] Sixteen years later he was to tell George Steevens, "An^{y} & Cleopatra I reviv'd Some Years ago, When I & Mrs Yates were Younger—it gain'd ground Every time it was play'd, but I grew tir'd, & gave it up, —the part was laborious."[6] Steevens replied, "Your Antony and Cleopatra was a splendid performance; but you were out of love with it because it afforded you few opportunities of showing those sharp turns and that coachmanship in which you excell all others."[7]

Why did the play not meet the manager's expectations? It was prepared and presented in a decade of spectaculars and was, in a sense, Garrick's answer to John Rich at Covent Garden. In this age of operas and pantomimes Garrick produced *The Fairies* and *The Tempest* and then offered his lavish presentation of *Antony and Cleopatra*, one of the grandest of tragedies. The version he worked out with Capell was published two months before the

---

of £200 on opening night and three other nights, a high of £210 on the fourth night, and a low of £150 on the final night, 18 May. The Winston Manuscript figures, when available, indicate, as usual, a few pounds less.

2. *Letters*, I, 284.
3. *Dramatic Miscellanies* (London, 1783), II, 368.
4. *Diary*, Folger Shakespeare Library. *London Stage*, Part 4, II, 704.
5. *Letters*, I, 307.
6. Ibid., III, 982.
7. James Boaden, ed., *The Private Correspondence of David Garrick* (London, 1831–32), II, 222.

first performance; a full house ("Nothing under Full Prices will be taken during the Performance," the playbill indicated) awaited with excitement. But the management expected better than it received, and the play was soon shelved. George Winchester Stone, Jr., has suggested several reasons for the discontinuance of the play.[8] One was the attitude of the critics regarding the acting. Davies, who played Eros, remarks,

It must be confessed, that, in Antony, he [Garrick] wanted one necessary accomplishment: his person was not sufficiently important and commanding to represent the part. There is more dignity of action than variety of passion in the character, though it is not deficient in the latter. The actor who is obliged continually to traverse the stage, should from person attract respect, as well as from the power of speech. Mrs. Yates was then a young actress, and had not manifested such proofs of genius, and such admirable elocution, as she has since displayed; but her fine figure and pleasing manner of speaking were well adapted to the enchanting Cleopatra. Mossop wanted the essential part of Enobarbus, humour.[9]

John Genest later reported on Garrick and Mrs. Yates: "His own person was not sufficiently important for Antony; and Mrs. Yates had not perhaps at this time displayed abilities equal to the representation of Shakespeare's best female character, Lady Macbeth excepted."[10]

The fact that Garrick's stature did not very well suit the figure of Antony may have played a decisive part in the play's being dropped from the repertoire, along with the fact that the relatively narrow range of the role did not give him much opportunity to display his astonishing versatility as an actor. Another factor which has been mentioned is the cast, which was not, as Joseph Knight pointed out long ago, specially strong, "except Garrick as Antony, Tate Wilkinson as Candidius, Davies as Eros, Mrs. Yates as Cleopatra, and Miss Hippisley as Charmian, few of the names would now be recognized."[11] Still another possible reason for shelving the play has been cited by almost every commentator on it until 1937, when that reason was effectively demolished by Professor Stone: This is the suggestion that Dryden's *All for Love* was too firmly intrenched and too much admired for maintaining the unities and standards of decorum to allow Shakespeare's play to take root, even with Garrick doing the honors for it.[12] Says Stone,

---

8. "Garrick's Presentation of *Antony and Cleopatra*," *Review of English Studies*, 13 (January 1937), 36–37.
9. *Dramatic Miscellanies*, II, 368.
10. *Some Account of the English Stage from the Restoration in 1660 to 1830* (Bath, 1832), IV, 546.
11. *David Garrick* (London, 1894), p. 171.
12. For example, Joseph Knight says, "So popular was 'All for Love,' an alteration, for such it must be considered, by Dryden, that it has held from the Restoration until far into this [the nineteenth] century possession, all but undisputed, of the stage" (*David Garrick*, pp. 170–71). George C. D. Odell maintains that "The public preferred Dryden's All for Love, as they soon showed they preferred Tate's Lear to Shakespeare's" (*Shakespeare from Betterton to Irving* [New York, 1920], I, 367). Charles Harold Gray remarks, "The thirty-eight scenes in *Antony and Cleopatra*, which take place in Alexandria, in Rome, in Syria—and where not?—extending over who know

As a matter of fact, a glance at the records of the theatres will show that if any play drove *Antony and Cleopatra* from the stage it was Murphy's *Orphan of China* and not Dryden's *All for Love.* For the latter play, however popular during the Restoration and during the early eighteenth century, was played but six times at Drury Lane in the fifty-three years from 1747–1800 and but twice during Garrick's whole term of management. It was, during these last fifty years of the eighteenth century, played at Covent Garden only sixteen times—not a popular record even on the basis of eighteenth-century standards.[13]

He indicates that Murphy's play had novelty in its romantic subject and setting and that it was more easily produced, preserving as it did the unities of time, place, and action. Zamti was one of Garrick's most successful roles, as was Mandane for Mrs. Yates.

Despite its brief run on the mid-century stage, Garrick's *Antony and Cleopatra* holds the distinction of being the first known revival of Shakespeare's play since the author's own time. And Garrick presented, in this instance, unadulterated Shakespeare—Shakespeare cut, indeed, and somewhat rearranged, but virtually pure Shakespeare.

In preparing the play for the stage, Garrick had the services of his friend Edward Capell, who was in the process of editing Shakespeare and, in doing so, was making use of books from Garrick's own library. Their idea was to fit the play for the eighteenth-century stage by cutting it down to size and by rearranging some parts of it to facilitate production. As a basis they used a 1734 edition of Nicholas Rowe's 1709 text, in which the play is first divided into acts and scenes and for which needed stage directions were first included. Rowe's text contains five acts and twenty-seven scenes, a number maintained in the Garrick production, even though the shifts in place along the Mediterranean are reduced in the interests of ease of production.[14]

If one uses eighteenth-century typesetting as a basis for counting lines,[15] the Garrick-Capell version reduces Rowe's text by six hundred lines and a small scattering of single words. Only twenty-one lines are revised, but a number are transposed to other parts of the play, most notably Enobarbus's

---

how many years [*sic*], were discarded for Dryden's *All for Love*, which concentrated upon the final phase of the drama, and in preserving the unities sacrificed the breadth and sweep of Shakespeare's play for a sharp, distinct effect of another kind" (*Theatrical Criticism in London to 1795* [New York, 1931], pp. 18–19).

13. "Garrick's *Antony and Cleopatra*," pp. 36–37.
14. The Folger Shakespeare Library has the marked copy from which Capell worked in preparing the text which was published in 1759, shortly before the Garrick production. It includes cuts in ink by Capell and a few additions of stage business, along with some further cuts in pencil. There are only minor and unimportant differences between the marked copy and the printed version. It is not a promptbook.
15. In order to compare effectively the four editions of *Antony and Cleopatra*, it was necessary to employ the customary eighteenth-century method of setting lines. All new speeches begin on the left margin; thus the number of lines in a Shakespeare play is greatly increased over the count in the *Variorum* texts, for example, or in those of George Lyman Kittredge.

classic description of Cleopatra on the River Cydnus from II, ii, to the end of the first scene of act I. A number of scenes are telescoped in order to avoid shifts in setting, particularly short scenes, as in the amalgamation of Shakespeare's III, viii, ix, and x, into the Garrick-Capell III, ii. A few single words are added to the dialogue, and the drinking song in II, iii, is expanded by six lines. The number of characters is reduced from thirty-four, not including the walk-ons, to twenty-three plus the Clown and the walk-ons.

The most striking changes are found in act I. Here at the outset Thyreus and Dolabella, of Caesar's party, take the lines of Philo and Demetrius. Antony, refusing to see the messengers from Rome, leaves with Cleopatra to "wander through the streets and note / The qualities of people," whereupon Thyreus steals Enobarbus's great speech from act II to tell Dolabella about the famous meeting of the two lovers. So ends scene i, but not to the satisfaction of all, as Genest makes perfectly clear:

> For the convenience of representation it was right to reduce the number of characters, but this is done without any regard to propriety—the speech with which Philo opens the play, and the famous description of Cleopatra on the Cydnus (taken from Enobarbus) are given to Thyreus—if a change were to be made it should certainly have been made in favor of some Roman of consequence on Antony's side, not in favor of Thyreus, who was Caesar's freedman and who had never seen Cleopatra til he was sent with a message to her, as in the 3d act of the play.[16]

The idea behind the shift of the most famous scene of the play to the first act, surely Garrick's brainchild, was to establish at the outset Cleopatra as a gloriously wonderful woman.

As the play moves on through the first three acts, cuts are made to reduce the amount of history and politics as opposed to the love element, four lines here, thirteen lines from the next scene, an entire scene of fifty-two lines next, and so on, as indicated in the textual notes. In the interest of staging the play, the scenes in Parthia and Athens are eliminated entirely; these omissions indicate Garrick's close supervision of the alteration. Removing such characters as Philo, Demetrius, Scarus, and Ventidius from Antony's train and Menecrates and Varrius from that of Pompey, no matter how badly missed, reduces the complexity of the plot.

Act IV begins with Shakespeare's scene iv, the striking scene in which Cleopatra and Eros arm Antony. Gone is the famous opening scene of Caesar's rage at being called a boy by Antony and the next, the powerful "last supper" scene in which Antony confuses Cleopatra and makes Enobarbus "onion-ey'd." Shakespeare's short scene iii, in which the soldiers foreshadow doom for Antony, is also gone. The omission of the first two of these scenes–but particularly of the second, or banquet, scene–is most difficult for modern readers to accept. Act V suffers least, only seven lines of the Clown being omitted in the interest of good (eighteenth-century) taste.

As Shakespeare's play is basically one of character, it is interesting to see what has happened to the major ones. Cleopatra is not harmed at all: having seven fewer lines could not cause the slightest change in that magnificent

16. *Some Account of the English Stage*, IV, 544.

character. Antony suffers somewhat more, particularly in being denied the "last supper" scene, one of Shakespeare's important steps in elevating his character to tragic importance. The loss of his scenes with Octavia in Rome and in Athens takes something away, but other lines cut, often political in nature, are of minor importance. Antony pretty much remains Antony, as Caesar remains Caesar, even though the lines eliminated reduce the picture of him as the cold, unfeeling, man-of-destiny type. For with some extensive cuts in his lines of a political nature we find that his interest in—and disillusionment with—Antony is emphasized; in attitude he is closer to Philo in the original play. His call to Antony, "Leave thy lascivious wassails," is all the more poignant for the cuts. The Garrick-Capell team apparently sought to humanize the man.

Enobarbus does suffer—he loses his most famous speech and a number of his dry, satirical lines,—but it would be difficult indeed to hurt him a great deal without eliminating him entirely. He keeps his job, so to speak; the treasure scene and the death scene are there for their original purpose: to enhance the character of Antony.

Even more do Octavia and Pompey suffer: both become bit players, and Mrs. Glen and Mr. Austin were not taxed beyond their capabilities. Austin, in fact, had time to play Proculeius on the side, as his only appearance as Pompey was in the galley scene of act II. Octavia suffers most in the omissions: she loses her betrothal scene and her domestic scene in Athens. Withall, she remains "most wretched" and becomes for the reader-viewer of the play the woman Cleopatra envisions her to be: "Dull of tongue, and dwarfish!" Mrs. Glen had time to spend in the Greenroom.

But the poetry of Shakespeare was preserved; there was here no Nahum Tate to "improve") the lines. Also, the play could be performed within a reasonable number of hours and, from the point of view of stage management, with a not too unreasonable number of set changes. Critics might carp, as did Genest later when he complained, "What the Soldiers and Scarus say in the 3d and 4th acts is absurdly given to Diomedes, who was only Secretary to Cleopatra and could have nothing to do with military concerns" and "That Capel [*sic*] and Garrick should not take the trouble to read Plutarch's Life of Antony is inexcusable—but even Steevens seems to have contented himself with consulting Sir Thomas North's translation, without referring to the original."[17] But Garrick was not presenting a lecture in ancient history; he was treating the public to a rare spectacle indeed in the eighteenth century: virtually unadulterated Shakespeare. And even though the play did not meet Garrick's expectations, Professor Stone rightly points out that he never played it to an empty house.[18]

A Note on the Text: We have reprinted here the first edition of the Garrick-Capell version of *Antony and Cleopatra* without the special typographical effects which Capell added to the edition in order to aid the reader in visualizing the action and reading the play more dramatically. The original edition of 23 October 1758 has the lines cluttered with six different marks:

17. Ibid., 544, 545.
18. "Garrick's *Antony and Cleopatra*," p. 38.

a dash at the top of a letter to indicate a change of address; a dash at the bottom of a letter to indicate a change of address within a speech; a cross to indicate a thing pointed to; a double-barred cross to indicate a thing delivered; a point (a raised period) at the top of a letter to indicate irony ("often so delicately couch'd as to escape the notice of the attentive reader"); inverted commas (double quotation marks) to indicate an aside. Capell explained his system in the preface to *Prolusions, or Select Pieces of Ancient Poetry* (London, 1760). The first example of the use of each mark in the text is indicated in the notes.

TEXTS

*D*1 1st edition. London: J. and R. Tonson, 1758.
*D*1a London: J. and R. Tonson, 1758.
*D*1b London: J. and R. Tonson, 1758.
*D*2 Dublin: Peter Wilson and William Smith, 1759.
*D*3 *Bell's Edition of Shakespeare's Plays.* London: John Bell and C. Etherington, 1744, VI, [259]–366.
*D*4 London: John Bell and C. Etherington, 1776.
S Standard Shakespeare texts.

Note: D1a, D1b follow D1 except for arrangement of preliminary materials. Although the Bell texts follow Shakespeare act for act and scene for scene, the omissions indicate the critical perception of the play later in the century and are therefore here collated. Francis Gentleman's introduction to the Bell texts is as follows: "Whether this play, tho' excellently wrote, has any chance for long existence on the stage is very doubtful. Twenty years since, that very able and successful Dramatic Modeller, Mr. Garrick, produced it under the most probable state of reformation; yet, tho' elegantly decorated and finely performed, it too soon languished. Antony and Cleopatra are the chief marked characters in it: he is a flighty infatuated slave to an excess of love and luxury; she a tinsel pattern of vanity and female cunning, which work the downfall of both. A double moral may be inferred, namely, that indolence and dissipation may undo the greatest of men; and that beauty, under the direction of vanity, will not only ruin the possessor, but admirer also."

[DEDICATORY POEM]

11. Pharian] pertaining to Pharos, a former island in the bay of Alexandria, celebrated in antiquity for its lighthouse; by extension, Egyptian.

[I, i]

2. o'erflows the measure] cannot be measured.
3. files and musters] ranks.
4. plated] armored.
5. office . . . view] all their attention.
6. tawny] dark-skinned. front] brow.
8. temper] moderation.
10. gipsy's] Egyptian's.

12. triple pillar] one of the three Roman Triumviers.
15. there's beggary] one is a beggar. reckoned] measured.
16. bourn] boundry.
19. grates] annoys. sum] substance.
23. mandate] command.
28. dismission] recall.
30. process] written orders.
33. Caesar's homager] does homage to Caesar.
36. ranged] wide.
39. thus] (they embrace).
40. I bind] I put (the world) under bond.
41. weet] know.
46. himself] i.e., a deceiver.
49. confound] waste. conference] conversation.
50. stretch] pass.
59. qualities] characteristics.
64. indeed] magnificently.
65. devised] invented.
77. fancy] i.e., the painter's imagination.
83. Nereids] sea nymphs.
86. a seeming] one dressed as a.
88. yarely] quickly, skillfully. frame the office] do their duty.
93. vacancy] making a vacuum.
103. ordinary] dinner (in a tavern).
107. cropped] gave birth.

[I, ii]

3–4. charge . . . garlands] thoroughly deceived, he will decorate his cuckold's horns with flowers.
19. companion me] make me thus equal to Cleopatra.
22. proved] experienced.
32. oily palm] (indicated lecherousness). fruitful prognostication] (indication of fertility).
42. go] have children.
49. loose-wived] married to an unfaithful woman.
62. Roman thought] a thought about Rome.
70. time's state] political situation.
72. issue] success.
80. as] as though.
88. home] to the point. mince not] don't soften.
91. licence] freedom.
93. winds] First Folio; Warburton emends to *minds*. still] idle (uncultivated).
94. earing] plowing.
106. importeth] is important for.
107. forbear] leave.
111. by revolution] by a turn of Fortune's wheel.
113. could] would if it could.
125. noise] rumor.
126. moment] occasion.
137. broached] set in motion (the civil war).
139. business] i.e., the affair with Cleopatra.

142. light] frivolous.
145. love] First Folio; often emended to "leave."
148. our . . . friends] friends who are making plans for me.
153. throw] transfer.
156. blood] spirit.
156–157. stands . . . soldier] assumes the position of leading warrior.
157. quality] aspirations.
158. sides . . . world] whole empire.
159. courser's hair] horsehair, fallen in water, was thought to come to life as worms or serpents.

[I, iii]

13. tempt] test. I wish, forbear] I wish you would stop testing him.
17. breathing] utterance.
19. sides of nature] bodily strength.
35. shake] make tremble.
37. mouth-made] spoken but unfelt.
40. color] pretext.
41. sued staying] asked permission to stay.
44. none our parts] no feature of mine.
45. race of heaven] godlike.
50. a heart] courage (to repay injury).
54. in . . . you] for your use.
58. scrupulous faction] disagreement on issues of little consequence.
63. quietness] peace. of rest] through resting.
64. particular] personal reason.
71. garboils] tumults.
74. sacred vials] bottles of tears, to be placed in funeral urns.
78. are] will be continued.
79. fire] sun.
82. affect'st] desirest.
83. lace] corset-lacings.
89. told me] i.e., I have an example of your faithfulness in your treatment of Fulvia.
96. meetly] well done.
98. target] shield.
100–101. become . . . chafe] plays well the part of an angry person.
110. idleness] foolishness.
111. idleness itself] foolishness personified.
112. Sweating labor] i.e., of childbirth.
115. becomings] attractions.
122. abides and flies] stays and goes.

[I, iv]

6. Ptolemy] Cleopatra was widow of Ptolmey XII.
7. gave audience] saw my ambassadors.
9. abstract] epitomy.
13. spots] stars.
15. purchased] acquired.
20. keep . . . tippling] alternately drink healths.

[I, iv]

23. composure] make-up.
25. foils] disgraceful acts.
25–26] bear . . . lightness] are so seriously affected by his frivolities.
27. vacancy] spare time.
28. surfeits] indigestion. dryness . . . bones] a symptom of syphilis.
29. confound] waste.
31. state] great position.
32. rate] scold.
34. to] against.
42. Give] declare.
44. the primal state] since the beginning of society.
47. body] people.
48. vagabond flag] common iris.
49. lacquying] lackeying, following a leader.
50. motion] mere movement.
53. ear] plough.
56. Lack blood] turn pale.
58. strikes more] is more effective.
59. war resisted] forces embattled.
65. patience] endurance.
66. suffer] show.
67. stale] urine. gilded] scum-covered.
68. deign] not disdain.
76. lanked not] did not become lanky, thin.
85. be able] muster in the way of troops.
86. 'front . . . time] cope with this situation.
93. bond] duty.

[I, v]

3. mandragora] mandrake root, used to induce sleep.
15. unseminared] emasculated.
23. arm] armor.
24. burgonet] helmet.
28. with . . . black] tanned by the sun, her lover.
31. great Pompey] meaning the *son* of Pompey the Great and Cleopatra's earlier lover.
33. anchor his aspect] fix his gaze.
34. his life] his reason for living.
47. piece] piece out.
50. arm-gaunt] thin from bearing heavy arms.
72. brave] splendid.
77. paragon] equate.
81. salad days] youth.

[II, i]

5. like himself] in a way worthy of his position.
9. I . . . today] would not be bearded by Caesar.
11. stomaching] resentment.
20. compose] come to agreement.

30. the rather] all the more because.
32. curstness grow to] anger enter into.
53. practice] plot.
54. question] concern.
55. intend] mean.
59. was themed for] concerned. your . . . war] the war was waged in your name.
60. your business] the matter.
61. urge me] claim he fought for me. it] into it.
64. Discredit . . . yours] rebel against both of us.
65. stomach] inclination.
66. alike your cause] equal reason to be displeased.
67. patch] make.
68. As . . . with] you have no facts on which to base your claim.
77. attend] witness.
78. 'fronted] opposed.
81. pace easy] cause to move easily.
85. impatience] i.e., because I was in Egypt.
86. Shrewdness of policy] i.e., to get me home.
96. what . . . morning] my earlier good control.
102. article . . . oath] agreement you swore to.
116. make . . . greatness] humiliate me.
126. atone] reconcile.
134. considerate] silent (as a).
137. conditions] dispositions.
139. staunch] leak-free.
148. of] because of.
157. That . . . utter] beyond words (ie., for themselves).
159. import] bring.
164. present] unconsidered.
175. fairly] promisingly.
177. grace] reconciliation.
179. sway] control.
187. strange] unusual.
195. Mount Misenum] a promontory west of the Bay of Naples.
200. fame] report.

[II, ii]

9. come too short] is inadequate.
11. angle] fishing tackle.
25. tires] headdresses.
26. Philippan] used at Philippi.
45. tart] gloomy. favor] look.
48. formal] normal.
58. honest] worthy.
60. mark] generally "make" in Shakespeare.
62. allay] alloy, lessen.
63. good precedence] earlier good report.
76. spurn] kick.
79. ling'ring pickle] brine which will preserve you.
85. boot] make amends.
114. So] even if.

122. unequal] unfair.
127. undone] ruined.
136. inclination] disposition.

[II, iii]

1. Pompey] an aside to Pompey.
2. have known] have met.
9. said] said truly.
17. divine] predict.
19. policy] political expediency. purpose] arrangement.
23. conversation] deportment.
29–30. his occasion] what was necessary for him.
35. high-colored] flushed with drink.
39. foison] plenty.
49. out] stop drinking.
70. epicure] atheist (Kittredge).
73. merit] my merit.
77. held . . . off] shown deference to.
93. pales] encloses (literally *fences in*). inclips] encircles.
124. reels] those who are reeling drunk.
126. Alexandrian] i.e., what Antony is accustomed to in Egypt.
127. Strike the vessel] broach the casks.
140. Make battery] assault.
142. holding] refrain.
155–156. wild . . . all] the mumming has almost made us professional actors.
157. try you] drink again with you.
161. have] took, siezed.

[II, iv]

22. not so good] not favorable for Octavia.
28. station] standing.
50. As . . . it] lower than she would want.
58. harried] mistreated.
59. no such thing] nothing much.

[II, v]

1. Condemning] having contempt for.

6. Caesarion] Cleopatra's son by Julius Caesar. my father's] Octavius was adopted by Julius Caesar.

9. 'stablishment] government.
13. they exercise] the troops drill.
23. queasy] nauseated.
29. spoiled] took his territory. rated] given.
53. borne men] been filled with procession-viewers.
58. ostent] ostentation, fittling display.
67. pardon for] permission to.
71. eyes] spies.
88. determined] predestined.
91. mark] range.

92. ministers] those who minister, servants.
98. large] unrestrained.
100. potent regiment] authority.

[III, i]

3. forespoke] spoken against.
6. denounced] declared (Rome had declared war against Cleopatra).
10. merely] altogether.
13. puzzle] confuse.
46. Ingrossed] gathered in masses. impress] forced enlistment.
48. yare] light, swift.
64. head] promontory.
70. power] troops.
73. Thetis] Antony refers to Cleopatra as a sea goddess.
77. a-ducking] by water.
83. the power on't] what is best.
92. distractions] divided actions.

[III, ii]

6. jump] chance.
8. battle] army.
12. admiral] flagship.
18. cantle] part.
27. breeze] a pun on air and a gadfly.
32. looft] having turned the boats to wind (Kittredge).
42. what . . . himself] true to his abilities.
45. thereabouts] thinking that.
48. attend] await.

[III, iii]

3. lated] belated, out too late.
13. that] that which.
18. Sweep] pave.
19. lothness] reluctance. hint] opportunity.
21. leaves itself] is not true to itself.
37. like a dancer] i.e., sheathed.
40. dealt on lieutenantry] depended on his lieutenants.
41. squares] squadrons.
44. unqualitied] without his usual qualities.
68. young man] Octavius.
69. palter] equivocate. shifts of lowness] dodges of lowly men.
79. full of lead] heavy.

[III, iv]

4. argument] sign.
10. petty] unimportant. ends] affairs.
21. circle] crown.

30. Bring] escort. bands] troops.
35–36. perjure . . . vestal] make even a vestal virgin break her vows.
37. edict] determination of reward.
40. becomes his flaw] adapts himself to his fate.

[III, V]

6. ranges] squadrons.
9. nicked] made a fool of.
11. mered] main, entire.
12. course] chase.
18. so] if.
22. grizzled] grey, salt-and-pepper.
32. gay comparisons] fine equipment.
33. answer] meet. declined] fallen in fortune.
36. Unstate his happiness] lower himself. staged . . . show] shown on a stage.
37. sworder] gladiator.
38. parcel] part.
39. inward quality] mind, character.
40. To . . . alike] so that both decline equally.
41. all measures] both prosperity and failure.
42. Answer his emptiness] will meet Antony without his usual power.
48. square] quarrel.
81. require] request.
87. universal landlord] ruler of the world.
91. In deputation] by you as my deputy.
95. doom of] judgment on.
99. grace] the favor.
104. As] as if.
111. kite] sparrow-hawk.
113. muss] scramble for something thrown.
132. abused] betrayed.
133. feeders] servants.
135. boggler] evader.
146. Luxuriously] lasciviously.
151. quit] repay.
161. fever] frighten.
169. orbs] spheres.
177. terrene moon] earthly moon goddess (Cleopatra).
182. ties his points] a valet (who laces the doublet and hose).
188. determines] melts.
190. memory . . . womb] my children.
191. brave] noble.
192. discandying] melting.
194. buried] devoured.
199. fleet] float.
200. heart] courage.
203. earn our chronicle] earn our place in history.
207. maliciously] savagely.
208. nice] pampered (Kittredge).
211. gaudy] full of revelry.
226. estridge] a kind of hawk.

[IV, i]

4. thine . . . on] i.e., mine that you have, on me.
9. false] i.e., that's the wrong place for that piece.
19. squire] one who arms the knight.
25. betime] early.
32. well blown] a fair warning.
35. that] i.e., piece of equipment. well said] well done.
38. check] reproof.

[IV, iii]

6. three-nooked] three-cornered (i.e., Europe, Asia, Africa).
7. olive] symbol of peace.
19. have entertainment] have been accepted (by Caesar).
26. on] i.e., when I was on.
38. bows] error for *blows* (bursts).

[IV, iv]

2. our oppression] the oppressive force against us.
6. clouts] bandages.
11. bench-holes] holes for privies.
12. scotches] slashes.
13. serves] stands.
19. sprightly] cheerful.
21. halt] limp.

[IV, v]

2. gests] deeds of valor.
5. doughty] sturdy, bold.
8. clip] embrace.
13. day] light.
15. proof of] impenetrable.
21. grey] i.e., hairs.
24. Get goal] win point.
31. carbuncled] jewelled.
34. targets] shields. owe] own.
38. royal peril] war, the sport of kings.

[IV, vi]

2. court of guard] guards' mustering place.
3. embattle] battle formation.
6. shrewd] tough.
17. dispunge] release your poisons.
24. particular] person.
25. register] its record.
39. raught] reached.
40. demurely] in muffled sound.

[IV, vii]

5. foot] foot soldiers.

9. appointment] the appearance of their ships.

11. But . . . charged] unless we are attacked. be still] will not move.

15. joined] i.e., in battle.

23. fretted] checkered.

29. Triple-turned] i.e., from Pompey to Julius Caesar, from Caesar to Antony, and now from Antony to Octavius.

32. charm] charmer.

37. spanieled me] followed me like a dog, fawningly.

38. discandy] dissolve.

43. crownet] coronet, crown.

44. fast and loose] a trick knot, apparently a difficult one, which can be loosed at a pull.

52. monster-like] like a freak.

53. diminutives] dwarfs. dolts] idiots.

60. shirt of Nessus] which defeated Hercules.

61. Alcides] Hercules.

62. Lichas] see Ovid, *Metamorphoses*, IX, 117 ff.

[IV, viii]

2. Telamon] lost the shield of Achilles to Ulysses. boar of Thessaly] sent by Artemis to revenge Thessaly for omitting sacrifices to her.

3. imbost] embossed, enraged (a hunting term).

4. monument] the tomb Cleopatra had prepared for herself.

6. rive] rend.

[IV, ix]

1. thou yet behold'st] can you still see me, or am I too much diminished.

9. black Vesper's] approach of evening.

12. rack] clouds. dislimns] umpaints.

22. Packed cards] stacked the cards. false-played] cheated.

27. sword] ability to fight, thus *manhood*.

35. unto thy hand] for you.

45. Does . . . labor] normally you would have been killed for bringing this bad news.

49. thy continent] what contains you.

55. length] i.e., of life. torch is out] Cleopatra is dead.

57. Mars . . . does] is useless.

57–58. force . . . strength] my efforts so entangle themselves as to nullify them.

58. Seal] i.e., the seal of death.

61. port] bearing.

62. want troups] be outadmired.

63. all . . . ours] all shall resort to us.

69. made cities] so numerous as to seem very cities.

73. exigent] exigency.

84. windowed] standing at a window.

85. pleached] folded.

87. wheeled seat] chariot.

119. record] history.
129. period] end (i.e., of the world).
137. enter . . . him] win a place in his service.
150. found] i.e., to be true.
151. disposed] made terms with.

[IV, X]

7. As . . . it] as Antony.
29. brooched] ornamented.
32. still conclusion] calm reasoning.
33. Demuring] looking on demurely.
37. sport, indeed] ironical reference to their former pastimes.
38. heaviness] grief.
44. Quicken] i.e., to life.
50. huswife] hussy.
51. offence] offensive language.
68. wou't] will thou.
72. crown] leader, chief.
74. pole] probably the Maypole (cf. "garland" and "boys and girls").
75. level] equal.
89. injurious] hostile.
92. is sottish] becomes a fool.
98. Our lamp] the light of my life.
102. case] body.

[V, i]

2–3. mocks the pauses] makes his hesitation seem ridiculous.
6. thus] i.e., with a drawn sword.
17. breaking] i.e., of the news.
19. shook] i.e., as an earthquake. civil streets] of cities.
22. moiety] half.
40. steer] govern.
45. launch] lance.
48. stall] live.
50. sovereign] potent.
52. In top] at the top. design] enterprises.
59. looks out of] is evident.
67. ours] our men.
74. passion] grief.
77. eternaling our triumph] make our victory procession eternally memorable.
90. writings] messages to Antony.

[V, ii]

4. minister] servant.
6. accidents] chances.
7. sleeps] brings sleep (i.e., death). palates . . . dung] gives a taste of this vile world.
16. to be] if I am.
30. pray . . . kindness] ask aid in doing kind deeds.

40. suprised] captured.
49. languish] misery.
66. varletry] rabble.
83. employ me] use me as messenger.
107. dolphin-like] kingly; the dolphin was often considered to be king of the animals.
109. crowns and crownets] kings and princes.
110. plates] silver coins.
117. size] capacity.
118. vie] contest.
152. extenuate] make light of your offenses.
153. apply] submit.
180. pomp is followed] great people are served.
193. parcel] add an item to.
196. immoment] of no value. dignity] value.
197. modern] ordinary.
199. Livia] Caesar's wife.
200. unfolded] exposed.
213. make prize] haggle.
222. words me] tries to delude me.
227. it] i.e., the asps.
246. puppet] a character in a puppet show.
251. drink] inhale.
253. lictors] officers (probably those impowered to whip whores).
254. scald] scurvy.
255. Ballad us] make ballads about our misfortune. quick] i.e., quick of tongue.
259. boy my greatness] a child actor will burlesque her majesty.
268. Show] display.
272. chare] chore.
281. placed] fixed.
283. fleeting] inconstant.
286. Avoid] depart.
290. immortal] i.e., mortal.
298. fallible] i.e., infallible.
303. his kind] as is his nature.
333. This] i.e., Iras's dying first.
337. intrinsicate] intricate.
341. Unpolicied] with no skill in statecraft.
376. Brav'st] most magnificent.
377. leveled] guessed.
386. trimming up] straightening.
392. As] as if.
393. toil of grace] snare of her beauty.
395. blown] swelled.
406. clip] embrace.

Cymbeline

Cymbeline was the ninth Shakespearean play Garrick altered and adapted for Drury Lane Theatre. In the opinion of G. C. D. Odell it was "the last really important Shakespearean production on Garrick's stage, during his lifetime."[1] Although it was not produced until 28 November 1761, the role of Posthumus had fascinated the actor for a great many years. As a manager Garrick would have known of this play and its performance record before his time. Altered by Thomas D'Urfey in 1682 under the title *The Injured Princess; or, the Fatal Wager*, it had been played successfully fifteen times at Lincoln's Inn Feilds between 1702 and 1720. It had been revived at Covent Garden as late as 1736–37 and played four times that season, and again on 20 March 1738. Theophilus Cibber had announced the play for his theatre in the Haymarket as "Shakespeare's" and perhaps played it on 8 November 1744, only to have his theatre closed by a local magistrate before he could attain a second performance scheduled for 10 November.

Certainly by 14 September 1746 Garrick was expressing a decided interest. On this date he replied to a letter from his friend, the Reverend John Hoadly, remarking, "I am glad to hear you have dock'd & alter'd Cymbeline & beg you will send it up immediately directed for me, at my lodgings in James street, Cov^t^ Garden; you will give me great pleasure & may do me a service by it, so I shall forbear to urge any stronger arguments in my favour. What character have you fix'd for me in y^r^ mind? Pray let me know when you sent it."[2] While there is no evidence to demonstrate that Hoadly ever dispatched his alteration, or, if he did, that Garrick received same, there is a slight clue in the matter next to be discussed.

We may be sure that Garrick took note of a Covent Garden production of *Cymbeline* in the *1758–59* season, an alteration of the play by the distinguished Oxford professor, William Hawkins. This version had a run of six nights, with two benefits for the author, and an additional command performance by the Prince of Wales.[3] The printed version of Hawkins's alteration contains an interesting introduction by the author in which he complains, "It will be proper to acquaint the reader, that, this play, was recommended some time since by a person of the first distinction, to the manager of the other theatre; who declared, that he had the very same altered play in his possession, and that it was designed for representation on his stage. Our *Cymbeline* therefore was obliged to take up his head-quarters at *Covent-Garden*, where he has contended not only with the *usual* difficulties, but also with *others* of an extraordinary nature—Mrs. Bellamy's declining the part of *Imogen* has done the play incredible prejudice."[4] Three seasons later Garrick brought out his own version! Whether this was based upon the earlier Hoadly alteration, or whether Garrick actually required three seasons to complete "the same altered play in his possession," no one can say at this date. But the fact remains that the manager had informed Hawkins that he had such an alteration ready for production thus early. Lacking corroboration for such speculation, we must reluctantly join Garrick's contemporaries and later scholars in supposing the version he produced on 28 November 1761 was his own.

1. *Shakespeare from Betterton to Irving* (New York, 1920), I, 372.
2. *The Letters of David Garrick*, I, 85.
3. *The London Stage*, Part 4, II, 711–12, 721.
4. (London, 1759), p. vii.

Professor Hawkins politely defended his strange alteration in these words: " . . . I have ventured publicly to defend this great *dramatic* Poet in the liberties he has taken; but still *Shakespeare* himself needs not to be *ashamed* to *wear* a *modern dress*, provided it can be made tolerably to fit him."[5] In altering *Cymbeline* to the classical strictures of eighteenth-century tragedy, Hawkins indeed preserves the unities of Time and Place. Scenes requiring a time span are telescoped by exposition, and the places are confined to ancient Britain—the royal palace, royal apartments, royal castle, the forests of Britain—no matter what happens to Shakespeare's drama. Iachimo is cut from the cast of characters, as is Cymbeline's Queen; Pisanio becomes a villain by the name of Philario; Cloten is made a serious character; and Bellarius's boys are called Palador and Cadwal.

Cymbeline refuses tribute to Rome and orders his heir, Cloten, to kill Leonatus (Posthumus) when and if he should return to Britain from Italy. We learn that Pisanio has travelled to Rome at Cloten's order to tell Leonatus of his wife's infidelity. Philario persuades Imogen to flee the court in male attire.

Act II consists of the discovery of Imogen's flight and her welcome by Bellarius and the boys at their cave in the forest. Act III includes a test of Imogen which proves her innocence, her taking of the drug, the death of Cloten by Palador's hand, the finding of the supposedly dead Imogen, and the dirge sung by Cadwal.

Acts IV and V are entirely new inventions. Act IV takes place on a battlefield, where Cymbeline accepts Bellarius and the boys and Philario into his service. A disguised Leonatus rescues Cymbeline in battle, Palador kills the treacherous Pisanio and retrieves an incriminating letter revealing Cloten's evil design. Leonatus, convinced of his wife's innocence, is honored with the others by Cymbeline. The whole party then departs for Bellarius's cave in the forest. Act V finds the assembly at the cave in time to witness the recovery of Imogen, who forgives Philario and is reunited with Leonatus. Cymbeline, now aware of Cloten's villainy, pardons Bellarius and receives his two sons in exchange. Genest comments on this alteration: "Some of Hawkins' additions are far from bad, but the similarity between them and the original play is not very discernible—on the whole this is a wretched alteration—D'Urfey had before altered Cymbeline—that he, Tate, Cibber, and others, should, at a time when Shakespeare was out of fashion, think themselves entitled to mangle him at pleasure, can no longer be wondered at, when Hawkins, Professor of Poetry in the University of Oxford, could in 1759 present the public with such an alteration as this."[6]

In his advertisement to the first printed edition of *Cymbeline*, Garrick explained his method: "It was impossible to retain more of the play and bring it within the compass of a night's entertainment. The chief alterations are in the division of the acts, in the shortening of many parts of the original, and transposing some scenes." Rather than follow Hawkins's method of "regularizing" the drama to suit eighteenth-century taste, Garrick persuaded

5. Ibid.
6. *Some Account of the English Stage, 1660–1830* (Bath, 1832), IV, 564.

his public to enjoy the beauty of Shakespearean verse and altered only as indicated in his advertisement. Such had been his custom when adapting these plays to the length of mainpieces, always excepting *The Winter's Tale.* It might be worth mentioning here that when Garrick speaks of bringing the play "within the compass of a night's entertainment" he means leaving sufficient time for an afterpiece entr'act features, etc., in his always varied program.

Act I, i, is Shakespeare's except for giving Pisanio the lines of the First Gentleman and adding such lines and words necessary to adjust to this change.[7] The scene includes all of the scenes in the original, i, ii, and v. In other words, Garrick is able to compress all the action taking place in Britain in his first scene, thus saving himself many more scene changes and making his story line clearer. Act I, ii, uses Shakespeare's I, iv, at the end of which the "fatal wager" is made.[8] Garrick cuts only I, iii, where Cloten is introduced in conversation with the two Lords. He allows Cloten to be characterized earlier through the remarks of other characters.

Act II is divided into five scenes, comprising Shakespeare's acts II and III. Cloten appears; Iachimo visits Imogen's bedchamber; while Cloten serenades Imogen in the early morning—with a spectacular dance of masquers adding novelty for the spectators. As the act closes, Imogen discovers the loss of her bracelet.[9]

Act III is divided into seven scenes, only one of which takes place in Rome. The first scene includes the boasting of Iachimo over his pretended conquest of Imogen and the reaction of Posthumus. The succeeding six scenes take place in Britain—Cymbeline refuses to pay tribute to the Romans; Pisanio receives instructions to murder Imogen; Bellarius and the boys are discovered at their cave. After including part of Shakespeare's act III, v, Garrick ends the act with III, iv, when Pisanio and Imogen find themselves near Milford-Haven.[10]

Act IV consists of six scenes. Scene i begins with Cloten's plan to pursue the missing Imogen to Milford-Haven.[11] Scene ii introduces Imogen to Bellarius and the boys.[12] Garrick then uses Shakespeare's act IV in scenes iii and iv to present Cloten's death and the burial of Imogen with his headless body.[13] The dirge is changed and reduced to a very few lines. A brief scene v takes place in the palace, where Cymbeline is made aware of the approaching demise of his Queen and the arrival of the Roman army. Scene vi returns to Shakespeare's IV, ii, and Imogen's awakening, her mistake in taking the body of

7. I, i, 1–159a; I, iii, 4–39a; I, v, 4–87; II, i, 62–70.
8. I, iv, 1–185.
9. Scene i: I, vi, 1–110; scene ii: II, i, 1–37, II, iii, 40–68, II, i, 35–62; scene iii: II, ii, 1–51; scene iv: II, iii, 1–14; scene v: II, iii, 15–35, 69–161.
10. Scene i: II, iv, 1–152; scene ii: II, v, 1–35; scene iii: III, i, 1–87 (14b–46 omitted); scene iv: III, ii, 1–84; scene v: III, iii, 1–107; scene vi: III, v, 1–65; scene vii: III, iv, 1–196.
11. III, v, 70–162.
12. III, vi, 1–97.
13. IV, i, 1–30.

Cloten for that of her husband, and her acceptance by Lucius as a member of his retinue.[14]

Act V is again in six brief scenes, using Shakespeare's IV, iv, and V, i, ii, iii, and v. The first scene has Guiderius and Aviragus joining Cymbeline's forces.[15] Scene ii finds Posthumus changing his garb to join also.[16] Scene iii, a field of battle, presents the confrontation between Iachimo and Posthumus, in which the villain is set free.[17] Scene iv shows the Britains winning their battle, and the spectacular valor of Bellarius, Posthumus, and the boys.[18] Shakespeare's V, iv, the prison scene, is cut. Scene v consists of a soliloquy in which Posthumus declares himself ready for "ransom's death" and wishes to expiate his crime against Imogen.[19] Scene vi finds Cymbeline in his battle tent, as all ends with the inevitable disclosures and reconciliations.[20]

Garrick's arrangement of scenes was a practical one for his stage. Twenty-six scenes were done in a minimum of fourteen settings, but the transitions were carefully plotted. Act I required but a single scene change; act II, a minimum of three different sets; act III, four sets; act IV, three; and act V, two. Unless new scenes were acquired (Garrick provided them for this production), the whole could be performed in stock settings which were easily and rapidly moved in the groove system of his theatre.

While over 610 lines were cut from Shakespeare's play, 524 of them in act V, Garrick succeeded in giving his age its first experience of *Cymbeline* as a fully fleshed drama. His first-rate acting text was developed without in the least sacrificing clarity of plot or the loss of a single important character. G. W. Stone, Jr., has counted 132 performances of *Cymbeline* during the years of Garrick's management, 102 at Drury Lane and 30 at Covent Garden. There followed 31 other performances before the close of the century.[21] In Posthumus the actor-manager had found a magnificent role suitable for his many-faceted acting personality, and when he had played it 23 times (1761–62 and 1762–63) he turned it over to future generations of leading men, who lost little time in reviving the play to their advantage and the audience's continuing pleasure.

Garrick's contemporaries were forced to reevaluate this drama. Of course Dr. Johnson thought Garrick's efforts were superfluous. Arthur Murphy has preserved Johnson's comment. "It has many just sentiments, some natural dialogue, and some pleasing scenes, but they are obtained at the expense of incongruity. To remark the folly of the fiction, and absurdity of the conduct, the confusion of the names, and manners of different times,

14. Scene iv: IV, ii, 1–269; scene v: IV, iii, 1–46; scene vi: IV, ii, 291–403.
15. IV, iv, 1–54.
16. V, i, 1–33.
17. V, ii, 1–7.
18. V, iii, 1–54 (lines of Posthumus now spoken by Pisanio).
19. V, iii, 66–83.
20. V, v, 1–485. (V, v, 23–68, concerning the Queen's guilt and death, were omitted after the opening night's performance.)
21. "A Century of Cymbeline; or Garrick's Magic Touch," *PQ*, 54, No. 1. (Winter 1975), 311.

and the impossibility of the events in any system of life, were to waste criticism upon unresisting imbecility, upon faults too evident for detection, and too gross for aggravation."[22]

Murphy agreed with the great man in part, but he deferred to Garrick's skill in providing a practical acting text: "In the play before us, all is confusion, a wild chace of heterogeneous matter. The poet may be said to have placed in view a monster fifty furlongs in length. And yet Garrick thought fit to revive the play, because he knew that amidst all its imperfections, a number of detached beauties would occur to surprise and charm the imagination."[23]

In 1770 Francis Gentleman belatedly added his critical view. "The plot of this play has too strong a taint of romance, and the absolute annihilation of unities is rather offensive. Notwithstanding Mr. Garrick's pains, there are absurdities of a very gross nature. We remember to have seen an alteration of this play by one Mr. Hawkins, played at York, and think it has considerable merit; however, we view Shakespeare between these two gentlemen as a stately tree, abounding with disproportionate superfluities; the former has been so very tender of pruning, that a number of luxuriances remain; and the latter admired the vegetation of his own brain so much, that he has not only cut the noble plant into the stiffness of an yew hedge, but decked it like a may-pole, with poetical garlands, which prove rather gaudy than useful ornaments. Mr. Garrick's is, no doubt, best calculated for action, but Mr. Hawkins's will stand a chance of pleasing every fanciful reader better, because he has in many places harmonized the expression, and rendered the obscure passages more intelligible; however, we wish he had retained more of the original, and Mr. Garrick less."[24]

While no theatre has ventured to stage Garrick's alteration in modern times, we agree with Odell: "Garrick revived the original play with so little alteration that I do not hesitate to pronounce it, as printed the following year, the most accurate of Eighteenth-Century acting versions. Changes there are in the text, but nothing worth quarreling about."[25]

TEXTS

D1 1st edition. London: J. and R. Tonson, 1762.
D2 Dublin: Printed for R. Watts, and W. Whitestone, 1762.
D3 London: Printed for H. Woodfall et al., 1767.
D4 London: J. Rivington *et al.*, 1770.
D5 London: John Bell, 1773.
W1 *Dramatic Works of David Garrick.* [London]: n.p., 1768, Ill, 79–164.
W2 *Dramatic Works of David Garrick.* London: Printed for R. Bald, T. Blaw, and J. Kurt, 1774, I, 269–340.
O1 London: J. Wenman, 1777.

22. Quoted by Arthur Murphy in *The Life of David Garrick* (London, 1801), II, 358.
23. Ibid., pp. 359–60.
24. *The Dramatic Censor* (London, 1770), II., 95.
25. *Shakespeare from Betterton to Irving*, I, 370.

[I, i]

8. referred] handed over.
15. bent] inclination.
29. Cassibelan] the younger brother of Lud.
30. sur-addition] another title.
40. time] age.
45. sample] example.
46. glass] mirror.
75. leaned unto] condescended to.
117. sear up] dry up.
130. fraught] burden.
134. remainders] persons left at Court.
144. touch] twinge or pain.
160. neatherd's] cowherd's.
212. orisons] prayers.
228. Allayments] antidotes.
271. liegers] ambassadors.

[I, ii]

2. crescent] just emerging in importance.
5. tabled] set down, listed.
10. words] describes.
14. extend him] increase his reputation.
21. stranger] foreigner.
71. convince] overcome.
81. moiety] an indefinite share.
112. I . . . lay] I will not permit it to be wagered.
117–18. commendation] introduction.
118. entertainment] welcome.

[II, i]

12. Change you] do you blush?
17. out of door] external.
19. Arabian bird] the phoenix.
37. Partition] distinction.
41. mows] moues, grimaces.
50. raps] transports.
94. snuff] burning candlewick.
131. empery] empire.
146. ramps] prostitutes.
149. runagate] renegade.
164. mart] bargain.
165. stew] brothel.
179. witch] dominating, fascinating person.
180. into] unto.
189. fan] test.
190. chaffless] pure grain without chaff.
201. factor] an agent.
226. tender] presentation.

[II, ii]

1–2. kissed the Jack] in a game of bowls, hit the small bowl.
3. take me up] admonish.
16. jack-slave] lewd fellow.
56. derogation] detraction.

[II, iii]

14. Tarquin] Sextus Tarquinius, who raped Lucrece.
16. Cytherea] Venus.
28. arras] hangings of tapestry.
29. story] illustrated by embroidered tapestry.
31. meaner moveables] knickknacks and occasional small furniture.
36. Gordian knot] Alexander cut this knot binding yoke to chariot pole, the chariot belonging to Gordius, King of Phrygia, making Alexander king of all Asia.
39. madding] maddening.
40. cinque-spotted] five-spotted.
47. The Tale of Tereus] Tereus, the Thracian king, dishonored Philomela, his sister-in-law, and to prevent discovery cut out her tongue. But the lady wove the assault into her tapestry.

[II, v]

8. Marybuds] marigold buds.
11. consider] reward.
13. unpaved] castrated.
74. south-fog] polluted air.

[III, i]

18. statist] statesman.
159. colted] possessed sexually.
179. limb-meal] limb from limb.
184. pervert] divert or turn.

[III, ii]

8. nonpareil] unequalled.
11. pudency] modesty.

[III, iii]

19. Muhmutius] a former king of Britain.

[III, iv]

56. franklin's housewife] a yoeman's wife.

[III, v]

27–28. Such . . . uncrossed] one who is supported by fops who pay the reckoning.
70. demesnes] domains.

[III, vii]

138. Titan] god of the sun.

[IV, iv]

11. journal] daily.
154. clotpoll] head.

[V, i]

6. render] an account.
15. quartered fires] campfires.

[V, ii]

5. wrying] swerving.

[V, iv]

34. chaser] pursuer.

[V, vi]

77. razed out] erased.
206. staggers] dizziness.

A Midsummer Night's Dream

The applause with which *The Fairies*, Garrick's "opera" version of *A Midsummer Night's Dream*, received at Drury Lane Theatre prompted the actor-producer to undertake a revival of Shakespeare's original. It was an unfortunate decision as far as putting on a successful play is concerned, for the play was a complete failure and Garrick was damned for it by the critics. Yet a careful examination of the production—and Garrick's part in it—by George Winchester Stone, Jr.,[1] has proved George Colman to have been the villain of the piece, not Garrick. For it was Colman's version that failed on the night of 23 November 1763.

Garrick had a hand in the production, of course. He had been working on a version of the play since before September 1763, probably with the aid of Colman. Garrick's adaptation, made in a 1734 edition published by Tonson, is preserved in the Folger Shakespeare Library. At any rate, when, discouraged with the personal attacks being made on him and in ill health, he determined to leave the theatre for travel on the Continent, perhaps never to return to the boards, he left Drury Lane in the hands of Colman, together with his working copy of *A Midsummer Night's Dream*. Colman was given a fairly free rein in operating Drury Lane during Garrick's two-year absence

1. "A Midsummer Night's Dream in the Hands of Garrick and Colman," *PMLA*, June 1939, pp. 467–82.

from the stage, along with advice to stress musical and spectacular productions.[2]

Garrick's concern over the fate of *A Midsummer Night's Dream* is reflected in one of the many letters the actor-manager addressed to Colman regarding the offerings at his house. He advised Colman: "As for Midsummer Nights, & I think my presence will be necessary to get it up as it ought—however if you want to, do for ye best—& I'll Ensure It's [*sic*] success."[3] With this support Colman felt he had a free hand to revise the working copy Garrick had left with him, to alter it as completely as he wished. He had, indeed, offered Garrick a considerable number of suggestions for further alterations on the actor's version, as a sheaf of notes in Colman's autograph and dated 19 June 1763, three months before Garrick's departure for the Continent, indicates.[4] The four and a half pages of notes, in which Colman comments on casting, music, spectacle, rhyme, and needed alterations—for example,

ACT 2

Can Miss Wrighten from Ranelagh be got to play *Puck* or any other of the Fairies? I hear a great character of her.

. . . .

P. 27 I'll follow you &c. [Puck's speech, III, i, 95–100.]
I think all this speech sh^{d} be set to Musick, and after Puck has spoken it he sh^{d} sing it—If well set, it must have a good effect; and the words are of a kind that does half the composer's business to his hand—
P. 28 Scene third—a Fairy Dance might very properly be introduced in this scene.

. . . .

P. 45 *Go bid the Huntsmen wake them with their horns.*
Here as they are supposed to be in the wood to observe the Rite of May, it w^{d} have a very good effect to awaken the sleepers with soft Musick accompanied with a song in honor of May Morning—or rather, as the Poet seems to have intended, with the noise of the *Horns* accompanied with a *Hunting Song*—a song however, of some sort or or [*sic*] other, by all means! Suppose you introduce y^{r} ingenious Mr Lee's—

ends with the comment, "On the whole I think it may with care and attention be made a most *novelle* and elegant entertainment—but may tumble for want of amending a few absurdities, and altering some trifling circumstances wch make it uncouth and unsuitable to the taste of the present times. I live in hopes of seeing it a favourite entertainment of next Winter."

Garrick accepted a number of Colman's suggestions, but not all of them. He is not, as Professor Stone has pointed out, nearly so obsessed with Shakespeare's rhymes in some of the love scenes as Colman is. Garrick's friend noted that the rhyming lines on pages 7, 8, and 9 of the Tonson edition are

2. George C. D. Odell, *Shakespeare from Betterton to Irving*, 2 vols. (New York, 1920), I, 376.
3. To George Colman from Paris, 8 October 1763. *Letters*, I, 387.
4. In the Folger Shakespeare Library. In addition to these notes the lot includes a list of songs to be sung, in Garrick's autograph, Prompter Cross's call book giving names and disposition of characters when coming onto the stage, two cast lists with alterations, and a song sung by a fairy, in Edward Capell's hand.

"very uncouth," unfit for the Drury Lane audience. These include such passages as the following, which Colman duly omitted in his 1763 version. Hermia says (I, i, 171–78),

By the simplicity of Venus' doves,
By that which knitteth souls, and prospers loves,
An by that fire which burned the Carthage Queen,
When the false Trojan under sail was seen;
By all the vows that ever men have broke,
In number more than ever women spoke,
In that same place thou hast appointed me,
Tomorrow truly will I meet with thee.

Markings in the Tonson copy, probably made by Colman ("I have marked them a little . . . see the crochets?) would have the lines read,

By the simplicity of Venus' doves,
By all the vows that ever men have broke,
In that same place thou hast appointed me,
Tomorrow truly will I meet Lysander.

Yet the only line decisively marked out, undoubtedly by Garrick, judging from the styles of the two alterers, is the line, "In number more than ever women spoke." Colman, in the 1763 version, reduces the speech still more, getting away from the "uncouth" rhymes: "By all the vows that ever men have broke, / Tomorrow truly will I meet Lysander." He recommended that the rhyming lines on pages 22 and 23 "be thrown out of rhime into plain blank verse–It may be easily done, & will have a much better effect." Among the offending lines are Hermia's (II, ii, 92–98):

How came her eyes so bright? not with salt tears,
If so, my eyes are oftener wash'd than hers,
No, no, I am as ugly as a bear;
For beasts that meet me run away for fear.
Therefore no marvel, tho' Demetrius
Do (as a monster) fly my presence thus.

A more telling example is found in Shakespeare's II, ii, 145–54, Hermia's appeal to Lysander, which Garrick retains:

Help me, Lysander, help me! Do thy best
To pluck this crawling serpent from my breast.
Ay me, for pity, what a dream was here?
Lysander, look how I do quake with fear.
Methought a serpent eat my heart away,
And you sat smiling at his cruel prey.
Lysander! What, remov'd? Lysander, lord!
What, out of hearing? Gone? No sound, no word?
Alack, where are you? Speak, and if you hear,
Speak of all loves. I swoon almost with fear.

Colman, in the 1763 text, breaks up the rhyme (italics ours):

> Help me, Lysander, help me! Do thy best
> To pluck this crawling serpent from my *bosom.*
> Ah me, for pity! What a dream was here?
> Lysander, look how I do quake with *horror.*
> Methought a serpent eat my heart away,
> And you sate smiling at him.—Ha! *Lysander,*
> Lysander! What, remov'd? Lysander, Lord!
> What, out of hearing gone? Out of *sight!*
> Alack, where are you? Speak, and if you hear *me,*
> Speak of all loves. I swoon almost with fear.

Indeed, Colman wanted all scenes except those between the fairies "thrown out of rhime" and cites scenes v, vi, vii, and viii of Shakespeare's act III as proving that "a good deal of the writing in this act is uncouth & wants alteration."

Another striking difference between Garrick's version and Colman's is found at the end of the play. In his four-and-a-half-page commentary on Garrick's alteration Colman referred to the "palpable gross play of Pyramus & Thisbe" and the running commentary thereon of Theseus and Demetrius, insisting that these passages "be shortened as much as possible." Garrick had, in fact, indicated the omission of twenty-two verse and prose lines (in the Tonson printing), fifteen of them comments on the Pyramus-Thisbe play by Theseus and Demetrius. But in the 1763 text Colman removed the "Palapable gross play" entirely. And whereas Garrick cut the whole of the last scene of act V,[5] Colman argued for its retention: "I think it very ill judged to attempt to cut out the concluding Fairy scene.—Restore it with Songs Dances &c at all events." When Colman prepared his stage version he retained the opening eighteen lines of act V, which include the "lunatic, the lover, and the poet" speech of Theseus, but otherwise completely rewrote the act to emphasize the fairies.

That it was Colman's alteration which failed miserably on the night of Wednesday, 23 November 1763, is made clear not only from the published text but from the commentary of William Hopkins in his *Diary*: "This piece was greatly Cut & Alter'd. the 5th Act Entirely left out & many Airs interspers'd all through; got up with a vast deal of trouble to everybody concern'd in it but particularly to Mr. Coleman, who attended every Rehearsal & had alterations innumberable to make. . . . The Sleeping Scene particularly displeas'd. Next day it was reported. The Performers first Sung the Audience to Sleep, & than went to Sleep themselves."[6] It is hardly likely that all of Colman's alterations are to be found in the printed text, as the "Book of the play" was advertised as being available for purchase on opening night.

Professor Stone has shown that the "alteration innumberable" of Col-

5. Scene iii in the Tonson edition. There is no scene division in the standard Shakespeare texts. The omission begins with V, 354.
6. *London Stage*, Part 4, II, 1021.

man include the cutting of 561 lines which Garrick had retained and the extension of some scenes.[7] Nearly every speech is cut, from a few words to a number of lines. Colman also assigned some of the action to characters different from those Shakespeare used, as Professor Stone explains: "In Colman's version the separation of Demetrius and Lysander in their attempted duel is accomplished by Oberon. In Garrick's version, which follows the Shakespearian text, it is done by Puck in a pleasant scene of thirty-two lines. Colman trimmed the number to nineteen and transferred Puck's lines to the Fairy King. The following scene, in which Puck is supposed to put Hermia to sleep and to arrange for a reconciliation, Colman trimmed likewise of four of its lines and gave all of Puck's words to Oberon and another fairy. Puck's part, of which Garrick was interested in keeping as much as possible, loses significance in the Colman version."[8]

A manuscript in the Larpent Collection of the Huntington Library, entitled "New Additions to the Midsummer Night's Dream," contains the annotation, in a second hand, "Garrick's 1763."[9] It gives, in addition to fifteen songs not in Garrick's alteration and some new lines, the seventeen-line dialogue and a four-stanza song added to act I intended to improve the first meeting of Bottom and his artisans. All these changes are made in the 1763 edition, Garrick being on the Continent when they were given to the Lord Chamberlain. Of this addition only the four-stanza song is indicated in Garrick's alteration, and that only by a number, 6. That Garrick intended to include it is proved only by a sheet in Garrick's hand, included among the sheaf of miscellaneous papers relating to the play. He indicated that the song to be added on page 12 of the Tonson edition, song 6, is to be a "Comic Characters Epilogue–Bot. or B." The remainder of the addition is Colman's and appears only in his play–more proof that the printed version of the alteration is more Colman's than Garrick's.

Garrick's alteration indicates the inclusion of twenty-five[10] songs and an opening and a closing chorus. All but two of these are identified in the sheaf of manuscript notes mentioned above. On a single sheet Garrick has indicated, by giving the page number of the Tonson text, where songs are to be inserted, often identifying them with some opening words. And in the Tonson edition we have Garrick's clear indication of where the songs are to be inserted. Only Bottom's "The ousel-cock" song (III, ii, 111–19), which is one of the two songs in Shakespeare's text, and No. 19, a duet between

7. Stone, p. 474. Seventeen lines of dialogue and a song added to the end of act I are credited in the *Variorum* (pp. 43–44) to Garrick but are not indicated in his alterations on the Tonson text.
8. Stone, p. 477.
9. Larpent MS. (6S [1763]).
10. Of the twenty-five songs, Garrick adds a note on "Come, follow, follow me" (No. 10), "May sing or not," and on "You spotted snakes" (No. 11) and "How calm's the sky" (No. 14), "May sing." One speech, Puck's "Up and down" (Shakespeare's III, ii, 396–99), Garrick had first intended as a song, but the word is marked out and "Said" is indicated. This revision seems to be Colman's.

Helena and Hermia, are omitted, the latter inadvertantly.[11] The songs indicated in Garrick's alteration include thirteen from the opera *The Fairies*, of which six are taken from Shakespeare (one, however, being changed to "said," probably an emendation in Colman's hand). On this list Garrick did not mention Oberon's "Flower of this purple dye" (Shakespeare's III, ii, 102–9) and Bottom's "The ousel-cock, so black of hue" surely because they are integral parts of Shakespeare's text. Six of the songs on Garrick's list are marked "New."

Colman's printed version of the play contains thirty-three songs and a chorus, twenty-two and the chorus from the Garrick version and eleven others, three of which are from *The Fairies*.[12] Eight are new, including "Kingcup, daffodil and rose," which Colman has substituted for Shakespeare's "Where the bee sucks," from *The Tempest* (V, i, 88–94), and which Garrick had used in *The Fairies* and again in his *Midsummer Night's Dream*. Colman, then, added more to the play than Garrick had done, cut more of Shakespeare than Garrick had done, and in general did not show the high regard that Garrick held for the purity of Shakespeare's texts.[13]

Garrick, stopping in Naples, read the review of Colman's effort which appeared in the *St. James Chronicle* the day after its single performance, the reviewer chastising the house for bad acting by the adult actors, poor singing, and a "flat and uninteresting" love story and celebration of the Theseus-Hippolita marriage. "The poor Mids. Night's Dream I find has fail'd," he wrote to Colman on 24 December,[14] perhaps recalling his earlier insistance, "as for *Midsummer Nights, &c.* I think my presence will be necessary to get it up as it ought." Clearly it had not been got up as it ought, for only the fairy scenes pleased and only the acting of the children was held to be satisfactory, particularly as they had "to struggle under such a Heap of Rubbish."[15]

The time was probably not propitious for a revival of Shakespeare's fanciful comedy—the speeches of Theseus, the same reviewer remarked, "are fitter for the Closet than the Stage"—and it is by no means to be supposed that Garrick's version would have fared much better. But Colman did rescue something from the "Heap of Rubbish"; three days after its single performance he produced *A Fairy Tale*, an afterpiece of two short acts built upon the fairy scenes and centered on the Oberon-Titania dispute. Hopkins noted

11. Shakespeare's songs are "You spotted snakes" (II, ii, 9–24) by the Fairies and Bottom's song (Shakespeare's III, i, 111–14, 116–19). In addition, a Fairy song and dance is indicated at V, i, 383, but the lyrics are not given.
12. "Sigh no more, ladies, sigh no more (III, vii), "Orpheus, with his lute, made trees" (III, vii), and "Hark, hark, how the hounds and horn" (III, viii).
13. Note, for example, Garrick's taking trouble to make even minor changes in the Tonson text to restore Shakespeare's reading: for example, in I, i, 62, he corrects Tonson's "earlier" to Shakespeare's "earthlier"; in I, i, 182, he changes Tonson's "your words I'd catch" to Shakespeare's "yours would I catch"' and in III, ix, 84, he changes Tonson's "on, you canker" to Shakespeare's "you canker."
14. *Letters*, I, 397.
15. *St. James Chronicle*, 24 November, 1763.

in his *Diary* that it was well received, and it played often through the season. Hopkins wrote, "Mr. Colman thought it was a pity so much pains and expense as was bestowed on the *Midsummer Night's Dream* should be thrown away,—he luckily thought of turning it into a farce, which alteration he made in one night,—and now I think as pleasing a farce as most that are done."[16] So Garrick was at last pleased, writing to his brother George from Naples on 31 January 1764: "Tell Colman I love him more and more & thank him most cordially for his Fairy Tale." The farce had made up at least in part for the financial disaster which had been Colman's production of Shakespeare's play.

TEXTS

G Garrick's prompt (and call book) made on the Louis Theobald text published by J. Tonson "and the rest of the Proprietors." London, 1734. Colman also made emendations in this copy.

S *A Midsummer-Night's Dream.* London: J. Tonson and the rest of the Proprietors, 1734.

[1, i]

4. lingers] tediously postpones fulfillment.
5. dowager] a widow with a dower.
19. triumph] public display.
39. immediately] expressly.
44. kind] respect. voice] approval.
50. concern] befit.
61. blood] passions.
62. earthlier happy] happier on earth.
66. patent] privilege.
83. protest] vow.
92. estate] bestow.
94. well possessed] well off.
100. head] face.
118. Against] in preparation for.
119. nearly that] that closely.
139. fancy's] love's.
143. respects] regards.
166. golden head] the arrowhead that kindles love.
167. simplicity] harmlessness.
175. fair] beauty.
176. loadstars] guiding stars.
177. tuneable] musical.
181. favor] physical qualities.
194. Phoebe] Diana, the moon.

[1, ii]

2. generally] severally (a malapropism).
3. scrip] list of actors.
20–21. condole] lament.

16. Hopkins diary—MacMillan. *London Stage*, Part 4, II, 1022.

22. Ercles] Hercules. to tear a cat] to rant.
24. Phibbus'] Phoebus'.
60. aggravate] meaning *modulate*.
67. discharge] perform.
68. purple-in-grain] dyed red.
76. obscenely] meaning *obscurely*?
79. Hold . . . bowstrings] probably meaning *be there*.

[II, i]

9. orbs] fairy rings.
10. pensioners] bodyguards.
23. lob] lout.
27. passing . . . wrath] very angry and wrathful.
30. changeling] a person, especially a child, surreptitiously put in exchange of another. Fairies were said to steal babies and leave their imps in their place. Here the idea is given from the point of view of the fairies: the child taken is called a changeling.
37. square] quarrel. that] so that.
47. gossip's] a gossiping woman's.
48. crab] crabapple.
55. quire] assembly.
56. waxen] wax, increase. neeze] sneeze.
65. step] mountain.
66. Amazon] Hippolita, queen of the Amazons.
67. buskined] wearing high boots.
71. Glance at] attack indirectly.
74–76. Perigune . . . Antiopa] reference to women Theseus had loved.
78. spring] beginning.
82. ringlets] round dances.
85. chiding] Shakespeare's "childing," fruitful.
90. original] source.
94. henchman] page.
141. Since] when.
151. vestal] virgin.
161. love-in-idleness] the pansy.
199. impeach] make questionable.
205. privilege] protection.
209. respect] regard.
214. Apollo . . . chase] in the myth, Apollo pursued Daphne; here the woman pursues the man.
215. griffin] a monster, part lion, part eagle.
217. stay thy] stay to hear.
233. oxslip] a flower like a cowslip or primrose.
234. woodbine] honeysuckle.
235. eglantine] sweetbriar.
239. Weed] garment.

[III, i]

1. roundel] a dance.
3. cankers] little worms.
4. rearmice] bats.

7. queint] quaint, but meaning fine, dainty.
11. Newts] salamanders. blindworms] limbless lizards.
13. Philomel] the nightingale.
29. ounce] a wild cat resembling a small leopard.
30. Pard] leopard.
64. approve] put to the test.
86. owe] own, possess.
100. sphery] starlike.
142. prey] preying.

[III, ii]

3–4. tiring house] dressing room.
10. By'r lakin] by our lady. parlous] perilous.
18. eight and six] lines of eight and six syllables, alternating.
29. defect] meaning *effect.*
46. disfigure] meaning *figure forth.*

[III, iii]

3. toward] about to begin.
18. brisky juvenile] brisk youth.
20. Ninny's tomb] the tomb of Ninus in Ovid's tale.
38. translated] transformed.
43. ousel] blackbird.
46. quill] pipe.
49. plain-song] simple melody.
50–51. Whose note . . . nay] reference to the fact that the cuckoo's note resembles the sound of "cuckhold" and thus falls unhappily on a husband's ear.
61. gleek] scoff.
68. still] always.

[III, iv]

26. Squash] an unripe peapod.
30. patience] endurance under hardship.

[III, v]

3. in extremity] extremely.
5. night-rule] business of the night.
9. patches] clowns.
13. barren] stupid.
17. nole] head.
29. latched] fastened, sealed (i.e., moistened).
33. force] necessity.

[III, vii]

8. Tartar's bow] the Siberian Tartars were known for their skill in archery.
21. fond] foolish.
26. sport alone] unique sport.
28. prepost'rously] in wrong order.

[III, viii]

4. nativity all truth appears] such vows are obviously true.
23. trim] neat, used ironically.

[III, ix]

14. Injurious] insulting.
22. artificial] skilled in art.
32–33. Two of . . . crest] two bodies (as in double coats in heraldry, one the man's and the other his wife's) but a single heart and therefore a single crest.
56. perserve] persevere.
57. mouths] faces.
61. argument] subject of a story.
85. canker-blossom] worm that destroys blossoms.

[IV, i]

8. sort] turn out.
15. wrong] insults.
20. virtuous] beneficial or potent.
30. night's swift dragons] the goddess of Night had a team of dragons.
31. Aurora's harbinger] the morning star.
42. drawn] with drawn sword.

[IV, iii]

2. coy] caress.
28. neaf] fist.
28–29. leave your courtesy] don't doff your hat.
31. Cavalero] cavalier, gentleman.
36–37. tongs and the bones] crude musical instruments.
40. bottle] bundle.
45. exposition of] disposition to.
49. woodbine] bindweed.
73. Dian's bud] perhaps *agnus castus*, said to be a preservative of chastity.
83. these five] Bottom and the two couples.
103. *Wind*] blow.

[IV, iv]

2. observation] ritual of May Day.
3. vaward] forefront, earliest part (vanguard).
13. chiding] noise.
18. flewed] large-chapped. sanded] sandy colored.
21. mouth] voice. It is said that Elizabethan huntsmen developed packs of hounds whose voices were harmonious.
22. Each under each] with different notes.
37. Saint Valentine . . . past] traditionally birds begin to mate on Saint Valentine's Day.
88. parted eye] unfocused eyes.

[IV, V]

5–6. go about] try.
8. patched fool] clown.

[IV, vi]

2. transported] transformed.
11–12. thing of nought] wicked thing.
20. hearts] fine fellows.
29. preferred] requested.

[V, i]

3. toys] trifles.
8. compact] composed.
11. Sees Helen's . . .] visualizes Helen of Troy when looking at an ordinary girl.
26. constancy] certainty.
49. abridgment] pastime.
52. brief] schedule of events.
54. battle . . . Centaurs] Hercules and Theseus took part in such a battle at a wedding.
58–59. The riot . . . rage] Orpheus was torn to pieces by drunken women at a Bacchanal.
65. sorting] befitting.
83. unbreathed] unpracticed.
103. Takes it . . . merit] takes the will for the deed.
104. clerks] scholars.
107. periods] full stops.
116. my capacity] my understanding.
117. addressed] ready.

[V, ii]

0. Vaughn] an actor in Garrick's company.
7. upon points] about punctuation, and about trifling matters.
8–9. the stop] a term from horsemanship.
12. government] control.
27. hight] called.
35. broached] stabbed, opened.
50. sinister] left.
81–82. Limander. . . . Helen] meaning *Leander* and *Hero*.
83. Shafalus . . . Procrus] Cephalus, Procris.
88. 'Tide] betide, come.
103. fell] fierce.
110. lanthorn] lantern.
118. for] because of.
119. in snuff] in need of being snuffed.
144. dole] grief.
152. thread and thrum] the warp and the loose threads of a piece of cloth.
153. Quail] overpower. quell] kill.
181. means] complains. *videlicet*] as follows.

193. Sisters Three] the Fates.
197. shore] shorn.
201. imbrue] make bloody.
208. Bergomask dance] rustic dance from Bergamo, Italy.

Hamlet

The 1742–43 season brought the official closing of Giffard's theatre in Ayliffe Street, Goodman's Fields, and the advent of David Garrick as the most important actor on the roster of Drury Lane. Once installed as a member of the Drury Lane Company, Garrick lost little time in appearing in all the leading roles which had made him popular at Goodman's Fields. In rapid succession he gave the new audience at Drury Lane his interpretations of Chamont in *The Orphan*, Bayes in *The Rehearsal*, Richard III, Clodio in *Love Makes a Man*, Captain Plume in *The Recruiting Officer*, King Lear in *King Lear and His Three Daughters*, and Fondlewife in *The Old Bachelor*. Then on 16 November 1742 he made his first London appearance as Hamlet. Thomas Davies remarked on this transfer to Drury Lane: "Mr. Garrick now considered himself in a different situation from that in which he had hitherto been placed. As manager and actor of Goodman's Fields playhouse, he thought himself warranted to act with somewhat less caution, and to venture at bolder hazards, than when he found himself ranked as the principal actor in the King's theatre of Drury Lane . . . Hamlet was a part which he knew the public expected from him. He had prepared himself for the able discharge of this task, by having very carefully acted it in Ireland."[1]

Garrick had spent the summer prior to his opening at Drury Lane acting with Peg Woffington at the New Theatre in Smock Alley, Dublin. At the end of this brief season, in which he raised a "Garrick fever" and gained for himself the appellation of a new "Roscius," he gave the Irish his interpretation of *Hamlet* on 12 August 1742 and repeated his performance some days later. Leaving Ireland in August he had ample time to improve upon his experiment before his first appearance as a regular member of the Drury Lane company. After a round of his usual roles, he introduced the Londoners to his Danish prince on 16 November 1742. Evidently his interpretation was slow in catching the fancy of this more sophisticated audience despite a number of "Command performances," for there is a manuscript note to the effect that his first benefit night, 13 January 1743, was "not crowded, opened lobby to dispose of tickets."[2] However, Garrick eventually became *the* Hamlet for most eighteenth-century playgoers, playing the role eighty-seven times before his retirement in 1776. He took his place with the great Hamlets, Thomas Betterton and Robert Wilks. Indeed, G. C. D. Odell writes: "This play . . . was handed down from Betterton to Wilks, by him to Garrick, and by Bell to Kemble, almost unchanged in its acting estate. The "frenchifying" of it by Garrick 1772 was the only break in the inheritance."[3]

1. *Memoirs of the Life of David Garrick, Esq.* (London, 1808), I, 59, 62.
2. 13 January 1743. *The London Stage*, Part 3, II, 1027.
3. *Shakespeare from Betterton to Irving*, II, 33.

Betterton first appeared as Hamlet at Lincoln's Inn Fields on 24 August 1661, playing an alteration of the tragedy based on Sir William Davenant's alteration of a 1637 quarto. The drama "being too long to be conveniently acted," Betterton cut it drastically but retained its dramatic structure. Gone were Voltimand and Cornelius, all matters concerning Fortinbras except the ending, Claudius's speech on the state of government, Polonius's advice to Laertes and his brief scene with Reynaldo, Hamlet's advice to the players, Polonius's lines on hypocrisy and the comment of the King, the flattery of the King by Rosencrantz and Guildenstern in the oratory. Additional lines of dialogue were reduced: Horatio's interpretation of the preparations for war, Claudius's reproof of Hamlet's melancholy, the soliloquy "O that this too too solid flesh would melt," Polonius's and Laertes's advice to Ophelia, Hamlet's comments on Danish drinking habits, the first colloquy with the Ghost, the conversation with the First Player and the Player's recitation, the Mouse-Trap, and the Queen's closet scene. This text was published in 1703 by Richard Wellington.

At Betterton's death in 1710, the role passed to Robert Wilks, who became the popular Hamlet in London. His acting version was carefully made in collaboration with the poet-playwright John Hughes and aimed at restoration of more of Shakespeare than had been offered in the Davenant-Betterton alteration. Wilks cut the Dumb Show and the Fortinbras ending, but restored such passages as "Angels and Ministers of Grace defend us!" and Hamlet's instructions to the players. The Hughes-Wilks text was published in 1718 by J. Darby and was reprinted at least five times. While Wilks was followed in the role by such actors as Henry Giffard at Goodman's Fields, William Mills and William Milward at Drury Lane, and Lacy Ryan at Covent Garden, these actors were soon eclipsed by David Garrick, whose interpretation became the accepted one for the next thirty-four years.

Garrick began acting the Hughes-Wilks alteration and, as the seasons wore on, on the advice of scholars and friends[4] and his own intuitive resources, he cut, added, and revised this text from time to time. At least *two* texts altered by Garrick appear to have been published in succeeding years. The first was that of J. and P. Knapton &c. in 1751, the year in which Garrick and his wife first visited the Continent. To date, scholars have not identified this printing as Garrick's; indeed, its title page reads only, "As it is now Acted by His Majesty's Servants." But a comparison with a second altered version published by Hawes and Company &c. in 1763, one we are certain was Garrick's, shows little change except for brief omissions or restorations typical of Garrick's continued study. The 1763 text even includes the same verbal changes appearing in 1751, such as I, ii: Saw! who? (*for* Saw who?); II, ii, 584: O! what a wretch (*for* O! what a rogue); III, i, 72: The pangs of despis'd love (*for* The pangs of dispriz'd love); V, i, 201: Alas! poor Yorick. I knew him well, Horatio (*for* . . . I knew him, Horatio); V, ii, 374: And choirs of angels (*for* And flights of angels). All this is a reminder that Garrick was continually at work on his revisions.

The 1751 alteration follows the Hughes-Wilks text of 1718 except for

4. Dr. Samuel Johnson and Bishop William Warburton.

several important omissions. Charles Beecher Hogan's *Shakespeare in the Theatre, 1701–1800* identifies these as follows: Act I–Horatio's description of the portents of Rome, Marcellus's lines on the celebration of the Saviour's birth; ii–the King's message to Norway; iii–Laertes's advice to his sister, Polonius's advice to Laertes; iv–the passage beginning, "So, oft it chances in particular men;" v–Hamlet's lines to the Ghost in the cellarage. In Garrick's customary manner of breaking up long speeches, the Ghost's "O horrible!" is spoken by Hamlet. Act II, i–Polonius's scene with Reynaldo; ii–the return of Voltimand and Cornelius, lines of Hamlet to Rosencrantz and Guildenstern about Fortune and "a king of infinite space," Hamlet's lines about child actors, the description of Pyrrhus, and from the soliloquy, "O, what a rogue and peasant slave am I!," the lines about John-a-dreams. Act III, ii–bawdy lines before the play, the Dumb Show, the Player King's discourse on will and fate; iii–Rosencrantz and Guildenstern flatter Claudius, Hamlet's refusal to kill the King at prayer; iv–some fifty lines from the closet scene. Act IV, i–the King's anxiety and his determination to send Hamlet abroad; iii–Hamlet's discourse on worms, the King's plan to have Hamlet killed in England; iv–Hamlet's scene with the Norwegian captain, and the soliloquy, "How all occasions do inform against me;" v–the Gentleman's description of Ophelia's madness, the song "By Gis and by Saint Charity," the King's speech about "the poison of deep grief;" vii–the description of Ophelia's drowning. Act V, i–Hamlet's comments on a lawyer as "a great buyer of land"; ii–the schemes for Hamlet's death and that of Rosencrantz and Guildenstern, Hamlet's reply to Osric concerning Laertes, and the Fortinbras ending.[5]

The 1763 alteration was published by Haws and Company while Garrick was abroad on his second trip to the Continent, a time when, because of ill health, critical attacks, and a period of unpopularity, Garrick seriously contemplated retirement. Except for the usual brief omissions and restorations it was no major improvement on the 1751 text. In fact this printing omits the cuts previously marked for omission in 1751, so that it consists of a mere seventy-two pages.

Upon his return from the Continent, a command performance of *Much Ado about Nothing* brought Garrick renewed confidence in his reception by audiences and a renewed interest in Shakespeare. He continued to play *Hamlet* in his latest revision until the 1772–73 season, when he brought out his long-planned new look at the tragedy. In this venture he had much encouragement from friends such as George Steevens and John Hoadly. Steevens wrote him in 1771 to say, "I expect great pleasure from the perusal of your altered "Hamlet." It is a circumstance in favour of the poet which I have long been wishing for. Dr. Johnson allots to this tragedy the praise of variety; but in my humble opinion, that variety is often impertinent, and always languishing on the stage." After discussing his dislike for what he terms tragicomedy and offering *Hamlet* as a prime example, Steevens continues: "I think you need not fear that the better half of your audience, (as Othello says,) *should yawn at alteration* . . . I cannot answer for our good

5. II, 187–88.

friends in the gallery. You had better throw what remains of the piece into a farce, to appear immediately afterwards. No foreigner who should happen to be present at the exhibition, would ever believe it was formed out of the loppings and excrescences of the tragedy itself. You may entitle it, "The Grave-Diggers; with the pleasant Humours of Osrick, the Danish Macaroni."[6] Hoadly wrote to Garrick on 10 January 1773 in much the same vein: "As to Hamlet, we have before now talked of the possibility of altering it; and as it was resolved at last, I am sorry I knew nothing of the matter. By your account, and twenty-five lines only added, I fear too little has been done."[7]

But it was certainly the experience of his second visit to France and a deepening of the influence of French criticism that determined Garrick to enter upon the unprecedented venture of relieving this tragedy of what he termed "the rubbish of the fifth act." On 18 December 1772 he appeared in still another alteration, to the dismay of many critics and the enthusiasm of London audiences for novelty at any price. William Hopkins, the prompter, commented on the occasion: "The Tragedy of Hamlet having been greatly Alterd by D. G. was perform'd for the first time Mr. Garrick playd divinely & Merited the great Applause he receivd It is Alterd much for the better in regard to the part of Hamlet & I think the alteration very fine & proper."

George Winchester Stone, Jr., discovered Garrick's preparation copy for the 1772 alteration in the Folger Shakespeare Library and described it at length, publishing the final act in its entirety.[8] The complete text printed herein is now published for the first time with the kind permission of the Folger Library. With notes, cuts, and emendations in Garrick's own hand, we are now able to assess what he wished to accomplish.

It was not made from Garrick's 1763 alteration, or that of 1751. Instead, he returned to a 1748 printing of the old Hughes-Wilks text he knew so well. Having decided to eliminate Shakespeare's act V, he had to restore much from the earlier acts which had not been played for over fifty years. Dr. Stone writes: "He was not interested in merely leaving out the Grave-Diggers and Osric, as the critics suppose; having cut the greater part of the fifth act he had to restore almost as much in the preceding part of the play, and in restoring some six hundred and twenty-nine lines he succeeded in giving the eighteenth-century audience a new interpretation of almost all the characters in the play."[9]

By 1772 a considerable volume of scholarly material on Shakespeare had appeared. All this Garrick seems to have consulted, especially Johnson's edition. In a letter to Madam Necker he describes his intentions succinctly: "The first act which is very long in the original is by me divided into two acts—the third act, as I act it, is the second in the original—the third in the original is the fourth in mine, and ends with the famous scene between Hamlet and

6. James Boaden, *The Private Correspondence of David Garrick* (London, 1831–32), I, 451–52.
7. Ibid, I, 515.
8. "Garrick's Long Lost Alteration of *Hamlet*," *PMLA*, 38 (September 1934), 890–921.
9. Ibid., p. 897.

his mother—and the fifth act in my alteration consists of the fourth and fifth of the original with some small alterations, and the omission of some scenes, particularly the Gravediggers."[10] Actually Garrick made no serious alterations in the action prior to the concluding act, which is quite brief. James Boaden claims to have witnessed a performance of the alteration, and in his *Life of Kemble* he describes act V.

He cut out the voyage to England, and the execution of Rosencrantz and Guildenstern. . . . He omitted the funeral of Ophelia, and all the wisdom of the prince, and the rude jocularity of the grave-diggers. Hamlet bursts in upon the King and his court, and Laertes reproaches him with his father's and his sister's death. The exasperation of both is at its height, when the king interposes; he had commanded Hamlet to depart for England, and declares that he will no longer bear this rebellious conduct, but that his wrath shall at length fall heavy on the prince. "First," exclaims Hamlet, "feel you mine"; and he instantly stabs him. The queen rushes out imploring the attendants to save her from her son. Laertes, seeing treason and murder before him, attacks Hamlet to revenge his father, his sister, and his King. He wounds Hamlet mortally, and Horatio is on the point of making Laertes accompany him to the shades, when the prince commands him to desist, assuring him that it was the hand of Heaven, which administered by Laertes "that precious balm for all his wounds." We then learn that the miserable mother had dropt in a trance ere she could reach her chamber-door, and Hamlet implores for her "an hour of penitence ere madness end her." He then joins the hands of Laertes and Horatio, and commands them to unite their virtues (a coalition of ministers) "to calm the troubled land." The old couplet, as to the bodies, concludes the play.[11]

In Dr. Stone's analysis of the first four acts of the alteration he notes that ninety-four lines were restored in the first act, especially the scene in which the ambassadors depart for Norway. Since Garrick wished to include the soliloquy, "How all occasions do inform against me," he had to restore Voltimand and Cornelius and the matters concerning Fortinbras. Forty-three lines in act II were restored to the domestic scene between Polonius and his children, and the entire speech of the Ghost was restored. The command of the Ghost that Horatio and Marcellus swear on Hamlet's sword is given but once, sacrificing some seventeen lines of the earlier text. Act III included for the first time the Polonius-Reynaldo scene and more information about Fortinbras. Garrick followed his own earlier alterations in cuts from the Rosencrantz and Guildenstern scene with Hamlet, and portions of the Players' first scene, but he restored twenty lines of the speech about Pyrrhus and Priam. His soliloquy, "O! what a *wretch* and peasant slave am I," followed the earlier texts, beginning with that of Wilks in 1718. In act IV the Dumb Show was omitted, but the Mouse-Trap play was restored in its entirety for the first time. Restored also are the plot to get Hamlet out of the country, the whole of the King's prayer and Hamlet's reactions, and many lines formerly cut from the Queen's closet scene.

To the surprise of many critics, including Boaden, who declared that the alteration "was written in a mean and trashy common-place manner, and in a word, sullied the page of Shakespeare, and disgraced the taste and

10. *Letters of David Garrick*, III, 1095.
11. I, 111–12.

judgment of Mr. Garrick," public reaction and that of newspapers and magazines was enthusiastic. The *Westminster Magazine*, 1773 (p. 35), rejoiced: "The tedious interruptions of this beautiful tale no longer disgrace it; its absurd disgressions are no longer disgusting. . . . many other inaccuracies are obviated by the simple effects of transposing, expunging, and the addition of a few lines.—Necessary innovations! when introduced by the acquisition of such splendid Advantages. We have now to boast that this brilliant Creation of the Poet's Fancy is purged from the Vapours and Clouds which obscured it; and, like his own Firmament, it appears to be finely fretted with Golden Stars."

Garrick played his alteration twelve times, then turned the role over to other actors such as Gentleman, Smith, and Henderson. It was played twenty-two more nights prior to Garrick's death and then abandoned. According to Dr. Stone, "Garrick received during his four remaining years on the stage £3426.14.10 for this alteration alone. Scarcely any other play brought in more box receipts. An average full house brought the managers £160. Garrick's first three performances of this altered version brought £284.5.6., £272 and £264.13 respectively."[12] But later critics have been uniformly hostile, ranging from Garrick's early biographers and John Genest to the present. *Town and Country Magazine* (December 1772) warned: "How far the critics will approve these mutations we will not at present determine; but the admirers of Shakespear must certainly be displeased, whenever they find his immortal works thus mutilated."[13]

With the alteration in its entirety now before us, we hope to vindicate in some measure Garrick's impudence. He himself admitted as much to Sir William Young in the last months before his retirement: "I have ventured to produce Hamlet, with alterations. It was the most imprudent thing I ever did in all my life; but I had sworn I would not leave the stage till I had rescued that noble play from all the rubbish of the fifth act. I have brought it forth without the Grave-digger's trick and the fencing match. The alteration was received with general approbation, beyond my most warm expectations."[14] We agree with Dr. Stone that Garrick's alteration is "an effective play, has lost a few 'drops of that immortal man' as was consistent with his scheme, has restored hundreds of lines to enrich every part, has with care adopted Shakespeare's text in many cases, and has added but thirty-seven lines of his own."[15]

And before we smile too broadly at Garrick's imprudence, it might be well to remind ourselves that we are not much changed in our own taste. During World War II Maurice Evans and a troupe of entertainers created what became known as *The G. I. Hamlet*, a version especially adapted for United States military audiences around the world. Evans, who had already played *Hamlet* in professional cut versions and a full-length version, wanted the play to speak with rapid action to the troops. In his preface to the

---

12. "Garrick's Long Lost Alteration of Hamlet," p. 894.
13. *The Theatre*, No. 41, p. 658.
14. *Letters of David Garrick*, II, 845–46.
15. "Garrick's Long Lost Alteration of Hamlet," p. 902.

printed text he describes how he and director George Schaeffer went about preparing their text.

Comparison with the full text will reveal the considerable ingenuity with which the objective was achieved, but all our labours with the blue pencil could not compress the second act sufficiently. A final count showed that we were still a full fifteen minutes overtime. I reviewed the cuts in other acting editions and simply could not stomach them. Most of them left out the "How all occasions" soliloquy—an unthinkable omission in a performance before soldiers—and many of the valuable little scenes in the middle of the act where the play acquires almost a "cops and robbers" flavour. . . . It wasn't until I lighted on an old prompt script of David Garrick's that I felt emboldened to follow his example and strike out altogether the graveyard scene. Not only did this give us the fifteen minutes which we considered more valuable, but it also removed from the play an inconsistency of which, probably, only those who have played Hamlet are fully aware. At the end of the graveyard scene Hamlet rushes from the stage, frenzied with grief over the death of Ophelia and shattered by his encounter with Laertes; yet he is required to re-enter only seven lines later, chatting blithely with Horatio about his adventures with the pirates on the high seas and his crafty disposal of Rosencrantz and Guildenstern. This sudden transition is as impossible to make with any kind of grace or conviction that I believe there are very real grounds for guessing that the graveyard scene was an addition to the original text, and that it was written in for some reason as simple as that Shakespeare had forgotten to include a part for the Globe's favourite comedian."[16]

Not only was the Evans production popular with the troops, but it was produced by Michael Todd at New York's Columbus Circle Theatre on 13 December 1945 for a run of 147 performances. Whether the scene is Drury Lane in 1772 or New York City in 1945—theatre audiences do not differ much in taste.

[1, i]

17. Dane] the king of Denmark.
42. pole] the polestar.
55. buried Denmark] Hamlet's father.
70. Norway] Fortinbras the elder.
71. parle] parley.
72. Pole-ax] Polish infantry. Early editions printed "pollax."
83. foreign mart] foreign trade.
84. impress] conscription.
93. emulent] envious.
99. seized on] owned.
100. moiety competent] equal portion.
101. gaged] pledged.
108. Sharked up a list] enlisted indiscriminately.
109. For food and diet] for cannon fodder.
110. stomach] courage.
116. head] origin.

16. *Maurice Evans' G.I. Production of Hamlet by William Shakespeare* (New York, 1947), pp. 12–13.

117. romage] bustle.
119. sort] be fitting.
130. doomsday with eclipse] see Matt. 24:29.
136. soft] hold.
150. partisan] pike.
166. extravagant and erring] abnormal. hies] hurries.
168. made probation] established proof.
174. strike] cause evil influence.
175. takes] bewitches.
178. russet] red-brown.

[I, ii]

8. sometimes] former.
10. defeated] reluctant.
11. auspicious . . . dropping] pleasant . . . tearful.
13. dole] grief.
31. gait herein] proceeding in this purpose.
38. dilated] detailed.
63. thy fair hour] thy youth.
64. thy best graces . . . will] your virtues give you self-control.
65. cousin] kinsman.
68. i' th' sun] sunshine of king's favor, a pun on sun/son.
69. nightly] dark.
77. particular] personal.
104. in grace whereof] in honor of which.
107. solid] some scholars argue for "sullied." "Solid" is the reading of the first folio.
132. I'll change . . . you] I'll exchange friendship.
137. what . . . makes you] what is it you are doing.
148. hard upon] soon after.
151. my dearest foe] my most hated foe.
170. waste] darkness. "Waste" is the reading of the first folio and the second quarto.
172. *cap-à-pie*] from head to foot.
175. oppressed] startled.
191. even] just.
206. beaver] visor, face guard.
215. Very like] to be sure.
219. grizzled] gray.
237. doubt] fear.

[II, i]

7. a fashion and a toy] a fad and a whim.
9. Forward] premature.
11. but so?] but that?
13. crescent] maturing.
14. thews] strength. waxes] matures.
16. withal] simultaneously.
17. cautel] deceit.
22. carve for himself] choose for himself.
38. chariest] most discreet.

41. canker galls] cankerworm ruins.
42. buttons] buds.
53. reaks . . . reed] heeds not his own advice.
64. character] inscribe.
85. Marry] an oath.
94. tenders] offers.
97. Unsifted] untested.
107. fashion] fad. go to, go to] come, come.
110. springes] snares.
120. larger tether] more opportunity.
121. In few] in short.
122. brokers] pimps.
126. This is for all] this is my last word on the subject.
128. slander] disgrace.

[II, ii]

1. shrewdly] bitterly.
2. eager] sharp.
7. held his wont] was accustomed.
10. Rhenish] Rhine wine.
17. breach] neglect.
28. cerements] graveclothes, shrouds.
39. impartment] disclosure.
64. the Nemean lion] lion killed as one of Hercules's twelve labors.
66. lets] hinders.
98. eternal blazon] revelation of eternity.
111. Lethe's wharf] bank of the river of forgetfulness in Hades.
115. process] account.
140. secure hour] unguarded hour.
141. hebona] poisonous plant in fiction.
148. eager] acid.
150. tetter] eruption of the skin. barked about] scabbed.
151. lazar-like] leprous.
156. Unhouseled, unappointed, unaneal'd] without the sacrament of communion, unabsolved, not anointed with extreme unction.
162. luxury] lust.
176. table] notebook.
177. fond] foolish.
178. forms and pressures] images and impressions.
187. word] motto.
195. Hillo . . . boy] traditional falconer's call.
206. arrant] unqualified.
210. circumstance] details.
222. honest] real, actual.
248. giving out] hint.

[III, i]

8. Danskers] Danes.
21. forgeries] inventions.
28. drabbing] whoring.
33. quaintly] delicately.

37. Of general assault] common to all youth.
48. prenominate] previously named.
50. closes . . . consequence] agrees with you as follows.
52. addition] title.
63. o'ertook in's rouse] drunk.
66. *Videlicet*] namely.
68. reach] awareness.
69. windlasses . . . bias] winding courses and indirect attempts.
76. in yourself] with your own eyes.
78. ply his music] carry on.
83. closet] sitting room.
86. down-gyved] hanging down in coils.
110. ecstasy] madness.
111. property forgoes] quality destroys.
121. quoted] noted.
122. beshrew my jealousy] curse my suspicions.
124. cast beyond ourselves] to overcalculate.

[III, ii]

6. Sith] since.
32. full bent] entirely (a bow bent its farthest).
49. Hunts . . . sure] does not exercise cunning.
56. grace] honor.
58. main] principal subject.
69. borne in hand] deceived.
83. likes] pleases.
122. *numbers*] verses.
124. *machine*] his body.
134. fain] willingly.
140. given my heart a winking] tried to be unconcerned.
151. watch] wakefulness.
164. centre] center of the earth.
171. arras] decorative wall hanging.
179. board] accost.
195. by] about.
207. honesty] decency.
214. happiness] aptness.
229. the beaten way of friendship] as old friends.
233. justly] honestly.
237. color] conceal.
241. consonancy] congeniality.
242. dear] important.
243. even] honest.
246. of] on.
249. moult no feather] be undamaged.
257. express] precise.
263–64. Lenten entertainment] a meager reception.
267–68. foil and target] rapier and shield.
278–79. picture in little] miniature.
290. clouts] clothes.
291. Haply] perhaps.
296. Roscius] Cicero's favorite comic actor.

303–4. scene undividable] plays written observing the unities of time, place, and action.

304. poem unlimited] plays unrestricted by the Unities. *Seneca*] Roman tragic playwright.

305. *Plautus*] Roman writer of farce-comedy.

312. Jephtha . . . Israel] title of a ballad, see Judg. 11:34–39.

318. row] line. rubric] direction in a prayer book.

321. valanced] bearded.

324. chopine] thick-soled shoe of fashion.

327. quality] artistry.

333. Aeneas's] Virgil's hero in the *Aeneid*. Dido] queen of Cathage.

334. Priam's] the king of Troy.

335. Pyrrhus] son of Achilles.

336. Hyrcanian beast] a tiger.

347. Repugnant] disobedient.

349. fell] deadly.

350. Ilium] Troy's "topless towers."

351. his] its.

359. against] before.

360. rack] formation of clouds.

365. Cyclops'] giants who assisted Vulcan, the gods' smith.

366. Mars] Roman god of war. proof] trial.

371. felloes] fellies, rims of wheels.

372. nave] hub.

376. jig] brief farce or interlude.

377. Hecuba] Priam's queen.

378. mobled] muffled.

382. clout] rag.

384. o'erteemed] exhausted from childbearing.

393. milch] moist.

398. bestowed] housed.

440. presently] at once.

446. tent] probe.

[IV, i]

2. confusion] pretense of madness.

32. closely] secretly.

58. to] compared with.

77. contumely] humiliation.

79. office] officialdom.

81. *quietus*] release.

82. bodkin] dagger. fardels] burdens.

85. bourn] region, boundary.

93. With this regard] because of this.

94. Soft you] Hush!

109. honest] chaste.

119. sometime] formerly.

146. on't] of it.

159. blown] blooming.

166. disclose] outcome.

197. groundlings] lowest class of spectators.

200. Termagant] Saracen god represented as a fiend in early morality plays.

Herod] violent melodramatic representation of King Herod in early English drama.
205. from] away from.
208. pressure] image.
215. indifferently] tolerably.
218. barren] stupid.
236. election] choice.
256. chameleon's dish] air; chameleons were thought to exist on air.
274. country matters] rustic fornication.
285. *Mallicho*] sneaking crime.
286. argument] plot.
292. naught] wicked.
296. posy] motto.
299. Phoebus' car] chariot of the sun god.
300. Neptune's salt wash] the sea. Tellus] Roman earth goddess.
303. Hymen] god of marriage.
309. distrust you] fear for you.
312. hold quantity] match in amount.
328. instances] inducements.
335. validity] strength.
355. seasons] ripens.
365. anchor's cheer] hermit's fare.
382. Tropically] a figure of speech, a pun on *trap*.
385. free] innocent.
386. winch] wince.
388. a chorus] actor who speaks plot information not acted.
390. the puppets dallying] Ophelia and a lover making love.
396. Hecate's bane] curse of the goddess of witchcraft.
403. false fire] fireworks or a blank discharge of firearms.
408. ungalled] uninjured.
424. choler] anger or bile.
426. purgation] bodily and spiritual cleansing.
452. these pickers and stealers] hands.
459. "while the grass grows"] a proverb: "While the grass groweth, the horse starveth."
465. this pipe] a recorder.
499. Nero] Roman emperor who murdered his mother, Agrippina.
506. the terms . . . estate] his position as king.
513. peculiar] private.
515. noyance] injury.
516. weal] health, well-being.
517. cease] cessation or death.
518. gulf] whirlpool.
532. tax him home] rebuke him sharply.
534. meet] suitable.
541. eldest curse] curse of Cain after Abel's murder.
572. limed] trapped, as with bird lime.
573. engaged] ensnared.
579. scanned] looked over carefully.
585. audit] life's account.
612. idle] foolish.
617. rood] cross.
627. ducket] ducat, gold coin of worth.

642. custom have not brazed] habits have not hardened.
652. contraction] marriage contract.
659. front] forehead.
661. station] stance.
669. leave] stop.
670. batten] gorge gluttonously.
673. waits upon] is subject to.
680. cozened . . . hoodman-blind] cheated you at blindman's buff.
682. sans] without.
701. vice of kings] the fool and mischief-maker in morality plays.
702. cutpurse] pickpocket
716. Conceit] imagination.
729. capable] receptive.
731. effects] deeds or plans.
732. want] lack.
739. habit] garment
768. remains behind] is yet to come.

[v, i]

11. brainish apprehension] mad fancy.
18. providence] foresight.
19. *short . . . haunt*] tightly reined and solitary.
26. ore] precious metal.
43. level] well aimed. his blank] its target.
57. replication] reply.
75. distracted] bewildered, confused.
77. scourge] punishment.
78. bear all] manage everything.
103. tender] hold dear.
123. hold'st at aught] value at all.
125. *hectic*] fever.

[v, ii]

4. conveyance] escort.
15. farm] rent.
17. ranker] greater. in fee] outright.
21. straw] argument.
22. imposthume] festering ulcer.
31. discourse] understanding.
59. continent] receptacle.
69. Spurns enviously] shies suspiciously.
84. *cockle hat*] a cockle shell worn in a pilgrim's hatband as he returned from shrines abroad.
85. *shoon*] shoes.
96. *Larded*] decorated.
101. dil'd] dild, yield or reward.
103. Conceit upon] brooding upon.
107. *betime*] early.
116. *By Gis*] by Jesus.
119. *By cock*] by God.
138. greenly] foolishly.

148. *Swissers*] Swiss guards.
151. over-piercing of his list] overflowing his bounds.
153. in a riotous head] leading a riot force.
174. fear] be alarmed for.
189. stay] prevent.
198. life-rend'ring pelican] contemporaries believed the pelican tore her breast to feed her young.
235. wheel] spinning wheel.
240. document] lesson.
242. herb of grace] rue is associated with repentance.
243. difference] variation of heraldry in coats of arms.
247. passion] grief.
248. favor] winsomeness.
255. *poll*] head.
274. splenetive] fiery.
287. eisell] vinegar.
291. *forbear him*] leave him alone.
310. *Entranced and motionless*] in a swoon.

The Tempest

When Garrick produced *The Tempest* on 20 October 1757, a year and a half after the last performance of his ill-fated opera version, he did much to establish his credibility as a defender of Shakespeare's text. For on that day the Drury Lane audience saw what George Winchester Stone, Jr., has called "one of the very best of the Shakespearian texts of the eighteenth century."[1] And London audiences heeded the call to worship at the temple, for it became a regular offering of the theatre throughout the remainder of Garrick's managership; in fact, it was presented each season except for two, 1759–60 and 1767–68, during the nineteen years remaining to the actor-manager.

The quality of Garrick's version of *The Tempest* negates the comment of Frank A. Hedgcock, a leading detractor of Garrick's Shakespeare productions, that the actor "was not capable of appreciating Shakespeare as a poet; fanciful pieces like the *Dream* or the *Tempest* were to him formless and barbaric compositions."[2] His alteration of the text is limited almost entirely to tightening the play by cutting its length, the few lines added being required for clarity. The lines omitted amount to only about three hundred ninety-eight, including four cut from the Epilogue,[3] surely minimal cutting when one considers the liberties which directors take with Shakespeare today. In act I a seventeen-line exchange during the storm, the end of Shakespeare's scene,

1. Shakespeare's *Tempest* at Drury Lane During Garrick's Management," *Shakespeare Quarterly*, Winter, 1956, p. 5.
2. *A Cosmopolitan Actor: David Garrick and His French Friends* (London, [1912]), p. 64.
3. The exact number of omissions depends on the typography of the Shakespeare text, as the play contains some prose. I have counted partial lines as half lines and totaled the whole.

is omitted. In I, ii, there are five short excisions totaling twenty-eight and a half lines, the largest single cut being of ten lines. Eighteen and a half of these reduce Prospero's long account of how he and Miranda came to the island, two omissions eliminate minor statements by Prospero to Ariel and to Caliban, and one partial line eliminates Miranda's "Good wombs have borne bad sons," undoubtedly out of respect for nice eighteenth-century ears. Only one line, part of an aside by Prospero, is cut from I, iii (Shakespeare's I, ii).

The opening scene of act II takes the heaviest toll in cuts, a hundred ninety-six in all. The largest, two excisions of fifty-six and thirty-three lines, reduce the exchange among Sebastian, Antonio, Gonzalo, and Adrian near the opening of the scene. These cuts include lines for Adrian, who is omitted entirely from the play. The remainder are minor excisions of one to five and a half lines except for five, all dealing with the conversation among Sebastian, Gonzalo, Antonio, and Alonso—and the joking at the expense of Gonzalo—and the conspiracy of Antonio and Sebastian to murder Alonso, totaling some eighty-four lines.

Only about eleven prose lines are eliminated in II, ii, all dealing with the taunting of Caliban by Trinculo and Stephano. Again, act III escapes with only the most minor excisions, ten and a half lines, mostly from Prospero's asides, in scene i, no cuts in scene ii, and twenty-one lines from scene iii, the longest single one, eleven lines, again as aside of Prospero.

Seventy-eight lines are eliminated in act IV, the two most extensive being forty-six lines from the Iris-Ceres-Juno exchange before the singing (Iris and Juno are omitted in the Garrick version) and twenty-one from the conversation of Ferdinand and Prospero regarding the masque. The remaining cuts are from a half line to three lines and are of inconsequential nature.

Act V loses twenty-nine lines, fifteen in the first scene, all trimming Prospero's speeches a line and a half here, four lines there, and fourteen in scene ii, the only one of any length being a nine-line speech of Gonzalo celebrating the successful end to the adventure. The Epilogue loses four lines of Prospero's summation of the events of the play.

The additions to the play are minor, twenty-one and a half lines in all, the most extensive dealing with the Ceres-Juno masque in Shakespeare. All are found in II, i, and IV, i. In the first scene of act II Alonso is given three lines to reinforce his hope that his son is alive (II, i, 45–47). A few lines later he is given two and a half lines of exchange with Gonzalo regarding their weariness. About forty lines later, at Garrick's line 90, we have the addition of a simple question from Sebastian, "What mean you?" to take the place of fifteen lines which have been omitted. In IV, i, the added lines all have to do with the masque presented for Ferdinand. Shakespeare's masque is composed of forty-six lines of verse by Iris, Ceres, and Juno and a twelve-line song of Juno and Ceres. Garrick omits the verse and expands the singing to thirty lines, of which fourteen are not found in Shakespeare. After the singing, where twenty-one lines are omitted, including the comments of Ferdinand and Prospero on the masque and the final speech of Iris, one short line, "Break off, break off," is added to make the transition to the remainder of the scene. This line completes the additions to the play.

What is lost in the cutting amounts mainly to a shortening of the initial storm scene, a reduction in the length of Prospero's account of his bringing Miranda to the island, the conversation among the four lords associated with Alonso near the beginning of act II and the conspiracy of Antonio and Sebastian against Alonso, the shortening of the masque to the singing only, and some slight trimming of Prospero's lines, mainly in act V. The only serious omission by modern standards—and this one does not affect the action of the play—is Prospero's "We are such stuff / As dreams are made on, and our little life / Is rounded with a sleep," a curious omission in that the remainder of the speech is given, only these well-known lines of it being cut. Trinculo, to be sure, loses something more than a dozen lines, and Gonzalo philosophizes the less,[4] his description of the ideal commonwealth being omitted from the production.

The songs in the play are Shakespeare's, and none has been omitted; only the song in the masque of Ceres has been expanded. The reading in Ariel's song in V, i, "Where the bee sucks, there *lurk* I," taken from the earlier eighteenth-century editions of Louis Theobald and Thomas Hanmer, has been retained, perhaps in deference to the editors. No songs from the Davenant-Dryden-Shadwell operatic versions or from Dryden's *Tyrannick Love* mar the text. Shakespeare's songs in the play were printed and distributed free of charge on opening night.

The state of mid-eighteenth-century taste and dramatic criticism is indicated by the lengthy—and tiresome—notes which Francis Gentleman included in the printed version of the play, Bell's edition of 1773. The "Authors of the Dramatic Censor," as Gentleman identifies himself in this edition, would have altered the play far more than Garrick did had Gentleman had his way. Indeed, in his introduction he says that Shakespeare's original is "not so well supplied with humour or business as Dryden's" and suggests that a better play could have been made by "properly blending" the Dryden version with Shakespeare's text. In a note on the last part of I, i, Gentleman writes, "This scene we think very ill written; in Dryden's alteration, which seems to us a better acting play than that before us, it is mended."[5] And he deplores such "indelicate and unnecessary" lines as Trinculo's "Monster, I do smell all horsepiss, at which my nose is in great indignation" (IV, i, 154), a line which for Gentleman "conveys a nauseous idea, without a gleam of humour." But Garrick refused to be driven by the critics and on 20 October 1757 gave his audience Shakespeare in a fine acting version. The long run of this play—sixty-one performances up to the time of Garrick's quitting the stage,—its popularity with actors when choosing plays for benefit performances, and its financial success[6] indicate that Garrick was right in restoring

4. Professor Stone says that only Gonzalo has "lost anything significant by excision" ("Shakespeare's *Tempest* at Drury Lane," p. 6).
5. Gentleman's explanatory notes are added to this edition of the play as textual notes.
6. Stone ("Shakespeare's *Tempest* at Drury Lane," p. 7) notes an income of £4,783 for the thirty-two performances for which there are records in the Cross *Diary* in the Folger Shakespeare Library. There are no records of receipts for twenty-nine performances.

Shakespeare in a play which had long been neglected in favor of operatic versions.

TEXTS

D1 1st edition. London: John Bell, 1773.
D2 London: J. Rivington, W. Strahan, J. Hinton, etc., 1775.
S The standard Shakespeare texts.

Note: A duodecimo published for Thomas Walker in Dublin, 1775, "As it is performed at the Theatre-Royal, Smock-Alley," is not Shakespeare's play or Garrick's adaptation, but the old Davenant-Dryden-Shadwell version.

[1, i]

3. Good] i.e., my good fellow.
yarely] quickly.
5. yare] yarely.
6. Blow . . .] addressing the storm.
7. room enough] we are far enough from shore.
24. complexion . . . gallows] born to die by hanging.
29. main-course] mainsail.
35. warrent . . . drowning] assure that he does not drown.
37. ahold] windward. two courses] foresail and mainsail.
38. off] i.e., off shore.

[1, ii]

4. welkin's] sky's.
13. fraighting] forming the cargo.
15. amazement] dismay.
26. meddle] mix.
35. perdition] loss.
36. Betid] befallen.
48. Out] yet.
55. remembrance warrants] memory assures.
59. backward] past.
67. piece] masterpiece.
70. no worse issued] not worse born.
78. teen] trouble. turned you to] made you recall.
79. from] beyond.
85. signiories] dominions.
95. lorded] given power.
101. substitution] being deputized.
102–03. executing . . . prerogative] performing royal functions without full power.
106. screen] barrier.
107. temporal] worldly.
111. dry] thirsty.
117. condition] i.e., the details of his double-dealing. event] outcome.
124. in . . . premises] in return for promised payments.
126. presently] immediately. extirpate] root out.

136. hint] suitable occasion.
141. impertinent] irrelevant.
148. With . . . ends] disguised their evil intentions with pretenses.
156. loving wrong] i.e., sighing in pity, the winds buffeted them even more.
162. decked] covered, sprinkled.
164. undergoing] courageous.
173. steaded much] been useful. gentleness] kindness.
184. vainer] spent uselessly
192. zenith] height of good fortune.
194. omit] neglect.
204. qualities] equals, associate spirits.
206. to point] exactly.
208. beak] prow.
209. waste] waist, middle part of the upper deck.
210. flamed amazement] burned so as to astonish onlookers.
220. constant] evenly balanced. coil] uproar.
235. sustaining] buoying.
241. in . . . knot] folded.
248. still-vexed] storm-ridden.
253. flote] float, sea.
261. glasses] hours (by the hourglass).
262. preciously] carefully.
263. pains] painful tasks.
274. bate] abate, shorten my term of service.
279. envy] malice.
283. Argier] Algiers.
292. blue-eyed] shadowy-eyed.
297. hests] commands.
303. vent] cry out.
323. correspondent] responsive.
324. sp'riting] spirit's duties. gently] graciously.
342. miss] dismiss.
350. quaint] clever.
357. southwest] a hot wind, carrying infection.
360. urchins] goblins.
361. vast] vast expanse.
397. red] bubonic. rid] kill.
414. whist] stilled.
415. featly] nimbly.
416. burden] refrain.
427. passion] grief.

[I, iii]

5. brave] handsome.
8. something] somewhat. stained] marred.
19–20. vouchsafe . . . know] let my prayer cause you to tell me.
20. remain] live.
22. bear me] conduct myself.
24. maid] mortal.
32. single] solitary.
35. at ebb] without weeping.

41. control] correct.
43. changed] exchanged.
45. done . . . wrong] not spoken the truth.
53. Soft] quiet.
58. ow'st] ownest.
72. entertainment] treatment.
75. Make . . . him] don't judge him too harshly.
76. gentle] a gentleman. fearful] afraid.
78. foot] inferior (in years).
80. ward] fighting stance.
94. affections] tastes.
101. spirits] energies

[II, i]

3. hint] occasion.
5. merchant] ship. the merchant] the shipowner.
14–15. against . . . sense] to injure my sensibilities.
34. loathness] reluctance.
35. Which . . . bow] which should weigh heavier.
43. time] suitable time.
57. heavy offer] i.e., the opportunity to sleep, which your drowsiness suggests.
65. quality] nature.
74. speaks] bespeaks, names.
99–100. your . . . fortune] your good fortune content you.
105. feater] more neatly.
110. Candied] sugared.
116. wink] closed eye.
117. morsel] bit of manhood.
118. Should not] so that he cannot.
119. tell the clock] say that the time has come.
128. fall] drop.

[II, ii]

3. inchmeal] inch by inch.
6. firebrand] will-o'-the-wisp.
9. moe] grimace.
17. mind] notice.
20 bumbard] bombard, leather cup or bottle.
25. Poor John] salted dried fish.
29. doit] coin of small value.
34. garberdine] cloak.
54. four legs] a four-legged creature.
61. recover] cure.
63. neat's] cow's.
65. after the wisest] sensibly.
67–68. I . . . much] no price will be too much.
68–69. he . . . soundly] the purchaser will pay dearly for him.
72. Come . . . ways] come on.
73. cat] proverbial idea that drink will make a cat talk

78. Four . . . voices] Trinculo's head protrudes from the cloak by Caliban's feet, and vice versa.

delicate] rare.

81. Amen] well done.

85. long spoon] reference to the proverbial saying that one should have a long spoon when supping with the devil.

90. siege] excrement.

90–91. mooncalf] freak.

94. constant] steady.

106. kiss the book] take a drink.

113. when time was] at one time.

115. dog . . . bush] they accompany the Man in the Moon.

129. crabs] crabapples.

143. trencher] wooden platter.

[III, i]

1–2. their . . . off] the delight they give offsets the labor.

3. most poor] poorest.

6. quickens] makes lively.

13. forget] forget to work.

43. hest] command.

47. best regard] closest attention.

52. owed] owned.

53. put . . . foil] destroyed its effect.

66. condition] rank.

70. flesh-fly] a fly which lays eggs in flesh. blow] swell (with the deposit of eggs).

77. event] outcome.

[III, ii]

2. bear . . . 'em] board the vessel, i.e., drink like a man.

8. set] glazed.

14. standard] standard-bearer.

15. list] please. standard] i.e., he cannot stand.

23. case] condition.

24. deboshed] debauched.

28. natural] idiot.

53. compassed] achieved.

58. pied ninny] multicolored fool (jester). patch] fool.

62. quick freshes] fresh springs.

65. stockfish] dried fish which must be beaten before it is cooked.

72. murrain] plague.

82. paunch] stab in the bowels.

83. weasand] windpipe.

85. sot] stupid person.

87. rootedly] firmly.

88. brave utensils] fine furnishings.

110. troll the catch] sing a round.

117–18. Nobody] referring to the picture on the title page of the c. 1606 play *Nobody and Somebody*. Nobody is all head and limbs.

[III, iii]

1. lakin] little lady (the Virgin Mary).
3. forthrights] straight lines.
6. attached] seized.
25. drollery] puppet show.
30. want credit] lack belief.
41. muse] wonder at.
61. proper] own. You fools] the hearers have drawn swords.
64. bemocked-at] ineffectual.
83. clear] blameless.
90. base] bass, say in a deep voice.
95. o'er] all.
99. bite the spirits] cause mental anguish.
101. ecstasy] madness.

[IV, i]

6. strangely] exceptionally.
8. boast her off] boast of her.
12. Against an oracle] even though a supermundane oracle would say otherwise.
14. purchased] acquired.
16. sanctimonious] sanctified.
18. aspersions] benedictions.
19. grow] i.e., into marriage.
23. As Hymen's . . .] as you hope the god of marriage will illuminate your wedding.
28. genius] nature.
31. Phoebus' steeds] who pull the chariot of the sun god. foundered] lamed.
43. vanity] slight demonstration.
46. with a twink] in a twinkling.
50. mop and mow] gesture and grimace.
54. true] faithful to your promise.
60. liver] thought to be responsible for passion.
75. foison] abundance.
91. beat the grass] dance.
97. Avoid] avaunt.
102. moved sort] troubled state of mind.
110. all . . . inherit] all earthly creatures.
111. baseless] insubstantial.
112. rack] whisp of cloud.
115. If . . . pleased] if it pleases you.
119. Come . . . thought] you have come at the instant of my thinking of you.
133. Advanced] raised.
136. goss] gorse.
138. mantled] scum-covered.
142. stale] bait.
145. Nurture] moral discipline.
148. cankers] festers (with malice).
149. line] linden or lime tree.
153. Jack] knave.
161. hoodwink] blind you to.

176. King Stephano . . . from a ballad.
179. frippery] used clothing shop.
185. luggage] worthless encumberments.
189. Mistress line . . .] reference to crossing the Equator ("line") and resultant suffering from scurvy by sailors, who reputedly lost hair as a result. This is a fur-trimmed jacket.
192. line and level] plumbline and carpenter's level, i.e., methodically and accurately
195. pass of pate] example (thrust) of wit.
196. lime] birdlime, used in snares.
199. barnacles] a kind of geese.
209. pard] leopard. cat o'mountain] panther.

[v, i]

2. crack not] work properly.
2–3. Time . . . carriage] all plans are on schedule.
12. weather-fends] shields from weather.
19. reeds] thatch.
31. rarer action] finer behavior.
38. standing] still.
41. demi-puppets] fairies.
45. solemn curfew] the nine o'clock bell which signaled spirits to walk abroad.
52. spurs] roots.
59. staff] magic wand.
66. even sociable] in sympathy with.
67. fellow drops] companionable tears. apace] quickly.
70. ign'rant fumes] mental confusion.
83. discase] take off my magic gown.
99. presently] at once.
101. Or ere] before.
110. abuse] deceive.
114. crave] require.
120. age] aged self.
138. woe] woeful.
154. admire] wonder.
155. devour] lose in wonder.
157. natural breath] gasps of astonishment.

[v, ii]

33. hers] her father, i.e., I welcome her into the family.
38. heaviness] sorrow.
46. still] ever.
51. blasphemy] blasphemous boatswain.
56. glasses] hours.
57. yare] seaworthy.
75. moping] in an unconscious state.
77. diligence] diligent one.
83. infest] disturb. beating] harping.
84. picked leisure] a selected time.
85. single] I alone.
87. happened accidents] occurrences.

94. Coragio] courage. bully-monster] my hearty monster.
95. spies] eyes.
98. fine] finely dressed.
100. badges] clothing (stolen).
101. true] honest (servants).
104. demi-devil] Caliban is son of a demon and a human witch.
113. gilded] flushed.
116. fly-blowing] i.e., because he is filthy from the pond.
138. accidents] events.
147. take the ear] spellbind.

Roster of the Drury Lane Company

For biographical information we are indebted to several standard sources, but we are most heavily indebted to *A Biographical Dictionary of Actors, Actresses, Dancers, Managers, and Other Stage Personnel in London, 1660–1800*, prepared by Philip H. Highfill, Jr., Kalman A. Burnim, and Edward A. Langhans (Carbondale and Edwardsville: Southern Illinois University Press, 1973–). We are particularly in debt to Professors Highfill, Burnim, and Langhans for permission to consult their unpublished files on the stage personnel of the period.

Ackman, Ellis (d. 1774). A utility actor at Drury Lane for twenty-five seasons, he made his debut as Lennox in *Macbeth* on 23 April 1750. His reportory was heavily Shakespearean, with minor or secondary roles in Garrick's revivals of the Bard. Other than these parts he played infrequently and mainly in the most minor roles.

Aickin, James (c. 1735–1803). Joined the Drury Lane Company in 1767, making his debut there as Young Belmont in *The Foundling* on 6 November. He remained for his entire career, also playing most summers at the Haymarket. His forte was portraying "honest" men, eccentrics, and Irishmen, and he was useful to Garrick in both major and minor Shakespeare roles.

Ambrose, Miss E. (fl. 1756–87). The younger sister of Mrs. Egerton. After many years playing in Ireland, she engaged at Drury Lane in 1772–73. She went to Covent Garden in 1775 and continued there through 1781–82. She was known for her portrayals of Lady Macduff and Regan.

Atkins, Charles (d. 1775). Dancer, acrobat, and actor of minor roles, he began his career presumably at Covent Garden in 1748–49—at least Mr. Atkins danced there through the 1750–51 season. Presmumably he is the Atkins who danced in *Harlequin Ranger* at Drury Lane on 26 December 1751, remaining on the payroll through 1760–61 as dancer and bit player, chiefly in comic roles.

Austin, Joseph (1735–1821). A skilled actor and a good theatre manager, Austin began his career at Drury Lane on 22 February 1757, playing Bertram in *The Spanish Friar*. By the next season he had important parts in such plays as *Henry VIII*, *The Tempest*, and *King Lear*. He became a regular player of Shakespearean roles, including Candidius in *Antony and Cleopatra* (although the printed text assigns to him the role of Proculeius), Burgundy in *Lear*, and the Dauphin in *King John*. Later he became manager of a provincial circuit.

Baddeley, Robert (1733–94). Reputedly a pastry cook, he first appeared at Drury Lane on 20 October 1760 as Sir William Wealthy in Foote's *The*

Minor, having made his debut in the same role in June of that year at the Haymarket. Noted for low comedy roles, he was the original Moses in Sheridan's *The School for Scandal* (1775) and played the part more than two hundred times. He left his house for the use of indigent actors, stipulating that the interest from £100 be used annually to provide Twelfth Night cakes and ale to Drury Lane actors, a tradition which continues today.

Bannister, Charles (1741–1804). Early enamored of the stage, he applied at the age of eighteen to Garrick for a place at Drury Lane but was not hired. He worked for Rich a while and finally came to Drury Lane as Merlin in *Cymon* (22 September 1767). He became a regular at Drury Lane through the 1786–87 season, then shifted between Covent Garden and Drury Lane, playing most summers at the Haymarket. He retired after the 1797–98 season, having been a leader in the founding of "The School of Garrick" club after the actor's death.

Barry, Ann (1734–1801). The wife of Spranger Barry, she began her career in the provinces, married William Dancer, an actor in the York company, moved with him to Dublin, where Spranger Barry undertook her instruction as an actress, and after the death of Dancer remained with Barry, eventually marrying him. Both moved to Drury Lane in 1767, where she opened as Sigismunda in *Tancred and Sigismunda* on 14 October. After continual disagreements with Garrick, both Barrys moved to Covent Garden for the 1774–75 season.

Barry, Spranger (1717?–77). An Irish actor who made his debut as Othello at the Aungier Street Theatre, Dublin, on 15 February 1744, emerging at once as a first-class actor. He played with Garrick at the Smock Alley Theatre, then made his debut at Drury Lane on 4 October 1746 as Othello, playing the Moor fourteen times in his first season. He continued at Drury Lane when Garrick became manager in 1747, but at the close of the 1749–50 season he and Mrs. Cibber went to Covent Garden. He appeared as Romeo on 28 September 1750 and opposed Garrick's production of the tragedy in "the Battle of the Romeos." With Ann Dancer Barry, his second wife, he returned to Drury Lane in the season of 1767–68 and remained through 1773–74. His last appearance was at Covent Garden on 28 November 1776.

Barton, George (d. 1784). A singer of no great renown, George Barton first appeared at Drury Lane on 29 April 1749 and continued as an occasional singer there until November 1776. One of his roles was undoubtedly Anthonio in the opera version of *The Tempest*. He was one of the bass singers in the Handel Memorial Concerts at Westminster Abbey and the Pantheon in 1784.

Beard, John (1716?–91). The most celebrated English singer in the middle of the century, he was a protégé of Handel and began his adult career at Covent Garden. He came to Drury Lane for the 1737–38 season, remained there (except for one season) until 1743, returned to Covent Garden until 1748, and then came again to Garrick's house to remain until his retirement in 1767.

Bennett, Elizabeth (1714–91). A spinster, she played in minor theatres until she joined Drury Lane in 1735–36 as a dancer. She advanced to minor comic roles beginning with the 1738–39 season and continued there for the next twenty-six years, specializing in roles of the pert maidservant, the gossip, the mistress.

Berry, Edward (1706–60). An actor, dancer, and singer, he began his long career at Drury Lane on 6 February 1729 as Hobinal in *The Village Opera* and ended it there as Sir Epicure Mammon on 15 March 1759, the year he took on his last role, that of Enobarbus in *Antony and Cleopatra.* He acted in virtually all the important plays of the Garrick period and was considered to have more merit in comedy than in tragedy. Among his many roles were Caliban in *The Tempest*, Gloucester in *King Lear*, and Jaques in *As You Like It.*

Blakes, Charles (d. 1763). A journeyman actor, he began his career at the Haymarket on 27 May 1736, was acting at Goodman's Fields in 1740, worked at Covent Garden in 1741, and first played at Drury Lane in 1743 as the Bailiff in *The Committee* on 9 October. He remained at Drury Lane to the end of his career.

Bradshaw, Mary (d. 1780). Probably the wife of Bradshaw the Drury Lane boxkeeper, she made her debut at Lincoln's Inn Fields on 7 January 1743 as Nell in *The Devil to Pay* and the next month played Lucy in *The Beggar's Opera* there. She joined the Drury Lane Company for the 1743–44 season and remained, with some small exceptions, for thirty-seven years. She was famous as Garrick's wife in *The Farmer's Return from London.*

Bransby, Astley (d. 1789). A member of the Drury Lane Company from Garrick's first season, 1747–48, he remained there throughout the management, playing minor supporting roles for some thirty-three years.

Bride, Elizabeth (d. 1826). Possibly the daughter of the Drury Lane sceneshifter. She made her debut there on 18 October 1760 as Lucia in *Cato.* The following season she appeared as Imogen in *Cymbeline* on 28 November 1761. After a final season in 1763–64 she left the stage in the keeping of John Calcraft, married a Mr. Lefevre, and later married John Samworth of Greenwich.

Burton, John (d. 1797?). An actor and dancer, he was the son of Edward Burton, a Drury Lane player, and first appeared on that stage as Master Burton, the Page in *Love Makes a Man* (28 October 1762). He played similar child's roles until the 1767–68 season, when he began to be billed as J. Burton and played mature roles. He remained a utility actor at Drury Lane through the 1795–96 season.

Cape, Master (fl. 1768–79). Edward Cape Everard appeared at Drury Lane in the 1768–69 season. By 1777–78 he was known as Cape Everard and played the minor theatres through 1778–79.

Cautherley, Samuel (d. 1805). Rumored illegitimate son of Garrick and certainly his protégé, Cautherley made his debut at Drury Lane in a children's performance of *Miss in Her Teens* on 28 April 1755 and his adult debut as George Barnwell in Lillo's play ten years later (26 September 1765). For the years remaining to him as an actor his meager abilities confined him mostly to secondary roles, although he was allowed to play *Hamlet* with Mrs. Baddeley and *Romeo* with Mrs. Barry, both times to cool receptions. He last played at Drury Lane on 26 September 1776, exactly ten years after his first adult role there, as Rivers in *The Note of Hand.*

Champness, Samuel Thomas (d. 1803). Featured bass singer at Drury Lane between 1748 and 1774, he was famous for singing in Handel's oratorios. It was reputedly Handel who had given him a start as a boy, and the composer eventually wrote several songs expressly for him in the oratorio *Joseph and His Brethren* (Covent Garden, 2 March 1744). When he retired from the stage at the end of the 1773–74 season Garrick played in *Zara* for his benefit (13 May 1774).

Cibber, Mrs. Susanna Maria (1714–66). Second wife of Theophilus Cibber. As Miss Arne she became established as a first-class singer, and after her marriage was tutored by Colley Cibber as an actress. She made her debut at Drury Lane on 12 January 1736 in *Zara*, and before the season ended was playing Indiana in *The Conscious Lovers*, Amanda in *Love's Last Shift*, and Andromache in *The Distrest Mother*. In 1736–37 she added Desdemona, Isabella in *Measure for Measure*, Monimia in *The Orphan*, and other roles. Her acting career was interrupted by the lawsuits surrounding her husband and William Sloper, and she began afresh in Dublin in December 1741. In Dublin she also was acclaimed for her singing in Handel's *Messiah*. After an engagement at Drury Lane from 1747–48 through 1749–50, she and Spranger Barry deserted to Covent Garden and began the "War of the Romeos" in 1750. She returned to Drury Lane in 1753–54 and remained with that company the rest of her life. Her final season was 1764–65.

Clive, Catherine Raftor (1711–85). A famous comedienne and Garrick's colleague throughout his career, Kitty Clive apparently made her debut as a page in *Mithridates, King of Pontus* in April 1728, and by the next season she began to be recognized for her comic genius. But she had other distinctions as well: Handel chose her to sing Dalila in his oratorio *Samson* in 1743, and she was a friend of Samuel Johnson. When Garrick became manager at Drury Lane she became the comedy mainstay of that house.

Clough, Thomas (d. 1770). An actor in minor theatres and fair booths, he joined the Drury Lane Company in 1752–53, first appearing as Jeremy in *The Double Disappointment* (11 October). After a season of barnstorming, he returned to Drury Lane and remained for fifteen years, closing his career there on 5 June 1770 in *The Jubilee*. He is pictured by Zoffany as a watchman in the famous portrait of Garrick as Lord Brute in *The Provok'd Wife*.

Collet, Miss Catherine, later Mrs. Tetherington (fl. 1767–1800). A dancer and actress, she made her debut as a child dancer in Garrick's *Cymon* on 2 January 1767. By 1780–81 she had matured, and on 24 January 1781 sang the title role in Arne's *Artaxerxes* for the first time. She was known for flirtatious chambermaid roles in *The Clandestine Marriage*, *The Provok'd Husband*, and *The Lying Valet*.

Curioni, Signora Rosa (fl. 1754–62). Coming from Italy to debut in London opera, she sang in *L'Ipermestra* on 9 November 1754 at the King's Theatre. Although she is listed in the bills to play Lysander in *The Fairies*, the opera version of *A Midsummer Night's Dream*, Cross's Diary assigns the role to Guadagni. She did play Ferdinand in the opera version of *The Tempest* on 11 February 1756 and five subsequent performances. After a return to Venice she again sang in London opera during the 1761–62 season.

Davies, Thomas (c. 1712–85). Actor, bookseller, theatrical historian, Davies apparently began his career as an actor with Fielding's company at the Haymarket on 27 May 1736, playing Young Wilmot in Lillo's *Fatal Curiosity*. After a brief career at Covent Garden, he acted and managed in Edinburgh, joined Thomas Sheridan's company in Dublin, played summers at Richmond and Twickenham, and eventually came to Drury Lane, where he remained for more than a decade. His first role there was Ross in *Macbeth* on 16 October 1752. His parts included Claudius in *Hamlet*, Nerestan in *Zara*, Eros in *Antony and Cleopatra*, and Carlos in *The Fatal Marriage*. About 1760 he opened a bookshop, which he maintained to his death. Indeed, he is best known in literary history for having introduced Boswell to Dr. Johnson in 1763. His own works include *Memoirs of the Life of David Garrick* (2 vols., 1780) and *Dramatic Miscellanies* (3 vols., 1785). Upon leaving the stage after the 1762–63 season he complained to Dr. Johnson that Garrick's temper at rehearsals was the reason. Garrick replied that the careless preparation of Davies for his roles prompted that temper.

Egerton, Mrs. (fl. 1728?–58). Is first mentioned on 19 July 1728 when she played Aurelia in *The Wife's Relief* at Lincoln's Inn Fields. On 12 May 1729 she played Arabella in *The Committee* at Drury Lane. In the 1740–41 season she engaged at Drury Lane, where her first role was the Nurse in *Love for Love* on 9 September 1740. Playing there through the 1743–44 season, her roles were Mrs. Sealand in *The Conscious Lovers*, the Nurse in *The Relapse*, Audrey in *As You Like It*, Mrs. Wisely in *The Minor*, Mrs. Security in *The Gamester*, and the Nurse in *The Fatal Marriage*. She ended her career at the Jacob's Wells Theatre in Bristol.

Evans, Master (fl. 1753). Appears to have had but one acting role, a Fairy in *The Fairies* at Drury Lane on 3 February 1755.

Fawcett, John (d. 1793). Having learned singing from Dr. Thomas Augustine Arne, to whom he was apprenticed, Fawcett first appeared at Drury Lane in the juvenile role of Filch in *The Beggar's Opera* on 23 September 1760. After a time at Covent Garden and the King's Theatre, he returned to Drury Lane on 23 September 1766 as Gildenstern in *Hamlet*. For thirty-three years a useful actor in supporting roles in the theatres, he played Dorilas in *Cymon* and Lennox in *Macbeth*.

Fleetwood, Charles the Younger (d. 1784). Son of the Drury Lane manager who first hired Garrick and from whom Garrick and Lacy purchased the patent to the theatre, he made his debut on 28 September 1758, playing Romeo. Prompter Cross noted that he "was receiv'd with great & deserv'd Applause.: On his third night in the role, 13 October, he gained dubious fame by running a fellow actor, Austin, who was playing Paris, in the belly during the duel scene, having a sword instead of a foil at his side." Cross tells us that it was "a Small Wound, & he is recover'd." After playing Caesar in *Antony and Cleopatra*, his fortunes seem to have waned at Drury Lane: by the 1760–61 season he is no longer there. He shows up at Covent Garden for the 1768–69 season and therafter appears with groups performing at the Haymarket, where his name is last seen in the 1770–71 season as one of the group of actors authorized to give benefit performances.

Ford, Harriet (c. 1755– ?). Daughter of George Colman's mistress, Sara Ford, who had been born in Jamaica and had been a servant before she was "seduced and debauched" by the actor Henry Mossop, Harriet's father, Miss Ford was employed as a dancer at Drury Lane by 1761 and was perhaps the means of her mother's support before the latter's liaison with Colman. Harriet played infant roles between 1761 and 1767 and is listed in the printed text of Garrick's *A Midsummer Night's Dream* as playing Titania (she would have been only about nine years old). The *Public Advertiser*, however, lists her merely as a Fairy. Fanny Burney described her in 1771 as "about sixteen, very genteel in person . . . and very well educated." Garrick referred to her in a letter to Colman as "my dear little Ford" (20 April 1766). She later married a Mr. Wilkinson. When Colman took over Covent Garden in 1767 she appeared there occasionally for a year or two.

Fox, Joseph (d. 1791). Having begun his career at Covent Garden as Fenton in *The Merry Wives of Windsor*, he spent some thirty-three years in the theatre, ending his career as a theatre owner in Brighton on 7 December 1791. He played journeyman roles at Drury Lane from 1758, having made his debut as a slave in *Oroonoko* on 1 December and playing there every season (except 1765–66) through 1767–68. His roles included Rosencrantz in *Hamlet*, Burgundy in *King Lear*, and Mat in *The Beggar's Opera.* Later he played at Covent Garden and the Haymarket, was keeper of the Shakespeare Tavern and Coffee House in Bow Street, and leased and managed theatres at Brighton.

Glen, Mrs. Ann (fl. 1755–66). Made her debut at Covent Garden on 24 February 1755 as the Countess of Rutland in *The Earl of Essex*. Her benefit as Lady Townly in *The Provok'd Husband* at Drury Lane on 21 October 1756 was termed "insipid" by prompter Cross. After a season at Smock Alley, Dublin, 1756–57, she returned to Drury Lane in 1758–59 to portray Anna Bullen in *Henry VIII*, Lady Macduff in *Macbeth*, Octavia in *Antony and Cleopatra*, and Lady Wronghead in *The Provok'd Husband.* Her last London role was as Indiana in *The Conscious Lovers.* Between 1760 and 1766 she acted at Norwich.

Griffith(s), John (d. 1801). As actor and prompter he appeared on the London stage scene for some twenty-four years, mostly in minor roles—Francisco in *Hamlet*, the Officer in *Venice Preserv'd*, the Physician in *King Lear*, Austria in *King John*, and others. He was a prompter at the Haymarket but was engaged for the winter at Drury Lane for twelve seasons.

Guadagni, Gaetano (fl. 1751). A castrato, he first sang at Drury Lane as

Edward, the king's son, in Garrick's production of *Alfred*. He had sung Orfeo in the first performance of Gluck's opera in Vienna in 1762 and again created the role for its first performance in London in 1770. He played Lysander in Garrick's *The Fairies*.

Havard, William (1710–78). First appeared in a booth at Bartholomew Fair on 20 August 1730. He soon moved to Goodman's Fields, where he played several seasons before going to Covent Garden and on to Drury Lane in 1737–38. There he opened as the Duke in *Rule a Wife and Have a Wife* (3 September). He remained at Drury Lane for nine seasons, playing Edgar to young Garrick's King Lear on 3 May 1742. He wrote several plays, Garrick playing the title role in his *Regulus* on 21 February 1744. After a season at Covent Garden he reappeared at Drury Lane on the first night of Garrick's management (15 September 1747) as Bassanio in *The Merchant of Venice*. He played Lelio in the premiere of *Albumazar* on 3 October of that year and thereafter played primary and secondary roles for Garrick during the next twenty years.

Hippisley, Miss Jane (Mrs. Henry Green) (1719–91). Daughter of comedian John Hippisley, Jane made her debut at Drury Lane as Rose in *The Recruiting Officer* on 11 January 1740. She played Prince Edward in *Richard III* on 19 October 1741 when Garrick made his debut at Goodman's Fields, and as Jane Green she was among the company of seventy which Garrick assembled in his first season as manager of Drury Lane, 1747–48. She played Mrs. Tatoo in *Lethe*, Armelina in *Albumazar*, and Mrs. Heidelberg in *The Clandestine Marriage* (at Covent Garden), and was the original Mrs. Malaprop in Sheridan's *The Rivals* (17 January 1775).

Holland, Charles (1733–69). Making his debut at Drury Lane on 13 October 1755, he played Oroonoko to Mrs. Cibber's Imoinda and later that season was Florizel in Garrick's alteration of *The Winter's Tale*. A warm friend of Garrick, upon whose acting he modeled his own, he was at Drury Lane for the remaining fifteen years of his career. He acted in many of Garrick's important productions: Horatius in *The Roman Father*, Sir John Melvil in *The Clandestine Marriage*, Moody in *The Country Girl*, Ferdinand and Prospero in *The Tempest*, Thyreus in *Antony and Cleopatra*, Young Knowell in *Every Man in His Humour*, Osman in *Zara*, and Richard III in *The Jubilee*.

Hopkins, Mrs. Elizabeth (fl. 1761–76). Wife of William Hopkins, Garrick's prompter. A utilitarian actress of great dependability, she joined the Drury Lane Company for the 1961–62 season and remained throughout Garrick's management. She played Hippolita on the opening night of George Colman's *A Midsummer Night's Dream* on 23 November 1763.

Hunt, Mrs. Henrietta (Mrs. William) (fl. 1769–79). Henrietta Dunstall Hunt made her debut at Covent Garden on 14 April 1769 as Sally in *Thomas and Sally*. After her marriage she spent several seasons in the provinces, returning to Drury Lane 1 October 1771 for Leonora in *The Padlock*. Later roles that season included Rosetta in *Love in a Village*, Patty in *The Maid of the Mill*. She played two more seasons at Drury Lane in the chorus of *Romeo and Juliet*, *The Elopement*, and

Macbeth. Then she removed to provincial playhouses at Birmingham and Bristol.

Hurst, Richard (d. 1805). Played in London and provincial theatres for more than forty-eight years. He made his debut at Covent Garden on 26 October 1754 as Tressel in *Richard III*. He may have been in the opening of *The Chinese Festival* at Drury Lane on 8 November 1755 and definitely was there in the 1765–66 season, playing Cornwall in *King Lear* on 22 October. He played Orasmin in *Zara*, Traverse and Sterling in *The Clandestine Marriage*, Macduff in *Macbeth*, Claudius in *Hamlet*, Antonio in *The Tempest*, and Posthumus in *The Jubilee*, remaining at Drury Lane through Garrick's management and into the fourth year of Sheridan's, through 1779–80.

James, Harris (d. 1751). Actor and dancer, he played Pert in *The Inconstant* at Goodman's Fields on 14 October 1732. He remained at Goodman's Fields through most of the 1733–34 season, then he went to Covent Garden for the seasons of 1734–35 through 1747–48. He played at Drury Lane from 1748–49 through 1750–51. His specialty was secondary roles: Samson in *Romeo and Juliet*, the Town Clerk and Dogberry in *Much Ado About Nothing*, and once as Polonius in *Hamlet*. His last appearance was as Blunt in Lillo's *London Merchant* at Drury Lane on 14 May 1751.

James. Mrs. Harris (fl. 1736–54). Actress and singer, she made her debut as a maid in *Love's Last Shift* at Covent Garden on 10 May 1736 and rose quickly to roles such as Lucy in *The Beggar's Opera*, Queen Elizabeth in *King John*, the Duchess of Gloucester in *Richard II*, the Hostess in *2 Henry IV*, Isabel in *Henry V*, and the Bawd in *The Chances*. She and her husband moved to Drury Lane in the fall of 1748, where she played the Nurse in *Romeo and Juliet*, Doll Common in *The Alchemist*, among others.

Jefferson, Thomas (1728?–1807). Making his debut as Rossano in *The Fair Penitent* on 31 October 1753, he remained a utility actor there through most seasons of Garrick's management, later playing at York and Plymouth and for a time being manager at Richmond.

Jefferson, Elizabeth (Mrs. William) (fl. 1753–58). Wife of Thomas Jefferson, who founded the Jefferson family of actors in England and America, Elizabeth was a member of the Drury Lane Company from 1753–54 through 1757–58. She played the part of Hippolita in *The Fairies*.

Johnston, Mrs. Helen (fl. 1762–78). The wife of Roger Johnston, housekeeper at Drury Lane from 1762 until 1775 and a scene painter and country theatre manager, she first appeared at Garrick's house in 1760–61 and became a regular member of the company in 1767. She remained throughout the 1780–81 season. Garrick thought Mr. and Mrs. Johnston to be "persons of great merit" (letter to A. R. Bowes, 23 April 1777).

Kear, James Thomas (d. 1796). A singer in Marylebone Gardens about 1754, Kear first appeared on stage under Theophilus Cibber at the Haymarket on 17 October 1757 singing "Dorus and Cleora" by Bryan and "Rule Britannia." In 1760–61 he engaged at Drury Lane, first performing in the funeral procession in *Romeo and Juliet* (20 October). He played Hymen in the adaptation of *The Tempest* in 1765 and obscure roles in

Macbeth, *A Peep Behind the Curtain*, *The Jubilee*, *Harlequin's Invasion*, and *Alfred*, appearing there into 1778.

Keen, William (1740–75). First listed in the Drury Lane bills on 16 May 1765, he was a supporting actor there until May 1775.

Kennedy, Lawrence (c. 1729–86). Actor and manager, he acted with his wife in the provinces for twelve years, then made a debut at Drury Lane on 29 December 1760 as Blunt in *The Committee*. In the 1761–62 season he played Capulet in *Romeo and Juliet*, the Lord Chamberlain in *Henry VIII*, followed by Tressel in *Richard III*, Laertes in *Hamlet*, Philario in *Cymbeline*, and Paris in *Romeo and Juliet*. Not being articled after his second season, he went back to the provinces and became a provincial manager.

King, Thomas (1730–1805). First brought to Drury Lane by Garrick as the Herald in *King Lear* (unannounced, 8 October 1748), King was soon given a variety of roles, including Fribble in *Miss in Her Teens*, the Fine Gentleman in *Lethe*, and Valerius in *The Roman Father*. After two seasons in the provinces he returned to Drury Lane in 1762 and grew in popularity until he achieved eminence as a comic actor with his Lord Ogleby in *The Clandestine Marriage* on 20 February 1766. He became Garrick's close friend, and after that actor's death became manager of the theatre (1782).

Lee, John (d. 1781). An actor and manager, he first appeared at Goodman's Fields in 1745, playing Sir Charles Freeman in Farquhar's *The Stratagem* and the Ghost in *Hamlet*. His name appears on the Drury Lane bill of 14 November 1747 as the Bastard in *King Lear*. After a season at Covent Garden (1749–50) he returned to Garrick's house in 1750 to play George Barnwell in *The London Merchant*. He was also the Poet in *Lethe*. Later he went to Edinburgh as a manager.

Lewis, Philip (d. 1791). Acted at Drury Lane, 1755–56, Covent Garden 1761–62 through 1767–68. He was acting in Dublin in 1757 through 1759 and at the Haymarket in the winter seasons, 1776–77, 1778–79, 1781–82, and 1788–89.

Marr, Henry (d. 1783). Actor, singer, and dancer, called "Dagger," he made his debut at Goodman's Fields on 22 November 1740 as Pedro in *The Spanish Fryar*. In the same season he played Sir John Gates in *Lady Jane Gray*, Mortimer in *1 Henry IV*, Ludovico in *Othello*, and Catesby in *Richard III*. He also danced in *King Arthur*. He played Drury Lane in 1742–43 and again in 1745–46 through 1776–77 in small parts.

Minors, Miss Sybilla (later Mrs. John Walker, 1723–1802). Played hoydens and pert chambermaids at Drury Lane from 1742–43 through 1755–56.

Moore, Master (fl. 1754–57). Appeared as a Fairy in *Queen Mab* at Drury Lane on 5 November 1754 and Puck in *The Fairies* on 3 February 1755. He played at Drury Lane in 1755–56 and the Haymarket on 17 June 1757 and 31 October 1757.

Mozeen, Thomas (d. 1768). Giving up a legal career for the stage, Mozeen made his first recorded appearance at Drury Lane on 20 February 1745 as Pembroke in *King John*. His wife, the former Miss Edwards, played Polly in *The Beggar's Opera* on 30 September 1746. After a season in

Dublin with Sheridan, the Mozeens reappeared in London, where he played Young Fashion in *The Relapse* at Drury Lane on 15 September 1750. Later he played Benvolio in *Romeo and Juliet* and Cob in *Every Man in His Humour*. His two-act farce, *The Heiress; or, The Anti-gallacian*, was performed for the benefit of Mozeen, Ackman, Scrase, and Harrison at Drury Lane on 21 May 1759. Prompter Cross labeled it "Indiff."

O'Brien, William (d. 1815). Making his debut as Captain Brazen in *The Recruiting Officer* at Drury Lane on 3 October 1758, he played the Fine Gentleman to Garrick's Lord Chalkstone the next month and ended his acting career as Lovet in *High Life Below Stairs* on 7 April 1764, when he eloped to America with Lady Susan Strangeways, eldest daughter of Lord Ilchester. Some years later he returned to London as a playwright and produced two pieces, *The Duel and Cross Purposes*, on 8 December 1772, one at Drury Lane and the other at Covent Garden.

Packer, John Hayman (1730–1806). Making his Drury Lane debut on 19 September 1758 as Selim in *The Mourning Bride*, he remained at that theatre until 18 June 1800, last playing Brabantio in *Othello*. As "a Gentleman" he had appeared for one night at Covent Garden on 24 January 1758, playing Johnson in *The Rehearsal* and the Frenchman in *Lethe*.

Palmer, John (1742?–98). Called "The Younger," he was the son of "Gentleman" John Palmer and first played at Drury Lane on 9 November 1763 as Blunt in *1 Henry IV*. He was the original Brush in *The Clandestine Marriage* and died on the Liverpool stage during act IV of *The Stranger*, 2 August 1798.

Parsons, William (1736–95). Coming to London from York and Edinburgh, he made his Drury Lane debut on 21 September 1762 as Filch in *The Beggar's Opera* and appeared last there on 19 January 1795. Zoffany painted him as the Old Man in *Lethe*, with Bransby as Aesop and Watkins as the Servant. He died of asthma in the severe winter of 1795.

Passerini, Signora Christina. A soprano introduced by Telemann to Handel at the Hague in 1750. The family reached London in 1752 and she sang in opera in 1753–54: *Deborah*, *Alexander Balus*, *Joshua*, *Samson*; the same season she sang *Messiah* and *L'Allegro*. The family went to Dublin in 1762 and remained there for nearly thirty years.

Perry, James (d. 1783). An actor at Drury Lane from 1758 through 1773.

Pritchard, Hannah (1711–68). First known as Miss Vaughan, she began as a performer at Fielding and Hippisley's booths at Bartholomew and Southwark Fairs, 1733–34, engaged briefly at the Haymarket, and then joined Garrick's company as Mrs. Pritchard, wife of William Pritchard, Drury Lane treasurer. Her final perfomance was as Lady Macbeth on 24 April 1768. She was the first and only player of Dr. Johnson's Irene.

Raworth, Master (fl. 1763–73). Played a Fairy in *A Midsummer Night's Dream* at Drury Lane on 23 November 1763. The following season he was a Fairy in *The Fairy Tale* on 22 September 1764. He was a singer not only at Drury Lane but also at Marylebone Gardens and the King's

Theatre in 1768–69. From 1770 through 1773 he was engaged by Tate Wilkinson at York.

Reddish, Samuel (1735–85). After a debut in Dublin on 12 October 1759 as Lord Townly in *The Provok'd Husband*, he eventually came to Drury Lane on 18 September 1767. He became a lunatic in December 1785 and was placed in an asylum in York.

Reinhold, Frederick Charles (d. 1815). Trained in the St. Paul's and Chapel Royal choirs, Master Reinhold first appeared at Drury Lane on 5 February 1752, replacing Master Vernon in an unspecified part in *Queen Mab*. He sang infrequently for two seasons, appeared at Marylebone Gardens in the summer of 1758 and thereafter, and was one of Handel's singers in the *Messiah* on 27 April 1758. He sang a half dozen times at Drury Lane in the spring of 1759, was in Norwich the next year, back in London at the Haymarket opera in 1761, and reappeared at Drury Lane on 15 February 1765 to sing Arthridates in Bates's opera *Pharnaces*. For the 1769–70 season he was at Covent Garden, singing Giles in *The Maid of the Mill*, and remained there until 1784, thereafter appearing only sporadically until his retirement in 1797.

Reinhold, Thomas (1690?–1751). An esteemed singer with an "excellent bass voice," he sang in opera and at Vauxhall, Ranelagh, and Marylebone Gardens. Born in Germany, he was reputed to be the natural son of the Archbishop of Dresden. He came to London to join Handel's company.

Scott, Mrs. John, née Isabella Younge (1741–91). A mezzosoprano, she first appeared as Miss Younge at Drury Lane in 1747–48. She was with Handel's company from 1755 to 1759, continued at Drury Lane as Miss Younge through the 1767–68 season, and as Mrs. Scott sang there through 1775–76.

Scrase, Henry (1717–1807). A bit player, he was at Drury Lane from 1750–51 to May 1762, apparently first playing Fenton in *The Merry Wives of Windsor* on 22 September 1750.

Sherry, Katherine (1745–82). First appeared at Drury Lane on 25 April 1772 as Lady Macbeth. She was the first Lady Sneerwell in Sheridan's *The School for Scandal*.

Smith, Maria, née Harris (fl. 1772–96). Wife of the pianist and composer Theodore Smith, she made her Drury Lane debut on 20 October 1772 as Sylvia in *Cymon*. She remained at that house until May 1785 and retired from the stage in 1796. Hopkins notes that she sang Sylvia to "vast Applause."

Taswell, James (d. 1759). A comedian, he appeared at Drury Lane on 16 January 1739 as Obadiah in Mrs. Centlivre's *A Bold Stroke for a Wife* and remained with the company until 9 November 1758, after which time he went to Dublin.

Usher, Howard (d. 1802). A bit player at Drury Lane beginning with the 1747–48 season, when he played Gildenstern in *Hamlet* on 22 September. He appeared at Covent Garden in 1753 and was again at Drury Lane through 1758–59.

Vaughan, Henry (d. 1779). Mrs. Pritchard's brother, he first appeared at

Drury Lane on 29 October 1751 as the Constable in *Eastward Hoe*. He retired from the stage in 1766.

Vaughan, William (fl. 1750). May have also been a brother of Mrs. Pritchard. A Captain of Marines who fought in the American Revolution, he made his debut 14 September 1751 as the Tailor in *The Relapse*. He acted at Drury Lane from 1750–51 through 1755–56.

Vernon, Joseph (d. 1782?). He first appeared at Drury Lane as a boy soprano in Mallet's revision of *Alfred* on 23 February 1751, and with Michael Arne he wrote the music for *Linco's Travels*.

Walker, Mr. (fl. 1766–67). A utility actor at Drury Lane during this period, he is also listed in Beard's company at Covent Garden.

Wilder, James (1724–?). A painter and actor, he made his debut at Drury Lane on 29 March 1749 and remained there until May 1756, when he left the stage for an appointment at Somerset House. He composed *The Gentleman Gardener*, an opera produced in 1751.

Wilkinson, Tate (1739–1803). The son of a clergyman and educated at Harrow, his passion for the theatre led him to join Garrick's company in 1757. He later went to Dublin with Samuel Foote but returned to Drury Lane and continued acting until he became manager of the York-Hull-Leeds circuit in 1766. He was known for playing Shakespearean roles, including Lear, Hamlet, Othello, Romeo, Hotspur, Richard III, and Petruchio.

Winstone, Richard (1699–1787). A friend of James Quin, his name appears on cast lists between 1734 and 1753 and as a member of Garrick's company beginning 1747–48. He also played at Goodman's Fields, the Haymarket, and Bristol.

Wright, Mr. (fl. 1767–76). Played at Drury Lane from the 1767–68 season through 1775–76. A Mr. Wright, possibly the same actor, played at Richmond, Bromgrove, and Norwich in 1767.

Wrighten, James (1745–93). Trained as a copperplate printer, he early left his occupation to join the provincial theatre. He made his Drury Lane debut on 21 February 1770 as Burgundy to Garrick's Lear and remained with that theatre until January 1793, serving as prompter beginning 1786.

Wrighten, Mrs. James, née Mary Ann Matthews (1751–96). Wife of the actor James Wrighten, she played and sang at Drury Lane from her debut on 8 February 1770 as Diana in Issac Bickerstaff's *Lionel and Clarissa* through the 1775–76 season. Later Mrs. A. M. Pownall, she also performed in America.

Index to Commentary